THE UNTH

JOANNA O'NEILL

J O'Neill

May 2023

WOODEN HILL PRESS

THE UNTHANK BIBLE

Published by Wooden Hill Press

ISBN: 978-1-8384387-0-8

PROLOGUE

THEY WERE SPEAKING ENGLISH. CLARA HEARD THEM OUTSIDE in the hall. They switched to German when they came into the drawing room.

'Mutti.'

'Anders.'

Clara spoke without raising her eyes from her needle. She knew Anders had stopped in the centre of the carpet, right on the medallion motif, as was his habit. There was a patch worn quite threadbare.

She also knew Gertrude had entered, half a step behind her husband as usual, and was watching. Clara didn't acknowledge her at all.

Her son cleared his throat. 'Mutti. I have to tell you that we have brought forward the date. There are – things to see to. We are leaving on Tuesday. You may have heard them packing.'

Of course she had heard them packing. Clumping about on the floor above, up and down the stairs, boxes colliding

1

with walls, Ernst shouting – what a one for shouting he still was – Franz moaning about his dogs…

Marilena had told her anyway. She had slipped in after breakfast, her sweet face stricken with woe. *I don't want to go, Grosmami. And if we have to go, I want you to come too.*

Clara had softened; *the little bird…* But Marilena was the only one who did want her. The boys didn't care one way or the other, all so grown up now, their interests only in outdoor things, shooting and chasing and making so much noise. They wanted to stay and join in the war, reckless, wooden-headed fools, too arrogant to imagine they could be killed. She did not blame Anders for taking them away, only for making it so clear he did not much want to take his mother too.

You might consider whether you will come with us, he had told her. *It is an uncomfortable journey at your age and you have been here so long now.*

So of course she had told him she had no intention of leaving England. What else could she do? Pride makes its demands. And Gertrude behind it all, no doubt.

Well. She was eighty-six now and her old bones didn't let her forget it. She might as well finish her days here as anywhere, and if she missed Marilena, well, the girl was seventeen; she would be getting married soon wherever she lived, and unlikely to visit her grandmother once she had her own household.

But such haste! Half the boxes to follow on behind, it seemed. Gertrude concerned only with her nice things, her gowns and coats, her jewellery, Anders packing up his financial affairs, the boys fretting and laughing in turns over their guns and their saddles and finding homes for their horses.

And little Marilena, the little bird, so wistful, so sad… Clara wanted to tell her: *Don't worry, Little Bird, you will come back one day because I am leaving Unthank to you; it will be yours and yours only.*

But she didn't. If Anders learned that she had altered her will then so too would Gertrude, and if Gertrude knew then Clara was afraid of what lengths the woman would go to in order to overturn her wishes. Try to have her declared mad, probably.

So she said nothing. She watched them all depart. And then she turned away from the window.

...

BOOK ONE

CHAPTER 1

IT WAS DARK, IT WAS RAINING, SHE WAS TIRED, AND SHE missed the turning, just as she'd been warned. 'There's a bridge and then a bend and then go dead slow because the gate is hidden by trees and you'll overshoot if you're not careful.' But it's hard to go dead slow immediately after a bend, even if you seem to be the only driver in the county, and Maddy was worried that something, a truck or a motorcycle, might rocket up behind her and not brake in time, so she slowed a bit but not enough and glimpsed the gateposts as they slipped by.

'Blast.'

She had to drive over a mile before she found a farm track with enough curtilage for a three-point turn. It was bumpy, and the rain that had accompanied her most of the day must have been falling here too because the ground was liquid mud, but there was a solid base and she didn't get stuck. Thank God. Getting stuck here, now, would be a seriously bad thing.

No traffic passed while she was manoeuvring, so perhaps 'dead slow' was safe after all. The turning would be on the right somewhere around–

'*Blast!*'

She had been on the road for the best part of eight hours now, about four times as long as her longest-ever drive before today, and now that she was nearly at the end she had begun to feel desperate and even a bit weepy. It was too cruel to keep missing the turning like this.

It had felt like an adventure at the start, setting her alarm clock early and pulling out into the pre-rush-hour traffic: delivery vans and road sweepers and milk floats. It took an hour and a half to get clear of London, but north of Biggleswade the A1 opened up and driving got easier. She stopped to stretch her legs and grab a bite at services outside Grantham. After that there was a slow thirty minutes around Doncaster and then a warning of road works just north of Durham, so in a moment of reckless bravery she had cut off south of the city and followed road signs through villages and farmland.

The countryside looked old-fashioned, timeless, the fields small and separated by heavy, ragged hedgerows; some arable but lots of sheep. Really *lots* of sheep. Trees gathered in clumps in fields or marched along distant horizons, their skeletal forms twisting and reaching like members of a modern dance company. Houses were squat and square and without gables, mostly stone or stucco; no friendly red brick to be seen.

When she was a couple of miles from Hexham, the rain that had washed her windscreen most of the day began to hammer down so that her windscreen wipers could scarcely cope. She found a car park in the town and sat, enjoying the respite from concentrating on the road, hoping the clouds would helpfully rain themselves out.

She had some leeway; she didn't have a specific appointment. R J Pattison had been remarkably easy-going. 'He'll be here,' his receptionist had assured her. 'I'll tell him to expect you some time after two. You might have to wait a few minutes, is that all right?' But it carried on raining, so Maddy got into her coat and pulled up the hood.

Peering through the rain, she could see that she had parked far below the walls of the abbey and would have to climb a slope that seemed brutally steep to someone who had been sitting in a car all day. She reached the top breathless, and paused to look about. The receptionist had told her to go through the market place and down a side road – vague instructions Maddy had thought, but Hexham was compact and there weren't many options. At more or less half past two Maddy had walked into the office, and more or less twenty minutes later emerged with a bundle of keys in her bag and a sheet of handwritten directions. 'Turn right in Kirkwitton,' Mr Pattison said cheerfully. 'There's a bridge and then a bend and then go dead slow because the gate is hidden by trees.'

And so she had embarked on the last leg of her journey, and driving was different all over again. The wider stretches of road had fallen behind and she was confined to narrow lanes that swooped and wound through a landscape that seemed scarcely to have changed in centuries. The countryside now was bleak: grey stone walls with jagged hawthorn and low, wind-warped trees; grey stone houses with mean little windows; grey stone barns, some of them with exposed rafters or without roofs at all. Fields were more of heather and clumps of brown reeds than grass, and there were rocky outcrops and small, shaggy sheep, and the sheep all had horns. What did sheep want horns for? Beyond the scrubby fields were high moors, alien and bare, unmistakable even in the gloom. A wild and woolly place, Maddy had thought, her spirits darkening under the darkening clouds.

She was in the back of beyond. There was no one behind her, had been no one behind her for miles, and she had met – two, was it? – cars coming the other way: a different world.

A dank and shadowy world. The clouds were fearsome, and at barely half past three it seemed like evening. The road was not quite single-track but it was narrow, and the edges of the tarmac had disintegrated, making it even narrower. There had been potholes as well, nasty, sheer-sided things that caused a jaw-clenching jolt and made driving fraught. Maddy had been immensely relieved when a sign on a boulder planted in the verge told her she had safely reached Kirkwitton, the last-named stage point before her destination.

The village appeared to be a triangle of grass separating five houses, and there was only one right turn so she had taken it.

Another narrow road. On the right a dry-stone wall imprisoned sheep in a steeply sloping field; on the left, trees loomed over the road making it still darker. The days are short in February and shorter still in Northumberland than in London. She realised now she should have set off earlier, before dawn, the city streets well-lit and much easier to navigate than these twisty, tricksy lanes.

She had travelled half a mile or so and arrived at the bridge. She took it very slowly indeed because the hump looked brutal, slowed again before the bend, wondered if despite the odds something was behind her, and overshot the gates. And then she had turned around and overshot them a second time.

FEELING SLIGHTLY DESPERATE NOW, Maddy drove back over the evil bridge, half a mile to the village green, turned around, drove over the bridge for the third time and then really crawled her way round the bend. A snatched glance in her rear-view mirror showed her a Land Rover on her tail but she'd be damned if she was going to overshoot a third time, so she started indicating left and *there*, there was the gap between the trees. She eased in with relief. The Land Rover accelerated and was gone and Maddy was alone under the dripping canopy, with her bumper almost touching a pair of high wooden gates between stone gateposts the size of coffins.

It was still raining hard. Maddy squirmed back into her waterproof and got out to investigate. She couldn't see a house name but this surely must be the right place. The gates were tall, above her head, and made from solid vertical planks, thick, like railway sleepers. There was an iron latch with a twisted iron ring, such as you find on the door of a medieval church, and bolts that dropped into a chunk of concrete buried in the ground.

Maddy swung each gate back and was surprised to see a stone building tucked away to the left, almost hidden behind bushes. The wall facing her had a ponderous bay window projecting into the branches, but everything else about the place looked pretty compact. A gatehouse? She had inherited a gatehouse as well?

But it was wet and she couldn't think about it now. She brought her car inside and shut the gates behind her.

Why?

It feels safer.

Well, that was stupid. The place had been empty since the death, and apparently no-one had visited for years before that thanks to Uncle Claude's policy regarding callers. 'It's a bit basic, I'm afraid,' Mr Pattison had said.

'But it's okay?' Maddy asked. 'It is habitable?'

'Oh yes, it's sound enough. The roof's on.'

Well, that was all that mattered for now. No need to splash out on bed-and-breakfast if there was a house available. She had a hold-all on the back seat and a sleeping bag, and two supermarket carriers of supplies: supper tonight, breakfast tomorrow, and enough to make a packed lunch for the homeward trip.

The tyres crunched; it looked as if the drive might once have been laid with gravel but was now well covered with leaf mould and debris from the enormous trees lining the way. What were they? They were clothed in needles but didn't look at all like Christmas trees. They weren't as regimented as the Holland pines, straight as telegraph poles, in the plantations she saw from the motorways down south; these were more individual, more organic, more primitive, Maddy thought, like the sheep. She was conscious of her ignorance.

The trees linked fingers above her, forming a tunnel that sheltered her from the worst of the rain. She could hear it pattering on the branches instead of on the car roof as she made her way cautiously along the drive, which seemed interminable − a huge distance between the gate and the house and always climbing.

And then she rounded the last bend and the tunnel of trees released her. Ahead was a sharp grassy incline and at the top, against the dark clouds, an even darker hulk: the house.

The house. Her house. It was waiting for her − or rather, Maddy thought, waiting for what was to unfold for it next. Deserted and cold, it had finished with the era of Grandmother Lawrence and Uncle Claude and stood poised now, aloof and impassive, marking time until a new age began.

Her house. Unthank.

Bloody hell.

CHAPTER 2

MADDY HAD ALWAYS EXPECTED TO DIE WHEN SHE WAS twenty-nine. Not absolutely as soon as she was twenty-nine, not on her birthday, but during that year, just as her father had and her grandfather. Things happen in threes and she was the third; thirty seemed for her unattainable, and the fact that for most of her thirtieth year it would be 1984, a date loaded with literary baggage if ever there was one, seemed ironically appropriate. So when she was woken by the doorbell on the morning of her twenty-ninth birthday, she opened her eyes without enthusiasm and with the sense of a cool hand closing around her heart.

Yes, it was superstition, thus by definition silly. Her mother had told her so often enough: *Look at me! Forty-seven and starting my fourth life!* But her mother wasn't a Lawrence, not by blood; the curse didn't apply to her.

Norma, Maddy's mother, was starting her fourth life because after three years of persistent and kindly courtship, her New York boyfriend (such an inappropriate term for someone middle-aged) had persuaded her to say Yes, and Norma had married him and emigrated to a spreading modern house in Long Island, with a bungalow in Florida for vacations. Bill was a lawyer and had money. They had met during one of his business trips to London: they fell into conversation on Waterloo Station when their train was cancelled – he was going to meet his cousin in Richmond and Norma was going home after meeting hers at the South Bank – and one thing led surprisingly swiftly to another. Generous Bill paid off the mortgage on the flat in Twickenham and Norma made it over to Maddy in entirety. *I feel like I'm running out on you, but you know I love you, don't you?*

Of course she did. Her mother had been a brilliant single mum: the third of her four lives. Her second life had been marriage to Maddy's father before he died – aged twenty-nine – and the first life, of course, was her youth up until her twentieth year when she met and married the dashingly handsome Ivan Lawrence. That second life had been brutally brief – five years from engagement to funeral, with Maddy's birth more or less in the middle. She was just three when her father died and didn't truly remember him at all, although photographs taken out and pored over can start to feel like memories.

Ivan died from undiagnosed meningitis; they thought he just had a headache. Theo, Ivan's father and Maddy's grandfather, had died in a car crash. No connection at all, as her mother had often pointed out, but still, both aged twenty-nine…It loomed.

And on her twenty-ninth birthday it wasn't just Fate that had its grip on her. She was sleeping in because the battle with the developers, drawn out for months, had been lost – or won, if you looked at it from Ted's point of view, as the price finally settled was a nice top-up for his pension – and the camera shop where she had worked for nearly ten years had been gutted and boarded up and was now awaiting demolition. She had so far failed to find a new job. On top of that, the arts centre in Camden had decided to cut a swathe of its classes including hers. She had been teaching several (Get to Know Your Camera, Composition in the Frame, Darkroom Techniques) and benefitted hugely from free use of the studio and darkroom outside class time too, and now she had nothing.

The flat was hers outright but there were still rates and utilities and the service charge, not to mention food. The running costs on her car too, a Volvo originally owned by her mother, who always insisted that they have a solid, resistant car rather than a smaller run-around type because of Theo Lawrence's fatal crash.

And that was another thing: some idiot in a yellow hatchback had made a serious attempt to wipe her out two days ago on the way to Bath, where she had been intending to cheer herself up with a day's architecture photography. It had roared over the brow of a hill, straddling the white line and heading straight for her. Only swerving onto the verge and ploughing to a halt in the bumpy grass had saved her. Volvos are tough but even they can't protect you in a head-on. After her heart steadied and she felt less sick, she found the nearside wheels were mired in a ditch, and although she had RAC breakdown membership it took them ages to come out. By then half the day was gone and she was in no mood for photography.

Two days too early, she thought. *That wasn't supposed to happen until next week.* And she wasn't supposed to have survived. Well, she had, but no doubt there would be another attempt.

The doorbell had been rung by the postman, who wanted a signature. Maddy signed and took possession of a business-sized envelope: thick, cream-coloured paper, franked.

Not a birthday card, then.

She opened it in the kitchen. The letterhead was in Times Roman: *R J Pattison & Co, Solicitors.*

Oh no, she thought, what now? She opened the envelope reluctantly. It was bad enough to lose her job at the shop *and* the studios at the arts centre in the same month. What else was going to go wrong: compulsory purchase of her flat for half its value? Notice that she was being sued for having spilled that bottle of fixer solution in the darkroom?

But as she unfolded the letter, she noticed that the envelope was postmarked Hexham. In Northumberland.

Not the fixer, then.

She read the letter. Then she sat down, leaned her elbows on the table and read it again. After that she stared out of the window for a bit, and then read the letter for the third time, slowly, and with care.

Solicitors don't usually make mistakes, she thought; not about legacies.

R J Pattison, in Hexham. She pulled out her ancient school atlas and estimated it would take her at least six hours to drive there – more than six with traffic and stops. A day, basically.

Which day? As of this week she could take her pick. Tomorrow, even.

Unthank.

Well.

SHE HAD PLANNED her route and written it out in large letters on a sheet of A4 she could keep on the passenger seat beside her – road numbers and major towns along the way. It looked like most of the first half would be dual carriageway, although once past the Midlands the roads would be smaller.

Maddy told the Jacksons opposite and the Chattertons below, packed clothes, a towel and some food, and turned down the heating. She checked tyre pressures, topped up the screen washer, and put a sleeping bag on the back seat (it was The North) all the while feeling slightly giddy.

I am going to claim my inheritance.

How do you do that, exactly? She had asked the receptionist what she needed to bring, and her passport and birth certificate were in her shoulder bag along with the most recent bank statement and electricity bill. Her credit card statements and phone bill were there too, which were not apparently needed but which she threw in anyway. Belt *and* braces. And her driving licence. Was that really all one needed? You waved these bits of paper in front of a solicitor and he handed you the keys to a pile of real estate? It seemed scarily open to fraud.

She rang her mother, horribly expensive. 'I think Uncle Claude has left me his house.'

Norma's voice came from three thousand miles away but sounded as if she were next door: 'Unthank? Really? Oh goodness!'

'Did you know? Did he tell you he was going to do this?' Grown-ups frequently conspired, Maddy thought, and even aged twenty-eight – no, twenty-nine now – she felt the gulf between their generations. There was still a sense of Them and Us.

But her mother said, 'No. Not at all. I used to sort of hope. I mean, he never married, there were no other descendants. But they were so reclusive, those two. Never wanted to communicate with me at all. I think,' she added, 'your grandmother was a bit mad.'

'What about Uncle Claude?'

'He was madder.'

Then she rang best friend Liz. Liz had put on a fairly poor accent and said, 'Eh, lass, you goin' oop north?' and Maddy had said, 'I am, but you're doing Yorkshire. Northumberland's two hours further up than that. Kirk-witton is nearer to Edinburgh than York.'

'Crikey.'

'Yes.'

Born-and-bred Londoners had little geography beyond, say, Cambridge or the Cotswolds, Maddy thought; everything above that on the map was a kind of generic, jokey 'North'. No doubt she would be just the same had it not been for those trips to visit Grandmother Lawrence while her mother was still trying to hold the generations together.

A lost cause. Her father had cut all ties with his family long ago, and by the time Maddy was seven her mother had given up the battle to reinstate the connection. Norma had depths of steel, Maddy knew, and it must have been a hopeless situation if even she abandoned it. Maddy didn't know when her grandmother had died; wouldn't even have known that she *had* died if it weren't for this.

What was the house like? Detached at any rate, with a large garden, she remembered that; she had got lost in it. Northumberland property prices would be pretty low, but surely a biggish country-ish house anywhere is worth quite a bit? An influx of cash would save her life right now.

Exactly how big was it?

Memories of those childhood visits played in her head. There weren't many, just a handful of moments, like tableaux: Grandmother Lawrence, ramrod straight and a daunting figure to bewildered little Maddy (everyone had liked her up until then); silent Uncle Claude wheeling in a trolley of tea things – stacked plates, sandwiches, a teapot wearing a woolly tea-cosy; a wooden crate full of cooking apples in the kitchen and the amazing smell that emanated from it; herself creeping into a spare bedroom on the way to the bathroom and finding a book open on the patchwork bed cover full of close handwriting in a language she couldn't read, interspersed with numbers, odd diagrams and arrows linking things.

She remembered how intrigued she had been, and how she had turned the pages without thought. She remembered also the cold fright that settled on her when she realised she had lost the original page, and making her best guess with her fingers crossed before finding her way back downstairs, certain that someone at Unthank was either a wizard or a spy.

Who had owned that book? Maddy had never dared to ask, aware she had been trespassing. Come to think of it, she still didn't know, but of the two of them – Grandmother Lawrence and Uncle Claude – surely Claude was the more likely? 'Do you like puzzles?' he had once asked her, tentative and awkward, and his shyness despite being a grown-up had frightened her.

What else? The fuggy smell of the kitchen, where unfamiliar food simmered on an enormous cooker and all the surfaces were higher than at home – a giant's kitchen, like the one waiting for Jack at the top of the beanstalk. Losing her way after she'd been ordered to go and play in the garden, full of fear that she would never get back in; it had been raining and the trees dripped on her. She remembered the way the passages indoors were dimly lit, gloomy and echoing and not at all like home. It was all stone floors and high windows, and when later a school trip went to Hampton Court, the eeriness of the worn steps to the royal kitchens took her back.

And she remembered how, when they drove away, Grandmother Lawrence would disappear back into the house as soon as their car started up, and only Uncle Claude would remain in the yellow doorway, watching as they crunched down the drive until the trees at the corner cut off the view. Waving goodbye, or making sure they'd gone?

Maddy's mother had embarked on an uphill struggle when she set about mending fences there; whatever had caused the rift between Grandmother Lawrence and her father wasn't going to be fixed by a twice-yearly visit and cards at Christmas.

And now Uncle Claude had left her everything. But what did 'everything' mean? The house, apparently, but money too, or just debts?

CHAPTER 3

Now, DRIVING SLOWLY, MADDY STARED. IT WASN'T A BIGGISH, country-ish house at all; it was a massive pile of stone, square and high, weighted into the earth like a castle. The roofline was crenelated like a castle too. Hell's teeth, it *was* a castle.

Three stone steps and a hefty stone porch jutted from the front facade. Maddy pulled up alongside and switched off the engine. She had spent practically her entire day with the undercurrent of motor noise growling away and now she sat for a moment experiencing the emptiness. Quiet, just the rain and the faint grumble of distant thunder.

But getting ever darker. Maddy pulled her hood over her head and got out. The porch sheltered her while she sorted through the keys, found the one labelled *Unthank front* and pushed it into the lock. It turned but the door wouldn't open. She rattled and shoved, and only then recalled Mr Pattison saying, 'I suggest you use the back door. The front door seems not to have been used and is bolted inside.'

Stupid to forget. But where was the back door?

Maddy sighed, pulled out the key the solicitor had shown her, the old-fashioned sort with a long straight shaft and a card label strung through the handle: *Unthank back*. She zipped up her raincoat.

Left or right? She chose left and followed the walls of the house to the rear, where she found herself in a square court-yard, cobbled and mossy and sloping to a centre drain cover clogged with leaves. On her left were outbuildings with stable doors, all shut, and in front of her a wall with small, high windows. In the far corner, a tall stone step and a door with flaking grey-green paint; a boot scraper was parked beside it.

The way in.

An overflowing gutter above the door was making a wide waterfall that bounced off Maddy's sleeve as she pushed her arm through, but the key slipped in, jiggled a bit and then turned with a reassuring scrape. Maddy opened the door.

It was cold. There was that damp-plaster smell of an unlived-in house. And it was dark – not *dark* dark, not like night time, too dark to see, but the lateness of the hour and the heavy clouds combined to produce a deep gloom.

The spatter of the overflowing gutter was loud behind her and she shut the door. The water was still audible. Maddy shivered.

She was reassured by the key having worked. With no name on the gates, it had crossed her mind that she might be trespassing in some quite different, unknown house. But still, she found she was reluctant to touch anything: the walls, the furniture, the floor; she almost wanted to walk on tiptoe. She felt like an intruder with no right to be there, and especially no right to be there alone.

24

Don't be silly. This is mine.

Which was true in the general, everyday sense. Legally, the deeds would not pass to her until probate was completed – six months or so, Mr Pattison had said – and there would be death duties to pay. But apparently Uncle Claude had had savings that should cover those, and the will was quite clear.

'This is mine!'

Her voice sounded unpleasantly loud, bouncing off the bare walls and floor, but it was a touch of normality and helped Maddy propel herself along the passage. Her shoes were wet but she didn't feel inclined to take them off. And anyway, the passage was laid with stone slabs and those wouldn't come to any harm from a few wet footprints.

Her soles on the stone made an alien sound, utterly unlike the tiles or carpet in the flat; utterly unlike any domestic floor she'd ever encountered, in fact. Churches sprang to mind, castles and churches.

On one side were the windows she had seen from the yard, set high above her head but letting in enough light – just – to see by. On the other were doors leading to a series of small, bare rooms like cells, devoid of furnishings apart from shelves of wood or slate, immensely deep. One had a low, narrow sink running the full width of the far wall, and they all had floors that sloped gently to a centre drain. Store rooms, Maddy presumed, for food in a day before refrigeration. The last one held a washing machine and a mangle.

Maddy followed the passage past a long, low oak bench, several pairs of boots and a row of hooks with coats and scarves: signs of habitation.

Beyond the coats was another door. Maddy pushed it open and stepped over the threshold into a kitchen, where she stood, dumbfounded. It hadn't been a quirk of childhood memory at all, that notion of the giant's kitchen at the top of the beanstalk. She had thought everything had looked so huge to her then because she was small.

Wrong. Everything looked huge now, too.

It wasn't just the floor space: the distance to the opposite wall, the yards and yards that separated the sink from the table and the table from the dresser. It was the scale of the sink and the table and the dresser themselves. They were mighty: vast chunks of tree trunks hewn into working furniture fit for an ogre.

Maddy drifted, looking, not touching (yet), trying to adjust. The game had changed. She had come believing she would stay overnight in a rather nice, rather big, four- or even (if she was very lucky) five-bedroomed house with a wrap-around garden in a Northumbrian village – probably not smart, given that it had been owned by a bachelor in his sixties, but certainly very saleable. A desirable property, one the estate agents would happily take onto their registers. And instead, here she was in something out of the Brothers Grimm.

Hulking under a brick fireplace at one end of the room was a range cooker, a massive one. Hansel and Gretel would have no difficulty fitting a witch into that. On another wall was planted a ceramic sink she could have taken a bath in, with a rack for plates above and a wooden draining board set on heavy, turned legs like those of a billiard table. The taps were dull brass and set up high, above exposed pipes.

There was a wooden table, also huge, with raw, square chairs set around it, and taking up most of the end wall was a mighty dresser with open shelves above and cupboards and drawers below; the shelves bore a jumble of crockery and books, candles and jars. A china lamp sat on the dresser, and propped against a mug was a spiral-bound calendar still showing January. Nothing had been written on it.

More crockery, fancy crockery, was behind the glass of a painted and glazed cupboard that filled an alcove. Otherwise, it was more stone slabs, high windows along one side, and a door with an iron latch that opened to reveal a larder. The larder was lined with narrow shelves bearing tins and packets but nothing perishable (happily). There was an air brick through which Maddy could smell rain.

She closed the door again. It was extraordinary. Where was the fridge? Her eye fell on a Brown Betty teapot on the dresser. *I bet it's the same teapot.* The tea-cosy was probably somewhere about too.

Uncle Claude had been stuck in time.

It was bitter. She would have to find the boiler and turn it up, but perhaps she'd just see a bit more of the house first.

Maddy left the kitchen. She had gained a little confidence now and walked more briskly to the heavy panelled door at the end of the corridor. She heaved it open and paused.

She was looking at the first signs of any of the comfort you normally expect in a residence. There was a carpet for a start, and the walls weren't stone or plaster but dark wood panelling, and there was a hearth with a grate and a basket of logs beside it. A staircase, wide and impressive, led to a gallery above, and the ceiling was far in the distance.

It was a hall, just a hall, and yet you could have fitted most of her flat into it.

She was exaggerating, but only slightly. The amount of walking you could do while staying inside this house was phenomenal. Maddy, like most, had been to National Trust properties and straggled from room to room behind the looped cords that protected the rugs and furniture, but to be in such a huge house alone and at liberty to walk anywhere was utterly different. And it was *hers*.

Her head was spinning. Maddy sat on the stairs and tried to be objective.

Mr Pattison had told her that the will was quite clear, and although there was a bit of number juggling to be done before probate came through, there was no reason she should not live there.

'In simple terms, if you have to sell the property in order to pay death duties, and you can't sell it because you've set fire to it and it's burned down, then you'll have to find the funds else-where to pay what's due,' the solicitor had told her. 'However…'

Maddy had faced him across a desk reassuringly scat-tered with family photos, a collection of ballpoint pens in an earthenware mug. There was a small figure, four inches high and dressed in judo clothes, standing next to the in-tray. *Luke Skywalker*, he had said, following her look, but had left his explanation at that.

'However,' she said, following his logic, 'if it were broken into while empty and *someone else* set fire to it…'

'Exactly.'

In any case, Pattison's, as executors, had taken out insurance to cover the period of probate. So it was her choice. And, apparently, Uncle Claude's wish.

'I always ask,' Mr Pattison said. 'Beneficiaries often live a long distance away and it's daft for them to be in a hotel when the house that will soon be theirs is doing nowt. Mr Lawrence was emphatic about you having the keys as soon as possible.'

Maddy liked that he used words like *daft* and *nowt*. He was about forty, she guessed, neither old and crusty nor young and slick, and she liked the Luke Skywalker as well, especially that he felt no need to explain its presence. One presumed he had a ten-year-old son. She had been happy to trust him.

It seemed now to Maddy inexplicable that she had never thought about inheriting the house. Why not? She had known Claude was her father's only sibling, had known Claude had never married or had children of his own. There were no cousins lurking, although probably some distant relatives in Switzerland. The estrangement had been so final somehow, so fierce, that she had literally never given the idea any thought. Yet here she was, sitting on the stairs with a bunch of keys in her bag: the new owner of Unthank. Effectively, as far as she could make out, the owner of a fortune.

Maddy climbed the stairs to the gallery and paused to stare out of the window. The sky was purple-grey and the unknown trees of the tunnel were quite black. When Maddy turned her back on the panes the house seemed suddenly gloomier than ever.

She had no torch, and glanced about for a light switch. There was one, the old-fashioned bulbous brass sort, and when she flicked it, an upturned wall light came on and Maddy breathed out with relief. *So* much better.

Actually, she could now see well enough to notice that the strip of carpet running along the floorboards was coloured in soft neutrals not by design but from age; it was threadbare, the dull warp exposed and the coloured wools faded to chalky pastels. The floorboards on either side were dusty, and not neatly patterned parquet blocks but wide, uneven planks with gaps here and there between them. Ogre floorboards.

And ogre furniture. Not a lot of it, not a lot of furniture at all, but here and there a low, wide book case, a carved chest or a cabinet, and all of it weighty and dark. She walked the passages and opened doors. The beds were wider than they were long and high enough to warrant steps, and in the corner of one room a massive free-standing mirror stood like a sentinel. Cobwebs arced across corners where walls met ceilings and in window recesses; dead flies littered windowsills and dead spiders, curled and grey, lurked on the carpets.

Thunder was rumbling closer. She ought to be getting on. Her bags were still in the car and she hadn't found the boiler yet. It was freezing.

I'll take a quick look up here first though.

There was a narrow staircase beyond the last door, and Maddy climbed, her shoes clumping on the bare wooden steps. A shorter staircase this time, and at the top she found herself in smaller, more constricted quarters: square rooms with small windows set high and nothing to cover the bare floorboards but flaking paint. Servants' rooms. Poor things.

Although come to think of it, they were no smaller than her own bedroom at home. How one's perceptions get messed with, and how swiftly.

Maddy found a bathroom with a narrow but immensely deep bath and a toilet with an overhead cistern, and what must be a linen cupboard with slatted shelves. She was on her way back down the stairs when there was a crash like a hundred metal doors slamming and a blaze of white light at the same time – a thunderclap directly overhead – making Maddy jump inside her skin and grip the hand rail.

And the lights went out. All of them.

PITCH BLACK. Beyond the windows now the world was utterly dark, not a star, not the moon, not even a hint of a rent in the clouds. And it was still pouring, the rain hammering against the window panes. Lightning continued to flicker but the thunder had moved on – she could hear it heading for the hills, leaving Unthank behind.

Thanks a bunch. The power was out and she didn't know where the fuse box was, didn't know where to begin looking for it. Where did people put fuse boxes in massive old houses like this? At home it was on the wall just inside the front door but that didn't seem likely here.

Why hadn't she thought to bring a torch?

When the thunderclap deafened and startled her, Maddy

had instinctively frozen, gripping the rail, her priority to keep safe and not fall on the stairs. Once she had gathered herself, she felt carefully the rest of the way down to the landing and paused to think.

She could see a bit. As her eyes adjusted, she could definitely make out the window at the far end, and knew that about half way along would be the main stairs down to the hall. She also remembered there being furniture against the walls, although that was invisible now. She would have to be circumspect.

Cautiously she made her way along the wall, feeling for obstructions and working her way around them. The stairs were detectable – just – when she reached them, the yawning mouth visible in a shadowy way, and she groped for and found the banister. Feeling hindered and vulnerable, her arms stretched wide, each step tentative, Maddy slowly crossed the open expanse of the hall (horrible) and with relief reached the back corridor, forgetting about the step at the threshold and stumbling. From here it was easier – clear walls, little furniture. She made it to the kitchen and from there to the back door.

Outside it was still raining but a little less heavy, she thought. The open air, even wet, was very welcome, and as a wonderful bonus there was, after all, some light outside. Hard to see where from – the sky didn't offer much promise – but there were at least shapes out here. The open space beyond the house, while black, was somehow less black than the stone walls and the trees. Through there and around the corner, her car was waiting by the porch.

She had forgotten to unbolt the front door from the inside. Idiot.

Maddy pulled up her hood and walked, lifting her feet high to avoid stumbling on the unseen cobbles. It was surprising how treacherously uneven the ground felt when she couldn't see it.

She slipped behind the steering wheel, turned on the cab light with a sigh of pleasure, and considered.

Options…

One: She could drive off in search of a bed-and-breakfast for the night.

Not appealing. There had been nothing obvious in Kirkwitton, nor for miles back the way she had come. The road would be even nastier in the dark, the lurking pot holes invisible, and anyway she was fed up with driving. Heading off with no idea of a destination seemed insane.

Two: There was no telephone at Unthank but Mr Pattison had said there was a public call box in Kirkwitton. Provided she found it she could ring Pattison's and hope like mad they hadn't all left for the day. What time do solicitors stop work? It was five fifteen now; if someone was still there, even if it was a cleaner (would a cleaner answer the phone?) they might be able to recommend a pub or something reasonably close by. Or not.

Three: She could take her stuff inside. She could try making sandwiches by feel, spend the night in the sleeping bag, and deal with the power cut in the morning.

There wasn't much of a choice to be made. She would be cold, cheerless, uncomfortable and probably hungry, but the house was here and it was dry; she didn't have to drive to get to it and she wouldn't have to make any more decisions today.

Choice made.

Maddy drove round to the back door. Then she took a grasp of her holdall, her camera bag and the supermarket carriers, shoved the sleeping bag under her arm, and got the lot indoors with minimal wetting from the overflowing gutter.

The car could stay unlocked. She doubted a thief would come by.

SHUTTING her eyes and testing how long she could go without opening them had been a recurring childhood game. *What would it be like if...*with the comfortable assurance of being able to open them again at any time. That time always came quickly; little Maddy never made it to more than a minute.

Now, eyes shut or eyes open made no difference. Everything Maddy did, she had to do by feel: ferrying her stuff along the passage to the hall in turns, only able to carry as much as she could manage with one hand so that the other could stay in contact with the wall. She dumped the bags immediately inside the hall, just to the left of the doorway, where she would be able to find them but wouldn't trip over them.

Then food. She decided against taking the carrier bags to the kitchen. What would be the point? Everything there would be invisible and frankly she didn't care to take cleanliness on trust. Instead, Maddy sat on the bottom stair and rummaged inside the plastic bags on her lap. She had brought salad stuff for ease, not wanting to get involved with a strange cooker. Now she pulled the outer leaves off a cos lettuce and chomped her way into what was left, ate her way down half a cucumber, bit into a tomato and hoped she could suck up the jelly and seeds without spilling. No salad dressing, of course. She ate a roll without butter and tore off pieces of sliced ham. It was a relief when the meal was over.

The truly horrible thing was that she couldn't stop herself from *trying* to see. She would become aware that her eyes were wildly wide, straining for a glimmer of illumination that would lend form to her environment, and would blink, forcing her eyelids to relax, but in no time they'd be stretched wide again, staring in hopeless desperation. It was exhausting. The muscles of her face ached.

Somewhere there must be matches and candles, or for that matter, a torch; somewhere probably not too far away either. But she had no idea where. Blundering about blind in an alien place seemed less than wise; better to sit it out until morning and then look.

So reluctantly and with bad grace, Maddy experimented with the sleeping bag here, on the floor, at the foot of the stairs. It was horribly hard. When she packed, she had anticipated stripping one of the beds of all its linen, but had expected to have a mattress under her. That seemed unnecessarily difficult without sight, and in the end she felt her way back along the kitchen corridor to the rack of coats, filled her arms with whatever was hanging there and used that, bundled up and patted into rough shape, to buffer her against the wooden floor of the hall.

She rolled up her raincoat to use as a pillow (crackly and too many zips) and squirmed into the sleeping bag, fully dressed and with her car key still in her pocket. It dug into her hip periodically, but there was no way she was going to be separated from her means of escape.

It was hopeless at first, far too early to be going to sleep, and her mind was fizzing. But at some point, as does happen, she stopped thinking, because when she opened her eyes there was light, not electric but daylight, and morning had come.

CHAPTER 4

MADDY BLINKED, ROLLED OVER, AND SIGHED. SHE WAS actually quite comfortable now and still sleepy.

But not very comfortable, and the key had found her again.

There isn't much to recommend sleeping in one's clothes without having washed or brushed one's teeth. Maddy felt creased and stale and sorry for herself. She was also desperately in need of a loo, and first port of call was the bathroom she had seen upstairs. The water was on – Mr Pattison had mentioned that – and the flush worked with a mighty clunk and whoosh. Rinsing her hands and face in icy water bucked her up considerably. Maddy returned to the hall feeling more like herself, even if she was dishevelled and still wearing her coat.

Next up: breakfast.

Other people's kitchens had never been her strong point. Uncle Claude might have been family, but he had been an old man living alone and Maddy opened cupboards gingerly, her fingertips alert for old spills and fluff.

It wasn't too bad: a bit sticky here and there, but nothing horrendous. She wiped one end of the kitchen table, smug that she had thought of bringing her own dish cloth, and took a dainty bowl and plate from the best cupboard rather than the plain crockery in daily use. A delicate film of dust had settled on them despite the closed doors, but she rinsed them, along with a knife and a spoon.

She served herself a double quantity of cornflakes and that refreshed her more than almost anything else could have done: the power of crisp cereal and cold milk. Toast was more of a problem. The cooker looked fearsome and was stone cold, and although there was an electric toaster, which looked like a trinket from a dolls' house in the ogre-sized kitchen, the power was still off. Maddy had switched on the kitchen light to test but there was nothing. So once again Maddy ate bread, but this morning she could at least spread it with butter and Marmite.

She ate with relish, allowing her eyes to rove. How many steps from the cooker to the sink? From the sink to the fridge? Oh no, there wasn't a fridge. How many to the larder, then? That triangle of traffic that kitchen planners talk about. In the flat everything was within three strides, pretty much.

Maddy went over to the cooker, looming vast and black in the chimney space, and then walked to the larder in the corner. Twenty-two steps. Nineteen diagonally to the sink. The room was probably larger than her kitchen and living room combined; basically, it was the size of a bed-sit.

She was pondering this when the light overhead came on. Power restored! Maddy toasted a slice of bread to celebrate. She also looked for but failed to find an electric kettle; there was only the flat-bottomed kettle sitting next to the range, so there would be no tea yet.

Maddy stacked the used plate and bowl in the vast sink and went in search of hot water. The passage past the store rooms seemed as likely as any, and sure enough she found a cupboard with a water tank and a switch for an immersion heater. A red indicator light glowed reassuringly when she turned it on, and she felt hopeful of real, actual hot water before too long.

In the meantime, she should turn the lights off. Maddy was conscious that along with the house came its utility bills. So she retraced last night's steps, up two flights of stairs and past all the bedrooms, switching off lights as she went.

Taking stock as she went, too. Touring the upper reaches of the house for the second time now, she noticed different things. For a start, it was abundantly clear that only one person had been living in the house for years. The beds were all bare and other furniture was minimal. It was as though sufficient furniture for, say, a nice three-bedroomed semi had been tipped into this hulk of a house and given a bit of a shake. The only thing that marked what must have been her Uncle Claude's room was the eiderdown and pillows stacked at the foot of the bare mattress and the electric bar fire in the corner, disconnected from the wall but ready to go.

Maddy looked at the plug lying next to the socket in the wainscot. Then she looked around the other walls. She walked round the foot of the bed and checked there too.

No radiator.

She went back to the room next door. No radiator there either.

Doubt stirred, like a small furry hamster curling up in her midriff. Maddy started to head for the stairs, but then thought again and returned to collect the electric fire. With that tucked under her arm, the lead looped up, she went down to the hall and ran her eyes around the walls there.

No radiators anywhere. Unthank wasn't heated.

Maddy sighed.

IT HAD BEEN HALF past seven when Maddy woke up. It was close to half past eight by the time she realised she had a new priority, even over boiling a kettle, which was to make fire. Still in her coat, still cold, she prowled the ground floor, discovering what there was, yes, but also looking for the best room to use as base camp.

Of course, she should have been leaving pretty soon. She had meant to check the place over, get a rough idea of how she would describe it to an estate agent, see a couple such in Hexham on the way south to get an idea of house prices, and be back home in time for tea. She could still do that. And yet…It would be silly to go away without having seen the place properly. Having been unable to use yesterday evening, she would need longer than an hour or so today to go over the house thoroughly, and there was still the garden to be explored, and that gatehouse too.

Maddy dragged open heavy doors, clumped across floors the size of school classrooms, stared into cupboards, gazed out of windows that all had heavy wooden shutters but no curtains.

This is mine. I own this.

She couldn't get her head around it. Unthank wasn't quite a castle. There was no moat, no tower, no dungeon (she hoped). But if not actually a castle then it was the next nearest thing. The size of the rooms and the quantity of them would have suited a hotel.

Unthank Hotel.

It didn't sound welcoming.

Why *Unthank*? Where did the name come from? What did it mean? Questions she had never thought of before.

There was a second hall, long and narrow, running from the galleried hall where the staircase began to a *third* hall with double doors into a square stone porch. Beside the porch stood a large and imposing grandfather clock, which Maddy was childishly excited about. She had never dreamt she would have her own grandfather clock. Whatever happened, that was going home with her.

But there were too many halls. She'd have to give them names: the Entrance Hall, the Long Hall, and the Main Hall. That would do.

The front door, made of oak and without a window, had black iron hinges and fittings and was bolted at top and bottom. When Maddy tried to slide the bottom one open, she couldn't make it shift. She'd need something to whack it with. Or a man. It could not have been in regular use. Presumably Uncle Claude hadn't opened the front door.

Maddy was beginning to suspect her mother was right about Uncle Claude being mad.

There were three huge rooms downstairs, oak-panelled from floor to beamed ceilings, all opening onto one another as well as onto what she had named the Long Hall, and none of them inviting. But at the far side of the Back Hall, behind the staircase, was a much smaller, friendlier room with a wing chair and a card table and a bookcase: a snug. Instead of an open hearth, there was a closed stove. Maddy instantly decided to adopt it while she was here. It would warm up far quicker than the larger rooms, and from the stacks of books on the floor and the ash tray on the table, she guessed it had been where Uncle Claude had spent most of his time too.

Not quite mad, after all.

By then she was utterly fed up with being perpetually cold, and she plugged in the electric fire in the kitchen and sat in front of it as the bars began to turn to dull red and then orange-yellow, until for the first time in hours and hours she felt warm. The smell of burning dust was unpleasant but she stopped shivering. Bliss.

It was ten o'clock. Where had the time gone? She could simply collect her stuff, lock up and go; have lunch in Hexham. Try to describe Unthank to some estate agents; tell them she'd give proper details later.

But later when? She didn't like the idea of letting agents borrow keys, roam around taking measurements and notes. The house was too peculiar, too special; she wanted to supervise, lead the tour, point things out and make sure nothing important got missed, but she didn't know her own way round the house yet. Somewhere this size and this old must have dozens of quirks she had yet to uncover. Besides, she hadn't even looked at the garden – 'the grounds', as they would no doubt be described.

Maddy considered. There were outbuildings to investigate too. This would take all day. She would have to stay another night and go home tomorrow.

That hamster inside her was stirring again. What now? It was stretching, Maddy thought, and relaxing: relief. She was relieved at having decided to stay an extra day.

Reluctantly she ventured into the chilly outdoors to hunt for coal.

The next hour was taken up with the primal need for warmth. Happily, she found not only coal in an open-sided stone shed but a store of logs too, and lugged a load into the snug using a great square of canvas there, with handles at the corners. After that, she searched the kitchen cupboards and found matches, which was good; but then she completely failed to find newspapers anywhere in the house at all.

She had to have something to get the fire started. There was her notebook, but there weren't many blank pages left in it and she wanted those. Reluctantly she returned to the snug and scanned the bookshelves for something cheap and replaceable that she could burn.

A lot of the books were obviously out of bounds: decent hardback fiction (the classics mostly), reference books (dictionaries, directories and field guides to this and that; a thesaurus; a great series of beige and maroon bindings optimistically called *The Book of Knowledge*), an impressive collection of Ordnance Survey maps (not current editions), and –

rather exciting – a number of handwritten notebooks that she told herself she would look at as soon as she was warm.

But there were a few paperbacks, thrillers mostly and detective novels, and Maddy pulled out one with a cover design of jagged bursts of black and red and, guiltily, began to rip out pages. Book burning. Well, needs must and no-one would ever know.

There was a basket of twigs and sticks next to the hearth. Dragging up vague memories of Enid Blyton and Girl Guides, Maddy laid the fire with scrunched-up paper first, followed by a wigwam of twigs, and managed to light it in three places before the match burnt out. If it didn't take, she'd be in trouble because although she had heard terms like 'drawing the flames' she had no idea how one actually did it.

At the moment the paper took hold and the fire caught the kindling sticks, it occurred to her that the chimney might be blocked or there could be a dead bird stuck up there, all kinds of horrible scenarios, and she sat back on her heels and held her breath. But nothing came down, nothing started to smell and no smoke billowed forth, so she assumed the chimney was in working order and she could stop worrying.

And she was in luck. The fire took, and when she added logs to it – the smallest, lightest ones – they began to smoulder too. Amid much popping and spitting, warmth began to radiate outwards, and Maddy unfastened her coat.

Heaven. This might be workable after all.

The fire gathered strength and Maddy added two more logs, wedging them against each other using the huge leather gauntlets that she had found nearby, and was retreating to the wing chair at the very moment that something hit the window like a handful of grapeshot and she realised it had started to rain again. Or - no, not rain but hail.

Good job she had brought enough logs in. She kicked off her shoes and tucked her feet up, then opened her notebook to a fresh page and uncapped her biro.

She was a maker of lists, always had been. Lists, Maddy believed, kept one on course, clarified one's thoughts and were extremely satisfying to tick off. She was looking forward to making one now.

Find out how to light the range.

She couldn't survive much longer without tea or coffee.

See garden and gatehouse

Can't do that until the hail stops.

Measure rooms; work out total floor area.

She needed a tape measure for that and had forgotten to bring one but it would be necessary to give the estate agents some idea of what she had to sell. Perhaps there was one here, or if not, she could pace it out. In which case…

Calculate my paces and convert to metres.

She needed a ruler for that and she didn't have one of those either. Surely Uncle Claude had had a ruler?

Sort out a bed.

Not bed linen, just somewhere half comfortable to put the sleeping bag.

This was better. This felt like organisation. Maddy scanned the list and wondered what else she could add. The most enticing job was to explore the garden, but hail was battering the windows and the sky was so dark it felt like evening. It was frustrating; it was barely midday and she wanted to be up and doing. A walk outside would have been perfect.

All right then, how about a walk inside? The layout of the house was still vague in her mind; she'd commit it to memory and stop being surprised whenever she turned a corner.

She set off. It was extraordinary to walk so briskly, stride out so strongly, indoors. Unthank Hotel, Maddy thought again, and this time the hamster quivered a little. A shudder? She imagined guests and staff and noise and bustle; mood music playing on a loop in the Back Hall, a commercial kitchen full of stainless steel surfaces, leaflets about local attractions in a rack by the stairs.

Completely horrible.

Deep in Maddy's mind a small voice chipped in: *What do you mean, horrible? What's it to you? You've only been here one day and you're off again tomorrow.*

All true. But it was horrible even so.

CHAPTER 5

TWO HOURS LATER MADDY ADDED ANOTHER JOB TO HER list.

Identify keys.

The bunch Mr Pattison had handed her was daunting; there must be a lot of locked doors in Unthank. She ought to know how to get into them, and now that the problem of boiling a kettle was settled the keys could jump to the top of the list.

Because she had, at last, managed to boil a kettle.

After walking around the house three times to fix the layout firmly in her head, Maddy had returned to the kitchen and searched drawers, cupboards, every nook and cranny she could find for information on how to work the range, but of course there was nothing. She found a lot of other stuff (gardening gloves, a jam jar of rubber bands, candles – hooray!) but nothing relating to the cooker. It wasn't surprising. Uncle Claude had grown up in Unthank; he would have known everything about living here without recourse to handbooks. Maddy opened oven doors, lifted lids and turned knobs on and off, but the range remained cold and dead.

She needed help. So despite the rain Maddy drove to the village.

When she reached the triangle of grass in Kirkwitton she bore right into a road she hadn't been along yet, and discovered there were more than five houses after all. There was a second small green with a phone box, just as Mr Pattison had promised, and on the far side a long, low pub with *The Swaledale* in green letters over the door and a picture of a sheep; there was a gravelled area to the side for parking and some tables and benches.

Alongside the green was a village hall with a noticeboard, and next to that a shop that had a Post Office sign above a window displaying vegetables, fruit, loaves and some enticingly rustic pies.

Maddy parked outside the shop and went in. She was immediately wooed by lovely yeasty smells. What looked like a small shop from the street went back a long way and then through into a second room, and seemed to stock a wide range of goods. The food was at the front: crates of fruit and veg, baskets of bread, tins and packets on shelves and a chilled cabinet for dairy. Further back were hardware items (dusters, disinfectant, bin liners), nets of kindling and balls of twine. Right at the back were bags of pet food and bedding.

Maddy collected milk and cheddar from the chilled cabinet and added a box of eggs, a bag of tomatoes and a couple of apples, and then went in search of chocolate digestives. Comfort food. You can do a lot with eggs, cheese and bread. This would tide her over for a day or even two. Just in case she chose to stay a bit longer.

She added a crusty cob and an appealingly lopsided pork pie that she would have for lunch, and while they were being wrapped, said, 'I wonder if you could help me with something else as well?'

The assistant was motherly and cheerful. She said, 'I can but try, pet. What is it?'

Maddy said, 'I'm staying in a house where the cooker is a range cooker and I don't know how it works.'

The woman showed no sign of surprise. 'Is it on?'

'No.'

'Is it oil?'

'Er…'

'It'll be oil. We're all on oil here. So first you need to check your oil tank's not empty.'

Maddy said, 'Right. Where is the oil tank likely to be, do you think?'

'This is Rosemount, is it?'

'Rosemount?'

'The holiday let?'

'No,' Maddy said, 'not that.'

There was a beat as the woman adjusted her assumptions.

'Are you in the village?' she asked.

'No, not really. A little way out.'

'Well, it'll be in your garden. Not too far from the house. You'll find it. Now, to light her up…'

Maddy dug out her notebook and started writing. Eventually everything seemed to have been covered, and the nice lady shopkeeper said, 'If you get into difficulty, just give us a ring.'

'Thanks,' Maddy said, 'but there isn't actually a phone.'

'No *phone*?' The woman literally took a backward step. Then she rocked forward again and rested her fingers on the high counter, like a dog peering over a wall. 'You're not talking about Unthank, are you? Are you from Unthank?'

'Um, not *from* it. I'm staying there though. Just for a couple of days.'

The backward step again. 'Away! Are you something to do with the executors, then? Sorting things out?'

'Not exactly. I've inherited it, I think. That's what I've been told. He was my uncle. I'm his niece.'

'Claude Lawrence had a niece!'

Maddy smiled shyly.

'Oh pet, you poor thing. There'll be a mountain of work for you there. He was a…Well, I won't say. He was your uncle.' She busied herself with a basket of rolls on the counter.

'It's all right,' Maddy said. 'I didn't know him. I only met him a few times, as a child. This has come out of the blue.'

'Well. He was funny, that's all. Never came out. Every-thing delivered. I expect he was shy.'

She didn't meet Maddy's eyes while she said this, though, and only after she had cleared her throat did she leave the rolls alone and look up. 'Look, now, pet. We're here all the time, so if you want anything, just ring. Oh no, you can't. Well, come by then. And if you want to use a phone and the call box is busy, you come in here and use ours.'

How kind.

Outside, the rain had stopped and Maddy was sure it was colder. The sky was lighter, the clouds high and pale. Frost tonight, perhaps? She definitely needed to get that Aga going.

First, she trekked back to the snug to put another log on the fire; she didn't want her only source of warmth to die on her. Then she went out and started looking.

Luckily, it wasn't difficult to locate the oil tank, which was a hulking thing shut away in the stable or shed or whatever it was nearest to the back door, which she was still using until she managed to unstick the bolts on the front one. She should have bought lubricating grease. Or perhaps there was some already here. Another item for her To Do list: *Nose about in the sheds*.

Notebook in hand, Maddy followed the shopkeeper's instructions and was greatly relieved when everything worked. In not too long there were distinct wafts of heat radiating from the range. Maddy rinsed out the flat-bottomed kettle in readiness. Soon she would have coffee, chocolate biscuits, a warm kitchen and a fire in the snug. This was *much* better.

Maddy opened her notebook and crossed off *Find out how to light the range* and wrote at the bottom *Identify keys*.

MOST WERE the kind Maddy thought of as picture-book keys – what you would draw if asked what a key looked like: a ring at the top, a straight shank and a ward at the other end that was more or less square. More or less. Some were oddly wide and thin, but they still fell into the same broad type.

Three were the modern, front door kind, with a solid disc above a serrated stalk. Two were short and stubby: padlock keys, Maddy guessed. And one was just a cylinder with a flat head and was labelled *Grandfather clock*. Excellent.

All of them were named, in fact. Someone had tied a card label to each one with string. *Unthank Gatehouse*, Maddy read, then *Outhouse 1, Outhouse 2, Outhouse 3, Cellar*. She had a cellar? *Attic*. That was creepy; why lock up an attic? *Larder*. Really? The larder had a lock? Bizarre.

When she had worked her way through the bunch, she discovered that not all the keys were named after all. There was one that had been forgotten, or had he – she – whoever – run out of labels? Or not known what the key was for? She would see if she could do better. Since she wasn't going home today, it could be her job for the afternoon: Find the Mystery Locked Door.

It took her well over an hour. She tested the labelled keys as she went, sliding each one into its lock and making sure it worked. She knew the front door was a problem and the back door was in use; now Maddy set to on the outbuildings.

She began with the row across the cobbled yard, and found dim, cold spaces full of mysterious countrylife stuff like sacks, pitchforks, tubs of chemicals and paint cans. There was a dusty bicycle, and a tin bath hanging on a wall, and gardening clobber (wheelbarrows, spades, an ancient, cobwebbed lawnmower). A roll of chicken wire was propped in one corner next to a witch's broom made of twigs (Grimm again). But there were more buildings than she had realised; there was a second yard behind the row of stables, with cracked and mossy concrete in place of cobbles. More outbuildings formed the other two sides, and they were shabbier. The centre section was a tall barn with wide doors at either end – for carriages? – and narrow wooden stairs to a scarily rudimentary flat above: two rooms and a poky lavatory. Maddy decided not to put the flush to the test and retreated.

On the farthest side of this second yard was a low building with a single door at each end. Inside that she found wooden stalls with iron hay racks and a shallow gutter running from one end to the other. Some lengths of wood leaned against the partition of one and there was a stack of dusty grey pallets. It smelled closed-up and dry.

She paused in the yard and surveyed the stone walls and wooden doors and thick, grey windows. Unthank was huge. It was less like a house than a small hamlet.

It was staggering to imagine this quantity of space. In London every square foot counts, every cubic foot utilized. When people move, they list every built-in cupboard, every alcove, all the little corners of space that could possibly be used for storage. There is a whole industry around designing shelves and cupboards to fit into the triangular area under staircases. You can buy boxes the exact dimensions to slide under your bed, yet even so, everything you no longer use – clothes, electronics, toys – gets jettisoned to make way for new stuff coming in.

Maddy thought of her mother's annual trawls around the flat, black bin liner in hand; she had taught her the Three Pile System: one pile to keep, one pile for the Oxfam shop, one pile to be chucked. It was a ritual: What They Did in the last week of the summer holidays. If they'd lived here instead of Twickenham, she thought, they could have shoved the whole lot behind one of these doors and never noticed the difference; they could have done it for years.

Perhaps it was just as well they hadn't lived here.

For a moment she pictured herself as a child, hammering her bike across the cobbles and hitting tennis balls against the walls. It didn't seem real; it belonged in another era, or at least another type of society. Nobody she knew had this much space to call their own.

It was very cold; her London coat wasn't up to this. The gatehouse would have to wait.

Back indoors, Maddy noted that the larder did indeed have a lock, as did the long cupboard lining the wall of the nearest pantry, and the mighty sideboard in the dining room, and the bookcase in the sitting room, and the cupboard in the panelling under the stairs. It came, Maddy presumed, from an age when property needed to be secured against theft from servants, for who nowadays locks cupboards?

The mystery key was still a mystery, though. Maddy sat on the stairs and looked at it. Less than two inches long, it was bright and simple. It didn't look like a key for a door but for something smaller, private, secretive. A cabinet? A chest? A box?

The key had borrowed the warmth of her skin; it wasn't so cold now, just a little cool. Maddy took it between finger and thumb and held it up in front of her. 'Come on, then. Where do you belong?'

If she was going to find the one whatever-it-would-be that this key could open, she would have to be methodical.

She had tried just wandering about and had got nowhere. She needed a plan.

'All right: start at the top and work down.'

The top was the attic. She had discovered a third flight of stairs, short and narrow and hidden behind a plain door on the second-floor landing, the servants' landing as it must once have been. She had already climbed these stairs and checked that the key labelled *Unthank Attic* locked and unlocked the door at the top, but hadn't gone in to look about. Now she did, and was pleased to find there was a bulb hanging from the rafters. She was not so pleased to find it had been left on. What a waste of electricity! Very negligent of Mr Pattison, or more likely his minion or whoever had secured the house after Uncle Claude's death.

It was freezing, like stepping into a fridge. Maddy walked along the centre. The ceiling there was high enough, but the atmosphere was stuffy, the cold air stale. On either side the rafters slanted down to meet the floor ten feet away, and Maddy felt unpleasantly closed in, conscious of there being only one exit, and the exit behind her at that.

Wedged into the angle where roof met floor were cardboard boxes, rolls of wallpaper, oddments of furniture – stick-back chairs, a footstool, a bedside cabinet. At some point she would have to go through all this.

Or would she? That was what house clearance firms did, didn't they? When the time came, she could just ring one of those and let them swarm through the house and extract all the junk and leave her with a calm, empty property to put on the market.

The hamster in her middle was twisting about again and Maddy's mouth was dry.

Why was there a lock on the attic door? Who had fitted it, and why? To keep people out? Or to keep something in?

She had gone forward some metres now and noticed a shape just ahead. It was an old-fashioned suitcase, made of scuffed leather and with reinforced corners. It could easily have been pushed to the edge like everything else, but instead it had been left on the walkway. It had been placed there.

Maddy crouched down. It was clearly much used, the edges battered and the leather that covered the handle worn away in places; and it had a brass plate at the front with a key hole in it.

The key fitted and turned. Maddy lifted the lid. Inside the suitcase was a book, a large one, of black leather worn smooth, the corners bumped and the lettering pressed into the hide softened with age: THE HOLY BIBLE.

Puzzled, Maddy lifted it out and saw that an envelope lay beneath.

It was the manila sort, newish and quite thick. And it was addressed to herself.

CHAPTER 6

ADDRESSED TO HERSELF.

Maddy switched off the light and took the bible and the envelope downstairs, leaving the attic with relief. She wouldn't have to go up there again. She couldn't say why, but she knew it would be much better if the house clearance guys did that.

The envelope was sealed.

Maddy wasn't foolish. She didn't expect the envelope to contain anything momentous. But it was peculiar of Uncle Claude to have left it for her in so unlikely a place, somewhere she might never have discovered had it not been for having time to kill and a certain persistent curiosity.

On the other hand, it was increasingly clear that Uncle Claude had been peculiar in all sorts of ways.

Saving up the little pleasure of reading his message to her, Maddy made a cup of tea – hot drinks still a novelty – before retreating to the snug to open the envelope. Her name, Madeleine Lawrence, was written in a careful italic hand, and for a moment she wondered whether there might be some other Madeleine Lawrence of whom she was unaware and who should really be opening the envelope.

But no, that was silly; the box had been positioned for her to find, its key was on the bunch to be handed to her, and Uncle Claude wouldn't have known she was always called Maddy.

She tore open the flap and drew out some folded papers with something small and hard inside that fell into her lap.

It was a key. Another one.

Maddy unfolded the letter and found it wasn't a letter at all. It was pages that had been torn from a notebook, covered in dense handwriting, a forward-sloping, cursive hand not at all like the one that had written her name on the envelope. The ink was a dirty blue and faded.

Maddy read.

My name is Lenka Midnight and this is my story. I'm writing in this book I found in the bottom cupboard of the bureau – abandoned, because the entries stop with October 1911 and it is now June 1918, and what was it doing in the study anyway? It's a beautiful book, too, a great big thing, over twelve inches tall and bound in leather. Bound in leather, just for recording how much sugar was bought last month and what candles cost!

Only the first half of the book has been used. A few pages at the back have been written on – stocktaking lists it looks like. Between the daily records at the front and the lists at the back are pages and pages of blank, beautiful paper, creamy white and smooth to the touch. I used to dream about paper like this when making do with the grainy stuff the candles had been wrapped in; paper to hoard; paper that begs for words.

Well, I'm having it. And what's more I'm going to sit at this desk to write in it. She won't come in here, and even if she does, what can she do? I've half a mind to leave anyway after that business this morning. It is now beyond reason, and if it weren't for the house I'd be on my way.

But that's the problem, isn't it? The house. This house.

How I find myself here I will never understand. I never wanted a roof over my head. I was afraid it would fall on me.

By the time I was three I had learned the story of Chicken Licken – I don't remember who told it to me but the chances are it was my father, Jeremiah Midnight, he of the wild yarns and uncharted past, because most of the stories came from him. Some of them were very good, worth laying down for possible future use if the right occasion arose, but although I liked the rhyming names of Turkey Lurkey, Cocky Locky, Henny Penny (although why was she not Henny Lenny?) I never cared for that repeating line: The sky is falling! It frightened me, and I would look up at the close boards of our wagon and imagine them caving in and killing us all.

Well, killing Benbow and me; it was impossible to imagine anything killing Jeremiah Midnight, although of course in the end something did.

Anyway, somehow the story turned itself around in my head and it was roofs I was always scared of, not the wide Cumberland and Northumbrian skies. I wanted to be outside always, and more and more the wagon became too close for me. I walked hundreds of miles with Black Jet, our cob, on one side and Benbow, our pepper-and-salt terrier, on the other, and I slept outside when the weather was mild enough, underneath the wagon when it rained, always dreading the onset of winter.

Then I made twelve and Jeremiah at forty-two decided he'd had enough of wandering. He swapped Black Jet and our lovely old Dunton wagon for a cottage, or so he called it, striking the deal with a fellow he met over a beer one day, and took the pans and books and blankets and me to a ramshackle pile of stones scarcely bigger than our home on wheels had been. My father said it was time to put down roots, that travelling wasn't the only way to live. He was no more a true Romany than my mother had been, shiftless rather than restless, preferring whole-coloured horses to skewbalds and without a trickle of music in him, and all the spells and charms and curses he sold to the poor, frightened, vindictive, gullible people on the road were ridiculous and worthless, the lot of them.

But he liked books. Oh, how he liked books. And he taught me to read and to write and to memorise, stories and poems and plays and histories, and there was always paper and ink of some sort to be had, although for sure most of it was rubbish and if there was ever any better stuff it would have been because he'd stolen it.

So there I was, keeping house (if you could call that heap of rubble a house) for my feckless father and hiring myself out for field work when it could be had, until a couple of months after my sixteenth birthday when everything changed.

Maddy looked for the next page but there wasn't one.

The writing had run out. There was no date, no name, no explanation. Maddy frowned, flipping over the sheets. Nothing.

Well, there was a name: Lenka Midnight. Who on earth is called *Lenka Midnight*? Maddy's friend Liz dabbled in family history, an on-going quest to trace her family tree as far back as she could, and to be companionable Maddy had sometimes gone with her to read parish records: a pleasant drive into the countryside, lunch at a pub, and a few hours spent photographing a church and graveyard while Liz ploughed her way through pages of faded, crabbed handwriting, rarely finding what she had hoped for. But even when her research drew a blank, Liz always found something of interest, including some amazing names from the past: *Maud Cramp* was one; *Abraham Silence; Gideon Cake.* Maddy remembered them without even trying; how can you forget a name like Gideon Cake?

Lenka Midnight.

Maddy picked up the key lying in her lap. It was very small and had a fancy, scrolling handle. And it was anonymous; another unidentified key for another unidentified lock. Someone was having a game with her.

Suddenly she remembered that notebook she had found twenty-something years ago, and its pages of mysterious script and diagrams and equations. Wizards and spies. Uncle Claude?

'Do you like puzzles?' he had asked her, but she had no memory of her response. Had she backed away, shaking her head, reaching out for her mother? Or had she nodded enthusiastically, stepping forward, eager to see what he might offer? She had no idea.

She looked at the key. She had seen something like this before. It was smaller than the first key, bright and brassy. Maddy shut her eyes and concentrated…

Yes. A piano. Liz played, and her piano had a lock on the lid over the keyboard with the key kept in it. Maddy had commented on it; it seemed strange to her and yet perfectly normal to Liz.

There was a piano in one of the huge ground-floor rooms. Maddy tried the key and it turned with a satisfying snick.

She lifted the lid. The keys were yellowish and a smell of old wood and stale polish rose to meet her. Lying across the keys was a scroll of paper covered in the same handwriting as before, and beneath it a second sheet of paper folded in four. She opened it out. It was a bill, an invoice on thin paper with a letterhead in italics: *Andrews & Son Ltd of Morpeth*. It was typewritten with gigantic serifs and lots of punctuation marks: *Mrs. M. E. Lawrence.*

Her grandmother. Maddy scanned the content. It appeared to relate to building work of some kind, the total to be paid *£8 17s 6d.*

She reached to lower the lid and then paused. The scroll and the invoice were not all that was hidden in the piano. Now she saw what had been beneath them.

ONE HAD BEEN INTERESTING, two annoying, but three was just silly. If Uncle Claude had thought he'd have a game with her *post mortem* he was mistaken. Good grief, what was he thinking? That she was some little girl to be teased and enticed and tricked? She was a grown woman (even if she didn't feel quite grown-up yet) with responsibilities (a spider plant in a pot) and things of her own to do (scouring the photography magazines for job adverts). She had a life (although not much of one right at the present, frankly).

Hmm.

Well, in any case she was absolutely not going to be sucked into some bizarre game of hints and secrets planned by some old guy who had by all accounts been eccentric to say the least. She would have the inheritance, thank you very much Uncle Claude, but not the shenanigans, no sir. She would read the scroll, obviously. I mean, obviously she would read the scroll. But after that, no more.

It was Lily Biddle – Lily Hopkins that was – who brought me to the German House, so in a way it was all her fault. Of course, she didn't know at the time; and in any case, you could just as easily say it was Sam Biddle's fault because if he hadn't broken his ankle Lily would not have sent for me.

Once you get onto that train there's no getting off.

It was Percy Whatmough's doing, because he barrelled round the corner without looking and cannoned into Sam on the ice; it was Mary Howie's doing when she decided not to marry Willy Tasker after all and left him without a bondage,r so that he took me to work on Halpin's farm in her place; it was all the fault of the tree root that met so unyieldingly the head of my father, Jeremiah Midnight, when he tumbled into the ditch in the dark. And in that case, then you must lay the blame at the door of the man who bought Jeremiah the spirits with which to toast his good fortune, because my father certainly did not have the wherewithal to obtain alcohol of that calibre for himself.

But he did, the man with the good fortune, and drunken Jeremiah took the fall and died in the ditch. Not fancying to live all alone – whatever else my father was, he was good company – I decided to try for a job outdoors so that during daylight at least I would be safe from the roof falling in, and took up my stand in the market square in front of Hexham Abbey on hiring day; and Willy Tasker, terrified he would lose his place for the coming year, thought I looked likely enough and took a gamble.

That was how Lily and I met. Lily was still Lily Hopkins then and only three years older than me, but she was a big woman even at nineteen, with a raw, red face and raw, red hands and a voice that on a still day or when the wind was blowing the right way could be heard by the men ploughing two fields away. She was working at Halpin's as bondager for her brother, Alf. That was how you said it: bondager for the man, the hind as he was called, not bondager to, because it was between the hind and the farmer that the bond was contracted. In Northumberland and the Borders, the hiring was for a man with a woman in his employ, and not all of those women were daughters or wives or sisters or sweethearts, although by then more often than not they were.

'We're called bondagers', Lily explained, 'because it's through us that the hinds can fulfil their contracts.' You yourself were free to take the work or not, which was exactly how Willy had got into a fix. 'She were here last year', Lily said, 'and a flibbertigibbet. Slow and complaining. I didn't like her one bit.'

Lily was a hard worker and she liked girls who kept up and didn't moan. I managed the one and refrained from the other, and reaped the rewards. There was camaraderie in the fields as we women, all dressed alike in striped skirts and lacquered hats, moved across the earth in a line, singling the turnips, hoeing between the rows, hooking the curved blades around the roots to lift the crops. Sometimes we used to race, for the hell of it, and always if there were men about. We had pride, and took satisfaction in making the effort. And I enjoyed the life; it seems common sense to learn how the earth can be cajoled into providing suste-nance; it was knowledge I was happy to gain.

So we hoed and singled and hoed again; turned and gathered hay in the summer and tied the corn sheaves in autumn; spread muck − that was ever the hardest − and sowed to start the cycle again, and we filled in the times between with all the sundry ongoing jobs around the farm, from hedging and fruit picking to rope making and mending tools. It was work as varied as you could ask, and in Lily I found a good friend to work alongside. She was strong, full of energy and determination and never shirked her share, and she was funny too. Where she got her jokes I never knew, for she had no more time than the rest of us to go off the farm, but she heard them somewhere and told them with panache, and she had a talent for mimicry too, keeping us grinning with her impressions of old Halpin, ancient Joseph Smith that stayed behind in the cowsheds, or prattling dairymaid Susan Greenway.

The only serious downside was that I could not see how I could ever move on. Labouring on the land was satisfying and worthy but I didn't want to be singling turnips for the rest of my life. I saved my pay but it wasn't clear to me what I was saving it for. Would a dressmaker or milliner take me on? The work wasn't appealing, and in any case the old problem lay before me as it always had: what jobs could I embark upon that did not involve being indoors? After all, that was why I had presented myself as a bondager in the first place instead of going into service.

I started at Halpin's in March 1911. Two years later, Lily's sister Emmy took her place in Alf's cottage so that Lily could move to Kirk-witton and marry Sam Biddle, and a year after that, Willy Tasker became affianced to a dairymaid called Ruby Ridley and told me I'd be out when Flitting Day came around in May.

I'd seen it coming, of course. And it wasn't unfair. The cottage provided on the farm was what you'd expect – a room hardly bigger than the Dunton wagon, with a hearth at one end and a curtained-off box bed at the other; I had the box bed, Willy slept by the hearth. Any man would prefer to live with his wife than with an employee. In fact, in the early days Willy made a few tentative approaches, but he quickly got the message. I was ready to take the poker to bed with me if he hadn't. He was a quiet lad, skinny and shy and sadly lacking in conversation, and I found it easier to understand Mary Howie's rejection of him than

Ruby Ridley's acceptance. But she was a silly girl, the sort that jumps at sudden noises and thinks she's seen a ghost when it's just a twist of mist around the chimneys.

And then Lily's message arrived, brought by the pot-and-pan man who had been at Kirkwitton a week before, and everything changed again.

That was it. Another cliff-hanger. Blast the woman. Or could the bible shed any light?

It was weighty, like having a small dog lying on her lap. A bit smelly too: not lovely new leather like a shoe shop, but back-of-the-throat old leather, veneered with the sweat and grease from countless hands, and when Maddy opened it a musty, neglected odour rose from the pages. It occurred to her that the bible had probably had many years of heavy use followed by decades of neglect. She doubted Uncle Claude had read from it every Sunday.

The tooling on the front was smoothed and indistinct. Still impressive though; it must have been a treasured possession once upon a time.

Maddy turned the first pages, the stained end papers and then the blank sheets before the text began, and found handwriting: names and dates. She paused to decipher the spidery script. Each line was different, either the colour of the ink or the size of the letters, some lines large and flowing, others compressed. They were lists of people and dates, presumably of birth, and it started a long way back. The first name – Josiah Alexander Dixon – was dated 1776.

1776! The year of the American Declaration of Independence – how extraordinary!

The names and dates ran on – lots of Dixons, followed

by a couple of Maxwells and then a run of Bells: *Mary Eliza-beth Bell: 27th November 1886; Joseph Franklin Bell: 23rd August 1888; Edwin Charlton Bell: 6ᵗʰ June 1890.*

Then the handwriting changed again and German names began. *Clara Maria Bircher: 19. IV. 1828* followed by *Anders Wilhelm Bircher: 5. VII. 1863*, and then a subtly different hand, as if the original scribe's style had evolved:

Ernst Maximilian Bircher born: 29. II. 1891
Jurgen Werner Bircher born: 5. X. 1892
Franz Dieter Bircher born: 15. VIII. 1894
Friedrich Maximilian Bircher born: 2. IV. 1896
Marilena Johanna Bircher born: 24. X11. 1897

And then the astonishing thing. In a new colour of ink – black, emphatic – and a new, bold, upright hand:

Lenka Midnight born: 31ˢᵗ October 1895

After that another change and a new, careful, forward-sloping hand.

My name is Marilena Bircher and I am the owner of Unthank.

and below that:

Theodore Kendrick Campbell Lawrence born:12ᵗʰ July 1896

With a little shock Maddy realised that Marilena Johanna must be her grandmother. How odd that she should write that sentence about being the owner. It was like staking her claim. Very imperious.

But what was Lenka Midnight doing there? What was her connection with Unthank? And what had Grandmother Lawrence thought on finding the family bible violated with a stranger's name? She must have been appalled! Perhaps writing her name that way, stating her legitimacy, was a way to draw a line under that unfortunate and regrettable act.

Theodore Kendrick Campbell Lawrence must be Maddy's grandfather, Theo. Quite a mouthful.

Claude Theodore Lawrence: 2nd August 1923
Ivan Kendrick Lawrence: 22nd February 1925
Madeleine Lawrence: 5th February 1955

And there it was, the second astonishing thing: herself, Maddy Lawrence, entered into the family record of births in the Unthank bible.

MADDY PLACED THE BIBLE, with care and respect – after all, it was over two centuries old – in the drawer of the card table. Then she folded the pages back into the envelope, slipping the builder's invoice inside with them, and dropped in the three keys – the one to the box in the attic, the one to the piano, and the third one, found inside the piano. It was probably a padlock key, she thought, stubby and modern...

But no.

She tapped the envelope against her other hand, thinking, then slid it upright into the book case in the snug, next to the maps.

Finished. End of story. The next time she took that out would be in preparation for the house clearance people. It was now nearly three o'clock, the light already growing dim, and she was going to pace out all the major rooms so that she could convert strides into proper measurements later, when she had a ruler. Then she'd have an omelette for supper, sort out a mattress for tonight, and leave bright and early tomorrow morning.

By this time tomorrow she would be home.

Uncle Claude's cunning little wheeze had run into the buffers.

PACING out the rooms was tedious. It was heartless too. Maddy found she hated defining Unthank as a string of numbers. Were the estate agents really going to describe it in square metres? It was a *castle*, for goodness sake! Surely all they had to do was wave a photo and say *There's a castle going here if you want one.* I mean, who wouldn't want one? Who honestly would not want to live in their very own castle in the middle of Northumberland?

Yet she did it, writing the figures down in orderly rows in her notebook, followed by a rough estimate of the outbuildings. Tomorrow, before leaving, she'd take a quick trot round the grounds just to get an impression of them. Then back to Twickenham.

She spent a while considering her options for the night. A bedroom was appealing because of having a proper mattress. On the other hand, who knew the history of those mattresses? They looked mostly okay, if a bit stained, but she decided *not* to start sniffing them as that way madness lies. She'd use her coat for a pillow again – everyone in the world drools into their pillow and she didn't fancy one of Uncle Claude's.

She did sniff the towels she found in the linen cupboard, though, and they were all right – a bit thin, but clean – so she could have a proper wash at last. She let the electric bar heater sit in the doorway of the bathroom first, then took it away and washed swiftly, standing at the basin. Next, she took the heater to the bedroom she had chosen, determined not to think about dead spiders and not to put her bare feet on the floor.

It was only like camping, she told herself, zipping up the sleeping bag. Spiders outdoors are fine.

Sleep came faster this time and she slept well, but when she woke there was something not quite right about the light, some quality she didn't remember being there yesterday: a brightness, a brilliance that was strange to her. And not just the light but the sound too was peculiar, muffled, too quiet even for this quiet place.

She had to fumble for her socks and shoes before she was prepared to stand up, and was circumspect in crossing the floor to the window, but once there all thoughts about spiders fled.

The courtyard, the roofs, the great evergreen trees were covered by a thick layer of diamond-white that sparkled in the early morning sunlight.

Snow. It had fallen in the night while she slept, and now lay deeper than she had ever seen.

Snow in cities down south is an impoverished, half-hearted affair that you can brush off and ignore. But this was at least a foot deep by the looks of it. Difficult to walk on; impossible to drive through.

She wouldn't be going home today after all.

She was snowed in.

CHAPTER 7

IT WAS EXTRAORDINARILY HARD TO WALK. RIDICULOUSLY,
Maddy was discovering this for the first time. You see television clips of farmers struggling out to feed their flocks in
deep snow but she had always thought the difficulty lay in
wrestling the bales of hay. Now she was shocked at the sheer
muscular effort needed to hoist each knee in turn high
enough for her foot to clear the snow.

The boots didn't help. She was using the wellies from the
hall, padded out with the thickest pair of socks she had been
able to find in Uncle Claude's chest of drawers, but they still
slopped about on her feet and threatened to stay behind with
every step. It was touch and go whether she would escape
toppling over.

Under the trees the snow was less deep, and when she
reached the gates Maddy found the road had been gritted
and her way to the village was far easier. Nevertheless, over-
sized boots and hidden potholes took their toll and she was
relieved to reach the shop, which was a dark cave. Snow

blindness; she had been squinting when she set off until her eyes adjusted, and now could hardly see a thing. She blundered into the newspaper stand by the door.

'Oops, steady!' Her friendly shopkeeper was behind the counter again. 'You alright, pet? Did you get the range going?'

'Yes. Thank you. It's fine now. But,' Maddy said, stepping carefully towards the counter, 'do you sell wellies?'

They didn't. 'Sorry, pet, you'll need Armstrong's for that. We've no space for all the sizes, you see.'

'And Armstrong's are in the village?'

'Oh no. But not far. Nine miles.'

'Oh.' Maddy's spirits drooped.

'You're never here with no wellies,' the woman said, not even asking the question. Maddy nodded glumly. The woman sighed. 'Ah, dear. What size are you?'

'Five and a half.'

'Then you're in luck. Hold on.'

She disappeared through a curtain.

Maddy held on. The door opened behind her, the bell tinkling cheerfully, and a thin, elderly woman came in, stared at Maddy, who smiled, and marched off towards pet food.

The curtain lifted and the shopkeeper was back. She held out a pair of black wellingtons, high above the counter. 'I'm a six. Try these.'

'Oh gosh!' Maddy hurriedly stepped out of Uncle Claude's boots and into the new ones. Bliss!

'Better?' The woman smiled. 'There you go then. You can borrow those until you can get to Armstrong's.'

'But won't you need them yourself?'

'I've more than one pair, pet.'

Maddy bit her lip. 'The thing is, though, I won't be able to get to Armstrong's until the snow thaws. My car is stuck.' She had no idea what Armstrong's was, but nine miles might as well have been ninety, and the snow might last for days.

'Mm. That's true. Well, how would it be if Jim picked some up when he's next there? I think he'll be going tomorrow; we need paraffin.'

'That would be fantastic!'

'There you go then. I'll ring you when he's got them. Oh no, no phone. Well, just come in tomorrow afternoon and I'll make sure he goes in the morning.'

The kindness of strangers. After that Maddy could hardly leave without buying something, and she picked up a wire basket and roamed the shelves, selecting treats for herself: grapes, salty biscuits, a tub of cream cheese and a carton of orange juice. Then a thought struck her, and she found rubber gloves, disinfectant, disposable cloths and bin liners. She took everything to the counter where the thin woman's shopping was being rung up. She turned bright eyes towards Maddy.

'You're Claude Lawrence's niece!' she said.

'I am,' Maddy responded, deciding to meet directness with directness.

'You don't look like him.'

There didn't seem to be an obvious answer to that. Maddy smiled and looked vaguely into the distance, aware she was still under scrutiny. She slipped a couple of poppy seed rolls into a paper bag and added them to her basket.

'But you do look like *her*.'

'Two pounds seventy-three, pet.'

The woman scrabbled in her purse. Maddy said, 'Do you mean my grandmother?'

'She was taller. Same nose.'

Okay, that was quite interesting to know. The thin woman paid for her groceries, said, 'I'll see you, Joan,' and left.

Joan took Maddy's basket. 'Sorry about Edna.' She began to ring up the goods.

'That's okay.' Maddy said, 'Thanks ever so much for the wellies. And I'm Maddy, by the way.'

'Short for Madeleine?'

'Yes.'

'Nice name, Madeleine.'

'Thank you.'

Maddy paused, then on the spur of the moment asked, 'Have you ever heard of someone called Lenka?'

'Lenka?'

'Lenka Midnight.'

'Lenka *Midnight!*'

Maddy said, 'I know. Crazy name. I just wondered.'

'Is she local?'

Maddy said, 'Um, maybe. I think she might have been here during the First World War.'

'You should talk to Edna. She's lived in Kirkwitton all her life. That comes to five pounds twenty-one. Shall I ask her for you, next time she's in?'

'Okay. Thank you.'

'We'll have your boots here tomorrow.'

Maddy stared at Uncle Claude's wellies, leaning where

she had abandoned them next to the baskets inside the door. She now had a carrier bag in each hand.

'Oh, come here. Give them to me and you can pick them up tomorrow.'

Rescued again! Maddy grinned sheepishly. Then another thought struck her. 'Do they have pillows at Armstrong's?'

'*Pillows!* No, pet, you'll need Dixon's for that.'

THE WAY HOME was infinitely easier, but walking through the deepest snow was still tiring, even with boots the right size. It was weird to feel resistance, start to transfer one's weight, and then have the ground collapse under one's foot. It turned walking into a four-beat rhythm: push-sink, push-sink, over and over. Maddy felt no inclination to investigate the gatehouse and just kept going. When she finally reached the door and set down her bags, she groaned with relief.

Coffee. Now.

But when Maddy had made her coffee she found she was carrying it out into the passage. The house was calling to her; she needed to wander.

The flat in Twickenham had two halls, both quiet and carpeted and too small to take furniture; there was the entrance hall behind the front door, from which doors led to the sitting room, the kitchen-diner and a cloakroom, and beyond the kitchen there was another hall linking the bedrooms. There wasn't much walking involved in getting from one room to another there.

Here it was utterly different. Here you could go for a hike indoors. With the time it took to walk from the back door along the rear passage, past the kitchen, through the astonishing, castle-like hall and up the stairs, she could have walked to the end of the road outside the flat; if you added in the length of the landing, the second staircase and the top floor, you'd be at the bus stop.

The passages weren't like those in any normal home, but they weren't like those in an office block either, or a public library. School, Maddy thought suddenly, that's what it's like: tramping the corridors between the form room and Hall for morning assembly, or the Old Chem Lab (the new labs had been in a modern extension), or the Music Room. Unthank was like her school!

Well, not that big, obviously. But sort of.

Coffee in hand, she rambled about, finding it comfortably familiar now. She pulled the flush for all three toilets (reasonably gushing) and turned taps on and off, testing the water pressure (serviceable). She opened cupboards and wardrobes; many were empty but some held Uncle Claude's clothes, bits and pieces of junk and household linen.

On the second landing, which she had begun to think of as The Servants' Floor, she was irritated to find the attic light was still on. What a waste of electricity. She thought she was more careful than that. She turned it off and checked the bedrooms to make sure she hadn't been careless anywhere else.

Eventually she satisfied her need for house prowling (it was extraordinary, like a drug she needed to keep topped up) and returned to the kitchen and the job that awaited her. Not a fun one, but essential if the snow was going to keep her here.

Cleaning. Maddy girded her loins.

The whole house would be impossible, of course; it would take a battalion of cleaners a week. But she set herself a goal that she thought achievable and would make a difference. She needed to be able to live without dodging spiders and grot. She needed living quarters within the living quarters. She needed a base.

The kitchen was essential, obviously, and a bedroom and bathroom, and the snug could continue to be her sitting room. Those, plus the connecting passages and stairs, would make her quite comfortable while she was in residence.

Maddy worked systematically, dusting everything first and then vacuuming with an upright cleaner she found. It was elderly but worked well enough. She fitted a slim attachment to it and poked into corners and up by the ceiling and along the skirting boards, and she moved the furniture that could be moved and got as far as she could under the heavy pieces like the wardrobe and the bed. Then she changed the attachment and vacuumed the upholstered furniture in the snug, too. Finally – and with care – she changed the bag and threw away the one full of spider and beetle and fly husks.

In the kitchen she emptied every cupboard and drawer and rinsed them all with dilute disinfectant, and washed up every item of crockery, cutlery and cookware too – a production line of sink to draining board to tea towel to cupboard, over and over again until the whole lot was sparkling and back behind doors and all the tea towels were sodden. And then she took all the food out of the larder, washed the shelves, and took stock while they were drying. She checked dates and discarded what was over, and also discarded anything open, like porridge oats and flour. Probably not necessary but she was squeamish.

When she was done, the larder looked depleted but reassuring.

Gosh, but there was a lot of space; you would never need to cram.

She was heartily fed up by then, but nevertheless took a bucket and cloths and washed every window in the three rooms, climbing on furniture to reach.

The banisters had a sticky patch, so she washed them. The handle into the bedroom was sticky too, so she washed all the door handles, inside and out, and the windowsills. And the basin and bath and splash backs, and, of course, the toilet.

Outside, night had fallen. Maddy's back was aching, her hands were raw and she was hungry. Her batteries had run down, but she felt happy and satisfied and could relax properly for the first time since she arrived, because for the first time her environment was clean.

She had run a marathon and crossed the finish line, and it felt good.

That night, despite the lack of a pillow, she slept soundly.

THINGS WERE BECOMING EASIER. She was getting the hang of it. A stand-up wash (the bath was gigantic and would take hours to fill) followed by cornflakes, toast and tea for breakfast, and Maddy was ready to start her day.

She already had a plan, formed the previous evening. After lunch she had to walk to the village and swap boots, but first she was going to put on Joan's wellies and explore the garden, even though it would be under its snowy blanket.

She set off clockwise, crossing the two courtyards, and then following a narrow path along the far side densely over-hung by conifers. On her right was the back of the stables, on her left a stone wall and, part way along, a five-bar gate. The path might once have been gravel, yellowish stones were visible in patches, but leaf mould and seed cases had taken over, speckled now with the snow that had worked its way through the branches. The seed cases were about the size of a marble and split open at the ends in a cross, like Brussels sprouts ready for the pan, but Maddy had no idea what they came from. She was sadly ignorant about things that grew.

At the far end of the path, where the buildings on her right stopped, was another gate, high and close-boarded with a curved top. It occurred to Maddy that if it was bolted on the other side she'd be stuck.

I'll have to climb over. There would be something in all those outbuildings she could drag around, surely?

But when she lifted the latch and turned the ring of twisted iron, the gate swung open. With relief she walked through.

Into the garden. Into *part* of the garden. Maddy paused in the gateway staring at the expanse spread out before her.

It was walled, and the walls loomed above her head and were brick, not stone. Spaced along them at intervals were espaliered trees, bare and grey now of course, their branches outstretched like arms. The ground was featureless under its blanket of snow, but looked to Maddy the size of a small prairie. At the precise centre of each span of wall was a door. She headed for the one opposite, *shush-squeak*, *shush-squeak*, taking childish satisfaction in breaking the flawless, sparkling cover.

The door wasn't locked but hung ajar, calling her onward with a tantalising vertical sliver of landscape, impressionistic only, the details cloaked by the snow.

Beyond the prairie was a second enclosure perhaps half the area. More trees held trained stances against the walls, this time like the canes of a fan, and at the far end the skeleton of a greenhouse stood, all but a few of the panes gone, the racking inside bare.

Maddy turned right, continuing to work her way clockwise around the house. There were more greenhouses, a long one with ornate ironwork and – jarringly – a small, modern one of the sort Maddy associated with the allotments that flashed past when she was on trains. Both were derelict, with missing glass and an air of neglect.

There were ranks of shallow boxes with glazed lids: *cold frames*, Maddy thought, and felt pleased with herself for knowing the name. And there was a row of compartments constructed from sleepers, each big enough to swallow a sofa, filled with debris and dead leaves.

There wasn't much else to see. Here and there, humps and lumps suggested things either growing or left lying about under the snow. Then Maddy dragged open another door and found herself in a new kind of place, one with a clear view instead of another wall. She paused to find her bearings. On her right the house fell back, leaving a great wide space that seemed to have no boundary at all. Maddy stared, trying to pinpoint where the grass gave way to fields and, beyond that, the fields became moorland, but it was impossible with the covering of snow. It was an incredible view.

She shook herself and brought her focus back to the garden. Perhaps fifty metres away and to the left, oddly stranded in the grass that she should probably call a lawn, stood a timber shed with large windows and a pitched roof, and Maddy was startled to remember running to peer inside, thrilled at finding a Wendy house in such an unlikely place.

It wasn't a Wendy house, of course. They had called it The Retreat, but seemed not to use it at all; it had been swathed in spiders' webs and the door handle was too stiff to budge, the door warped in its frame. Such a disappointment.

And then, while Maddy stood poised on the boundary between the kitchen gardens and the lawn, halted for the moment by her memories, snow began to fall again. A fresh wind whipped pinpricks of ice to sting her face, and she abandoned her exploration and scurried along the side of the house, hoping to find herself at the front, from whence she could navigate to the back door.

Success: at the far end, a stone archway led to the front drive. Maddy stepped under the wide arch and paused.

Someone had whistled.

She turned her head. Someone behind her, in the garden? Or in front, on the drive? She couldn't see anyone.

'Yes?' she shouted, and waited.

Nothing.

Maddy shrugged and headed on, but as she reached the courtyard she heard it again, very distant, and this time she thought it was a tune being whistled, although not one she recognised. She stood in the stinging snow and concentrated.

It was next to impossible to work out a direction, but if anything, it seemed to be coming from above.

She looked up. None of the windows were open, which was good because the snow was now blowing at an angle. And then the whistle stopped, and she wasn't entirely sure it hadn't been the wind anyway.

Maddy let herself into the house.

CHAPTER 8

Lunch, and then back to the village to swap wellies. Maddy took a carrier because she realised she was almost out of milk and would want more bread too. Those rolls were fantastic. She would ask if Joan baked them on the premises.

It crossed her mind to pause outside and listen, but she decided not to.

The gatehouse seemed shrunken beneath its heavy cape of snow. It looked icy and neglected.

'I'll come and look at you later,' Maddy told it.

She was getting pretty practised at walking in snow now. On the road the tarmac was showing through the layer of pinkish grit, but the snow on the verges was still white. Astonishing! Snow in London turns grubby in no time.

At the shop no-one was at the counter, but Joan appeared through the door behind within moments. Her sitting room, Maddy decided, must be very close.

She saw Maddy, nodded, and vanished again to re-emerge holding up a beautiful new pair of boots. They swapped and Maddy paid.

'I asked Edna about your Lenka Midnight,' Joan said as the cash register pinged.

'Oh yes? And?'

'Here's your change. She was housekeeper at Unthank back before your grandmother arrived. First World War, just as you said.'

'Crumbs.'

'Edna said there was some kind of scandal. Carrying on with the gardener, she thinks. Left in a hurry.' Joan slammed the drawer shut and leaned comfortably on the counter. 'What made you ask?'

'Oh, I…saw her name on something. Nothing really.' Maddy was reluctant to explain and didn't know why. 'Thank you, though. And do you by any chance have any aerogrammes?'

She didn't expect to be in luck, but she was. 'There's a couple of folk in the village have children overseas,' Joan explained, and Maddy slipped a packet into her carrier bag. She would write to her mother that evening, post it tomorrow; let her know the weird turn her daughter's life had taken.

Back at Unthank, Maddy lit a fire in the snug. She knelt until she was sure it had taken properly, and then stood up, intending to start her letter. But instead, her hand reached to the shelf where the old OS maps were, with the manila envelope in amongst them. She tipped the envelope and let the three keys spill into her palm, and then returned the two she knew about and looked at the third, the padlock key, that remained.

What do you put a padlock around?

A door that had a bolt. Gates fastened with a chain. A strongbox of some sort: a trunk or chest, perhaps.

It was nearly dusk; she didn't fancy venturing outdoors again today. So where might a strongbox be stored?

Maddy climbed the stairs to the gallery, climbed again to the servants' landing, and finally, reluctant without knowing why, climbed the third staircase to the attic.

The light was already on. Bother. She was as bad as Mr Pattison. She must make sure she remembered to turn it off this time.

Shivering, she made her way down the centre aisle, peering into the recesses on either side, straining to identify a padlock in the shadows. There were lots of shadows, the light from the single source interrupted by the clutter, and had Maddy still been seven years old she might have imagined eyes and twitchings and whisperings in the corners, in the dark, in the cold.

She wasn't seven, but she was imagining them nonetheless. There could be nothing in the attic with her except, probably, mice, and she could cope with those, yet her heart was bumping ridiculously and she kept thinking she could feel something touching her skin inside her clothes. Stupid of course, but horrible.

She needed to find this thing, whatever it was, and get downstairs, but that was easier said than done. The problem lay not in finding a strongbox but in finding one with a padlock. There were several suitcases, the old-fashioned leather sort, and a cute, round-lidded chest you could imagine a pirate stashing his pieces-of-eight in, but none of them had padlocks.

There was one thing with its own integral lock – a leather brief case with a dark stain across the top – and Maddy of course let the key nose at the keyhole, but it was far too small for the modern key.

Maddy shivered. The deep chill was so much sharper up here. She should have put her coat on.

There was the hint of something that looked promising at the far end, where it really was dark. Maddy bent down and groped towards the shape of something box-like under the rafters, lost her balance, wobbled, and flung out her hand. The knuckles scraped against the textured surface of wicker. The wicker creaked.

She stabilised herself and reached forward again, only to find the box she was aiming for was disappointingly made of cardboard, and the flaps opened freely. So much for that.

Still crouching, Maddy swivelled in order to retreat and hit the wicker thing again, and this time her knuckles touched metal. Metal on a basket? She explored with her fingers. The basket was the size of a trunk, a hamper that conjured up images of Edwardian gatherings, shooting parties and boating picnics: Ratty and Mole in *The Wind in the Willows*. It seemed to have leather straps either side fastened with buckles, but there was also a thick chain that ran right round its middle, and where the ends overlapped was a padlock.

Maddy fished in her pocket for the key, and a voice in her head warned her *Slow down and don't drop it!* Too true – it would be horribly easy to lose a key here, in the dark and the dust. Maddy sat cross legged and carefully brought out the key, her spare hand cupped underneath as a safety net while she fitted it into the lock and turned.

The padlock sprang open. Maddy released the chain, lifted the wicker lid, and reached inside.

Then the light went out.

THE DARKNESS WAS COMPLETE.

Maddy froze. This was very not funny. There wasn't even a thunderstorm.

Fortunately, despite jumping, she hadn't dropped anything. Now, with great care, Maddy put the keys, all three of them, the padlock key and the two new ones, in her pocket and crawled along the floorboards in search of the door to the outside world, trying not to scurry. Instinct told her that once she allowed herself to think about feeling…*anxious*…full-blown fear would come rampaging in, and that was simply unacceptable.

She crawled forward grittily, one hand grasping the book with the loose papers tucked between the pages. She had no idea what it was apart from old; her fingers recognized cloth boards worn smooth and bumped corners, and could even detect the slight indentation of a title on the front, but she couldn't decipher it by feel.

She had a fair idea what the loose papers would be, though.

Don't fall out the door! The stairs began immediately and she could die tumbling headfirst down those.

But the air changed as she reached the open doorway; it was less chill, less closed-off, less *old*. She sat back on her heels and felt for the door jamb, and then cautiously stood up, her free hand flat against the woodwork. The light switch should be about shoulder height. Maddy found it and flicked it up so that she wouldn't have to return to switch it off later. Then she felt her way down the narrow stairs and along the second landing, down to the gallery, down again to the Back Hall and at last into the snug, where the wavering, golden light from the fire had never been so welcome.

There were all sorts of things she should do next, including fetching one of the candles she had found in the kitchen, but the flames were throwing out enough light to read by and the temptation was too great. Maddy sat on the hearth rug and held the book towards the glow.

The title was in black on a very faded cover, probably once red but now a greyish pink: *A First German Primer*.

Maddy opened it at random and flipped pages. German and English bumped shoulders, and there were passages of text, lists of vocabulary and tables of conjugations. How odd. What was a German primer doing on Uncle Claude's treasure trail?

Maddy lifted the book and gently flapped it upside down, trying not to destroy the spine but hoping for some scrap of paper slipped amongst the pages that might give her a clue. But there was nothing.

She put the book on the table and turned her attention to the papers. Same handwriting, so she was right, but she'd need better light for them.

And finally, she looked at the new keys. One was small

and slender, like the piano key but without the fancy handle. The other was much larger, blackened with age and with a simple ward. She put them in the manila envelope with the others. Then she felt her way to the kitchen and then to the correct drawer, and was pleased and encouraged when she successfully had her hand around a candle. She took it to the snug, lit it in the fire, and wedged it firmly into the candlestick on the mantelpiece.

It worked surprisingly well. By candlelight, Maddy read.

Flitting Day was only six weeks away and Willy got Halpin's permission for me to leave early. We shook hands, as befitted business partners, and on Sunday, even before the milking started, I set out. I had twelve hours of daylight, from misty dawn to twilight, and expected the walk to take eight or nine of them.

I'd written down a list of villages, told to me by the pot-and-pan man. All I had to do was walk from one to the next until I arrived in Kirkwitton. 'Then it's over the bridge and on the left', said the pot-and-pan man, who had Northumberland's spider's web of lanes etched on his eyeballs. 'The first proper gates you come to, just on the bend.'

March in Northumberland is still winter; you have to look close to notice the buds on the hedgerows, tight as fists against the frosts, and trees loom grey and dormant in the mist. That month had been dry and there was little mud. It was a still day too, which was a blessing as by afternoon the way had become high and exposed, and a wind would have been whipping my skirt about my legs and hindering my stride. By then the roads were empty, the church-goers that had passed by in traps and on bicycles in the morning having returned home, and only the grating cry of rooks and the bleating of sheep accompanied my footsteps.

Walking is good at the start – the rhythm and the freedom, and marching forward with a purpose. I was ready for change, too; Halpin's had not been so wonderful that I wasn't happy to try something new.

What the new thing was to be I didn't know for sure as yet, but I had expectations. Lily was housekeeper at a big house and Sam the outside man, and if Sam was unable to do his job it was likely to be that work that I'd be doing, as far as I could. Not a bad prospect: hoeing a kitchen garden couldn't be so different from hoeing a field (less wind, surely?) and Sam would tell me what to do.

Then the road began to descend and the moors gave way to forest. At Shilston I couldn't find a fingerpost and had to ask a boy driving a cow, which paused to snatch a mouthful of grass from the bank while he pointed the way, and then I was on the last stretch; there were no more villages between me and Kirkwitton.

It is a funny thing that you can keep going for three hours or three days, but when the end is in sight you feel tired; it is as if the knowledge that you will be stopping soon makes it harder to carry on. Through those last three or four miles I was oh, so fed up with putting one foot in front of the other, and with the tramp-tramp of my own feet, and with the blister I felt forming on my left heel, and even with the croaks of the crows that had punctuated the cold air all day long. I yearned to take off my boots, make a cup of tea and sit down. Better would be if someone else made the tea for me, and handed it to me where I sat, somewhere the warmth from a stove could be taking the chill out of me. But that wasn't likely as Lily would be at work.

I realised I wouldn't know where to go. I had never called at a proper house before. Round the back, yes, but would it be obvious? Would there be a knocker on the door? What if Lily didn't answer but someone else did? Did they even know I was coming? I should have asked Emmy before I left Halpin's; she had been a scullery maid before deciding mud and muck suited her better than being up to her elbows in water and lye all day. 'Red and blistered up to here,' Emmy used to say, pushing back her sleeves. 'Give me muck any day!'

It sounded awful. Now I found myself in trepidation of what lay ahead for me. They'd better put me outdoors, I thought. I'll be off again if they don't.

Kirkwitton, when I reached it, was just a handful of cottages set around a triangle of grass. The bridge I needed wasn't in sight and neither was anyone to ask, but there were only two possible roads out and I tried the larger. I was lucky. The lane twisted and the bridge came into view.

Back doors, strangers, sculleries or not, at least the walk would be over.

There was no mistaking the gates, just round the bend as the pot-and-pan man had described, between stone gateposts the size of coffins. [That's what I said, thought Maddy.] *I pushed the gates shut behind me and was setting off along a drive between trees when my name was called from behind.*

I turned. There was a square lodge inside the gates. [Oh crumbs, yes, thought Maddy. I really must take a look at that before I leave.] *The door of the lodge was now open and a man filled the space.*

Sam Biddle. He had a crutch under one arm and was waving.

I retraced my steps.

'Lenka Midnight,' Sam said. 'You alright? Come inside.'

And of course I had to, even though the walls were so close together and the ceilings so low. The lodge as a whole was much bigger than Willy Tasker's cottage, but each of its rooms was, if anything, smaller. I won't manage this, I thought. I'll never sleep.

It must be that Lily had spoken to Sam, because he said, 'Don't worry, pet. You'll be at the flat tonight, we'll get you moved as soon as Lily's done.' As if that would make any difference.

But he did make me the tea! And sat me down by the stove.

He was a nice man, Sam Biddle. Lily did herself a good turn there.

By the time Lily came in with a crock of meat for our tea — our proper tea — dusk had set in, and the moon that night was only a paring, offering no usable light at all. But Lily knew the way and we did not fall in the ditches either side of the drive but walked with arms linked until at last the trees fell back and the German House was before me, blocking out the navy-blue sky, with arms stretching forward to — what? Greet me? Hug me? Or seize me?

What went through my mind that cold night, walking and walking towards that looming pile of stone? I remember still the queasy churning of my stomach, but was that excitement or fear? I know my clothes chafed my skin as if I were ill and over-sensitive, and I had no mind to reply to Lily's comfortable chatter about not minding Madam and my finding the kitchen gardens so easy after the turnip fields.

If you had asked me at the time, perhaps I would have replied that I sensed something momentous ahead of me, but that I did not know whether it would prove good or terrible.

For we none of us can know the future.

Maddy thought.

Clearly the German House was Unthank. She sat with the papers in her lap, feeling the weight of having inherited not just one house but two, because of the gatehouse. It was an estate. She was an estate owner.

Lenka Midnight. The scandalous housekeeper. Maddy frowned. The writing finished half way down one side, but she flipped the page anyway and was surprised to find more words on the back. Just a sentence, very brief, written with a ballpoint pen and in quite different handwriting: *It will get harder now.*

THE POWER CAME BACK on before bed time. Maddy returned to the second floor to turn off the landing lights there and saw from the yellow crack under the door that the attic light was on, although she knew she had switched it off.

Shivering, she climbed the stairs and flicked up the switch.

CHAPTER 9

THE THAW CAME TUESDAY NIGHT. THERE WAS A DISTINCT AIR of change late in the afternoon, when Maddy was rootling about in the cobbled yard looking for a long stick she could reach the ceiling with - there were cobwebs in the hall and she had the idea of draping a duster over the end of a pole. Through the open door of the outhouse, she became aware of a tonk-tonk-tonk which proved to be water dripping from the gutter onto the rusty drain cover. By the time the light was fading, pock marks were appearing in the snow as if someone had been round poking a stick into it, and there was less resistance under her boots.

When she woke on Wednesday morning almost all the snow had gone apart from corners where it had drifted. The gravel was glistening, the grass verdant; everything shone in the pale sunlight as if freshly washed, and all things seemed possible.

For a start, she was mobile again.

It was Wednesday: Day Eight. She had been at Unthank

for an entire week. Last Wednesday she had driven up from Twickenham and set her foot in the house for the first time since she was…seven? Eight? She had intended to stay just one night, and yet here she still was.

At least she had a better idea of what she had inherited now. She had even, finally, investigated the gatehouse, tramping down the drive on Sunday morning.

The air inside had been bitterly cold and the damp-plaster smell all-pervading. No radiators, of course. Experimentally, she twisted one of the kitchen taps but no water came forth; someone had turned it off at the mains.

She walked from room to room – there were no stairs. It was a symmetrical building with the front door in the centre and windows spaced regularly all around. Most of these had three narrow panes set between vertical stone transoms, but at the back the kitchen and bathroom had only single lights. The rooms opened from the hall and all you had to do was stand in the middle and pivot. The rooms on either side at the front were larger and used as a bedroom and sitting room; the kitchen and bathroom at the back were smaller – *even* smaller, Maddy thought, conscious that her perceptions had altered.

It had occurred to her, with a little kick of annoyance, that she still had neither tape measure nor ruler, and she returned to the main house.

Being snowed in had caused all sorts of problems. Maddy had been hand-washing her underwear and drying it on the giant wooden airer suspended from the kitchen ceiling, but she was desperate for a change of clothes.

She was also desperate for a pillow. And a warmer coat.

And slippers so she didn't have to walk about in shoes all the time. And if only Uncle Claude had installed a telephone…

So the thaw was wonderful, invigorating and full of promise, and immediately after breakfast Maddy started the engine – it caught first time, the Volvo had always been good for that – and drove.

The feeling of freedom was heady.

After a week buried in the depths of the wintry moors, Hexham seemed like a metropolis. When she rumbled out of the pot-holed, twisting, up-and-down lanes onto the smooth straight road and saw *traffic* – actual other cars – Maddy experienced a sort of sideways shift – no, more violent than that: a lurch – as if she had been time-travelling. It was like emerging from a storybook into reality. *Normal life will now be resumed.* It was a relief, but part of her was a little bit sorry.

She parked where she had before, climbed the steep hill to the town and took her bearings, standing at the edge of a small covered market opposite the Abbey. Narrow streets wound off in all directions. Maddy began to roam.

The first way she picked was cobbled. Not quite the metropolis, then.

It was nice. What she had expected, more or less, a random mix of shops and services: card and gift shops, opticians, hairdressers, dry cleaners, a pet shop, a dental surgery and a vet. There was an independent bookshop – always good to see – and in the smaller streets charity shops and antique shops jostled. There was also a stationer, which she dived into to buy a fresh notebook, and a miniature department store: Dixons, where she had been told there were pillows! And there were estate agents, of course, which drew Maddy's eye so that eventually she relented and paused to scan the notices in the window. It didn't help her much; there was nothing for sale remotely like Unthank. She'd have to go in and talk to someone to get any kind of figure.

She would do it. When she had measurements. When she didn't have to buy things.

In the department store she bought a pillow, some underwear, two basic tops and a pair of jeans, and slippers with fleecy linings. Then her eye was caught by some long-sleeved thermal vests and she took a couple of those too.

By the time she slung her purchases in the car she felt she had a reasonable grasp on Hexham. The sun had gone in and it was cold, so she tracked back to the café she thought looked the most appealing and sat in a first-floor window seat with a coffee and a slice of carrot cake, trying to decide what to do.

It was difficult.

She knew what she *ought* to do. She ought to go into one of the estate agents and start the ball rolling. Of course she should. But she didn't want to. She sat, thinking about doing it, about what she would say, how she would describe the property, what she would tell them regarding time scale, for she would have to wait for probate before she had the deeds; whether they would want to see it straight away in any case (they probably would, in order to get the business) and what it would feel like escorting them round.

It would mean staying on for longer. Which she hadn't intended to do. She ought to be getting back to the flat. Those poor baby spider-plants.

She would skip the estate agents for now. She would see them another time.

She finished her cake with a lighter spirit.

Before driving home she called in at Pattison's and spoke to the receptionist. 'I just thought Mr Pattison ought to know I'm still here.'

'I'll tell him. Everything alright? No problems?'

Another friendly, mothering sort. Maddy said, 'Well, some, but I'm finding my feet. People in the village are very helpful.'

'That's good. Well, if you need any help, just let us know.'

Maddy walked down the hill to the car park feeling buoyant and well cared for. People in Northumberland were very *nice*, she thought. As she turned the key in the ignition, she remembered she was supposed to have bought a tape measure.

Go back? The shops were still open.

Next time. Maddy slipped into first gear and pulled away.

It was lovely to put new clothes on. Rather than battle with heavy wet denim in the sink, Maddy investigated the washing machine and found she could make it work. It was beautifully simple – basically you put your clothes in the top, wrapping them loosely round the central paddle, sprinkled detergent over them and turned the tap on. It made quite a racket, but seemed to do the job. Putting the soaked clothes through the mangle was an experience, but that too was a lot more efficient than she had imagined, and in a little while everything was hoisted on the airer and she was drinking tea feeling competent and smug.

Before dusk, she walked into the village, but not to the shop this time. The phone box stood on the grassy triangle, its gentle yellow glow inviting her in. She stacked up her coins and dialled.

'Liz. It's Maddy.'

Her friend's voice came down the line, ordinary and familiar and as if she were just next door. 'Oh hi. When did you get back?'

'I haven't yet. I'm still here.'

'Oh.' Liz paused. 'Why?'

'I got snowed in. The Volvo was buried.'

'Oh no! Of course! I saw you had snow up there. So you're really stuck?'

Maddy looked through the glass at the wet road. 'Well, not anymore. We had a thaw last night.'

'That must be a relief. So you'll be home tomorrow?'

Home. Oddly, Maddy had been using that word for Unthank recently. Not aloud, but in her head; or was it her heart?

She said, 'Um.' And then she said, 'Look, Liz, do you think you could come up?'

IT IS EXTRAORDINARY, the energising power of decision-making. Maddy felt invigorated – fully charged, like a Duracell battery straight from the box, and all because she had made up her mind.

It had happened in the middle of writing a fresh list, this time of items she would need for Liz's stay, and didn't feel like something she was responsible for at all. It was just that as she wrote *Bed linen,* she thought she was covering herself for a couple of weeks, and as she wrote beneath it *duvet,* she knew she was going to move base. Kirkwitton was going to become Home for the next few months. She wasn't going to *stay* at Unthank; she was going to live there.

She paused, her pen hovering. What was the catch? Was there one? Mr Pattison had been perfectly clear: Unthank was hers to live in as she chose, and for her to sell as soon as probate came through. She would never again have the chance to live in a castle so she might as well make the most of it while she could.

She would have to go back to Twickenham and pack the car, close the flat properly, tell the neighbours and get the post redirected.

Rescue the spider plants.

She would do it when Liz left; give her a lift home and save her the train journey.

A new list: *Things to bring up: Clothes…*

By the time she had finished, or at least got down everything she could think of for now, Maddy was ready to eat. She opened the larder door and looked at the box of eggs, but then changed her mind and decided to try her luck at The Swaledale pub in the village. She felt bubbly and ready to cope with company. She would have a drink and see if they served food, and if they didn't she'd come back and have an omelette, but if they did she'd treat herself. She deserved a good supper. And anyway, it was her local now.

THEY DID. Standard pub fare with a couple of house special-ities, served on oak bench tables with a choice of cooked veg or salad, chips as a side. Maddy had a lamb chop, which sounded promisingly warming, with bread-and-butter pudding to follow, and it was very good.

She had driven, not wanting to walk on an unlit road in the deep dark. On the way home she stopped the car at the corner of the drive where the house came into view and turned off the engine. She got out and stood.

She listened.

The house was silhouetted, deeper black against a lighter black sprinkled with pinpoint stars; you could see the stars here, on clear nights: no light pollution.

She couldn't hear anything…anything at all…

Not even a whistle.

She concentrated.

No, nothing. Just the breathing of the cold air, and perhaps, maybe, the softest of sighs as a delicate breeze caressed the tops of the trees.

Maddy thought, *I live here.*

She slipped back behind the wheel and drove up to the door.

CHAPTER 10

Day Nine; she had been at Unthank *more* than a week and still she had yet to become familiar with the garden.

Maddy had lived all her life in a city flat; she could do summer window boxes of red and white geraniums and the more robust, independent kinds of house plant, but the rest of gardening was an alien world. Liz, on the other hand, had a house with a tiny yard at the front but a long, narrow strip at the back and she grew things: colourful things that she stuck in a vase near the front door; fresh, crisp things that she gathered for supper; perfumed things near the back step that she snipped and sprinkled in casseroles and sauces. Liz was a Gardener and a Cook; she would Know Things. Maddy wanted to have at least some idea of what lay beyond the stone walls of the house when she showed her friend around.

The ground was sopping and the sky was grey. Maddy wandered through the kitchen gardens, picking her way amongst decaying structures of planks and glass and chicken wire, pausing occasionally to gaze. Pale stems and seed heads leaned drunkenly above the low, sour-looking weeds that carpeted the soil; grass, thick and brutish, was colonising some of the beds, and there were isolated clumps of collapsed and rotting leaves. Everything was sodden and spoiled.

Almost everything. Here and there little green noses were poking through the soil and there was a swathe of snowdrops along one wall; almost all the fruit trees sported buds, and Maddy recognised lavender, low clumps of it forming a hedge around a gravelled bed.

Maddy liked lavender; there had been great bushes of it flanking the door of a holiday cottage, in the misty past when she was a girl, and the scent of it always filled her with nostalgia. She rubbed the leaves now and found the scent still there, even in winter.

She explored the greenhouses, long and draughty, housing ranks of pots in all sizes. The pots were not plastic but terracotta, mossy and chipped, and there were tools: spades and forks and trowels of various shapes with faded, wooden handles worn satin smooth. Underfoot, weeds struggled between paving slabs, and where there was open soil on either side, clouds of fairy-like fronds had reached thigh height, spiders' webs linking them in delicate swags.

Camera, Maddy thought, and went inside to fetch it. The light was flat, but nevertheless she spent a happy hour playing with views, angles, long shots and close-ups, getting to know what there was and how it might be captured under different conditions of light and weather. *And different seasons*, she thought, and the hamster woke up and twitched.

Feeling slightly sick, Maddy dragged her thoughts in a different direction. She had four days to prepare for Liz and she wanted to make Unthank as welcoming as possible. She felt it was immensely important that Liz should like it.

Her friend – her best friend really, although that sounded very junior-school – was giving her four days of her precious half-term holiday, which at short notice was pretty amazing and probably only happening because her husband Paul, also a teacher, was going to be decorating. 'He can do that by himself,' Liz had said on the phone. 'Just painting. No decisions.' They were getting their spare bedroom ready for possible guests. Liz and Paul were further along than Maddy but not yet out of sight: married, but no children.

'He won't mind?' Maddy had asked.

'No. I'm not allowed to paint anyway, not good enough apparently. I provide coffee and admiration. He can manage without that.'

Liz was breezy and confident, smart and funny. Maddy was really looking forward to seeing her and getting her view on this business of inheriting a castle.

After extracting the used film from her camera and replacing it with new, Maddy knuckled down to more cleaning. It was tiresome and tiring, but you can't invite a guest to a dusty, spider-ridden room. Thin, old-man's towels and blankets are hardly welcoming either, and Maddy planned to buy one decent set of guest linen including pillow and duvet, and a good, thick bath towel as well.

After attacking the next bedroom along, and then the remaining stretches of the landing, Maddy stayed with the vacuum cleaner and this time took it right around everywhere, sucking up all the grot that had collected in corners and using the nozzle to clear the windowsills. Now they would be able to walk safely without having their eyes drawn to soft, sinister debris. She got down and dirty with the other reception rooms too, if that's what they were called, and gave them the same care she had paid to the snug, vacuuming the upholstered furniture and washing the windows. The glass didn't look bad until you wiped it and saw the cloth black in your hand. She was coming to the conclusion that Uncle Claude had retreated to the kitchen and the snug years ago and left the rest of the house to itself.

What had he been like, this eccentric uncle of hers? It's all very well to write someone off as a recluse, but they still have to fill their hours, don't they? Twenty-four of them every day, just like everyone else. So far as she could see he hadn't spent them in the garden; surely even at the end of winter there's something to see in a well-tended garden, and not just lavender. The greenhouses were a disgrace; he hadn't even picked up the broken glass.

I need to do that before anyone comes.

She didn't mean Liz, of course; she meant estate agents, and after them, potential buyers.

There went the hamster again.

Alright then, Maddy thought, *let's just suppose.* She put away the cleaning things and washed her hands, then opened her notebook and drew a question mark in a circle in the centre of the page. She frowned at it for a moment, and then began to write.

After making a spider chart you are supposed to let it lie fallow for a while, so when her ideas had dried up Maddy made a cup of tea and took it to the snug. She had decided to look at Uncle Claude's notebooks while she took her mind off the chart. There were a lot of them. Perhaps he had been researching a hobby interest: local history or natural history (she thought of Selborne) or genealogy, although that would be tricky as the family was half Swiss.

Perhaps he had been writing a novel.

She hooked out one of the notebooks. It was smallish, case-bound in black cloth with a faded spine. The pages were the colour of very weak tea and the ink on them had faded too. What had once been black and white had become merely brown on beige, as if the colours were trying to merge.

Maddy flipped pages. There was a lot of text, but it was gobbledegook: sequences of numbers and letters, capitals or lower case, but not in any language. You couldn't read it. Here and there, drawn arrows linked blocks to one another, or a section was ringed, and many pages had letters arranged in a grid, like a word search puzzle.

The whole notebook was pretty much like that. Maddy felt a flutter of excitement as a spread of ordinary words flicked by, but when she went back to it she found herself reading a shopping list: *butter, tea, matches.*

She put the book down and tried a second, and then a third. The letters swarmed across the paper, occasionally changing ink colour, the handwriting sometimes larger, sometimes smaller, sometimes neater, sometimes pretty rough, but always the same hand. There were diagrams in some notebooks, but not of anything Maddy recognised; nothing concrete. They were geometry puzzles, interlocking circles and triangles, sprinkled with symbols some of which she recognised as Greek but most of which were strange.

It was mad. Uncle Claude was mad. Either that or he had been employed by MI5 as a cryptographer.

Maddy sighed and replaced the books. He had clearly been obsessed by puzzles, riddles and codes. Small wonder he had decided to leave her a trail of secrets as his final act, but it was annoying even so. It was like a treasure hunt without any treasure.

It will get harder now.

The really annoying part was that despite herself she had become interested in Lenka Midnight and wanted to read what happened next, but to do that she had to find out what the fourth key unlocked. Where to start? She had been around the house again, and while there were several locks, none of them accepted either of the current keys. He had said it would get harder and it had. Had he known how infuriating that would be?

Probably. It occurred to Maddy that the first instalments had come to her easily to lure her in, to whet her appetite and induce her to play the game, and she had fallen right in line.

Hmm.

Okay, back to the spider chart.

Maddy reviewed the page. It wasn't what you could call bursting with ideas. She had set down a few: arts centre, residential adult education, management training centre or outward-bound school, but the '?' that seemed the most promising was hotel or bed-and-breakfast.

The words swam about, bumping into her consciousness

like goldfish mouthing at her fingers. Guests, in her own private home. Having to look after those guests. Doing Things Right. Cooking and cleaning and smiling all the time, including when you were feeling grumpy or had a cold.

It sounded horrible. But even without the final numbers, Maddy knew enough to realise that Unthank couldn't just be a nice home in the country. Uncle Claude might have been able to stash away enough liquid cash to cover the death duties, but there was a real need for more money just to get the place straight. You really can't live in a house with only two thirteen-amp sockets in each room – well, Uncle Claude had but nobody normal could – and the overflowing gutter at the back door was not the only sign that maintenance was overdue. All the outside woodwork was flaking, some of it completely gone, and the windows were poor, draughty things and lots of them stuck. There was probably no loft insulation, and the biggest job of all, of course, would be to install heating.

The rough figure Mr Pattison had given her when she collected the keys wouldn't cover it. The bitter truth was that far from providing her with a delightful windfall, her inheritance looked like costing a small – or not so small – fortune…

Unless she sold it.

And she didn't want to.

But she would have to.

Guests. Horrors! Only three weeks ago all she had needed to worry about was unemployment, household bills and the likelihood that she would die in the next twelve months. It seemed a haven of peace and calm compared to the problems she was facing now. Such is the penalty for desiring the unattainable.

Had her uncle been kind or ingeniously cruel when he made his will? Was Unthank a blessing or a curse?

All those wretched keys.

Maddy considered. She would be driving into Hexham again tomorrow to stock up on groceries and buy the bed linen and towels for Liz. Perhaps she would drop in at Pattison's as well and ask if they knew anything about these mysterious keys. After all, the solicitor had been hired by Uncle Claude; presumably, ethically, Mr Pattison was still working for him.

BUT HE DIDN'T and he wasn't.

'I was contracted by your uncle to act on his behalf in this matter,' Mr Pattison explained. 'But once the client has deceased, the contract switches to the legatees and my responsibility is to them. Basically,' he said, 'I'm working for you now.'

They were in his office. Maddy had called in as soon as she arrived in Hexham and the friendly receptionist had said there was a space after lunch, so after shopping and killing time looking around the Abbey, Maddy presented herself back at the office and was now seated across the desk from the solicitor, who seemed not the least bit fazed by her accusation that he was in cahoots with a conspiracy fantasist.

I'm glad you called in,' he said. 'I was going to ask you to anyway.'

The time scale for probate was annoyingly, and to

Maddy surprisingly, lengthy. 'Out of my hands', Mr Pattison explained. 'Unfortunately these bodies don't have a personal sense of urgency and take their own time. Nothing I can do. But it shouldn't be too long.'

'What is "too long"?'

'Hard to say…'

Nevertheless, affairs had moved on and there was a figure now. Mr Pattison gave it to her orally and backed it up with a letter that he slid across the desk towards her. It seemed large but not huge. Maddy thought about the absence of radiators, the sparsity of electric sockets and the flaking exterior paint. She needed huge.

'This is it after all the death duties and things have been paid?'

'Yes. After all the costs and dues and taxes, that is a good approximation of what you will have left over. I can't be more exact yet but we're within a couple of thousand or so.'

Maddy folded the letter and stuck it in her bag.

His questions for her concerned how to pay the necessary taxes, the choices being out of cash or from selling some of Uncle Claude's shares, and when Maddy opted for the shares he asked her if she wanted to consult her own financial adviser or accept his, Pattison's, decisions. Never having had a financial adviser, Maddy was happy to go with him. He seemed trustworthy and she was glad to have some of this arduous thinking done for her.

After that Mr Pattison leaned back in his chair and said, 'Anyway, how are things going?' which provided Maddy with the perfect opening to tell him about the keys.

'That's exciting!'

'Well…yes and no,' Maddy grudgingly admitted. 'It is fun when I find something but I've come to a dead end.'

'Stone dead or just pretending?'

Maddy grunted. 'Pretending, I suppose. But I can't find a lock anywhere for either of these, so it's as good as dead.'

'Show me?'

Was it just Hexham solicitors who had this much time on their hands or did all solicitors keep space free in their afternoons for playing at riddles? Maddy fished out the keys. The solicitor turned them over in his hands.

'This one looks like a door key,' he said, waving the big black one.

'Yes. Can't find a door for it though.'

'And this one perhaps a cupboard?'

'Yup. Same problem.'

Mr Pattison did not appear to have the creative and devious mind Maddy had hoped. He handed the keys back and she dropped them into her bag. Oh well.

But when she was at the door he said, 'Have you asked at the library?'

Maddy turned back. 'Asked what at the library?'

'Oh, I don't know. About the house in general. Big old place like that, there might be information on it. Local history. That kind of thing.'

Local library? That was a thought. Maddy added it to her list.

CHAPTER 11

IT WAS RIDICULOUSLY EXCITING TO HAVE LIZ VISITING.

She knew she was being absurd but Unthank was like a wonderful new toy, and while she did not want to show off exactly, nevertheless she was conscious of the surprise Liz would surely feel when she rounded the last corner of the drive and saw the wild, crenellated hulk. She anticipated with thrilling pleasure the first tour, conducting her friend through the stone passages and oak-panelled rooms, watching while she took in the lofty ceilings and ogre-sized scale; standing her inside the gate to the first kitchen garden and letting her see how far away the walls were, and then showing her that there were other walled gardens further on, and then the ornamental gardens, and then the lawn.

There was the alien, folk-tale stuff like having candles on hand in case of more power cuts (two in a week did not bode well), cooking on the mighty Aga, and laying and lighting fires. Especially, she wanted the fires to go well.

Since her arrival Maddy had learned that running a

fire isn't especially easy, or not for a novice. Some evenings the wretched thing wouldn't take, and the logs just smouldered and blackened while she played around with the door of the stove, opening it a centimetre, half a centimetre, wider, narrower, while the chimney roared and the bed of cinders glowed but refused to bring forth any actual flames. One night she had to start it three times and use armfuls of kindling before the fire really got going and stayed.

But she was improving. She had instigated a new routine of topping up the log basket at lunchtime and laying the fire then. It felt easy and luxurious to enter the sitting room after supper with no more arduous duty to be done than lighting a match. (She had tried this after breakfast first, only to find, come evening, that the still-warm cinders from the night before had quietly destroyed her carefully laid paper, kindling, logs and all.) Laying the fire early also made the room look tidy and well-kept in case any visitors showed up. Not likely, but one never knew.

She collected Liz from Hexham Station in the afternoon, having stocked up on groceries before the train came in. Her friend's reaction as they emerged from the avenue was as satisfactorily awestruck as Maddy could have wished.

'Crumbs! It's like Bodiam!'

It wasn't, but Maddy saw the connection.

She parked by the back door as usual ('I haven't been able to open the front one yet') and put the food away, then spent a happy hour rambling about, first indoors and then out. As expected, Liz was especially interested in the gardens.

'Look at this! You could be self-sufficient with this much land. And the greenhouses. You could be The Good Life.'

Maddy snorted. 'The work would be never-ending.'

'Yes, but nice work.'

'Doesn't sound nice to me.'

They walked on, Liz whooping over the shiny green spears of bulbs poking through the soil and making little, darting forays between the beds and bushes and cold frames every time she caught sight of something interesting: 'Rhubarb forcers! And a lawn roller!'. Maddy watched indulgently. It wasn't that the notion of growing one's own food didn't appeal; it did. But Maddy was under no illusions about how easy it would be, neither the intellectual effort of learning what to do nor the physical labour that would inevitably follow. These walled gardens needed a team of trained horticulturists, not one lone city-girl.

Eventually they emerged from the last walled garden and stood with their backs to the gate to stare at the long, wide expanse of grass that merged gently into the distant moors.

'It's a football pitch,' Liz said. '*Two* football pitches.'

'Not quite.'

A flight of six steps took them onto a raised, gravelled terrace bounded by a low stone wall. They passed the glazed doors of the giant sitting rooms and peered in, seeing the rooms afresh from this new viewpoint. They looked dim, cold and unfriendly.

'Where did you sit when you went to visit, when you were small?' Liz asked.

Maddy said, 'I suppose we were in one of these, but I don't remember.' What did she remember? She frowned.

'They had a dog. That was exciting. Trixie…Trix. I think she was old, though. She just lay in a corner. And there was a curtain over the door.'

'A curtain!'

'Dark red velvet. It was supposed to keep out the draught. In fact, we *did* sit in these rooms because the draught came from the Long Hall. It was freezing out there.'

Twists and flickers of memory danced on the edges of her mind: the open coal fire; herself curled in a corner of a sofa, colouring; Uncle Claude bringing in the tea tray – it was always Uncle Claude that did that, never Nanna Lawrence.

Nanna Lawrence, tall and spare, permitting the talk to flow about her but scarcely joining in; Nanna Lawrence, catching her eye from time to time and planting a chilly, wobbly sensation in her stomach.

'It wasn't great,' Maddy said.

'Did you only go once?'

'I don't think so. A few times perhaps. I can't remember.'

Dusk was approaching. The lonely look of the rooms behind the glass made Maddy long for firelight and cake.

'Come on,' she said. 'Time for tea.'

Maddy had planned easy food, finger food, to minimise cooking, never her strong point. They took trays to the snug and ate crisps with the proper food, feeling bohemian and devil-may-care. Well, Maddy did at any rate. Liz talked about school and Maddy half listened and half wondered what was going to happen about the house. That seemed to be the way the issue presented itself: not *what she would do* but *what would happen*, as if she had no hand in the matter.

The obvious answer was that it would be sold and she would have enough money to stop worrying about getting a job for a while. She could go to university or tech college and change her career completely, *and* stash money away for the indeterminate future. Probably enough for a little judicious but fun spending too.

(There it was again: *it would be sold*, not *she would sell it*.)

What else could happen? It was hardly an option to let it. She wouldn't want to be traipsing all the way up here every time the tenants had a problem, and paying an agent would eat into the rent she could collect. In any case masses of work would have to be done to the place before any tenant would agree to live here.

Of course, all that would be a problem when it came to selling the house, too. It might appeal, maybe, perhaps, to someone with energy and enthusiasm and cash who was looking for a project, but Maddy doubted there were many of those about. And it was Northumberland, for heaven's sake, not Hampshire or Kent. You couldn't commute to London from here. You'd be lucky not to get snowed in most years, probably.

Wellies included. Please state your size.

'You're not listening, are you, Maddy?'

Maddy snapped to. 'Yes I am. No, I'm not. Sorry.'

'It's alright.' Her lovely, tolerant friend smiled. 'You're thinking about the house.'

'Yes.'

'What are you going to do with it?'

'Oh Liz, I honestly don't know,' Maddy said.

THE NEXT DAY brought the best weather since Maddy had left Twickenham, and at breakfast they decided to go for a walk, a proper one. 'Over the hills,' Liz said, not even bothering to ask if Maddy had already done such a thing. Maddy was not given to scrambling about in the countryside, or at least not unless she was after a particular photograph. It had occurred to her that she might explore beyond the boundaries of Unthank and the village, but it seemed a lot of bother and she wasn't confident with maps.

With Liz in charge it was much more doable, and they duly togged up. Liz had brought her walking boots as a matter of course, even on the train. 'Will you be okay in those, Maddy?' she asked, eyeing the wellies.

'Of course,' Maddy said, tucking her jeans legs carefully inside each boot. But although they were brilliant for plodding round the garden in the wet, she discovered a two-hour hike over the hills to be another matter. That tiny bit of slippage that was as nothing on the flat became annoying when scrambling up and down slopes of tussocky grass, and quickly began to rub. When she got home, she found blisters.

Liz had a barely concealed air of *told you so*. 'You need proper boots,' she said. 'Why don't we go shopping this afternoon and I'll help you.'

The shopping list generated from inheriting this house seemed never-ending, but Maddy supposed her friend was right. It had been extraordinary, standing on the high shoulder above the trees, seeing the remains of snow on the crests in the distance, breathing the ridiculously fresh air and hearing the wild, remote calls of crows. To her surprise, she wanted to do it again.

She didn't want to waste another morning in Hexham, though, so they asked Joan in the village, and then drove over the moors on roads with scary poles painted to indicate depths of snow that looked highly improbable to Maddy (*They aren't, though,* Liz told her, *so be careful*) to a village that boasted a camping shop, a nice pub *and* an interesting book-shop to explore.

They bought the boots first, Liz advising on fit and Maddy walking up and down a little ramp in the shop to test for comfort, and Maddy found she had bought a high-tech jacket and waterproof over-trousers as well, and the local Ordnance Survey map. Then they had lunch in the pub, which was called *The Handsome Jack* and had a horse painted on the sign, and finally spent a happy hour in the bookshop, which was much bigger than it looked from the outside and was very quirky. New and used books were all jumbled together, and it was full of things you don't usually find in a bookshop, like grandfather clocks and patchwork quilts and a stone head broken off a statue.

They split up to browse. Maddy chose some fiction and a second-hand book on gardening for beginners, just in case, and found Liz already at the till. 'What have you got?'

Liz spread out her books: children's novels with pictures of cats on the covers. 'Calpurnia and Mercutio!' Her friend's voice was breathy with rapture. Maddy must have looked blank. 'Didn't you ever read these? I had them from the library because they're all out of print. I'm going to read them to my class. And there's this, illustrated by Rebecca Mulligan; I love her drawings.'

Stories and drawing, literature and art, that had ever been Liz's bent; Maddy had been quite surprised when she chose history for her degree, but not when she went on to teach. She had always been bossy.

They loaded up the car and then wandered about the village a bit before driving home, while the cloud-streaked sky ran through a repertoire of colours like someone playing with a paint box.

They didn't pass a single car the whole way.

When they got home the sky was deep, soft blue. Maddy switched on the table lamp in the kitchen, and immediately the view through the window turned to black. Not for the first time she thought how much cosier was the glow from a lamp, a proper one with a shade, than under-cabinet strip-lighting.

Liz thought so too. 'You are lucky. Look at this kitchen! It's like a woodcut. A folk tale. A kitchen for baking in.'

Maddy said, 'Hmm.' She wasn't a baker any more than a gardener. The cake sitting on the table with clingfilm over it was one of Joan's at the shop.

Liz gave her a look. 'Cakes are really easy, Maddy, and so much nicer when they're home-made. Why don't we make one now?'

Maddy had cringed at the *why don't we make one* but brightened at the *now*. Cast iron excuse! 'No ingredients,' she said, hoping her relief didn't show. 'No flour.'

'Well, let's go and buy some then. I haven't seen Kirk-witton yet.'

Maddy deflated, but it was only five thirty and she knew Joan stayed open until six, so off they went again, not bothering with coats as Maddy knew she'd be able to park right outside the shop and they would only have to cross the pavement.

Joan was serving. Liz took charge and loaded self-raising flour, butter and sugar (*'The foundations'*) into the basket, then a roll of greaseproof paper (*'Essential'*), and finally a pot of baking powder, a bag of mixed dried fruit and a fresh lemon. (*'Cinnamon would be nice but you'll need the supermarket for that. I'll make a list for you.'*)

That sounded ominous. The trials of having a bossy friend.

They had plenty of eggs already so Liz said that would do, and they joined the queue. Joan was serving a thin woman in a wax jacket with two heaped baskets, and while they waited Liz started reading postcard adverts on the inside of the door. Maddy looked too. A litter of puppies for sale; a lost cat; a window cleaner and handyman – *No Job Too Small* (worth making a note of; was unbolting the front door not Too Small?); a toddler group in the village hall and a quiz night.

'Maddy.'

Maddy looked at the typed card that said:

EXPERIENCED GARDENER
All Jobs Undertaken
Weeding, Planting, Pruning, Mowing
Flexible Hours – Reasonable Rates
Ring Chris – 57722

'That's who you want,' Liz said. 'Take the number down.'

'No pen.'

'Here you are, pet.' Joan had finished serving and now pushed a biro across the counter. 'Write it on the back of your till receipt.'

What a resourceful woman! Maddy paid for the goods and did exactly that, torn between feeling energized by everyone's suggestions and resentful of them. She was being chivvied and wasn't sure she liked it.

'Going to have a nice evening in the kitchen?' Joan asked, folding her arms on the counter.

'We are!' Liz said, beaming.

Maddy said, 'Mm.'

'Ring Chris tomorrow because he's over at Eltons' tonight.'

'Right. I will.' Whatever Eltons was.

'And don't you girls get cold. You need your coats at this time of the year.'

'The car's just outside,' Maddy said, and then explained: 'I don't like walking on the road in the dark.'

'Of course not. But why don't you use the footpath?'

'Footpath?' Liz said quickly. Maddy could sense her sparking.

'Ah dear, you don't know about the footpath, and why would you?' Joan settled comfortably into teaching mode, as she had about the oil tank and then about wellies. She said, 'Now, I don't know how it looks at your end, but it runs alongside your field, through the woods and along the back of the Old Forge, and comes out opposite the green. There's a fingerpost. Keeps you off the road. Much safer.'

'Brilliant!' Liz said, but Maddy was struggling with the directions. The grass was on the west of the house but the village was to the east. How did the footpath get round to the woods? And it was a bit odd to call it a field anyway.

'I wouldn't call it a field exactly,' she said. 'It is a lot of grass, I know, but it's still a lawn.' She had been wondering yesterday how she would get it mown once it started growing in the spring.

'No, no, pet! Not your lawn, your field. Your twenty-acre field.'

Maddy stared. 'I have a twenty-acre *field?*' she said.

CHAPTER 12

'I HAVE A TWENTY-ACRE FIELD!' MADDY SAID, YET AGAIN.

They were standing with their backs to the five-bar gate half way along the path that ran behind the stables and led to the kitchen gardens, gazing across a vast plain of grass that was long, tussocky, rough and very much not a lawn. Maddy's field.

'This is mine,' she added, her mind full of wonder.

'Yes, it is,' Liz agreed, with remarkable forbearance.

Owning a field clearly didn't weigh much in her friend's life, but to Maddy it was momentous. The house and garden, despite being enormous, were still a house and garden: domestic. A field was a different thing altogether; it turned her from being merely an owner of property into an owner of land.

'You didn't know?' Liz had said as they drove back from the shop the night before.

'Not a clue. The solicitor didn't…' At least, she didn't think he had…

She had argued at first. 'There was nothing in the letter...Are you sure it belonged to Uncle Claude?' Then, when Joan had tutted and sighed enough to convince her, the doubt had set in. 'I don't know how to own a field,' she had said, her voice sounding unpleasantly plaintive. She knew she was being feeble but didn't seem to know how to stop.

Joan flapped her hand dismissively. 'Nothing to it, pet. Do what your uncle did: let Colin Chappell take a hay crop every June and the rest of the time ignore it.'

'Colin Chappell?'

'Local farmer.'

'Does he buy the hay, then?'

'No, because he does all the work, but he'll kill the weeds and mow the field for free in return for the hay. No payment either way and growth doesn't get out of hand.'

'Oh.'

So that was how the countryside worked. Interesting. Efficient.

Now they left the gate and forayed into the expanse of grass, making their way towards the far side where trees met a dry stone wall. There was no gate to be seen, yet Joan had said they could access the woodland path from the field and that the footpath in fact crossed the field. They reached the wall and began to walk alongside, and quickly found the crossing place – not a gate at all but a stile of sorts. Two big stones projected from the wall at its base, like steps, and there was a timber post driven into the ground that you could grab to steady yourself as you stepped over.

They walked as far as the village green, checking out the

route, and then turned back and walked the other way, past the stile and up the long, curving incline until they reached the summit, where rocks broke the surface of the grass like broken teeth and you could see for miles.

A wind had sprung up with nasty, stinging rain in it, so Maddy said, 'Cake?' and they retraced their steps, downward now, so easier but into the wind. They crossed the wall at the stile ('I suppose this is my wall too') and tramped through the field. The courtyards felt warm by comparison.

Maddy put the kettle on and took out plates; there were rock buns, baked yesterday evening. Liz had taken charge, unearthing baking sheets and issuing orders, and within an hour the kitchen had smelled divine. The buns, craggy and sparkling with sugar, were authentic and inviting on the cooling rack, and in truth the process had been neither difficult nor very laborious. And of course it was true: homemade tasted far, far better than shop-bought.

'Not so bad, was it?'

Maddy said, 'Alright, I could certainly make these again.'

'Exactly.'

Liz was smug but Maddy let it go. The rock buns were *very* good and they greatly enhanced coffee.

'So,' Liz said, folding her arms on the table. 'Your nutty uncle and all these keys.'

Maddy looked at her. Putting together her friend's bullheaded confidence, her energy (the hill walking was only half the story; Liz played for the county netball team too), and the enthusiasm in her voice, Maddy could tell she expected to solve the mystery at a stroke.

Maddy recognised that feeling. You watch someone

struggling to untangle string and you just know in your core that you could do it so much better. Crossword clues too; who doesn't ask if they can help, even when cryptic crosswords are not their thing at all?

Well, maybe Liz could get the trail moving again; a fresh take, and all that. She fetched the keys and tipped them onto the table. The papers – Lenka Midnight's journal, the builder's invoice, the German primer and of course the bible – she left on the bookshelves in the snug.

Liz fingered the keys. 'So, what's what?'

Maddy pointed. 'Box in attic. Piano. Hamper in attic. These two, who knows?'

Liz picked them up. 'Well, this one's for a door.'

'Yes, but which door? I haven't got a door that isn't already open.'

'What about in your gatehouse?'

Maddy perked up. 'That's a thought,' she said. 'We'll go and check.'

They did, and there wasn't a door, but Maddy was surprised to find how many locks of one kind or another there were. It was as if her brain had been sensitized to them and was noticing them everywhere: locks on cupboards, on the cabinets built either side of the chimney breast, and on the small ornate dresser. But none of them were locked and none of the locks fitted the mystery keys.

They dropped into the two chairs in the miniature sitting room. Liz looked about, tapping her fingers on the chair arm. 'This is perfectly livable-in.'

'Tiny,' Maddy said.

'Yes, but perhaps a holiday let? Very quaint. You could

have fun doing it up. Rustic-but-pretty. Rag rugs and prim-roses in milk bottles.'

Maddy pictured the gatehouse as Liz described it: bijou and romantic, perfect for young couples on a quiet country break. Kirkwitton was certainly quiet – it was hard to imagine a village more remote or a county less populated.

Could she rent it out? Would it be taken up? Would the income be enough to keep Unthank?

Of course not. The holiday season is short, probably even shorter in chilly Northumberland, and maintenance and electricity and water and taxes are ongoing. And besides, how could she be a proper landlady more than three hundred miles away?

The same question, the same problem, over and over again, and never a solution that worked.

Maddy sighed.

IT WAS Liz's last evening and they ate at The Swaledale. They walked through the dusk, using the footpath, and in the village the light was on in the phone box and children were playing in the road. Maddy's heart jumped when the raucous growl of an engine sounded behind her and a motorbike roared into view, but the children calmly mounted the bank and flattened themselves into the hedge to wait until it had passed.

The rider raised a hand to salute them as he went. Everyone seemed to do that here.

Imagine letting children as young as that toddle off and play football in the road. Was it just Kirkwitton parents who were bringing up their families with staggering nonchalance, or did everyone behave like this in rural Northumberland?

Yet there was no air of risk, Maddy realised, neither from traffic nor from predatory psychopathic rapists. She would be completely happy using the path by herself after dark, actually a lot happier than on some of the side streets in Twickenham. She had been living alone in Unthank for two weeks and had never once thought herself to be vulnerable.

Odd.

They ate steaks followed by ice cream, and finished with real coffee before heading home.

Home.

There was a full moon and no cloud, and the house was silvery, the moonlight glinting on the window glass. They went indoors and found there had been another power cut.

'I don't believe this.' Maddy rummaged for a candle but Liz said, 'Hold on, let's see what it's like by moonlight.'

So they made a circuit of the house, finding their way easily by the grey light that fell through the tall windows. The house was quiet, the air still, and Maddy felt again that Unthank was waiting to see what would happen to it next: what she would do. But what could she do?

'Do you hear that?' she asked suddenly.

'Hear what?'

They had come to a pause by one of the high, narrow windows on the galleried landing, and Liz was looking out. Plainly she hadn't heard the whistle. She said, 'You've got a summer house!'

Beyond the lawn the timber shed was floodlit by the moon and looked eerie and faintly gothic.

Maddy said, 'They called it The Retreat. It isn't floored properly though – just concrete. An old table, deck chairs. Spiders.'

'But you could tart it up.'

'Oh yes, you could do that.'

When Liz said 'you' she meant Maddy; when Maddy said it, she meant 'one': *One could tart it up. One could have rag rugs and primroses.*

The whistling had stopped. Maddy said, 'I'm not keeping this,' and immediately felt sick.

'No, I know. But it is insane.'

It was. More insane than anything that had ever happened to her in her life, and yet the clouds were closing in.

Her gaze had dropped to the windowsill. Liz said, 'Maddy!' and she raised it again to look obediently through the pane.

There was an animal, dark against the grass, picked out by the moonlight. Too still to be a dog, and not the right shape for a sheep – too svelte.

Liz said, 'It's a deer!'

Maddy thought, *This house is like a castle, and it has deer.*

And then she thought, *I don't want to do this.*

CHAPTER 13

TWICKENHAM WAS WEIRD.

How could Twickenham become weird in so short a time? She had only been away a fortnight – no longer than family holidays, and yet the sense of disorientation was immense. Because she had been alone for most of the time? Because of the enormous size of Unthank and its grounds? But she felt it in the streets too.

Maddy decided to put the strangeness down to the pressure of the whole deal: inheriting something approaching a fortune (she hoped) and having to make major decisions entirely by herself. She tried to put it out of her mind while she concentrated on the dense traffic, see-sawed her way along the side roads (all those ninety-degree corners) and finally reversed up to the hedge outside Melbourne Mansions.

No pulling up just anywhere; she had to align the Volvo accurately so that the parking spaces either side weren't impinged upon.

She let herself into the flat and felt a shock at how warm it was. Surely she hadn't left the heating on?

But she hadn't. The control was at minimum. It was just that the flat, with floors below and above, was kept warm by her neighbours. Maddy realised that for the past two weeks she had been wearing more clothes than she was used to – those lovely vests for a start, and the only time her cardigan had been off was when her coat was on.

In two weeks her perceptions had changed. Hmm.

In two weeks her opinions about space had changed too. The flat was *miniscule*. She felt she could stand in any room with her arms outstretched and touch opposite walls. She couldn't, of course, but that was how it seemed. A dolls' house; a Wendy house. And she'd shared this with her mother! She felt like Alice crushed into the White Rabbit's cottage.

It didn't last, thankfully. By the time she had turned up the thermostat, filled the fridge and was heating up a can of chicken soup, Maddy knew she was home and normality had returned. She made a cup of tea and stood at the balcony window.

So many roof tops, so many cars. It was normal, but was it nice?

I've been back an hour and already I'm missing it.

The beautiful thing was that this was, for now, temporary. One day here to sort things out and she'd be driving north again on Saturday.

She smiled. It was like being dropped into a fairy story, or like waking up in the middle of Jane Eyre or Northanger

Abbey. Unthank was her equivalent of time travel – a dip into a past before phones or fitted kitchens; a chance to play at Lords and Ladies.

The phone was a problem though. The next morning, she enquired about getting a line connected and was dismayed to learn that because Unthank never had been connected to a telephone and was so far out of the village there would be a delay of *months*. That was a blow.

Maddy worked her way through the items on her list: Redirect mail: tick. Turn off the water: tick. Her home insurance policy on the flat. *It's going to be empty for a few weeks, not sure how long yet.* A small addition to the premium but nothing major: tick.

In the afternoon, Maddy went shopping and found she was just in time to catch the winter sales, before the warm clothes all vanished. The shops were full of spring collections, laughably flimsy, but she wound her way through the lightweight tops and skirts to the bargain rails and came home with a couple of chunky cable-knit sweaters, several pairs of long socks and yet more vests. Best of all, she became the happy owner of a super-warm coat, thickly quilted with a fluffy hood. A coat warm enough for dashing between the tube station and the shops in London is not necessarily up to walking to the village in Northumberland, she now knew.

She returned her library books without taking any more out, and resisted buying anything to read because she thought it would be better, more loyal, to support the independent bookshops that were to be her locals up north.

In the evening she went to Liz's to be fed ('My treat, and it will save you having to get things in to eat') and to admire the freshly painted bedroom. She sat in the kitchen looking at the garden, lit by the windows. It was tidy and clipped and unbelievably compact, and she tried to work out how many times it would fit into one, just one, of the walled gardens at Unthank. No wonder Liz had been awestruck. Yet her friend was content here, happy and untroubled, not at all as Maddy knew she herself had been all day. Liz was still a Londoner; Maddy had changed.

In just two weeks.

The next morning, she loaded up her car and headed north.

THERE IS something so profoundly different, so transforming, about repeating an experience. Maddy had learned to use a photographic enlarger at the arts centre, watching the resident photographer explain the parts and then operating it herself under his guidance. She could still remember her second go, flying solo after hiring a session in the darkroom and finding with delight that her confidence had increased hugely. Instead of being an alien beast, the enlarger had felt familiar, the procedures understood and committed to memory. Maddy in the darkroom alone had been a different person from Maddy having a lesson, and now, unlocking the back door and carrying the first bags through to the hall, she was again a different Maddy from the version of herself who had arrived in the rain a fortnight ago.

Unthank was no longer a mystery; it had become familiar, commonplace even. She was competent with it.

Maddy propped the door open with her suitcase and went back to the car for the groceries, and finally the carrier bags of bits and pieces like shoes and the alarm clock. She had put the rear seats down to fit everything in. But the long drive – the second in three days – was over and for a while, at least, she was settled.

While the kettle was boiling, Maddy took her suitcase and bag of shoes upstairs. She left the case open on her bed and carried on up to the second floor, and then up the attic stairs to turn the light off.

She had mentioned the attic light to Liz, but not until they were on the way south. Maddy hadn't wanted to alarm her friend while she was sleeping in the house, and certainly didn't want to put her off staying. 'You're not worried about ghosts, are you?' didn't strike her as the best of greetings.

As it happened Liz wasn't worried at all and was actually pretty dismissive. 'You just forgot to turn it off.'

'I definitely did not! The first time, perhaps, but not after that. I started taking note.'

Liz shrugged. 'Dodgy connection, then. You need to get an electrician to look at it.'

Maddy found she was annoyed. She said, 'Well yes, that could be it. But it isn't just the light. It's really cold up there.'

'Maddy, it's really cold *everywhere*! That house is freezing!'

It was true, but the cold in the attic was different, Maddy thought – at least five degrees lower, like the quiet breath of an ice monster.

After that she had decided not to tell Liz about the

whistler. Her no-nonsense friend would doubtless say it was just the wind in the chimney, and Maddy wasn't sure she wanted to believe that.

She was aware that it was a little strange of her to *want* Unthank to be haunted, not to mention ridiculous; she had never believed in ghostly goings on before, and it was inconvenient too. Maddy was acutely aware how close she came to fear when she was up there, although normality always – or always so far – returned by the time she got back downstairs. But if the house *were* haunted – *if* it were – then it was her ghost and better kept secret.

The next morning, she used the call box in the village to call Chris-the-Experienced-Gardener. The phone was picked up by Chris's wife, who said he was out on a job but would ring her after lunch. Maddy explained that she had no phone and was using a public call box, and Chris's wife said he would come round then, and what was Maddy's address?

'Unthank,' Maddy said, 'Kirkwitton.'

'What's the name of the road?'

'I don't know. Do country roads have names? I'm at Unthank, the great big house just over the bridge coming out of the village. Big stone gate posts.'

'Oh! That place! I thought an old man lived there.'

'He did,' Maddy said. 'He was my uncle. I've inherited it.'

'Oh, well, congratulations! I mean, I'm so sorry. I mean –'

'I know,' Maddy said. 'Don't worry. We weren't close. It's fine.'

Chris's wife rang off, and Maddy pulled her boots on to

walk round the garden and remind herself of what was there and what needed to be done. Not that she really knew, even after Liz's visit. She had no intention of cultivating things, or of paying an Experienced Gardener to cultivate things on her behalf. She just wanted it to look less like a waste ground and more like a potential asset for the day she brought in an estate agent. She hoped very much that this Chris wouldn't be expensive. Without a job, she was living on her savings, an uncomfortable thought every time she drew cash out.

She felt the hamster shifting in her stomach. Neither she nor the hamster wanted an estate agent or an estate agent's lackey tramping round Unthank with a clipboard and a tape measure. He would bang on about mundane matters like central heating (none) and fitted carpets (also none), when all the time it was a *castle*, for heaven's sake! Who could care about fitted carpets?

I'll deal with it later. And in any case, Unthank wasn't actually, properly hers until probate came through. She couldn't ethically set estate agents going yet, could she?

As usual Maddy shoved the problem aside and went for a walk around the greenhouses, stepping carefully to avoid the broken glass. Once upon a time, these had been used for raising tender plants that couldn't cope with the Northumbrian winters. Liz had explained the principle of walled gardens to her. They weren't just about dividing the space into friendly chunks, like rooms in a house, but a scientific and practical device for increasing the growing season of fruit by absorbing and storing warmth from the sun in the porous bricks and giving it gently back to the trees that were trained, spread-eagled, against them. It seemed to Maddy elegant, efficient and surprising that people so long ago had worked it all out. But then, she was constantly surprised by what people from long ago knew how to do, whether it was extracting iron from rocks or turning sand into glass or building bridges that didn't fall down. She, secondary-school-educated in the twentieth century, knew none of these things.

She went indoors feeling disheartened and pessimistic about what any gardener could do for such a bomb site, no matter how Experienced.

But when the man himself turned up four hours later her gloom dissipated like mist in the sun. She quickly discovered that against Chris, pessimism hadn't a chance.

He rang the bell at the front door, a sound Maddy hadn't heard before and took a few moments to identify. When she did, she dashed out of the back door and pelted through the courtyard, skidding around the corners, fearful he would give up and go away. But he was standing outside the great square porch, his back towards her, gazing at the avenue. He turned at the sound of her footsteps and said, 'Beautiful cedars,' and came towards her with his hand outstretched to shake. 'Chris Beattie. Alright?'

Maddy slewed to a halt. She knew this one now. You didn't say, *I'm fine thanks* because the person wasn't asking if she was all right but saying Hello. Instead, she said, 'Maddy Lawrence. Thanks for coming.' They shook hands and Maddy said, 'Can I show you round?'

'Oh aye. Definitely. I've been hankering to see inside this place for years.'

He was very tall, which must be an advantage for a

gardener, Maddy thought; less need of a ladder for pruning and whatever else you did with trees. He was broad as well, though not fat, and exuded an aura of strength and competence that Maddy felt encouraging.

I must remember to get him to unbolt my door.

They went anticlockwise, starting with the ornamental garden alongside the terrace and then working their way through the walled gardens, Chris Beattie sweeping his knowledgeable gaze across the neglected ground, Maddy conscious of her ignorance of all things horticultural.

'I don't think my uncle had done anything with this for years,' she said. 'Decades, probably.'

'Not decades.'

'No?'

'No. This is just annual weeds. Two years at most, I'd say.'

'Oh.' Maddy mulled this over. 'But what about all the wreckage? It looks like an army's rampaged over it.'

'Storm damage.' Chris Beattie stirred an upturned pot with the toe of his boot, an impressively heavy-duty affair with a deep, ridged sole. 'Wind throwing things about. What's over here?' He struck out along one of the narrow paths towards the greenhouses and Maddy trailed behind.

'Mind the broken glass,' she called, conscious of her landowner responsibilities. 'It's everywhere.'

But Chris had reached the first greenhouse and stood surveying the derelict shelves.

'Now, he wasn't using these much.'

'No?' Maddy said again.

'No. These pots are ancient. This was just used for storage, I'd say.'

They mooched about, the gardener pulling weeds away from cold frames, rocking posts to test for stability or rot (Maddy wasn't sure), running his eye over the bare branches of fruit trees. He sniffed the contents of the compost heaps and picked up handfuls of soil just to drop them again. Maddy thought she could almost see his brain ticking.

Eventually they reached the courtyards and he said, 'All right. What do you want me to do?'

Maddy had prepared for this. 'I don't exactly know,' she said. 'Have you got time for a coffee and we can talk about it? And could you help me with a bolt too?'

Twenty minutes later she waved him off from the front door, open for the first time in eons, judging by the dust on the bolts. Chris Beattie had shifted them, although she could see they took even him a bit of effort, and then he fetched an oil can from the back of his van and got them sliding nicely for her.

He was a gentleman, and Maddy was sorry she wasn't going to be hiring him after all. Especially as he had been so keen on the prospect.

They had sat in the kitchen with mugs of tea and biscuits, Maddy having failed, despite her best intentions, to make more rock buns. Chris had insisted on taking his boots off at the door despite Maddy's assurance that the stone floors wouldn't mind a bit of mud and were freezing.

'Basically,' she said, 'I want it to look presentable.'

'What do you mean by that?'

'Not neglected. Reasonably tidy. Ordinary.'

Maddy was aware she wasn't really helping. She pulled a face.

Chris said, 'Do you want to grow things in it?'

'I don't know. I mean, it would be nice, but…'

The Experienced Gardener didn't even sigh; he had, Maddy thought, the patience of an infants' school teacher.

He leaned back. 'How about I give you some choices?'

'Oh, yes please,' Maddy said with enthusiasm. Choices sounded much easier.

'All right. First option: we aim to restore the garden fully, ending with a proper working kitchen garden and glass houses, and mixed border along the terrace. You'll have vegetables and fruit and cut flowers for the house, and the National Garden Scheme will want you to open to the public once a year.'

'Really?' Maddy was staggered. 'Is that possible?'

'Of course it's possible. But it will take me and two other gardeners a year to get to the point where one person can maintain it, and either you or I will have to put in a lot of hours a week from then on to keep it going. It's nice work, but hard work.'

'Oh.' Maddy deflated. 'Expensive, then.'

'Yes. Next option: I clear the weeds and junk, fix the broken things and make all the areas safe. I can do that in a few weeks if I fit you in around my other customers. The beds will be empty, and to keep them clear of weeds I'll cover them with light-proof lining material. All of them. You'd never keep them clear by just hoeing, the area's too great. You'll have to pick the fruit, of course, but I can help with that if you want. That's the minimal option.'

'Affordable.'

'I hope so.'

'But ugly.'

'Very. Boring too.'

'Are there any other options?' Maddy asked. She wasn't terribly hopeful but Chris said, 'Yes. And here's what I recommend.'

CHAPTER 14

Maddy couldn't wait for him to go.

He was a nice guy, kindly and straightforward and reliable, and his Third Option was sheer genius. But after they had done drinking tea, they took another quick circuit of the gardens for Chris to outline what he was proposing, and when Maddy had commented casually on the astonishing view from the terrace, Chris had said equally casually, 'Well, that's the point of a ha-ha of course.'

Maddy was surprised. 'There's a ha-ha?' She thought they only went with stately homes and palaces. Unthank was huge by ordinary domestic standards but hardly Blenheim.

'Didn't you know?'

Chris led the way off the terrace and across the lawn until they reached the edge and for the first time Maddy saw the drop.

'Gosh,' she said. 'You'd think Capability Brown had been here.'

'Aye, well, he probably was.' The gardener looked at her sideways. 'You know he was a local boy?'

'He wasn't! Was he?' Maddy wasn't sure if he was joshing her.

'Grew up in Kirkharle. Went to school in Cambo.'

'Well. Gosh.'

They turned back towards the house and it was then that Maddy saw it. Her heart missed a beat – corny but that was how it felt. Was it really there? She strained her eyes as they walked closer, and found she was holding her breath as she fought to focus beyond the straggly winter foliage of the border, the brown stems and blanched leaves of whatever tall shrubs had been growing at the back.

She was right; it was there.

They concluded business next to the van. Chris gave her his card with his house address scribbled on the back ('Just pop a note through the door') and Maddy thanked him yet again. She waited until his van had disappeared between the trees, which she now knew to be cedars, then flew indoors and grabbed the keys.

If they didn't fit, she'd cry.

She almost fell down the steps from the terrace and jogged along the border, searching for the place. And there it was, the tall stalks leaning drunkenly against each other and behind them, the small wooden door in the terrace wall.

The keyhole was a bit chewed up but the iron key went in sweetly and turned. Maddy pushed, and the door scraped open.

It was a large space, a room not a cupboard. The floor was earth and the ceiling a vault of stone blocks. Facing her was a stone wall which Maddy judged to be approximately where the wall of the house would be, so this space didn't extend under the floor.

It smelled damp and earthy. There would be creatures.

But she didn't have to stay long. Whatever it had been built for originally, it contained nothing now, not tools nor crates nor equipment, but simply one metal box. It was a little larger than a shoebox, and had a square plate at the front with a keyhole. Maddy squatted and unlocked it, and grunted with satisfaction as she drew out the papers she had expected, the key she had feared, and a slim brown envelope, stuck down.

MADDY CURLED herself up in the chair in the snug and read.

Did you see what I did there? Raised a question in your mind and left you with it, didn't I? Was the German House safe or dangerous? Would it be a haven or a threat? Should you be rejoicing with me in my good fortune or quaking with fear for my future? Oh, I know how to tell a story; not for nothing was Jeremiah Midnight my father.

I was to have the coachman's flat above the carriage house, where Sam had been sleeping until he married Lily. There was no coachman any more although there was cob and a trap. Tom, the horse was called. Sam had been looking after him, but the outside boy was going to take that on. 'Be good if you can keep an eye, though,' Sam had said over tea. 'Not patient, is Percy. Bit too quick with his fist.'

Lily led me across the yard and up the stairs, her boots clumping above my head. 'Here we are.' She stood back to let me see. 'You'll be all right here, won't you, Lenka? It's bigger than at Halpin's.'

Well, it was; longer, anyway, and there was just me in it, not Willy

Tasker as well. But the pitched roof came down to the floor at the sides and you could only stand up in the strip down the middle. I shuddered. It was dark, too.

'I'll light you a lamp. You'll be better then.'

I sat on the bed next to my bag and let Lily bustle. She was always a kind girl and it was making her feel better even if it didn't help me much.

'I'll just get the stove going. I'll show you how to do it.'

We were upstairs and there wasn't a hearth, but Lily was lighting a match and turning a knob and shutting the door of the narrow stove in the middle of the room, and a smell like tar reached me.

'Paraffin. Turn it off when you go to bed.' Lily stood with her fists on her hips. 'Well.'

'Thank you,' I said. Then, 'I'll be all right now, Lily. You go along back.'

'If you're certain…'

'I'm certain.'

So she went, and I unpacked my bits and pieces and found somewhere to put them, and later, when the place had warmed up, I got into my night dress but kept my stockings on, and turned off the stove and the lamp and huddled in the bed, trying not to think about the ceiling just above me and hoping my long walk had made me tired enough to fall asleep quickly.

And that was my first night at Unthank, although back then the people locally called it 'the German House' because the family spoke German. That was ignorance, though, because the Birchers spoke the German language but were not German at all. They were Swiss.

I say the Birchers, but by the time I arrived there was only one Bircher left, the others having departed soon after the outbreak of war, as Lily recounted to me during the first few days. They had sons, that was *part of it: sons full of notions of adventure and heroism, and one of them already eighteen. The language was the rest: being Swiss did very little to quell the rising anti-German emotions in the locality. Lily thought there was something about family property in Switzerland too, though what she couldn't say. In any case, they upped and left in October 1914, taking the boys with them but leaving the boys' grandmother – Madam. It was Madam who actually owned Unthank, Lily believed, although why an old Swiss lady of means should choose to buy an estate in the far north of England she did not know.*

'But why did they leave her behind?' I asked.

Lily shrugged. 'I don't believe they liked her much.'

It seemed a callous way to carry on, although I've since learned not to like Madam very much myself. She's not a very likable person.

So the family had shrunk from six to one. The kitchen maid and housemaid were dismissed and shortly after that the cook handed in her notice. (Ambitious, Lily said. She wanted to do dinner parties, not invalid trays.) Since she arrived, Lily had obliged by being scullery maid and kitchen maid and helped out the chambermaid too, so now she stepped up and started cooking. And then the chambermaid left, saying she was lonely and was going to try her luck as a bondager, or failing that, as a herring girl over at Seahouses come the spring ('Serve me right for blabbing,' Lily said. 'Made it sound too much like fun, didn't I?') which left Lily inside and Sam outside, and Percy Whatmough, the outside boy Sam thought was too quick to use his fist on a poor horse.

That was the household I joined: four of us to look after one old woman, the last of the Bircher family in England. Clara Bircher was her name. Frau Bircher we had to call her to tradesmen and the like, or Madam when we were addressing her, which I never did at all for the first few weeks because she never came outside and I never ventured farther into the house than the kitchen, where we took our meals.

Lily was right. Working in the kitchen gardens was a lot easier than working in the fields. There wasn't the wind for a start, and the tasks were diverse too. It was February, time for preparing the beds for sowing, finishing the pruning and washing the glass houses. I stone-picked and dug and raked and fed the soil with manure that I collected in a wheelbarrow from the muckheap in the stable yard, and even that wasn't half as bad as muck spreading on the farm had been, when you spent days and days on it and went to bed feeling like an old woman with aching bones and blisters on your palms. I sorted seeds in readiness and wrote labels to mark where they were to be sown, and Sam Biddle sat by on an old milking stool and talked and talked about vegetables so that eventually what he was telling me stuck. He was a good teacher, steady and quiet, and he was patient with me when I went wrong. He showed me where to make the pruning cuts and explained why – 'That branch is growing inwards, see? You want an outward-facing bud' – and taught me the names of all the varieties of apples and pears and damsons and soft fruit he had growing, all of which I was to be exceedingly grateful for, for reasons you shall hear in time.

And when my work in the gardens was done for the day, I walked down to the field where the cob spent his hours among the sheep and slipped his halter on to lead him back to the stable, because Sam was dead right about Percy, who was a skinny, orange-haired monkey, and I'd caught him cuffing the horse about the head on my second day. I like horses and missed Black Jet when Jeremiah sold him. The women had little to do with the horses at Halpin's, and it gave me pleasure now to take Tom out to graze each morning and bring him in at night. I filled the hay rack too, not trusting Percy an inch, and that left him only the mucking out of the stable to do.

Then one day Sam asked me, right there in the middle of the carrot bed, trickling seeds into the row I'd marked out, whether I would stay on after his leg had mended and be his outside boy in place of Percy.

I straightened up and stared at him.

'Only he's no good, that 'un, and he's all talk of going to be a soldier anyway. You can do everything he does, and better, so long as you don't mind. And you'll be a sight more use to me in the garden. He's got no interest, Percy, no interest at all.'

Outside boy? It was menial – bringing in the coal, taking out the water, cutting the grass. No harder than being bondager to Willy Tasker. Almost all of it was outdoors. Lily and Sam for company.

'Yes,' I said. 'Done.'

At the end of the week, we saw Percy Whatmough off the estate for the last time, and though he scowled a bit I think he was pleased enough. Country life was too dull for him, he said, and he wanted to join up and see the world.

Well, we know now how that turned out, but at the time we were just glad to see the back of him, Sam and me. And Tom.

So that left the three of us, or four if you count Madam, which we didn't. Lily coped with her and the house and the cooking, and Sam and I managed everything else, and it was fun. You always have something to show, when you're growing things, not like indoor work, flat out from when you get up to when you go to bed, sweeping and washing and polishing just to get back to where you started; chopping and boiling and scrubbing the pans and putting them away just for people to get hungry again. Where's the satisfaction in that? But taking some basic items and making something that wasn't there before, that's creative, whether it's soil and seeds and water or wood and hammers and nails.

We were like a family, we three, sharing our ups and downs, having a laugh sometimes. Lily had always been a mimic and could reproduce Madam's haughty, harsh German accent so accurately, making Sam and *me jump sometimes if she timed it right. We shared the excitement of the summer fair, and the harvest home, and the day when the man with the camera came and took our photographs. From Birmingham, he said he'd come, documenting rural life, and somehow or other he'd found his way to the German House and wheedled Madam into letting him document our own little slice of rural life in the kitchen garden. I asked him for a copy when they were done and he said he'd be sending it to Frau Bircher, but I got him to promise to send one to me, too, because Madam wasn't one to share with the servants.*

The months wore on. That winter was shocking, and I was glad indeed not to be at Halpin's but to have brick walls and glass houses to shelter me from the worst of the weather. When March came around again, I'd been at Unthank a full year and knew it had been the best year of my life.

Two years on and we were still settled. I had seen enough of the kitchen gardens now to know that was where my interest lay, and I would not willingly return to the open fields. There is much more variety, much more to think about, when raising food straight for the table.

That last winter was a vicious one, and slow to leave. April 1917 opened with a blizzard, but when the snow had finally cleared Sam and I started sowing again, and a month later the soil was throwing up green shoots, fat buds swelled on the fruit trees, and the days grew warmer and the evenings longer. Soon, I thought, I would be able to sleep out again as I always did, get away from that horrible roof, for lying under the low ceiling in the winter months was the only bleak side to this position for me. Apart from that, in every way my life had taken a turn for the better; that Percy Whatmough had done me two good turns, first by breaking Sam's ankle and then by being a bad sort. And I had become as fond of the cob, Tom, as I had been of Black Jet.

Then in September of my fourth year, Sam and Lily told me they wanted to take two days off together and go on the train to York, because Lily's aunt, who had been in service there, had died and Lily was her only surviving relative. She could have gone alone, but they decided to go together – it would be a holiday, a treat, a special time for them.

'I've cooked the meals,' Lily told me. 'You only need to heat them up, I'll show you how.' (I'd never handled a range in my life.) 'I'll pretend I'm going down with something. Influenza, I'll say. She'll never know.'

She was becoming infirm by then, Frau Bircher, and couldn't manage the stairs any more, so Sam had asked the knife grinder when he came and between them they brought a bed down to the parlour next to the drawing room, and in those two rooms Madam lived, day and night.

Lily showed me how to work the range, and where the food was kept, and how to lock up the house at night, and when the day came I waved them off – Kirkwitton Station was only a walk away – and set about holding the fort for the two days they'd be gone.

I'd been through York in the old days, with Black Jet and the Dunston, but never since; it would be fun to hear Lily talk about it when they got back.

I thought it would make up for having to cope with Madam and that range while she was away.

Maddy put down the pages. The worst of it was that she was interested in the story now. She wanted to know how Lenka Midnight fared while Lily was in York, and how she coped with Madam, and when the gardener would arrive with whom she was going to get up to no good, as it clearly wasn't going to be Sam Biddle.

Hadn't been Sam Biddle; this wasn't a story, it was the past. All this had already happened, and happened here at Unthank.

The other sheets of paper in the envelope were no help at all. Maddy read them, pondered them, and then slipped them back into the envelope to think about another time.

What a strange era, when three adults in their prime were needed to look after one old woman. How old had Frau Bircher been by then?

Maddy went to the snug and opened the bible. 'Madam' was easy to identify: Clara Maria Bircher, born in April 1828. The next name, Anders Wilhelm Bircher, born in 1863, must have been her son, and the following five, all born in the 1890s, her grandchildren.

April 1828. In September 1917 'Madam' had been eighty-nine.

She wandered into the Long Hall and looked down its length towards the Front Hall and the vestibule inside the porch, which she would be able to use now, thanks to Chris Beattie, Experienced Gardener and all-round good egg. If his idea worked it would be brilliant.

Seventy years ago, Lenka Midnight had stood in this hall, trodden the passage between the kitchen and the pantries, crossed the courtyards to the stables and laboured in the walled gardens. What a different life she had led from Maddy's own. How extraordinary that she had written so much down, and that it had survived. Where had Claude found it? And why had he taken all this trouble to get her to read it?

And why on earth had he made everything so bloody difficult?

CHAPTER 15

JOAN'S DIRECTIONS WERE GOOD. MANY PEOPLE'S ARE NOT. Maddy supposed someone running a Post Office and general store in the depths of the countryside would have plenty of practice at telling people where to go. Despite having been at Unthank for nearly two months now, it was the first time she had taken the east road out of Kirkwitton, and the way was twisty and steep for the first couple of miles. But then she reached the high ground and suddenly could see all the way to Scotland.

The hills in the distance were amazing.

A few miles further on, the road began to descend and she was between trees again. Maddy recognised the bridge Joan had described and took a left. Half a mile further and she pulled into the yard of Armstrong's, the country store, which looked like a warehouse. She felt nervous. This was not shopping as she knew it.

Metal racks laden with boxes and packets and tubs of… what? She paused and read a few labels: Swarfega; wood preservative; *rat poison!* There were shovels and forks, heavy-duty toolboxes, rope and string and black plastic bags. On one side was a horsy alcove full of complicated-looking bridles and brightly coloured nylon halters and a tub of brushes with wooden backs. The leatherwork smelled lovely, as new leather always does, and much nicer than the oil-and-tar scent of the rest of the store.

Dozens of cardboard boxes of screws and nails and washers; racks of hammers, screwdrivers and axes; reels of hose, of rope, of chains, and a stack of plastic buckets. Up ahead, shiny green and red lawnmowers were parked in a row, like push-along toys for grown-ups.

Voices drifted through an open door. Maddy stuck her head into a tiny room with a cash register and said, 'Excuse me?'

The two men paused and looked at her.

'Gloves?' she asked.

'What kind, pet?'

'Thick. Very thick. *Really* thick.'

'Work gloves up the stairs, pet.'

There was a short run of wooden steps beyond the lawn-mowers. At the top Maddy found clothing, mostly water-proofs and sweaters and mostly black, navy or dark green. Further along there were also hats and gloves, and − yes − work gloves too.

She roamed the shelves, hunting for a pair that would protect her for the job she had in mind.

'You alright there?'

'I want some heavy-duty work gloves,' Maddy said. '*Really* thick ones. Leather, I should think.'

154

Fifteen minutes later she was leaving with a pair of yellow leather gloves, padded and lined with cotton.

She'd bought a thinner pair too, with leather palms but cotton backs, in case the need for something more dexterous arose. One never knew.

Maddy felt bizarrely countryish, pulling out of the yard and joining the lane: competent and casual. She was now a person who could deal with country stores. Easy; what's next? But she knew it wouldn't last.

Her temporarily breezy mood was helped by the upturn in the weather. There had been another cold snap after Chris Beattie, Experienced Gardener, paid her a call, and although the snow had been light this time the temperature had plummeted and there was a sharp freeze. Unthank, never warm, had once again returned to arctic conditions, and Maddy had hidden away in the snug and the kitchen, keeping the electric bar heater in her bedroom. It had been too cold to venture into the rest of the house, too cold for more than the swiftest washing, and she had felt herself to be almost hibernating, like some small furry animal.

It hadn't been all gloom. With only a scattering of snow she had been able to wear her new walking boots to the village instead of the icy wellies, and her new coat was wonderfully warm too. But she knew in her heart she was marking time, allowing the freezing weather to put her on hold when she ought to have been making decisions, and once the milder weather began its advance, the combination of guilt, doubt and uncertainty hanging over her head all her waking hours made her miserable.

Then her bank statement arrived, successfully redirected, and Maddy realised she couldn't prevaricate any longer.

That had been Friday, and it had rained solidly for twenty-four hours. On Saturday the sun was out, though not warm, and the sky was clear. Everything was dripping, but Maddy's excuse for inaction had vanished, and she drove to Armstrong's to buy gloves.

It was still only eleven o'clock. Maddy braced herself and got started. But her new padded gloves proved too thick for the finger-and-thumb precision that was called for, and she abandoned them for the lightweight cotton-backed ones.

Now her hands were cold and vulnerable. Picking up the shards of glass had to be done in slow motion with immense concentration, applying enough pressure to take hold of the piece but not so much that the edges cut.

'Ow! Blast!'

After ten minutes Maddy threw down these gloves too and stomped back to the outbuildings to look and to think. There must be a proper way. Somewhere deep in her core an alien, trembling thing touched her as if with a tentacle. She took a loud breath in and out and wrenched her mind away.

She returned to the greenhouses with a spade and a battered sieve, if that was what it was called, and began shovelling dirt, stones and glass into the sieve and shaking the earth through until only glass and stones were left. Well, and shards of terracotta, and dry, fibrous roots, and sticks and leaves and the odd empty snail shell. She wasn't inclined to be picky. Everything caught by the sieve went into the bin bag in the wheelbarrow, and she was proud of herself for thinking ahead and starting a second bag before the first was too heavy to lift; but she also shivered inwardly at finding herself in the position of having to think of such a thing.

Her hands were freezing. She put the padded leather gloves back on.

Such a *boring* job. Hard physically too.

She tried bending with her legs spread and her elbows on her thighs, and she tried standing bolt upright with the sieve out in front, and she tried hunkering down on one knee. She tried shaking from side to side and back and forth, quick shivery shakes and large, rhythmic ones. Her back started to ache first and then her shoulders joined in, and the wind around her head was vicious. She really, really wanted to go in for a coffee and three times she very nearly did but had the self-knowledge to realise that once indoors she wouldn't come out again, and this glass absolutely had to be got rid of. It's one thing to have a no-go area for yourself, but if other people were going to come into the garden, she had to make it a safe environment for them.

At last the ground was cleared, but she still had to tackle the greenhouses. Thankfully the broken glass here was much easier to deal with because the floor was paved and she could use a broom. She swept up everything, glass, leaves, broken pots and plant labels, and trundled the wheelbarrow to the heap she had started. She would have to rent a skip; there was clearly going to be *a lot* to go in it.

After that she did permit herself to go indoors, shed her outside layers and filled the kettle. The weight of it, full, made her hand shake and she sloshed water when she put it down.

'Blast.'

She wiped up the spill and spooned instant coffee into a mug, and her hand was still shaking and almost scattered the granules, but not quite. She poured the hot water with intense concentration, and it occurred to her that if she scalded herself no one would hear her scream or come to her aid. She missed home, and knowing Ian Jackson was just across the hall in the opposite flat because he worked from home and almost always was there.

She missed Liz too, and she thought of walking to the phone box to call her but knew she wouldn't, partly because it wasn't the right time to be calling her and partly, she knew, because holding the phone would inevitably remind her about the *last* time she had held the phone, which was this morning at nine o'clock when she rang the estate agents and arranged dates and times for them to make their valuations. And it was when the memory of that struggled through to the forefront of her thoughts that she started crying.

AFTER LUNCH, which offered comfort in the form of a cheese sandwich with an apple, she felt a bit better. But there was so much still to be done – by her and by her alone – and not that much time, even though she would have two days before she met the estate agents. She had arranged for three, one either side of lunchtime on Tuesday and the last on Wednesday morning. The plan was to consider all three and make her decision on Wednesday afternoon, call the lucky guy and give instructions immediately so that the survey and photos could be taken Thursday. She thought they would get photos and descriptions done quickly, wouldn't they? She had never sold a property before and she was on her own.

And in the meantime, there was still this wretched garden. That she had been thrown a lifeline in that respect just made it harder right now because it meant she absolutely had to get it passably safe first, which just loaded more work on her plate (mixed metaphor but stuff it) and also, if she were brutally honest, because in her present mood she'd have quite liked an excuse to let it all go hang. Grounds that big had a role to play just by preventing anyone developing a housing estate or factory on your doorstep, and so what if they were left to slump into a hideous, overgrown, festering mess? It wasn't reasonable to expect her, a non-gardener aged twenty-nine and (it appeared after this morning's work) in possession of a dodgy back, to turn it into Sissinghurst in one season. So stuff that too.

Maddy had enough detachment to recognise that her true nature was not in charge today. The cheese sandwich had helped, but the trembly feeling was still there.

I wish it was next year and all this was over.

Yes. But.

She sat on an upturned bucket in one of the greenhouses, because a bitter wind had sprung up while she was indoors. Another thing to contend with. Northumberland was a hat-inducing county.

She had thought that looking at the house from outside might help. So far it hadn't.

She needed milk. Coffee was okay black but not tea, and no milk meant no cornflakes either. But she didn't want to go to the shop because Joan would want to chat and her first question would be 'Have you decided what you're going to do yet?'. Maddy didn't want to discuss the decision to sell, and not discussing it when it was enveloping her conscious mind like some vast thunderous cloud was just too hard; Joan would winkle out the truth and it would be in the public domain. That couldn't happen. The only way Maddy could see herself getting through this was to keep everything totally private until it was a fait accompli with no going back. Sympathy was the last thing she wanted; she hadn't even told Liz. She hadn't even told her mother.

Oh crumbs, her mother.

WHEN HER BOTTOM BECAME NUMB, she stood up and went for a tour of the grounds, right around the house, staring at the stone walls, and the rickety gutters, and the flaking paint around the windows, and then down to the gates to peer through the windows at the lodge, the key to which she had forgotten to bring, and then back to the field and right around the perimeter of that, for no real reason other than a vague idea of completeness. She stayed out until it was too dark to see properly, then went inside and made a tour indoors. Why? What was it all about? Trying to convince herself it was real?

No idea.

At five to seven she made scrambled eggs for supper and failed utterly to read until bed time.

She failed utterly to get to sleep for ages too, despite knowing she had a long drive the following day. Instead, she lay awake with her eyes open in the deep dark and her brain buzzing, thoughts whirling and colliding like dodgems at the fair. Her decision, heavy with portent, had been made but not yet implemented; at this point no-one even knew.

Suppose she got up tomorrow and just did the expected? It would be so easy, not scary at all. Lots of benefits; her road into the future clearly mapped and simple to follow. What could be more sensible? And nobody would ever know she had once plotted to do things differently. There would be nobody to call her a coward except herself.

Temptation pulled, but it pulled both ways. Maddy felt like the rope in a tug of war, hauled this way and that, never really moving from the unstable centre position. If only one side would get clear and *win*. It was the agony of having both futures open that tortured her. At this point, tonight, in the dark, she could still change her mind.

She groaned, rolled over and pulled the pillow over her head. If only this was over.

And suddenly she knew.

Go one way and she could, if absolutely necessary, go back; it would be expensive and a horrible waste of time and energy but it could be done. Go the other way and everything would be lost forever, leaving only the regrets and What Ifs that she would never be able to answer.

There, then: decision made. There really wasn't any choice.

CHAPTER 16

Spring was well advanced in Twickenham. The daffodils that were in full, bright flower in Northumberland and Yorkshire were beginning to brown and shrivel as she passed Milton Keynes, and outside London they were finished, the dead heads cut off. Extraordinary. She felt she had come from a different world.

In the bistro there were miniature white narcissi on the table. She found Liz and dropped her bag on the spare chair.

'We'll have a nice time,' Maddy said as she sat down, 'so long as you don't ask me anything.'

'What, nothing at all?'

'Nothing about what I'm doing. Or I'll cry.'

Liz, the trooper, said, 'Got it,' and returned her attention to the menu. She had bagged a good table near the back. It was early and the place wasn't full. The background hubbub was low enough that they could hear one another comfortably, which Maddy thought wasn't necessarily a great thing on this occasion. She had meant it about the crying.

Unfortunately, *what she was doing* was so vast, so all-engrossing, so elephantine in her mind, she couldn't think of anything else to talk about, or give proper attention to Liz's snippets of news, which seemed paltry by comparison: staffroom politics with a tedious colleague; whether or not to replace the bath with a shower cubicle; the rubbishy quality of current films.

'There's a cinema in Hexham,' Maddy said.

'Is it good?'

'Haven't been.'

Liz said, 'Oh.' Then she said, 'Have you been watching–'

And Maddy said, 'Haven't got a television.'

'Oh no, I forgot.'

After a beat, Maddy said, 'But I am getting a phone soon. Should do, anyway.'

'That's good.' Liz said tentatively, 'So…are you sorted now?'

Maddy sighed. 'Yeah. It's never been so shiny.'

It was true. After a day of full on, unceasing, super-efficient cleaning and tidying, every single room in the flat had been looking photogenic and, Maddy hoped, desirable. Aspirational but attainable. She had put fresh flowers all over the place for the photography, and when the last photographer had left, she crossed the hall and gave them all to a bemused Sue Jackson. The Volvo, seats down, was laden to the gunwales with stuff she didn't think would help sell the place; the estate agent had told her that buyers like to see cupboards with space in them – neatly folded towels, careful stacks of storage boxes, space between the coat hangers. She had wanted the estate agents to be able to park easily, so she had vacated her slot and taken the Volvo around the corner, hoping no one would take a fancy to her junk and break in.

There would be no trouble finding places for it all at Unthank.

After that she had put in a telephone call to her mother in Long Island, only to find it wasn't helpful at all. Lovely to talk, of course, and sort of reassuring that someone cared deeply about her, but America was so far away and Northumberland hardly seemed relevant. It was, as her mother said, her decision and only she could make it. In the end Maddy put down the receiver thinking it would be nice to be middle-aged with life's big choices behind you.

'Anyway,' Maddy said now, 'It's done. Maxwell and Swallow. They didn't give the highest valuation but he was the most convincing. At least he wasn't nineteen,' she added, recalling the ridiculously juvenile agent from the first outfit.

That's how you know you're getting old, isn't it? When everyone else looks young.

'I don't think I'm old enough to be doing this,' Maddy said. 'You realise I'm completely terrified?'

Liz reached across the table. 'You are *absolutely* old enough to be doing it. You've managed fantastically so far. Look at all you've achieved already!' She stabbed the table top with her finger. 'It's going to be marvellous.'

It is perverse but true that sometimes enthusiasm and loyal support from one's nearest and dearest make one feel worse instead of better. Tears rose behind Maddy's eyes. She blinked them as best she could and rummaged in her bag. 'Look. What do you make of this?'

She laid on the table the two sheets of paper that had

been folded into the envelope in the cellar strongbox, her latest infuriatingly cryptic find. She had read them several times but they raised more questions than they answered.

'Photocopies,' Liz said, picking them up.

'Yes.'

'May I read them?'

'Of course.'

They appeared to be notes: *Anders and Gertrud return October 1914...Treatment for arthritis?...Percy Whatmough siblings?* Opaque and far from gripping. But then: *Marilena Bircher inherits – arrives July 1919.*

'That's my grandmother,' Maddy said. 'My father was born in 1925 and Uncle Claude was two years older, so 1923. I know my grandmother's maiden name was Bircher, but I never knew her Christian name.'

Maddy's grandfather had died long before Maddy was born, and obviously Uncle Claude hadn't called his mother by her first name. So far as she could remember, which admittedly wasn't very far, he had called her "Mutti". She couldn't remember her father calling his mother anything, which was rather shameful really.

Liz said, 'So your grandmother inherited Unthank in 1919? Where did she arrive from? Newcastle? London? Zurich?'

'Don't know.'

'Did she have a German accent?'

'No idea.'

Her grandmother hadn't spoken much at all, so far as she could recall – a tall, straight, silent woman who always seemed to be watching her. Watching her and frowning.

That, coupled with Uncle Claude being so shy, meant that Maddy's mother did most of the talking, valiantly chirping away in a bright tone, rattling on about cooking and gardening and how she, Maddy, was doing at school. What a hero she had been, Maddy now realised, and all to no avail because the broken family ties were never mended. Or at least, so she had thought.

Their food arrived and Liz handed the papers back.

'What do you think?' Maddy asked, slipping the envelope back in her bag.

'Honestly?'

'Honestly.'

'I think,' Liz said, 'your Uncle Claude was a nutter.'

THE ROUTINE WAS BECOMING FAMILIAR. Maddy unpacked the Volvo but left the serious putting away until the next day. Instead, she lit the fire in the snug, made herself cheese on toast, and opened the mail that had arrived while she had been away: an aerogram from her mother, chatty and comforting and wishing her well with her decision; the quarterly electricity bill on the flat; and a letter from Pattison's asking her to make an appointment.

IT WAS GOOD NEWS...ISH.

The death duties would definitely be covered by Uncle Claude's investments. He had apparently been putting money away for years. 'I think he lived frugally,' Mr Pattison said.

I'll say, Maddy thought. He sure hadn't spent much on domestic comforts.

But after the tax had been paid, there wouldn't be a great deal of money left over, certainly not enough for rewiring and radiators.

It was time for Maddy to speak, and taking a tight grip on herself she told her nice solicitor that she was in the process of selling her flat. 'I can't afford to keep it going without a job,' she explained. 'It will give me breathing space while I decide what to do.'

'That sounds sensible.'

Maddy relaxed. But then Mr Pattison said, 'If you intend living at Unthank after probate, I strongly recommend you get in a structural surveyor. It can be surprising what serious issues can be invisible to the ordinary eye and you don't want a nasty surprise down the line.'

'What kind of nasty surprise might that be?' Maddy asked cautiously.

'Dry rot? Leaky roof? Dangerous wiring?'

Not a bright prospect. On the other hand, there would be quite a lot of ready cash once the flat was sold. Enough?

There'll be enough, Maddy thought. *I'll live frugally too.*

'You'll then need to get your own insurance,' Mr Pattison said.

'Yes, of course.'

Maddy wondered whether insurance was calculated on the basis of floor area or number of rooms. If it was rooms, did one include the servants' quarters?

That evening she settled down with the small notebook from her handbag. She had been jotting down thoughts for the last five days; now she would start sorting those notes into sensible, usable lists.

First there was the *TO GET* list, which seemed to be ongoing and inevitable.

1Insurance Obviously.

2Freezer She really needed one of those.

3Another electric fire.

Then came *TO DO.* She wrote:

1Structural survey She had taken Mr Pattison's advice to heart and really didn't want a leaky roof.

2Get chimneys cleaned Joan in the bakery had told her last week that a chimney could behave perfectly nicely while still harbouring a build-up of soot that posed a fire hazard. At this very moment her life could be under threat. Since learning this she made sure the fire had died down before she went to bed.

3Investigate generator Power cuts, as she had learned, were common and could last for days. Just about everybody around had a generator so that they could at least cook.

4Window cleaner She would ask in the village.

5Get carpets cleaned They were awfully old and probably filthy, and she was tired of being afraid to go barefoot after washing.

6Rewiring

7Central heating!!! She put that last because it was going to cost a fortune.

She read over the list. Too many tasks. One of the problems was that she still didn't have a phone and all this would need to be arranged from the call box on the green.

Oh well, nothing could happen until she had money to

pay for it, and that was now in the hands of Maxwell and Swallow. She hoped they would get a move on.

And in the meantime, she intended to enjoy herself. Starting tomorrow, she was going to have a *very* pleasant few days.

As WELL AS clothes and household items, Maddy had brought from the flat her most treasured possession: a photographic enlarger saved up for and chosen after much consideration of features and costs. It had travelled north swathed in a blanket and belted into the front passenger seat, and she carried it with care through the passage to the first of the pantries. Here she was going to make her darkroom, where the window was small and easily blacked out, where there were shelves for equipment and chemicals, and where there was running water and a large sink. Perfect, and best of all, she could keep it as a permanent darkroom instead of having to restore it to her bathroom, as she had done at the flat.

It had been far too long since she developed any photographs and she had three rolls of film as yet unseen. She couldn't wait.

CHAPTER 17

THE NEXT MORNING, MADDY GOT TO WORK TRANSFORMING the pantry into a darkroom. It was easy, if inelegant, to hammer in tacks to fix blackout material over the window, and she could always rig up something better when she had given it more thought. There must be a village handyman; she vaguely recalled a postcard in the shop. No doubt he would tell her off for making holes in the window frame, but it was her house…nearly.

She set out the trays and papers, filled a jug with water and boiled the kettle so that she could get the temperatures correct, and then shut the door and checked for darkness.

Absolute. Perfect.

She switched on the red safelight and got to work on contact sheets.

BY LUNCHTIME she was through and had a swift snack before unbolting the front door and hovering nervously in the

Reception Hall. She was still using the back door into the courtyard for convenience – and from habit – and tended to leave the front door locked, but visitors would be expected to try there and she was not sure how far the sound of the doorbell would carry. It was a beautifully crafted bell-pull sort that clanged impressively when you were nearby, but it wasn't possible to pull it and also be upstairs or in the kitchen to hear how loud it was, so Maddy sat in the hall and doodled on the pad she had ready. Taking notes would, she hoped, look businesslike and efficient.

When the doorbell did ring, she jumped half out of her skin. The massive oak door and stone walls did a great job of soundproofing the house and she hadn't heard anyone approach.

She dragged open the door. On the step was a tall, square-shouldered woman with cropped grey hair wearing what looked like a man's donkey jacket. Just behind and to one side was an Indian woman, slender and pretty, wearing tight jeans tucked inside long boots and a quilted jacket shaped at the waist. The tall woman said, 'We're from the gardening club. Evelyn Dodd.' And the other one said, 'And I'm Devyani.'

'Welcome,' Maddy said. 'Thank you so much for coming. Shall we get started?'

It was Experienced Gardener Chris's third option, the one he recommended: get in the amateur gardeners and make it a community project.

'What, schools and things?' she had said, taken aback.

'If they're up for it. And the WI. But start with the gardening clubs. There's an active bunch around Shilston that some of the Kirkwitton crowd belong to, and I reckon there'll be people wanting to come from Hexham too.'

'Hexham? Really? It's not exactly local.'

Chris shrugged. 'It's less than an hour. I don't think you realise what you've got here. This is an opportunity to restore an Edwardian kitchen garden and get it producing again as it once did. Chances like this don't come along often.'

Maddy considered. 'But it would be an enormous job.'

'Yes, it would. But this way you'd be spreading the work out so that everyone did what they wanted to and no more. And it would be fun, and very rewarding.'

Sharing the work out made sense, and Maddy definitely liked the idea of not having to pay people to do it. But would anyone really drive miles on a regular basis and put in hours of toil on land owned by somebody else? She wasn't convinced. And even if they did, it would be bedlam unless someone was in charge, and it couldn't be her because she didn't have a clue.

'How would it run?' she had asked cautiously, and took notes as Chris explained. Now, striding forth with Evelyn Dodd and Devyani in her wake, Maddy clutched her notebook and trotted out Chris's instructions, doing her best to give an impression of wisdom and authority.

It didn't last long. Before they even reached the walled gardens, she had been rumbled. Chris had kindly contacted the Shilston and District Gardening Club on her behalf and invited them to meet her and see what was involved. He had given them a little too much background.

'It must be quite a shock to have all this after your London flat,' Evelyn said conversationally. She was, Maddy guessed, about six feet tall and managed somehow to loom, even when behind.

'Um. Yes. Quite a shock.'

'A bit different from pansies in a window box.'

'Yes.' Maddy opened the gate and stood back to let them see the first of the walled gardens. Hopefully it would be impressive enough to stop that particular conversation. Inexperienced, yes, but she'd prefer not to come across as totally incompetent.

It was. Both women stood gazing at the abandoned beds and overgrown paths and bare but mature fruit trees trained against the walls.

'And this is just the first,' Maddy put in.

'Oh my,' Evelyn sighed, and Maddy breathed out.

In the event, she just let them wander and simply tagged along, answering questions when she could, admitting ignorance when necessary. By the time they reached the greenhouses they had progressed from quiet marvelling to animated discussion, most of which went over Maddy's head but which did, she thought, bode well. And when they eventually emerged onto the terrace and saw the bedraggled herbaceous border, Devyani asked, 'And will this be part of the project too?'

'Definitely,' Maddy said with conviction, not at all sure what needed to be done to it. All flower beds look dead in March, don't they?

Both women beamed. Maddy took a deep breath. 'Let's go inside and talk!'

They had tea from the big brown teapot and rock buns she had daringly made the day before. They were her first attempt at solo baking and weren't bad at all. She was feeling warm and buzzy, and intensely relieved that it looked as if this was going to work. Chris's remaining option, Option Four aka Last Resort, was for her to rent out individual areas of the gardens for people to cultivate as they chose, like a private allotment scheme. The idea of having to allow just anyone onto her property didn't appeal at all; the restoration scheme felt safer, kindlier, even if it still involved strangers.

She didn't need her notes much; Chris had briefed Evelyn well.

'Most of these projects have much less to go on,' she said, and Maddy decided it would be tactful to let her explain the stuff Chris had already taught her. 'Walled gardens were usually turned into ornamental gardens, or just grassed over. But here you have all the structures still in place. It will simply be a case of restoring them to working order.'

'It will be a massive job, though,' Maddy said, wanting to ensure everyone understood.

'Of course, but you're not under any time constraint, are you? You're not expecting to have it all up to scratch by the summer?'

'Oh crumbs, no. Loads of time. As long as it takes.'

'Well then.' Evelyn took a second bun. She was spare and not at all overweight, but her rangy frame probably took some fuelling. Maddy guessed her to be in her fifties or perhaps older, but she looked tough.

Devyani was different altogether, petite and birdlike, and very pretty. Maddy hazarded only a little older than herself - in her thirties anyway. She was wearing make-up and turquoise drop earrings. When she pushed a business card across the table ('Here's my number') Maddy was startled to discover her surname was Blenkinsopp.

Devyani Blenkinsopp. Hard to forget that.

The card said she was a painter.

'Landscapes and flowers,' she said.

'I'm a photographer,' Maddy said. 'Also landscapes, mostly. Black and white though.'

'I'd like to see your work.'

Maddy glowed. Devyani was being polite, but it was still warming. 'I'm going to be doing some printing this week,' she said, thinking suddenly of the contact prints drying in the pantry. 'Just stuff I've taken locally. And of this place, of course.'

'Will you be documenting the restoration?' Evelyn asked.

'Yes. Definitely.'

Maddy hadn't thought that far – it had seemed too nebulous to rely on. But the possibility was firming up promisingly. 'What do you do, Evelyn?' she asked.

'Retired. From teaching. Maths. Newcastle.'

Maddy said, 'And you both really think this can happen?'

The two women exchanged glances. Then Evelyn said, 'I think you'll have people queueing down the road.'

WHEN THEY HAD LEFT, Maddy wandered into the pantry-darkroom and looked again at her contact sheets. The nice thing about a Rolleiflex camera is that the film is large, which in turn means that each image on the contact sheet is also large: six centimetres by six centimetres – easily big enough to get a good idea of the picture. She ran her eyes over the sheets, comparing the photos of the gardens she had taken last month with the garden as it was now.

It had changed; things were definitely stirring. The daffodils were out of course, and there were other pointed spears pushing up now, and primroses in clumps of delicate yellow and cream. Buds on bushes had arrived from nowhere, and there was tiny white blossom on the waving twigs of an unknown shrub.

If this really happened, it could be marvellous.

Maddy leaned on the bench, propping her chin on her hand. Some of the photos had been taken from across the lawn, trying to place the house in its context, and showing the terrace and the herbaceous border Devyani had been so drawn to. At the foot of that sheet were four photos taken from still further back, showing the vertical wall of the ha-ha as a horizontal band across the image.

Her own Capability Brown ha-ha. Crazy.

Then she frowned and looked closer.

CHAPTER 18

WELLIES WERE NOT GOOD FOR RUNNING IN. IT HAD RAINED since the gardening club advance guard had left and the long grass would soak her shoes. That was another sign of the recent milder weather – the grass was definitely growing. She wondered whether the restoration project would include mowing.

But she wondered only briefly and her focus swiftly returned to the ha-ha. It had been about a third of the way along. Maddy descended the steps carefully, conscious of broken slabs, and jogged alongside the great ditch that separated the lawn below the terrace from the rest of the grass falling gently to the boundary below.

And there it was. Maddy halted. How could she not have noticed this before? It would have been within clear view each time she returned from the summerhouse. In fact, it had been in clear view when she took that photograph. Proof, if proof were needed, that one sees very differently when looking through a viewfinder.

Her mind had been on the large picture, the house in its setting, not on the detail. Only when she was inspecting the printed contact sheet had she noticed the break in the pattern.

The ha-ha was both the ditch and the retaining wall that supported the upper level. That wall should have been unbroken stone, but it wasn't. Part way along, there was a door. Maddy let herself down the drop, already knowing she would have to go back. The door was fastened with a latch and the latch was secured with a padlock, a big one, and it was closed.

Nevertheless, she rattled it, just in case, but she would have fainted with shock if it hadn't been locked. *Of course* it was locked. Of course.

Back to the house, then. She wished she had thought ahead and brought the key with her, but she hadn't. Indoors, she yanked her feet out of the wellies and trotted in socks to fetch the key from the biscuit tin. She had been labelling the keys, and only one was as yet unidentified: the key that had been in the strong box in the cellar beneath the terrace.

It was lightweight, the shank perhaps an inch and a half in length and with small wards and a flattened oval handle. It didn't look like a padlock key.

If it isn't, I'll cry.

Maddy dropped it into her pocket and returned to the ha-ha, only to find that she was right; the key didn't fit the padlock. It wouldn't even go into the keyhole.

Blast.

She didn't cry, but it was extremely frustrating. She

rattled the padlock again and wondered whether she could break it. Or take the latch off the door?

Maddy fetched a screwdriver from the tool box she had found in the outbuildings and had a go at removing the latch, but she couldn't get any of the screws to turn at all.

Saw through the wood?

No. She was being ridiculous now. It would be mad to start destroying things just to find another piece of Uncle Claude's puzzle. It wouldn't even be the next piece of the puzzle, because that, surely, was hidden somewhere that this key *would* unlock, and actually there might not be anything at all waiting behind this door.

I bet there is though, Maddy thought, and returned to the house feeling grumpy. The flurry of excitement had pulled her back into the game again. Distracted by the business of the last few days – sorting out the flat, sorting out the garden, sorting out the darkroom – she had been brought back with a bang to Lenka Midnight, the wicked housekeeper.

Although that was back to front. It was Lenka Midnight who was the distraction from real life, not the other way about.

'Oh, stuff Lenka Midnight,' Maddy said aloud. 'And stuff Uncle Claude.'

Nevertheless, when she was buying milk two days later and saw Edna, the brusque woman she had met briefly when she first arrived in Kirkwitton, she didn't hesitate.

'Excuse me,' she said, diving in unprepared. 'We met before. I'm Madeleine Lawrence, Claude's niece. Could I possibly ask you a few questions?'

So much for 'stuff Lenka Midnight'; Maddy walked home along the footpath preoccupied.

Edna turned out not to be quite the blunt-verging-on-rude person she had seemed when Maddy first met her, although certainly still rather…severe. She had responded to Maddy's request with a very cool look, but once Maddy had plunged in with 'Did you ever meet Lenka Midnight?' the door cracked open.

The thin woman peered into her purse as if avoiding Maddy's gaze, but she said, 'Not met her, no. Saw her once or twice.'

Only once or twice?

Maddy said, 'Did she not come into the village, then?'

'Rarely. Everything was delivered. Shut herself off, she did, in that big house.'

'Lenka?'

'No, not the housekeeper! Frau Bircher.'

'Oh yes, of course. Did you ever meet Frau Bircher, then?'

Edna snapped her purse shut. 'No. Not her. Never set foot outside the gates. She was a snob, my father said. Never liked her.'

'Your father?' Maddy was floundering.

Edna sniffed. 'He was a doctor. *The* doctor. He went up there a few times towards the end. Before she died. And after she died, of course. He wrote the death certificate.'

'And she died from…?'

'Heart. Just old age. Eighty-something she was, by then.'

'She died in her own home, then,' Maddy said cheerfully, just to keep things rolling.

Edna sniffed again.

Maddy didn't like the pause, afraid the prickly woman would shoot out the door as soon as she had been served. She said, 'Joan mentioned something about a scandal…'

A snort this time, then Edna said, 'They were up to no good, those two. My father caught them at it more than once.'

Wow!

'What, Frau Bircher and the housekeeper?'

'No! The housekeeper and the gardener.'

Ah yes, Joan had told her about this theory. To make sure she had the story straight, Maddy said, 'They were married, weren't they? The Biddles.'

'I don't mean the Biddles. The Biddles left when I was twelve. I'm talking about your Lenka Midnight, that took over after that, and the new gardener.' Edna paused fractionally and then lowered her voice. Maddy leaned in a little, since they were being confidential. 'My father used to wait *minutes* at the door, and when she opened it, she would be barely dressed. All askew. Buttons undone.'

'Goodness.'

'And sometimes there was *dirt* under her nails.' Edna straightened up and opened her purse again, clearly her favourite avoidance activity.

'Crumbs.'

Well, that was that, then: guilty as charged.

When Edna had left the shop and Maddy was paying for her milk, Joan said, 'Find out what you wanted?'

'Did you hear?' Maddy asked.

'Bits. Dirty fingernails.'

'Apparently.' Maddy took her change.

Joan said, 'I have heard tell that Edna was offered a job later by your grandmother. After the old woman had died. House maid. Daft idea, she was a doctor's daughter, but they probably did things different in Switzerland, do you think?'

'Probably,' Maddy agreed, having not the slightest.

'Anyway, she wouldn't go but her friend Effie did. Effie's dad was a farmer so that was all right. And Edna once told me that Effie told *her* that the house was all under dust sheets when she started. Nothing been done to the rooms for years. So what housekeeping that housekeeper was doing, I don't know.'

No indeed. How interesting. Maddy wondered why Lily and Sam had left, and how Lenka had coped with strangers coming in to replace them. Evidently quite well with at least one; she wondered who the gardener was and what he was like. Young and lusty, it would seem.

She also wondered where the next instalment of wicked Lenka's account might lie. She had been all over the house for the umpteenth time but had not uncovered anything the little key would fit. *So* frustrating.

She was processing test strips later for the photos she intended to print, when she remembered what Mr Pattison, the solicitor, had said.

SHE HAD DECIDED to go into Hexham for exotic groceries later in the week anyway, but a letter arrived on Monday from Maxwell and Swallow, the estate agents in Twickenham.

It was incredibly difficult selling property without having a phone, and the agent had not done a good job of concealing his impatience. But what could she do? She had asked for a line to be installed and could hardly dig up the drive herself.

However, the post still worked, and Maddy tore the envelope open to find that an offer had been made on her flat for only slightly less than the asking price – higher than she had expected to settle. The flat was sold.

She changed into clean jeans and set off at once, calling at the phone box on the way to ring Maxwell and Swallow ('I accept the offer') and Pattison's ('I've accepted an offer'). It had seemed sensible to instruct Mr Pattison to handle the sale of the flat.

'Have you arranged for a survey yet?' he asked as she was gathering her coat to leave.

'No. Must do that.'

'And a chimney sweep?'

'That too.'

It was nice to know she was being looked out for. Now, though, she needed the library.

It had been Mr Pattison's suggestion back in February, when she had shown him the mystery keys, and she had forgotten about it until that moment in the darkroom. There isn't much to keep you interested when printing test strips, just counting seconds between each exposure, and random trains of thought often floated through, such as her friendly solicitor's suggestion that there might be something about Unthank in the local history section at the library.

And of course he was right. But first she asked about the bible that had come out of the attic on that first full day in the house.

She had found the date of publication on the title page: 1698. So old. It had been gnawing at her, so she had brought the bible with her and flourished it in front of the reference librarian.

'Do you know anything about old bibles?' she asked. 'Is this valuable?'

The librarian, who was young and thin and bearded, looked a little taken aback but recovered quickly and jumped in. He found the title page swiftly and then skimmed over the rest of the volume.

'It's interesting,' he said, and Maddy stopped holding her breath. 'Interesting' is not the same as 'exciting', and sure enough, he continued: 'Sixteen ninety-eight is very old but to be honest so many of these were produced and well looked after, and so many still survive, it won't be tremendously valuable. Especially as it has been written in. Collectors don't care for that, unless it's someone famous, of course. Pepys, for example; or Newton. Sorry.'

'That's all right.' Maddy put the bible back in her bag. 'I didn't really think it would be.'

'I'm not an expert though. An antiquarian bookseller would value it for you.'

'Yes. Maybe. Anyway.'

So that was that. Then the librarian took her to the shelves where local history documents were filed and showed her how to use the microfiche viewer to access the index. 'Any problems, just shout,' he said breezily.

Maddy didn't encounter any problems, but was disappointed to find there wasn't much. She found references to the Women's Institute (in the 1960s Kirkwitton WI merged with Eastwitton WI and moved down the road), and to village shows and harvest suppers and farm auctions, one of which she was interested to note took place at Bank Foot Farm, belonging to one Mr Fred Halpin. But that was in 1948, long after Lenka's connection with the place, if indeed it was the farm that she had called simply Halpin's.

She was almost at the end of the last microfiche when she struck lucky. The capital U, always unusual, jumped out of the small print, and she read that there was a typescript in the archive of a pamphlet dating from 1898 called *Kirkwitton and Unthank*. She shuffled through the box file and there it was, typed on foolscap with a manual typewriter, two sheets stapled at the top left corner. She carried it to the desk.

'May I photocopy this?'

She could. In fact, she copied it twice so that she could send one to Liz, for fun, and in case it sparked any ideas in her. Reading it in the library, it felt like a real find, and when she got back to Unthank, she read it again.

Kirkwitton, Eastwitton and Unthank

by

A Warwickshire Traveller

In the wooded foothills below the Northumberland moors, a pleasant day's walk from Hexham, lies the tranquil village of Kirkwitton and its lesser cousin, Eastwitton. I arrived in Kirkwitton as the shadows were lengthening and the songbirds sounding their evening discourse, and can well attest that the traveller heading for the moorland heights on his way eastwards to the coast will find a welcome at The Swaledale Inn, whether he be seeking a hearth to warm himself by, a sustaining repast, or a bed for the night.

Kirkwitton is a moderately sized village of some dozen or so cottages arranged around a small green, and a handful more that border the lane from the south. The school, the inn, the forge, the bakery and butcher's shop present themselves as testimony to a comfortable and settled community, and the fields as I approached, whether freshly mown and punctuated by tidy stooks or stocked with the small, horned, local sheep and their growing lambs, looked well-managed and prosperous.

The innkeeper at The Swaledale could not have been more helpful to a weary traveller, and I was soon settled in the snug with a hearty supper of collops of mutton and turnips. Being early in the week, the inn was quiet, however, and with only one rather silent old local with whom to converse, I withdrew myself from his company in order to sit on the wall of the yard and sketch the front elevation of the inn (see below) before retiring early to my chamber, promising myself a closer investigation of the village before departing the next day.

And so I did. Following a breakfast that was sustaining if not of especial merit, I set forth and followed the lane that led away from the main road and which would, I had been informed, take me to the church and the school. Indeed, the top of the church tower was visible above the tree, and was not hard to find.

The church of St Cuthbert in Kirkwitton has much to interest the passing historian. A simple, unadorned exterior speaks of its roots in the troubled times of the Scottish raids in the fourteenth century, appearing more like a bastion for refuge from the marauding reivers than a place for worship and contemplation. Indeed, holes in the internal stone walls on either side of the door attest to the church having been barred against raiders. The interior is otherwise unremarkable; a carved coat of arms of a fourteenth-century knight here, an incised stone to a seventeenth-century grandee there. There is no stained glass to bring welcome respite to the interior, and the windows are small, but the font is medieval and the pulpit of oak, decorated with carved roundels, is very fine (see below).

It being a fine day and dry, I sketched the church from the eastern aspect (see facing page), and then wandered the graveyard encircling the church and paused to decipher some of the names. The good names of Northumberland were well represented, of course, and Armstrongs, Bells, Charltons and Dixons had all found their repose under those gentle mounds. I was considering these matters, when I rounded the western end of the church and discovered I had company in the shape of a woman on her knees, tending one of the more recent graves. I gave her a quiet "Good day" and would have walked on had she not straightened and set down her trowel as if ready for diversion. I therefore remarked upon the pleasant weather, and she agreed, but warned that she feared rain would fall by evening. Then, as we were conversing so easily, I asked if there were any other aspect of interest that I should visit before quitting Kirkwitton, and she replied that there was the big house, and that the occupiers were recently come to the neighbourhood from the continent, but would surely be pleased if I should pay them a call, so accordingly I did so.

The house is called Unthank, and is on the southern edge of the village, perhaps one mile beyond the last cottage and set well back from the lane, so that the building is entirely concealed by a fine stand of trees. I approached along a mature cedar avenue that curved around an incline, and in time revealed a miniature castle, complete with crenella-

tions, narrow, stone-transomed windows, and an imposing, square porch into which I stepped in order to pull the bell.

Fortune smiled on me, as the lady of the house was at home and without company, and kindly undertook to show me the place herself, and then to provide me with tea taken in the morning room, during which the lady continued to impart the tales and legends associated with the house.

Frau Bircher is a young lady with but two children as yet, both of these being small boys. Her husband's widowed mother lives with them, and also her husband's grandmother: three Frau Birchers all together. The family is Swiss, and the youngest, to whom I think I might refer, without giving offence, as "my" Frau Bircher, spoke English very prettily, with an impressive command of vocabulary and grammar, and only a delicate accent, which was most attractive.

Unthank, which is apparently to be referred to in this truncated form without the softening addition of a "House" or "Hall", possesses a wealth of "secrets" attached to itself, most of them of the traditional sort frequently found connected to large houses of two or three centuries' age. There is a Priest Hole accessed from the library by means of a mechanism, which the Birchers expect they will have disabled before their eldest son, named Jurgen, achieves the age at which boys have the tendency to explore and, unfortunately, pay small heed to instructions. (At this juncture, I acknowledged that I, myself, passed through just such a phase, and still possess the scars that bear witness to my brave but foolhardy exploits.) There is, too, a small chamber beneath the floor of the ice house, which has been expertly disguised to be quite indiscernible to any but those who know of its existence. This chamber was presumably excavated and lined in order to be a secure place of concealment for documents or valuables, but Frau Bircher assured me that the current *family do not make use of it, preferring to place their trust in banking institutions.*

The remaining secret is, it appears, no secret at all, for I was informed that the Unthank Bible is well known of in these parts. "We do not keep that in the Bank," Frau Bircher told me, "For it belongs to the house and should reside here, within its walls, just as it always has." Then she enquired whether I should like to see it, and of course I said I would, with great pleasure. The Bible is kept in a small cabinet in the library, awarded due care indeed, residing as it does in a walnut box lined with lead, commissioned from an Edinburgh cabinetmaker specifically for this object. The lady was so good as to bring it out for me to inspect. And very fine it is indeed, an exquisite edition, which I feel most honoured to have held in my own hands and seen with my own eyes.

And so I took my leave and returned to The Swaledale, where I enjoyed a cold lunch and spent some hour and a half sketching Unthank from memory, before setting forth. These drawings are therefore more flawed even than usual, but I hope will serve to render at least an impression of the house and its prize treasure.

I left Kirkwitton along the northerly lane and, half a mile on, walked through Eastwitton, which was, as I had been led to expect, a small number of dwellings without shop or inn, and from thence continued onto the moors.

That was it. It was a pity the helpful person who had copied the text hadn't been able to copy the pictures too.

And the Unthank Bible, with capital letters, eh? Maddy didn't think it was all that exquisite, although it was certainly interesting and impressively ancient. On retrospect, she supposed she too felt a bit honoured to hold something so old, with so much history attached to it. It was a pity more of the history wasn't available, though.

She had gasped when the priest hole was mentioned, and gasped again on reading about the ice house and the chamber underneath the floor. So that's what was built into the ha-ha; she should have guessed. There seemed little doubt that Uncle Claude had used both the ice house and its hidden compartment, but until she found the keys for them, she couldn't get inside either.

And for certain he had used the priest hole too.

She wondered what had become of the lead-lined box.

CHAPTER 19

M ADDY DIDN'T WANT TO BE TRAPPED FOR DAYS SO SHE booked the removals company to pack as well as transport the contents of the flat. It cost more but she was feeling rich. In terms of renovating Unthank her wealth wasn't huge but for day-to-day expenses – well, checking her bank account gave her a warm glow.

But then, on reflection, she decided to drive down a couple of days ahead of the move after all, not to pack, not that, but to give herself the chance to bid a proper farewell to the places where she had grown up; the places she used to call home.

'You will be coming back,' Liz reminded her. 'You're allowed to visit.'

Maddy knew that of course, but this relocation was momentous for all that. Melbourne Mansions had been her home since she was three – she couldn't remember the house they had lived in when her father was alive.

It wasn't just the flat either. Now that the time had come,

Maddy realised she would no longer be able to hop into London on a whim. It wasn't that she had taken the train up very often, not having much interest in Oxford Street shopping or, to be honest, art galleries or museums either, but she had always known she could, if she wished. That would no longer be the case, or at least, not without a great deal more bother and expense.

So on the Saturday she and Liz took the train into Waterloo and wandered along the South Bank, dipping into the second-hand book stalls, before crossing the river and heading to Covent Garden. It was a bright day if breezy, and London felt warmer than Northumberland. Busier too. Maddy found it hard to believe the crush of the crowds.

'This isn't like Hexham,' she grunted as she squeezed between one of the pillars and the very broad woman who was refusing to make way.

'It is Saturday,' Liz pointed out.

'Even so.'

They mooched around the more interesting shops and had lunch in a bistro they hadn't seen before. Maddy ordered a salad that seemed awfully expensive for a few raw vegetables, and thought about the rich comfort-food served at The Swaledale.

'I've changed,' she said, stirring the brightly coloured shreds about with her fork.

'You don't say?'

'It is weird, though. You realise less than three months ago I had no idea this was going to happen? *Three months!* And here I am, spoiled for the city. I've become a yokel.'

'Hardly.'

Maddy didn't argue but Liz was wrong. She felt like an alien, found herself shrinking from the bustle and jostle on the London pavements. Her thoughts kept straying to the openness and emptiness of Hexham, even Hexham on a Saturday, and the thought of Unthank, tall and empty, herself the only living creature in all that space, made her shiver with longing.

In the afternoon they made their way to Trafalgar Square and the National Gallery, which was Liz's favourite, cultured being that she was, and then, for Maddy, to the National Portrait Gallery next door. Maddy wasn't big on art but she was drawn to faces, particularly faces from long ago that yet looked contemporary – ordinary, believable faces that, if stripped of eighteenth- and nineteenth-century hairdos and costumes, would look unremarkable in a shop or at the bus stop. It was a game she had played for years (*That one, look, he could be a plumber!*) and she could play it in reverse too, picking out passers-by and zapping them into Georgian silks and wigs for a stately portrait.

She played it at Waterloo an hour later. There was a crowd already on the platform, noisy and excited – a school trip or youth club outing it seemed – and only marginally under control. Teenaged boys shoving each other about; it seemed easier to skirt them than try worming through. Maddy walked round, conscious of the edge of the platform on her left. She had never liked getting too close to that.

One of the kids blundered and almost pushed her, catching himself inches from the edge and letting out a crow that sounded like alarm quickly corrected to laughter. Very funny, obviously. *If I'd been a second ahead, he'd have sent me over*, Maddy thought.

She got past and scurried back to safer ground. She was suddenly aware, as she had not been for weeks, that she was twenty-nine, in her fateful year, and no attempts had been made on her life since that yellow sports car just before her birthday.

Well, she'd foiled this one.

It had been a mostly fair day but now a breeze was bringing light, stinging rain. They kept to the covered part of the platform but the wind came at them even so. When the train appeared she stepped up, looking forward to the warm, fuggy carriages. Not too close, of course, because there is that awful lure of the precipice, and few deaths sound quite so gruesome as falling under a train.

'Oh no,' Liz sighed.

Maddy glanced back and saw the crowd of kids flowing their way. She pulled a face. 'I hope they stay out of our carriage.'

It looked like they were heading for what would be the front of the train when it left the terminus. Maddy and Liz began to move the other way, happy to settle for the rear coaches, and squeezed – it felt like squeezing – between the boys and the track, Maddy keeping her eyes on her feet and concentrating on exactly where she stood.

The train began to pass her, a long process as it slowed, and with the boys gone on, she paused and faced the moving coaches. Liz had come around on the inside and was now standing to her left, she remembered that afterwards, and the man wearing a light-coloured jacket and carrying a holdall, an elderly man with silver-grey hair, was a few feet along to her right.

And then he wasn't.

Maddy had taken her eyes away, looking back at the train again, waiting for the moment when she'd be able to judge where the doors would stop, when she was yanked backwards and felt herself fall.

Not quite. The grip that had hauled her had become a grip that kept her on her feet, rocking to regain her balance.

'What on–'

She saw Liz's shocked face and followed her stare. The elderly man was on the concrete, his bag on its side, his arms spread wide. Maddy saw this, a brief impression, before he disappeared behind people moving in.

Her heart was walloping. 'What was that? What happened?'

'Idiot opened the door.' Liz looked pale.

'What?'

'Some guy on the train. Opened the door before it had stopped. Idiot.' Liz pursed her lips. 'Probably killed him.'

He hadn't, though. Even through the fence of helpers the old bloke's arms could be seen stirring. Someone said, 'Don't move, an ambulance is on its way.'

He wasn't dead. But Liz was right, he could have been.

There were a lot of people clustered about him; there wasn't much either of them could do. They boarded the train in silence, subdued by the drama and feeling suddenly tired.

Maddy thought, *I was too near the edge of the platform. If that old guy hadn't been there the door would have hit me instead, and if it had got me in the head, I could be dead.*

Unthank had never seemed so desirable.

THREE DAYS later the packing was done, her possessions stowed in the removal lorry and the key handed to the estate agent.

Maddy had moved.

...

BOOK TWO

CHAPTER 20

THERE WAS AN AEROBATIC DISPLAY GOING ON ABOVE THE lawn; it was like the Red Arrows in miniature. Birds were zooming low over the grass, missing each other by fractions, or so it seemed to Maddy. The speed was fantastic. Presumably they were taking insects in flight. How could they be so accurate?

Maddy wished she knew whether they were swallows or house martins. She had stared and stared, but their speed was simply too great and she could not for the life of her decide how long the forks of their tails were, or whether they had white rumps. A book on bird identification is not much use if you can't properly see the birds you're trying to identify.

It was the second week of July. Maddy had been in Northumberland for five months and for the last three of those Unthank had been her home – her proper home, her only home. She was no longer camping. The chain below the sale of her flat had been short and had completed within a month.

Unthank had swallowed the entire contents of the flat without so much as a blink and was still under-furnished. The mixture of styles was peculiar. Flat-pack bookshelves rubbed shoulders with ornate Victorian cabinets; white-painted MDF jostled with mahogany and oak. But it was brilliant to have her own things again, and Maddy immediately felt more deeply embedded, as if she were no longer pretending. Unthank had become more hers.

And it wasn't simply the import of her furniture. Other things were happening that made life more normal, if living in a castle could ever really be that.

For a start there was the garden reclamation. Chris Beattie, the Expert Gardener, had been at least half right and although there wasn't exactly a waiting list of volunteers desperate to get on board, there were five who were really keen and another six or eight semi-regulars, and between them they were making huge improvements to the poor deserted garden that had greeted Maddy in February.

Evelyn Dodd was more or less in charge, or so it seemed to Maddy, who was not involved in the decision making at all but stood on the side line and observed with interest. It was Evelyn who had regular phone conversations with Chris and then relayed the important points to the rest of the team. Devyani, who looked far too fragile to be trundling loaded wheelbarrows about but who nevertheless did, could only spare one day a week, but arrived every Wednesday without fail, whatever the weather, wearing beautiful clothes in bright jewel colours that made her easy to see from a distance, a butterfly amongst moths.

There was a frail man in his seventies called Jed, like some old cowboy in a Western, who didn't do any physical labour but was frequently consulted by Evelyn, and a husband-and-wife team in their thirties called Bob and Barbara who came every weekend, sometimes both days, and did a great deal of the heavy work.

Understandably weekends were the busiest times, when the most volunteers showed up, but people came in the evenings too, and there was often someone at work on weekdays. Maddy was torn between humble gratitude towards the selfless souls who were doing her this gigantic favour and saving her so much money, and a niggly resentment that her privacy could no longer be counted on. It wasn't reasonable and it certainly wasn't fair, but it was the truth.

On the other hand, nobody ever came indoors. There was an outside toilet that Maddy kept clean. There was also electricity in the nearest outhouses, and she had set up a refuge for the gardeners, with deck chairs and a kettle and even a small fridge. Unthank the house remained a castle aloof, its thresholds uncrossed, its walls never breached. Maddy could always hide.

Uncle Claude's hiding places had not been breached either, annoyingly. After considerable effort, poking and prodding and knocking and listening, Maddy had uncovered the priest hole behind the panelling in the library – an obvious place to start – and had felt triumphant and very pleased with herself when the side of the massive hearth scraped aside and showed her a compartment in the thickness of the wall about the size of a toilet cubicle. A rough metal chest like a tool box occupied the floor, fastened – of course – with a modern padlock; there was nothing else.

Maddy resolved not to dwell on gruesome and frightening history and instead seized the box and closed the panelling, but she was stumped yet again because none of the keys would fit the padlock. She now had no fewer than three uncovered hiding places of which she could access none. It was frustrating beyond belief. Once again she considered smashing her way in, but knew in her heart that it was out of the question – destruction on that scale was too heavy a price to pay for satisfying mere curiosity. Sooner or later, she told herself, she would find a keyhole for the outstanding key and the trail would get back on track. She must just be patient.

However, she did take the bible to be valued. Of course she did. It would have been madness not to explore all possibilities, and that date tantalised her. 1698. It was thrillingly old.

She went back to the public library in Hexham and this time asked at the reference desk where one might go to have a possibly rare bible valued. It was a different librarian, a woman with startlingly red hair who brightened visibly at being brought an unusual request, and she dived into her resources to come up with several names of auction houses and dealers specialising in old books. The nearest was in Edinburgh, and since Maddy did not want to consign The Unthank Bible to the post, she decided to start, at least, with that one. She rang first, and at once found herself being corrected. One did not, apparently, have an antique bible valued; one had it *appraised*.

Driving to Edinburgh took two hours and was almost entirely accomplished on single-carriageway country roads between stone walls and forests, occasionally dropping to thirty miles an hour through villages, always brief and quickly left behind. Now that she was actually doing it, she could hardly believe she hadn't driven to Edinburgh before. Two hours! In driving terms that was nothing. And all on country roads! You can't drive for two hours straight anywhere in the Home Counties without hitting a dual carriageway. The North… It really was a different country.

It had been a lovely spring day, a cliché really, soft, sunny, the leaves on the trees – lots of those – just opening. There were lambs in the fields and the sky was blue.

She reached the outskirts of Edinburgh around noon and found herself on urban roads at last. She worked her way along the streets, checking turnings against the directions she had written. Edinburgh's suburbs were nothing like as busy as Middlesex, and it wasn't too difficult to find the address. There was even a parking space just a few yards from the door.

Her spirits were high and she felt competent, mature and breezy. After all, she had in her possession The Unthank Bible, of which even The Warwickshire Traveller had been aware, and it was dated 1698. The librarian, the first one, might have been sceptical but what did he really know?

She knew her heart rate was heightened as she locked the car and walked back along the pavement, past a sewing machine repair shop and a hairdresser's to the door she wanted. It was painted bottle green with brass furniture, not shiny, and a green sign above the window next to it was inscribed *George Murray, Antiquarian Books, est. 1947.* She mounted the steps, turned the handle and entered.

An old-fashioned bell jangled above her head. She was in a small – a very small – shop. Three walls were lined with shelves floor to ceiling and the centre space was taken up by two scuffed leather armchairs either side of an equally scuffed pine farmhouse table. The chairs were of the deeply buttoned sort with the backs no higher than the arms – Chesterfields? – and one was occupied by a tabby cat, curled and asleep; books filled the shelves and more were stacked on the table.

The air was thick with the smell of old paper, old cloth, old leather and peppermint; Maddy wondered about the peppermint.

Running along most of the fourth wall was a counter with a glazed cabinet beneath and a bell on top. Maddy was lifting her hand when the door beyond opened and a man came through.

Maddy had played with images of an antiquarian book dealer on her way up. On the whole she had leaned towards over-fifty, middling-height, tweed-jacket and spectacles, all the while perfectly aware that this was a stereotype and the real thing might easily be thirty, six feet three and in a suit. Now it transpired that the stereotype was not far off. The man saying Good morning to her was at least fifty-five, probably sixty, of middling height and build, and wearing a corduroy jacket, which Maddy thought like enough to tweed. No spectacles, though.

'How can I help you?' he asked.

Maddy drew out the bible from the carrier bag and laid it on the counter.

'I rang yesterday,' she said. 'About having a bible valued. Appraised, I mean.'

'Ah.'

Spectacles came out of the inside breast pocket – the stereotype fulfilled after all.

'May I see? Thank you.'

How very courteous. Mr Murray – was it him? Although surely not the original one that established the business in 1947 – opened the bible and turned the first pages. Maddy waited, suddenly fluttery; the hamster was waiting too.

'Well, it is a good clean copy and interesting in its way. A pity about the genealogy, but not uncommon, unfortunately. This is your own family?'

'Yes,' Maddy said.

'And are you making a general enquiry or do you require a specific valuation?'

'Er – I'm not sure–'

'If you would like an idea of its value, I can give you that now. If on the other hand you intend to sell and want a more precise forecast of what it is likely to realise, than Mr Murray will look at it, but for that there will be a fee.'

Not Mr Murray then.

Maddy said, 'Well, perhaps a rough idea now and then I can think what to do?'

'Of course.' Not-Mr-Murray closed the bible and slid it towards Maddy. He took off his spectacles and tucked them back inside his jacket. Then he clasped his hands on the counter and said, 'First of all, please understand that the figures I am going to mention are not to be considered concrete. I am sure you will understand that there is no definitive price list for antiquarian books as circumstances dictate that each book is unique. Second, if you were to decide to sell your book, we would not be able to help you in that respect.'

'Oh, but–'

'It would be quite unethical for a bookseller both to appraise an item and also sell it. There would be a conflict of interest. I am sure you understand that.'

Maddy was being corrected again. 'Oh,' she said. 'Well, yes.'

'If you were to ask a different business but one such as ourselves to sell it on your behalf, I believe they would suggest a price between £2,000 and £2,500. Mr Murray will confirm more accurately. From that they would take fifty percent commission.'

Two thousand. *One* thousand.

'Alternatively, at auction a higher price might be achieved, and in general, auction houses take twenty-five percent commission. However, it is also possible that your reserve price might not be realised and the book remain unsold.' He straightened up. 'Do you have any questions?'

Maddy said, 'No. No thank you. I don't think so.'

The hamster had gone still. Maddy pictured it curled up in a corner with its head in its paws.

The disappointment was greater than she had expected, and ridiculous really since she had suspected all along that the bible wouldn't be valuable. Actually, two thousand pounds valuable and should have been exciting in ordinary circumstances, but value depends upon context and in the context of providing an income, two thousand or even two thousand five hundred pounds was as nothing. Useless. Wouldn't last twelve months.

For so little gain it didn't seem worth parting the bible from the house it belonged to. Maddy drove home and put it back in the snug. The Unthank Bible could stay at home.

The next step she had taken was to ask at the library about a local history society and she was given a contact name – Joyce Campbell – and a phone number that she rang that evening from the kitchen because finally, after months of waiting, she *had a telephone*. It was bliss, and not just because she could ring friends again. It also meant she could deal with tradesmen, make a dental appointment, query the bit on her electricity bill she didn't understand and, indeed, call complete strangers asking for favours. Now that she was connected, she wondered how she had managed without it for so long.

Joyce Campbell sounded starchy and Edinburgh and didn't seem to have a lot of time for her, but she did give Maddy another number to ring, and this time Maddy found herself talking to Joyce's polar opposite. Brenda MacSomething – Maddy didn't manage to catch her name – had a slow, comfortable voice like a squashy sofa, and was thrilled to learn Maddy was the new owner of Unthank. The big houses in Northumberland had been her pet interest for years and she had hoped to get to see the inside of all of them before she died.

Heart sinking in what she knew to be an ungracious

manner, Maddy said she would be pleased to welcome Brenda to visit Unthank any time, and was relieved (also ungracious) when Brenda thanked her but said she didn't think that was likely because her leg stopped her from going out now and those adventurous days were over.

Brenda rambled a while before they were done, but when Maddy replaced the receiver she had a deal. Brenda would give her a box file of research about Unthank and in return Maddy would present her with photographs of the outside and inside of the house, formal rooms, bedrooms, servants' quarters and offices all. It seemed more than fair.

The next week was spent documenting, developing and printing, and then Maddy drove to Gosforth on the edge of Newcastle and made the swap. She had feared Brenda MacWhatever would be living in a small house on a depressing urban street, this notion conjured up out of the bare facts of her being elderly and infirm, but she found her in a rather grand, genteel town house with bay trees either side of the step and stained glass in the windows, and the only thing wrong with the living room she was shown into was that everything was beige.

They had tea and shortbread (more beige), and Maddy explained how her inheritance had come out of the blue and that she had moved in permanently, and then about her father having died when she was a toddler and her mother having married an American, and after that about being a photographer (and unemployed), all because Brenda was so thirsty for gossip it seemed any news would do, even about people she had never met.

Back at Unthank Maddy was disappointed to find less in

the box file than she had hoped for. There were some photographs, which was fun, and then two stapled bunches of papers, the first somehow familiar. She started to read and realised she had seen these notes before. *Anders and Gertrud return October 1914...Treatment for arthritis?...* Yup, these were the same as the photocopied notes Uncle Claude had hidden for her to find. Brenda had said they had been left to the local history society by some researcher interested in Victorian and Edwardian kitchen gardens who had abandoned her project, uncompleted, in the nineteen-sixties, she believed.

The second sheaf was even more disappointing. A quick riffle through showed them to be mostly about Romany travellers, with family names and itineraries and stuff about wagons and horses. The relevance was lost on Maddy and she turned instead to the photographs. They were all old, most of them tatty around the edges and some of them creased. People and places long gone. Several featured cars, angular models with running boards planting them firmly in the nineteen-twenties or thirties, and a bloke astride a motorbike, the spidery pre-war type, with a leather helmet and a scarf round his neck, very Lawrence-of-Arabia, very Peter O'Toole.

Scarcely any were labelled. She would never know who these people were. The photographs were interesting as all old photographs are, but they didn't help.

After an evening of looking, Maddy had put the box file on the shelf in the snug. Once again the trail had gone cold.

CHAPTER 21

AND THEN AT THE END OF JUNE SHE WENT TO THE CINEMA – actually went to see an actual film – because after four long months in the North, she had a friend: Anthea.

Anthea arrived one day soon after the garden restoration began, turning up on the doorstep with a brilliant smile and shining blonde hair in a thick plait, and asked whether she might be permitted to see the garden project even though she would not be able to take part on account of having a seven-month-old son. Before they got past the terrace Maddy felt they were becoming friends.

The basics were there, of course; there was only a year between them in age. Anthea too had grown up in London, and had moved to Northumberland after marrying Matthew, who had switched career from computer programming to being a ranger for the Northumberland National Park and was now that perennially attractive notion: an intellectual man living a rugged outdoor life. I bet he's good looking too, Maddy had thought, and then she met him, and he was.

The Lancasters lived in a converted chapel on the edge of Shilston, a village four miles from Kirkwitton, which in Northumberland counted as local. The conversion was charming, quirky in the extreme, with original pews reused as dining chairs, gothic windows with stone tracery and stained glass, and steeply pitched ceilings in the upstairs rooms. But it had only a small garden, and although Anthea had roses around the door, courgettes and beans in tubs and sweet peas scrambling up the fence, she hankered for proper gardening in a way that Maddy certainly did not. Anthea, like Liz, wanted to grow things; Maddy just wanted the place tidy and not on her conscience.

Also like Liz, Anthea Lancaster was further along the road to being grown up, not only married but a mother too, and baby Ben, with his fat hands and perfect ears and astonishingly long eye lashes, was delightful. Matthew was happy to babysit while they went to what was undoubtedly a rather girlie film. In truth, the plot was fairly daft and some of the lines unintentionally funny, but it had been fun to go out. Maddy was driving and had stopped for a coffee at Anthea's afterwards, so it was not much before midnight that she drove over the bridge and the last thing she expected was to find a car blocking her gates.

She slammed on the brakes and then nosed carefully into the bank a few yards on. That should, she hoped, give the Volvo at least a chance if any other car came zooming around the bend. Before she could think further, there was a knock on the window. She jumped, and wound the window down.

It was a man. He was bending slightly to see her, and

perhaps her jump had been noticed because he tipped his torch upwards so that his face was lit and she could see him, and the first thing he said was, 'It's all right.' Then he said, 'Thanks so much for stopping. I don't suppose you have a plug spanner?'

Maddy wasn't a fool and she had spent all her life in London, yet having wound her window down she now switched off the ignition and then got out of her car. She was aware, faintly, of a small inner voice as if from a great distance calling *beware, beware*, but it didn't seem to weigh much against the immediacy of the voice next to her, which was deep and dark brown with a Scottish lilt, and was saying, 'It cut out right on the bend just back there. I was so happy to see this gateway. I just coasted in.'

Maddy said, 'Yes.' Then she said, 'The thing is, though, I didn't stop to see if I could help. I was turning in. I live here.'

'Oh what, here?'

What are you doing? nagged the little voice, but Maddy said, 'Yes,' and then, 'Do you have breakdown cover with anyone?'

'I do. RAC. But I didn't fancy walking along these roads until I found a phone box. Do you know where the next village is?'

His car was pointing towards Kirkwitton; he had come from the Morpeth direction. Maddy said, 'Actually it's only a mile further on but I agree about the road.' And finally she paid attention to the little voice of wisdom and said, 'Why don't I ring them for you?'

It took a bit of hassle to organise. First Maddy crossed

the lane and stood flashing the torch alternately left and right as a warning to any traffic that might turn up, while Doug – his name was Doug Ferguson – pushed his car back onto the road. Then they swapped and Doug flashed the torch while Maddy reversed back and drove through the gates and a few yards up the drive. And then they swapped yet again and Doug pushed his car through the gates too and stopped just behind her, leaving space for the RAC van when it arrived. Then Maddy drove – alone – up to the house and let herself in.

She locked the door behind her. Away from the influence of that chocolatey voice, common sense kicked in. What had she been thinking? She was slightly appalled by the ease with which safety-consciousness had melted away just because the guy was attractive. And how could she even tell that he was attractive when it was too dark to see him properly?

She knew he was though.

Almost certainly he was perfectly fine. Maddy did not subscribe to the Stranger Danger All Around lobby. But still, she would have been vulnerable if he was a wandering psychopath.

Hmm.

She made the call. Doug had copied the number and his membership details onto the back of a petrol receipt. She had suggested she take the card but he had pointed out that then she would have to come back out to return it.

The RAC operator told her it might be a couple of hours before they got to him because he was neither a woman alone (*No*, thought Maddy, *that's me*) nor had a medical condition, and being June it wasn't likely to snow. Then she sat in the kitchen and thought.

It was nearly midnight. She should just go to bed. The house was locked up. The RAC van would come, get him moving again and that would be the end of it. That was certainly what he expected her to do. It was what she ought to do.

She went back out. She made coffee first and filled a flask and took the packet of digestives, and put them both into a carrier bag so he could leave them for her to collect in the morning, and then drove back down the drive.

Doug had the bonnet up again, the torch propped so that it shone into the recesses of the engine. He looked around at the sound of her approach. When she said, 'I've made some coffee,' his face registered surprise, pleasure, gratitude and embarrassment in a blend that made it impossible for Maddy not to grin, and instead of handing over the carrier and turning back, she sat in the passenger seat next to him.

His accent was Edinburgh, but so much warmer than Joyce Campbell's had been. He was a chemical engineer working in the field of materials, and when Maddy asked what that actually meant, he said his team was developing a new insulator for circuit breakers to make them more reliable and thus improve power failures in rural areas, which sounded much less boring than she had thought at first. He lived in Durham, which wasn't too far away Maddy thought, and was on his way to pay a visit to family in Edinburgh, which was also promising. He had been diverted from his usual route by a bridge closure and had been driving impressionistically, and as a result had found himself on the Kirk-witton lane without much idea how far he was from anywhere.

And then he said the visit was to say goodbye for a while because he was flying to Boston, Massachusetts, where he would be working with MIT for the next couple of years or so. And that wasn't promising at all.

They shared the flask beaker.

Then it was her turn, and Maddy explained about her astonishing inheritance and how she had fallen under the spell of living in a castle, albeit a small one, and moved here permanently. 'Permanently for the time being,' she added, to be clear.

'A *castle!* Does it have a name?'

'Unthank,' Maddy said, thinking as always what a strange name it was. But Doug was unfazed.

'Ah, right.'

'What do you mean? Have you come across an Unthank before?'

'Oh aye. There are a few about. My sister lives on Unthank Road in Norwich. It means land settled without permission. A squat, basically.'

'Really?' Maddy mulled this over. So she owned a castle that was *without permission*. The original occupiers, the ones who had built it, had been chancers trying their luck, and apparently it had paid off. It was a beguiling thought.

'So, what are you going to do here?' Doug asked.

Maddy sighed. 'I don't know. That's the problem. I can't afford to just live in it, but I don't want to turn it into a hotel or conference centre or something horrible like that. I want to keep it private. But I can't. Any ideas?'

She expected Doug to pass on this, but instead he gave it thought. 'You're ideally placed for an outdoor retreat. Corporate days, or weeks maybe. Or school residential trips. You're not far from the Wall. History and archaeology, maybe.'

Maddy wasn't sure which sounded worse, middle management guys or school kids. She thought of the rabble of teenagers at Waterloo. 'Mm,' she said, cautiously.

Sitting in the car more or less forced them to stare at the windscreen. Maddy would have preferred to see his face but twisting sideways would have been a bit obvious.

He said, 'You're not keen.'

'Not on hordes of strangers descending, no.'

'Aye, I can see that. Not sure what else you can do with it, though.'

'No.'

Maddy sought for something else to talk about. She was worried that any minute he might say she needn't wait and ought to go in, and if he did, she couldn't think how to respond without coming across like an idiot. So she said, 'What are you going to be doing in Boston?' and that set him off. He was enthusiastic about his work, which was nice, and had the knack of explaining enough specialised stuff for you to follow but not so much that you got bored. Maddy listened with half her mind on what he was saying and half on how he said it. She liked his accent, which was distinctly Scottish but didn't batter her about the head, and his voice was lovely.

It was surprisingly deep and made her think of rich and delicious things to eat. It was the first thing she had noticed about him and was, she acknowledged, the hook. It was gorgeous.

The rest of him was at least a bit gorgeous too.

But he was going to America.

After materials, they talked about photography, which Doug was interested in as an amateur – he had a Pentax – and he asked some sensible questions about processing and printing. Then they talked about Northumberland, which was still new to Maddy although becoming less so and which Doug knew only from driving through it. Maddy gathered enough courage to ask what wall he had meant and discovered that Hadrian's Wall was not far from Kirkwitton and that there were forts and towers and small museums that she ought to visit.

To balance things a bit, Maddy mentioned Hexham Abbey and that led to a discussion of other abbeys and cathedrals, many of which they both knew, Maddy as a subject for photography, Doug because he was interested in history, especially medieval buildings. Then Maddy mentioned her priest hole, and the next thing she knew she was launching into the whole Uncle-Claude, Lenka-Midnight, keys-and-riddles shebang.

Doug was impressed.

'That is amazing. And you can't get into the latest box?'

'No. Which means there must be another hiding place I haven't found yet. It's a killer.'

'Aye. Well. And you've looked behind pictures and things?'

'Yes, done that.' She had. Not that there were many, but

those there were – a couple of hunting prints in the dining room, a clumsy painting of the Matterhorn – had been lifted off the wall and the panelling behind knocked and pressed and generally assaulted, but to no avail.

'You must have an attic in a place like this. Have you–'

'Yes,' Maddy said hurriedly. 'And no.'

Not quite true. She could have searched the attic more thoroughly but there was that question of the light that insisted on turning itself back on. She had stood at the foot of the stairs watching the light switch in its off position, daring it to defy the laws of physics, for ten minutes at a time, and then as soon as she turned her back it clicked and the light was on again. She even tried reversing away from it, like a courtier leaving the Royal Presence, and once she was round the corner – click.

So then she used a towel to protect her hand and unscrewed the bulb. That turned out to be the worst thing she could have done, because an erratic electric switch was one thing, explainable, blarneyed away using Liz's idea of dodgy electric connections, but to be all alone in a huge, dark house half a mile from the nearest other human being and see candle light flicker behind a closed door was ghastly. Her skin had turned to ice and she had been literally shaking when the next morning, in reassuring daylight, she replaced the bulb. It was not something she wanted to be reminded about, and certainly not something to tell this lovely man who she was hoping might like her. She wanted to be cool and competent, not a gibbering hysteric.

Doug said, 'Okay, have you thought about–' and then headlights showed behind them and the RAC had arrived.

Maddy hung around, feeling superfluous. Then Doug came over and said it was the ignition coil, as he had thought, and the van was going to give him a tow to the nearest garage.

And that was that. There was a bit of a circus sorting out the tow; Maddy drove the Volvo up the drive followed by the RAC van towing Doug, and while she tucked herself away in the courtyard the other two managed a stately three-sixty turn in front of the steps and headed away back towards the road.

Maddy watched them go and realised she hadn't even said goodbye.

Two days later a bouquet of white freesias arrived with a card that said, *Thanks for all your help – Doug.*

And then that really was that.

CHAPTER 22

THE DOORBELL CLANGED WHILE MADDY WAS UPSTAIRS. SHE was in the smaller of the front bedrooms, which she used as an ironing room. Objectively, it was squandering space to turn an entire room over to one job, and a job she only did once a week at that, but it meant she could leave the ironing board out and heaven knew the space was there to be squandered. Come the autumn she would return to using the kitchen, which would be warm, but for now this worked well.

She set the iron on its heel and trotted to the largest bedroom to open the door onto the porch roof, a balcony large enough for a dining table and chairs had she wished to lug them up there, and walled by crenellated stone. The car she was expecting stood on the gravel. Maddy leaned over.

'Hang on,' she shouted. 'Down in a tick.'

Then she returned to the smaller room, unplugged the iron, and cantered down the stairs feeling light-hearted and bubbly. The clouds could have been fewer, the breeze might have been lighter, and the letter on the kitchen table had been a blow, but she was going on a picnic and right now that was enough.

She grabbed the cartons of apple juice – her contribution – and went out to meet Anthea, who had the back door of her car open and turned now to say, 'Look at this!' Then she faced into the car again and said, 'Ben, let's show Maddy our new trick!'

Anthea was beautiful, stylish and graceful, and all in a casual, unselfconscious way that could have driven Maddy wild had she not also been such fun. She was now sticking her tongue out as far as it would go and waggling it, and after a moment or two the baby strapped into the child seat carefully extended the tip of his tongue between his lips.

Maddy gasped and the tongue vanished.

'Oh that's wonderful!'

And it was. Maddy had not anticipated being engulfed in baby-worship but she had been, and now found herself buying rattles and baby socks whenever she was in Hexham. This time she had a square book with four plump plastic pages. She swivelled in the front seat and handed it to Ben, who dropped his rattle to carefully take it from her hand and put it in his mouth. He watched her steadily over the top.

Maddy faced front. 'I did wash it first,' she commented.

'You ought not keep buying us presents,' Anthea said.

'I like it.'

There was no need for Maddy to hop out to do the gates. These days she left them open for the gardeners to come and go. Most evenings she walked down and closed them for the night, but sometimes she forgot and it didn't worry her. Unthank felt a very safe place.

They were going to a National Trust property as a treat; the buggy for the gardens was in the boot and they would take turns to carry Ben inside the house.

Anthea turned into the lane and changed gear. 'Ought I ask whether you've heard?' She had an unusual and rather appealing use of English, Maddy thought. She used words like *ought* and *might* and said *I fear* instead of *I'm afraid*.

Maddy herself was more blunt. 'Didn't get it,' she said.

'I'm sorry.'

'Yeah. Well.'

The job had been as a studio technician in the photography and printing department of a tertiary college, and was probably quite lowly but might have been a stepping stone to something better. But she hadn't got it, and the letter she had opened half an hour earlier, and which was still on the table, didn't suggest why or offer any encouragement but simply stated that she had been unsuccessful. Blast.

Maddy needed a job. She couldn't live on the proceeds of her flat forever. But she wasn't desperate enough yet to abandon photography and take a clerical job of some sort – even supposing she could land one of those. She had approached every camera shop within reasonable reach – which up here meant inside an hour's drive – going to the shop in person, dressed smartly and with typed copies of her CV in a folder, but not one of them had any vacancies. People who work in camera shops like what they do; staff don't move on. Still, she met a few managers, and when she was feeling upbeat and energetic she told herself she was making contacts and someone might remember her. When she was feeling low she thought it was pointless.

She was also compiling portfolios of her best prints to send off to magazines and agents, because now that she had a phone, prospective business contacts could call her. There was nothing like being *without* for a few months to make you appreciate being *with* again. Having a phone was delightful, and made so many things possible.

'Oh, and I've called your chimney sweep,' she said now, happy to change the subject. 'He's coming on Friday.'

HE WASN'T Anthea's chimney sweep exactly, but he did their chimneys and Anthea had recommended him. Joan in the shop used him too. Clearly the man to get.

Chimney cleaning was another aspect of life about which Maddy had zero experience, and it crossed her mind that she should have spread dust sheets all over the place, but in the event the guy (*'Call me Steve'*) did all that. Maddy watched him sweep the first chimney, interested to see what it entailed, but then drifted off to the kitchen while he worked his way from room to room. The job was costed per fireplace and it wasn't going to be cheap. After an hour she took him a mug of tea, and ten minutes after that he brought the empty back to the kitchen and asked her what she wanted done about the chimney with the cash in it.

'Cash!' she repeated.

How extraordinary! And jolly useful too, especially if it was a large quantity of cash. 'Where exactly is the cash?'

'Left hand side, about three feet up. An arm's length. Didn't you know?'

'I certainly did not.'

Intrigued, Maddy followed the chimney sweep up two flights of stairs to the second floor and into one of the bedrooms that had been empty of furniture. Steve showed her how to wriggle round and reach up with her hand, and Maddy's fingers found a brick that jutted into the flue. If she really stretched she could just about reach over the brick and scrape her fingertips against something smooth.

She withdrew. 'And the cash is in there?' she asked.

Steve looked at her doubtfully. 'That *is* the cash,' he said.

They stared at one another for a beat, and then the penny dropped.

'Oh – it's a *cache!*' Maddy exclaimed, and then wished she hadn't because now her error was evident.

Her chimney sweep was a gentleman. He didn't laugh, just moved on nice and quick. 'It's the third of these I've come across,' he said. 'Before they had banks, and that. D'you want me to see if there's anything in it?'

Did she heck!

'Go on,' Maddy said.

Steve reached in. It was easier for him, being taller. 'Probably nothing there.'

Maddy thought otherwise. She watched him scrabble, her skin tight and prickly. Then he frowned and grunted, grappling with something he couldn't see that was just beyond his grasp.

'Hold on.'

And then he had it. He straightened up and his arm reappeared, holding a metal cashbox. 'Here you go.'

'Thanks. That's amazing.'

'Aye, well. Anything in it?'

Understandably he was curious, but Maddy selfishly said, 'It's locked,' without mentioning that she had the key.

It nearly killed her to wait for him to finish and leave, but she did, and only when he had been paid, and they had chatted about chimney caches and priest holes and secret compartments in ice houses, and he had finally, finally driven away did Maddy fetch the key.

The key fitted.

Maddy opened the lid.

THAT RANGE COOKER. A monster, I was going to call it, but a monster roars and prowls and grabs you, and the range didn't do that at all but slumped there against the wall, huge and sullen and uninterested in me or what I might do. I wasn't interested in it either, and we'd both have been perfectly happy to turn our backs on one another and have nothing to do. But I couldn't turn my back because even after three days Lily hadn't returned and the food she had left had run out.

And she never did return, neither her nor Sam, not ever.

I never found out what happened. I've guessed. What could swallow them up in York, so completely that they could not even send word? Did they both succumb to disease – a sudden, devastating illness that swept the life out of them both in twenty-four hours? An accident? Did one of those motor cars run over the top of them in the street, where they were walking arm in arm not noticing what was coming upon them from behind? Or did Lily overbalance and tumble onto the railway track and Sam leap down to rescue her, only to die with her?

Or did they decide they'd had enough of Frau Bircher and her moaning and run off to London, leaving me in the stew? No. I don't believe that. But the thing is when they walked away down the drive that day it was the last I saw of them, and I have never found out why.

That range cooker, though. It was the heart of the household, you see. Everything depended on it. If the range wasn't running, you had no hot food, no hot water even, nothing to eat but raw stuff and no bread to help the raw stuff go down. Well, Lily had taught me how to light it in the morning and how to see it to bed at night, and how to clean the wretched thing at dawn, when it was finally cold, before setting it all going again for another day. If you didn't clean it, or didn't clean it properly, it would rust and stop working. On your knees you had to be, reaching in and around and behind and rubbing for all you were worth at full arm's stretch, which is the hardest way to work. I'd clean ten mucky stables and ten muddy horses any day before one kitchen range.

But the kitchen range was what I had, and I had to get on with it. I had to bring in the coal as well, and take out the ashes, and while we didn't have ten horses there was Tom and I still had to deal with him and his stable too.

The first week I didn't, not properly; I'd skip out the droppings left on top of the straw and shove him back in without dealing with what was underneath, and the mud Tom collected stayed on him. They'll come back tomorrow, I kept telling myself, and I'll catch up then, and I'd get on with weeding and picking the fruit and sowing the spring cabbages and onions. But the stable became disgusting and I couldn't bring myself to put the poor horse in, so I lugged out all the bedding and right heavy work it was by then, and swept the floor and made the bed anew, and I picked out his feet as well because horses can suffer and go lame if that's not done, but the mud on his coat where he'd rolled had to wait until I sorted out a routine for myself. I'm flat out, I told him when he looked at me under his claggy forelock, so you'll have to put up with it.

There were times when I glimpsed him dozing in the field and wished I were a horse and could do the same.

It was non-stop from before dawn to midnight, when no matter what was outstanding I downed tools and went to bed. If I didn't get some sleep nothing would get done at all and then where would we be? Frau Bircher, the old biddy, depended utterly on me. I depended utterly on me. It's no fun eating apples and cheese every day, and I was never so thankful for anything as I was that Madam wasn't steady enough on her legs to come looking for me. I've thought since that she must have been frightened, abandoned in that drawing room with no-one answering her call, and I'm sorry for it. But it was beyond me in those first days to service her every want while coping with everything else. Something had to make way, and it wasn't going to be me.

A day came when I stopped expecting Lily and Sam to walk through the door. Perhaps it was a week after, perhaps longer, but I remember that it was a Friday. I'd been serving us cold meat and salad vegetables until they ran out, and then eggs or cheese on toast, using the last drying remains of Lily's loaves, too stale to eat fresh, and then the only thing left to cook was potatoes so we had them, boiled and crushed with some butter. At that point there was nothing for it but to start cooking proper meals. I knew it, even if I didn't like it. And with cooking came the realisation that I had been coping, that's all – surviving moment to moment, nothing more. That couldn't go on. I had to decide how I was going to do this, and right then and there I knew that deciding how to do it took precedence over all the rest.

I washed my hands and tucked my hair behind my ears and put on the white apron that hung on the kitchen door. The apron kept you decent when you presented yourself to Madam, Lily said, and so far I'd remembered.

I walked all the way to the drawing room, knocked on the door and opened it without waiting to be bid. Madam looked astonished. Before she could speak, I said, 'Excuse me Madam but dinner will be later than usual.' Then I backed out and shut the door.

Oh yes, I remember that it was a Friday and I remember the satis-faction I felt all the way back to the kitchen.

I needed things to write with. Lily kept the accounts book in a drawer in the kitchen and I used that, turning it upside down and opening it from the back. It wasn't a smart book, not like this one I'm writing in now. I saw no transgression in using a page or two for house-hold planning.

I began with lists: one for daily jobs, one for weekly jobs, one for occasional jobs. Then I turned to a fresh page and started again, this time copying across only the tasks that were essential.

I finished and read it over. I could manage it, I reckoned. If I cracked on.

At that time it still seemed possible Lily would return one day.

And by now you should be asking yourself three questions.

Are you?

Maddy laid the pages down.

The extra thing this time, the cryptic addition, was a photograph. Faded and cracking, it showed three people standing in front of a greenhouse. Two were women, in long skirts and pinafores with their hair hidden under caps, and one was a man in outdoor clothes, a waistcoat over a shirt, trousers tied below the knees. They stood in a row, shoulder to shoulder, staring at the camera, unsmiling and suspicious. There was nothing written on the back.

Maddy gazed at the faces. Lenka with Lily and Sam, surely? But which of the women was Lenka?

'I think it's the slim one,' she said aloud. She fetched her loupe from the dark room and set it over the faded print. The woman's face stared back, magnified and relatively sharp although the contrast was woefully weak. If only she had the negative.

But of course she didn't have the negative. This photograph must be the one the visitor had taken, and then sent to Lily because Madam wouldn't have shared. What a cow.

The new key was the black iron, straight-shanked sort, with a wisp of frayed string looped through the handle. It was far too big for the padlock on the metal box she had retrieved from the priest hole, so she rammed her feet into shoes and went out to the ice house, where to her great relief it turned. She dragged open the door and a smell of stone and earth met her.

The hole in the ground was easy to find if you knew it was there, and thanks to the Warwickshire Traveller, Maddy did. She reached down and brought out a plastic storage box that rattled.

That would be the key.

She closed and locked the ice house and took her prize to the kitchen.

She was back in business.

CHAPTER 23

Jeremiah Midnight — my father, that is — was hopeless. Always had been. So charming he could be, loving and cheerful and stuffed full of romance, and with his curling red-gold hair and corn-flower-blue eyes it was easy to see how my mother fell for him. He wasn't a gipsy but he made friends with gipsies. He saw how they gleaned a living from seasonal work both legal — fruit picking, haymak-ing, beating for the autumn shoots — and not-so, which was mostly poaching whether with a rod, a snare or a ferret, and he added to that tutoring and scribing, teaching children that slipped through the fingers of the education boards to read and adults too, and writing letters or contracts for anyone who would pay. And the charm-weaving, of which the least said the better. My part had been to keep track of the books — who had borrowed what and fetching them back later, because Jeremiah would never stand for the loss of a book — and when I was old enough, to help with the teaching.

Why I'll never know, but Jeremiah loved literature with a passion greater than anything he felt for mere people, even us, his family. I think he kept me at home as much as anything so we could read together and discuss what we read. *'Do you see what he's done here?'* he would ask me, smoothing the page with the flat of his hand, like a horseman stroking the neck of his mare or a lover caressing a mistress, *'Do you see how he's done it?'* It wasn't just the words, you understand, but the way they were plied that he loved. And at least some of his passion has transferred to me. I have listened to a treasure house of words and it's nice to write some of them down and think how they will seem to those that read them.

So, did you ask yourself what questions I meant? The three questions that should have raised themselves from my account so far?

I'll tell you what they are.

The first question: Why did I stay at the German House after Lily and Sam vanished? I was strong, healthy, young and by now reasonably skilled in farming and gardening and could have expected to find myself a much easier position quickly enough.

The second question: If I wanted to stay, why did I not explain to Madam and get her to hire replacement staff?

And the third question – the really big question: How was I faring under the roof? Was I cowering like Chicken Licken, waiting for it to plunge down upon my head? And if so, how could I carry out the work?

I'll tell you.

Have you ever been in a wagon? A gipsy wagon, I mean, with the hooped roof and the beds on boxes? Or ducked your head under the lintel to enter a cottager's hovel, the kind provided for field workers? I'm a tall woman; I could only stand up at the apex, had to bend my neck nearer the eaves. Someone, never mind who, once said *Had I not been in a church?* Well, no I hadn't. Churches didn't figure with Jeremiah Midnight and even after he was gone, Sunday Service was never something that concerned me. It didn't seem relevant. I did my best to do right by people, even people I had never met – then, at least – but *saw that as plain common sense and what was right, done because I could imagine how I would feel in their shoes not because the parson or the Bible told me to. And you know I never set foot inside a schoolhouse.*

Have you not been wondering how I ate my meals at the Hall? I asked Lily to bring mine out to me on a plate, and at first she did. But then it was raining one day and she dragged me over the threshold and through the passage to the kitchen, and by the end of the meal I had had my revelation.

It was the ceilings, you see; they were so high. I never needed to bend my neck inside the German House; I had to tip my head back even to see where the ceiling was. I could walk and stand tall, open my shoulders and breathe deep, just as if I were in the open outdoors. At the German House I could be in the open indoors.

Oh, at first the old dread would settle on me as I approached the doorstep because a lifetime of habit will drag its feet leaving, but gradually that dread shrank to unease, a much less bothersome feeling, and eventually unease slipped away too and for the first time in my conscious life I could pass through a doorway from outside to inside without any trepidation at all. It became normal. I became normal.

And just in time too, because my life was now to be as much under a roof as under the sky. A house the size of the German House takes a deal of looking after just to keep it running, even with one old lady in sole residence.

In the event, that was one of the first decisions I made: not to keep the house running, or not all of it. It had been hard enough for Lily to cope with alongside the cooking, I knew from our conversations around the meal table that it would be impossible for me if I had to manage everything outdoors as well. No Percy Whatmough now, remember! It crossed my mind that I might regret seeing that boy off, but not for long;

he was a bad one, and it would have taken more of my precious time checking what he was up to than to do his work myself, I reckoned.

So I closed up all the rooms we didn't use, that Madam didn't use. They could be put in store until the day they were needed again, and I found dust sheets in one of the linen closets – I think they were dust sheets for they had a tired, stale air – and spread them over the upholstered furniture, the pieces that would be difficult to clean once dirty. Then I shut the doors and left them shut.

That brought the house down to six rooms in use: the drawing room where Madam sat all day, the dining room that had become her bedroom, the kitchen of course, and the bedroom and bathroom for my own use. The house had modern plumbing and hot water came out of a tap, thank God. I also decided to keep open a small parlour at the end of the Long Hall which Madam could use at meal times. It meant she could go in to eat and leave the table at the end of the meal, which she was used to and would give her a change of scene during her long, empty days. I was not mean, am not mean, and I did feel sorry for her, Frau Bircher, it was just that she was an impediment to me and my working schedule meant that impediments of any sort were desperately unwelcome.

An impediment and yet the point of it – a conundrum, I know. It was only the existence of Frau Bircher that caused me to be there at all, and the irony was not lost on me. I ran myself ragged trying to look after her while she sat idle and complained, and I confess there were times I felt I hated her, yet all the while it was her presence that allowed me to be living at the Hall instead of in some cramped, terrifying hovel or trying to sleep under a tree in the rain.

And I do mean living in the Hall, for that Friday I moved from the loft above the stables into the house, taking a room on the first floor, not the second. There were rooms on the second floor, less opulently furnished, with oil cloths on the floorboards and unlined curtains, and I left those alone. The ceilings were high enough, probably − far better than any I had encountered outside the Hall − but I didn't see why I should put up with anything but the best available. Why not? It would have been a waste of a good − a lovely − bedroom if I hadn't used it. And in any case, it seemed small recompense for the work I was doing. Madam never wandered the house any longer, her legs weak and apparently painful, so who would ever know?

Not that I spent many wakeful minutes in that room. I was up well before dawn and when I dropped onto the bed at the end of the day I was asleep in moments. I had thought I worked hard at Halpin's Farm but it was nothing to this, and there was never a half day off. I cleaned and lit the range first, then swept the hearth and laid a fire in the drawing room. I let the hens out and collected the eggs and in the winter I fed Tom before going round the gardens and picking what I needed for the day, and what I didn't need yet but which would have spoiled if left on the plant any longer. By then Tom would have finished his breakfast so I turned him out in the field and cleaned the stable; in the summer months he stayed out, thank God, and made do with grass to eat.

Then I took eggs, vegetables and fruit indoors, checked the range, made breakfast for Madam and set it out in the parlour, lit the drawing room fire, brought in the coal (two trips at least) and ate my own breakfast. And so it continued through the day, all the essential tasks I hadn't found a way to get rid of: the fire in Madam's bedroom after she was downstairs; the washing up; preparing lunch and, later, dinner, feeding the range, sweeping and dusting and scrubbing the flagstones, which I now did on a rota, and outdoors hoeing and hand weeding the vegetable beds, sowing, thinning, potting on and planting out in the spring and summer and digging, raking leaves, turning compost and checking our stored fruit and vegetables in the winter. In the evening, before dusk, I fed the range again so that there would be hot water for Madam's bath, then brought Tom back up and put hay in his stable, counted in the hens and shut the shed, took more coal in, washed up dinner, cleaned the bathroom and lavatory, lit the fire in Madam's bedroom and filled her hip bath by hand, scrubbed the kitchen table, and listened for the querulous call that told me the old woman had retired for the night, which was my cue to empty the bath, do the final washing up of coffee cups and cream jugs, close down the hateful range so that it would be cold enough to clean in the morning, and crawl upstairs to bed.

And that was just if I was left undisturbed to get on with it. Mercifully, Madam had no friends and we rarely got callers, because when we did – the Doctor mainly – I had to drop what I was doing and answer the door, and that wasn't easy if I was in the garden. I had to run, just run, and drop my hitched-up skirts down over my trousers and straighten my cap and shed my coat along the way, and there certainly wasn't time to wash my hands.

I took short cuts where I could. One of Madam's constant moans was that we now ate the same meal two days running. I cooked double in one go and then kept portions back to be reheated the following day; in frosty weather I could make it go three days. That tactic gave me an hour extra on alternate days to do the jobs I had otherwise to put off: grooming Tom once a week to keep him healthy and check for small injuries of the sort horses can do themselves; cleaning out the hen shed and checking the hens for mites; pruning and tying in and thinning the fruit, cutting back and forking in and pulling up and still more hand-weeding; washing windows, polishing silver (an astonishingly dirty job), mending (not Madam's clothes, which came to no harm in the drawing room, but my own, which suffered constant rips and splits and straight-forward wearing away), and writing up the household accounts.

I was tired and I was angry and the stark fact that there was *nobody to blame helped not at all. I believe I became a little mad; certainly I did some mad things. I talked to myself a great deal, indoors and out, and one day, when I had burned the dinner beyond recognition and had to serve cheese and bread, crashing the tray down on the table and rushing out of the door before Madam could speak, I lost my head and unable to face that horrible kitchen I went instead to the library and, without giving myself any warning, wrote my name in the family bible. It seemed to me I was working so hard to keep the house afloat I had as much right to be recorded there as any family member.*

Ridiculous of course. But I was so very close to the end of my tether. Simply put, I was doing the jobs of three full-time staff all by myself.

And that's the second question, is it not? Why did I not tell Frau Bircher that Lily and Sam had vanished and needed to be replaced?

Jeremiah said I was prickly. Like a thistle, he used to tell people, to my shame at first, when I was a little girl, although by the time I was ten I had become proud of my prickliness and felt it made me special, independent and strong. Later still I became indifferent; we all have our character traits and I'd rather be prickly than a fantasist like my father. But it is true I do not suffer fools gladly or even like people much, and part of what made my situation at the German House so valuable to me was that both Lily and Sam Biddle had been tolerable companions – more than tolerable in Lily's case, as evidenced by our friendship at Halpin's. I think Lily could be prickly too.

How would my position be if new staff arrived? The three of us had to live so close, working indoors and out, eating together, forced into social intercourse over and over throughout the day, every day. Frau Bircher might bring anybody in, they might be stuck up and full of pretentions from having worked for a large household, or spiteful and mean with the food, or just plain idiots with no conversation. Sam

Biddle had been a quiet soul but when he did speak he made sense, and I'd met plenty at Halpin's and elsewhere that didn't. I couldn't imagine living with people like that. It would be worse than hard work.

So I bided my time. I thought I'd see how things went, whether it was possible for me to keep up with what had to be done without collapsing. If it became too hard I could tell Madam then; until that time I'd manage. Because the worst outcome of hiring new staff seemed obvious to me: I'd get my marching orders. Forget prickly, I was far worse than that: I was an anomaly – an Outdoor Boy who was a woman – and if there was anything I'd learned in life it was that the vast majority of folk do not care for anomalies, do not care for them at all. And what folk with any power do with things they do not care for is get rid of them.

For the first time in my life, I was afraid. I could be easily got rid of by anyone who wished me gone. No family, no friends, nothing to my name but my clothes. I had no-one to stand beside me while I fought my battles and no-one to catch me when I fell. When those are your circum-stances it makes simple sense to avoid fighting battles at all, especially battles where your heart's desire is at stake.

And so we come to that remaining question. Why did I not leave of my own accord and return to life on the land?

The answer: because I had fallen in love.

Fallen in love? Fallen in love with whom? There wasn't anyone else there, Lenka had spent the last however many words explaining that. The mysterious new gardener, the young and lusty outdoor servant who had been making Lenka Midnight slow to answer the door to Dr Burden, who undid her buttons and messed her hair, had never existed. It had been Lenka herself, clad in trousers and boots, that Edna's father had glimpsed at a distance.

In that case, who had Lenka met, and why had she made no mention of him in the journal? She didn't say she was *soon going* to fall in love, but that she *had already* fallen in love and that was why she was struggling on alone.

What on earth was going on?

Maddy sighed and turned to the extra sheet. It was a letter, handwritten on good quality paper, the script loopy and faded.

It was in German. Maddy had failed her German O-level and forgotten most of the little she once knew. *Ja, nein, danke, bitte, Wie heisst du? Die Blumen sind schön*, that was pretty much it. She started working her way through the words, which always seemed so very dense in German, but it was hopeless and she gave up. Then, as she set the letter aside the edge flicked up and she saw there was further writing on the reverse, in a different colour of ink.

She flipped the sheet and saw friendly English words. It was a translation.

3.VI.1918

Dearest Mutti,

It is with a heavy heart that I write to you this day and warn you to prepare yourself for news of the gravest and most desolate kind.

Our darling Marilena, whom I know has been your favourite grandchild since she first made her appearance in this world, is present to light up our lives no longer. A malady of the throat took her last week, and swiftly gathered strength despite all that the best physicians could do. Our little bird, our little Christmas present as we used to call her, could not fight it, and she succumbed quickly, which is our only poor comfort, that she did not languish and suffer long.

By the time this doleful letter reaches you, little Marilena will have been consigned to the earth where her brothers Fritz and Franz await her. Of our beautiful children, none now remain.

Gertrud and I are leaving. The memories here are too strong and too heavy. We will buy a chalet close to Gertrud's sister and will not travel again.

There seems nothing more I can say.

You remain in our thoughts.

Your loving son always,

Anders

Maddy looked at the German side again. Had the word *tot* or *Tod* appeared she'd have recognised it, she thought, but despite the whole letter being to inform Frau Bircher that her granddaughter had died, the words for die, death or dead did not appear at all. Such is our reluctance to face these unhappy truths.

It sounded like Marilena had been very young, and her brothers had all died too. How ghastly.

Maddy was waiting for the kettle to boil when she remembered the bible, and went to the snug to fetch it. She made her coffee and sat at the table with the bible open in front of her.

There they all were, the poor, doomed Bircher family: Ernst, the eldest; Jurgen, the next, and then Franz and Friedrich, poignantly shortened to Fritz in the letter, and lastly Marilena herself, born at the end of 1897 so only twenty-one when she died. Dreadful.

Maddy was rinsing out her mug when it hit her.

CHAPTER 24

MADDY DECIDED TO SHELL OUT ON A TRANS-ATLANTIC CALL. It was expensive but she hadn't spoken to her mother since she sold the flat, so she reasoned a proper conversation was due anyway.

She waited until two because of the time difference, but when her mother picked up, the first thing she said was, 'You only just caught me. I heard the ring as I was shutting the front door. We're going to Maine for the weekend.' Then she said, 'How are you, love?' which made Maddy feel better, but straightway followed it up with, 'Is this urgent?'

'Well, no, not urgent. I mean nothing's wrong. I was just calling for a chat.'

Which wasn't quite true.

'It's not a great time, love. How about next week? We'll be back on Tuesday.'

'Yes, okay,' Maddy said reluctantly. She could hardly say anything else. But then, before her mother put the phone down, she added, 'Just quickly though, what was Dad's mum like?'

'Your grandmother? Oh, I don't know. Difficult. Why?'

Maddy dodged. 'Did she have a sister? Did Dad have any Swiss aunts?'

'Maddy, what on earth is this about?'

Her mother sounded exasperated, as well she might. Maddy said, 'I was just wondering whether she came from a large family. Whether there were any more of them in England.'

'Not as far as I'm aware. Thank goodness. She was a strange woman. She practically ordered us to call you Madeleine.'

'*What!*'

'But we liked the name anyway – it was that or Isobel – so we went with Madeleine and kept her happy. Look, love, can we talk about this next week? Only Bill's giving me looks.'

'Okay. Sorry. Go on. And have a nice weekend,' Maddy remembered to say just in time.

She put the phone down feeling bereft. It never occurred to her to keep her mother up to the minute with her affairs now they were so far apart, yet it seemed peculiar and not quite nice that her mother had her own schedule too. Maddy knew perfectly well that she and Bill were not sitting at home waiting for her to call, but nevertheless she sort of expected them to be there should she choose to.

Very unreasonable, obviously.

How extraordinary about her name.

Isobel, though! A narrow escape.

Maddy shook herself. On Tuesday she'd call again, but it wasn't likely her mother would be able to shed any light on the matter. She hadn't expected she would, but it was all so weird she felt she had to try.

She checked her watch: two twenty; Liz would still be at work, up to her elbows in end-of-year reports, school fetes and emptying the lost property box. Anthea would probably be at home, baking something or pegging out baby clothes on the line, but she hadn't yet broached the subject of her peculiar ancestry with her new friend and felt shy. Or rather, not shy, just that it would be an uphill struggle with lots of background to explain before she got to the meaty bit, which was what she wanted to share: The Strange Case of the Two Marilenas.

Feeling grumpy and hard done by, Maddy wandered into the snug and dropped onto the edge of the chair. The bible lay on the table but she didn't open it; she didn't need to. She knew what was written there by heart now, just as she knew the letter translation; reading either again wouldn't alter anything.

In 1918 Marilena Bircher died in Switzerland. In 1919 she proclaimed herself to be the owner of Unthank in Northumberland.

How?

Had she not died after all, but made a surprising and miraculous recovery? But Anders in his letter said they had buried her. It could hardly be more final than that.

There had been a lot of deaths. Why? An accident – all four boys off gallivanting somewhere and caught in an avalanche? Influenza was a big killer back then, Maddy knew. Had there been an outbreak of 'flu in Switzerland as there had been in Britain after the first World War? What must it be like to bring up five children and lose them all? It didn't bear thinking about.

Death was more common then, of course; infant death happened all the time. People re-used Christian names, recycling them through the family when a child died and a new baby arrived. But Marilena was twenty-one when she died and Anders and Gertrud clearly hadn't had any more.

Gertrud wasn't listed in the bible. Only for blood relatives, perhaps. Although Theodore, Maddy's grandfather, was there. Perhaps Grandmother Lawrence hadn't understood the tradition.

There had to be another Marilena. There must have been two different girls sharing the same name, one of whom had died and one of whom had come to Unthank. So if the daughter of Anders Bircher, the beloved granddaughter of Clara Bircher, had died in Switzerland, who exactly was the Marilena who became Maddy's grandmother? A cousin? That would work. Perhaps Anders had taken to her, sharing his daughter's name and probably being friends as they grew up. This other Marilena might have been of solace to them after their final, crushing bereavement. They had said they would not travel anymore; they might easily have decided to give the strange English castle-house to a beloved niece. Mightn't they?

Maddy sighed. It was all guesswork. Historical documents were all very well but she was longing for a proper account that explained everything – a book written by someone who knew. Historians used surviving records, letters and deeds and wills and so on, for their research – 'working from the source' – and must deal with gaps and holes all the time. It didn't appeal; Maddy wanted things all sewn up.

In the box from the ice house there had been a key too. Of course there had. It was a modern padlock key and Maddy had seen immediately that it wouldn't unlock the strong box from the priest hole, but she had poked it at the key plate even so. Useless. Infuriating.

So now there was yet another lock she had to find.

Maddy had dredged up memories of every mystery story, film and television drama she had read or seen – every locked-room murder, every fake-haunting, every lost-treasure plot she had ever heard of – and had thought long and hard about how they might apply at Unthank. She had walked the passages and counted her paces inside rooms and outside, measured where the doors and walls were, knocked and listened for hollow spaces and stamped on creaking floor-boards under rugs.

She had toured outside too, moving incrementally around the house, scouring the walls for irregularities in the stonework, counting windows and gauging angles. A house like this could easily have a hidden room, she thought, the door plastered over and the window bricked up. A priest hole in the fireplace was as nothing, Unthank could have a dozen of them under stairs and behind walls and in the spaces between ceilings and floors.

But if there were, she couldn't find them. No more ice houses, no more cellars under the terrace, and no more caches in chimneys. Yet the key – the seventh, it was now – must open something, and somewhere there must be a key that would open the priest hole's strong box. It was maddening, and Maddy rang Liz after supper to complain about it.

Her friend was distracted by end-of-term admin just as Maddy had feared, and was unsympathetic. 'It'll show up. When you're thinking about something else. How's the garden restoration?'

But Maddy didn't want to talk about digging and sowing. 'Where would *you* hide a key, if you had to?' she asked.

'I did have to. I locked myself out when Paul was in France. Remember?'

Maddy did. It made a good story although no doubt it was annoying at the time. Afterwards Liz had put a spare key in a jam jar and buried it in the front garden.

'I can't go looking for a buried jam jar here,' she said, dismayed. 'It would take me centuries!'

'Very true,' Liz said calmly. 'So you'll just have to hope it turns up, won't you? Now, what about that farmer?'

THE FARMER WAS COLIN CHAPPELL, who had left a note for Maddy at the shop in the village. It was proving difficult to spread the word that Unthank had a telephone these days. Joan passed the envelope to her with the poppy-seed rolls. 'Colin's been in,' she said, as if that explained everything.

The note was brief and scarcely warranted an envelope: *Mowing Tuesday if weather holds. Colin 42959*

The weather did hold and on Tuesday after breakfast Maddy took a book out to the field and sat on the gate to wait. She wanted to see what this entailed, and knew she wouldn't hear from the house. After an hour or so she became aware of an engine throbbing along the road, and then of it idling the other side of the trees. She put down the book and waded across the field, the grass above her knees now, to see a tractor coming through the gate down there.

She waved. The tractor rumbled to a standstill and a man swung down from the cab and walked towards her. They met amongst the seed heads of grasses and mead-owsweet.

'I'm Maddy,' Maddy said, holding out her hand.

'Colin. You alright?'

He was fiftyish, tallish, plumpish, wearing a faded polo shirt and denims, a flat cap and serious lace-up boots.

Maddy said, 'I've no idea how this works.'

The farmer gazed around the field, his hands on his hips. 'Right. I'll cut her today, the weather looks good, so leave her to lie and bring the baler in maybe Friday. Alright?'

'Fine,' Maddy said. 'Honestly, I don't know anything. And I don't have to pay you?'

She was confident about this but wanted to have every-thing upfront and settled.

'No, no, if that's okay with you I'll just take the hay.'

'And I don't need to do anything else? Tell me if there's something I should be doing.'

'No, no. Old Mr Lawrence, he never came out at all. Didn't see him. A bit of a recluse, I think he was.'

Maddy nodded. 'So I gather. A bit odd altogether.' She wondered what Colin Chappell would think if he knew about the trail of keys and riddles. 'By the way, there's a phone here now. This is the number.' She handed across the slip of paper she had written out.

'Ah. Right. Good. I'll get on, then.'

Maddy returned to the gate her side, following the swathe she had made through the long grass, and heard the tractor roll forward behind her.

In the evening she came out again and surveyed the rows of banked hay, lying to dry as it did every year in fields all over the world, every year for centuries. It was late, the sun was beginning to sink and the mounds cast shadows, striping the field as it fell gently towards the trees. The smell was divine.

Maddy leaned against the wall. She thought of all the variations of this scene stretching back in time, and of painters who had tried to capture it. Constable of course, and those lovely, swirling paintings by Van Gogh, and the stark golden haystacks of John Nash. Liz would know many more.

She breathed in the rich air laden with the scent of things that grow, and felt the cool ruffle of the breeze that was ever-present in Northumberland and that stopped even warm days from being oppressive and sweaty as they were in London. She could hear no traffic at all, nor voices, but in the distance sheep bleated and she could hear the caw of a crow. In a while, Maddy thought, she would walk through the courtyards and go into the house through the back door, make some tea and probably finish her novel before bed. And with that thought she realised quite suddenly that she was happy.

Happy? Maddy paused to consider. She needed a job and she needed an income. There was a lot to do on the house before it was really comfortable, and at the moment no money to pay for it. That was a worry. She was lonely sometimes, her life more solitary than it had ever been before, although there were people she could call on – Anthea for a start, and the restoration crowd, especially Devyani, and Joan at the shop, as well as people like Liz and her mother who were at the end of a telephone – which she now had at her command.

Her life was quiet too, with no television; she could buy one, and buy an aerial, and pay for someone to install it, but so far it hadn't seemed worth the bother. Perhaps in the winter, when the nights were longer. And there were times, lots of them, when she felt lost in this rural environ-ment, ill-equipped and ignorant and unsure what was expected of her or how she should behave. She was an alien, she knew, and knowing it was unsettling even when people were kind.

And yet she was definitely happy. She could feel it, feel her happiness, like warm honey in her veins. For all her worries – or perhaps not worries but concerns – she was more relaxed than she had ever been in London. She felt taller too, wider-shouldered, firmer on her feet. As if she could breathe better in this air.

Which she probably could. The traffic pollution in Twickenham had been dreadful.

She was so lucky to be here.

Maddy turned and began to walk. Unthank rose before her like the castle it was at heart, and she felt the familiar glow of pleasure at having so marvellous a place all to herself. She softened every time she thought about it. It was like being in love.

Maddy stepped over the threshold and headed for the kitchen.

WHEN COLIN CHAPPELL returned two days later he rang the front door bell. Maddy was surprised because she had assumed after their conversation that he would simply bale the hay and cart it away, but here he was on the door step.

When she opened the door he said, 'You alright?'

Maddy said, 'Hi. Anything wrong?'

'No, no.' He was holding a suitcase in each hand, modern ones, light grey with rounded corners. They were huge, the kind you take for a very long holiday. He raised them and said, 'These belong to you.'

MADDY SAT on the floor in the drawing room, where she had asked Colin to set down the suitcases. They were too heavy for her to lift. She opened one while he was there, saw the stacks of books, and felt a flutter of pure adrenalin spring up.

'Thank you. Thanks. Great.'

'No, no. I'm sorry I didn't remember before. My wife reminded me.'

'That's fine. No problem. Thanks.'

Maddy saw him back to the door and then poured herself a tall glass of lemonade and returned to the drawing room. She sat cross legged on the carpet and began to explore.

They were diaries. Apparently, weirdly, her grandmother

had given them to Colin Chappell Senior, this Colin's father, ten years ago. Colin – her Colin, the present one – said his dad had been a little bit sweet on Mrs Lawrence after his wife died. Didn't get anywhere with her, Colin said, but he reckoned she knew he had a soft spot for her because she gave him these suitcases of her diaries and asked him to keep them until after Claude Lawrence, Maddy's uncle, had died.

'Didn't want him to know about them,' the farmer explained unnecessarily. 'I suppose she knew she'd go at some point and didn't want her son to find them.'

'I wonder why she didn't just burn them,' Maddy said.

The farmer shrugged. 'Anyway, she told Dad that Claude Lawrence was going to leave this place to you, and she wanted you to have the diaries too. Only Dad forgot, and I didn't know, and it was only Sue having a turn out and asking what they were that jogged his mind. He's eighty-eight. Sorry.'

'Oh gosh, no, that's fine.'

Now she lifted out the volumes and took stock. They ran from 1919 to 1974 – ten years ago – and the last one was only part used, the last entry written on the seventh of September: *CC is mowing tomorrow and I'll ask him then.*

With a little chill, Maddy realised this must be the request to keep the diaries. There were no further entries because Colin Chappell Senior had said Yes.

Quickly flipping through volumes at random, Maddy could see her grandmother had been a serious and committed diarist.

How extraordinary. And how wonderful.

And what a lot of reading lay ahead.

CHAPTER 25

IT'S DONE, FINISHED, IN THE PAST. I'VE BEEN HERE TWO WEEKS now and can put it all behind me.

What a strange way to begin a diary.

Maddy had embarked on her grandmother's journal collection, entranced but also faintly uneasy – reading another's private diary carries a feeling of transgression even when the author is no longer alive.

Only faintly though. The book felt comfortable on her lap, much more pleasant than the poor torn-out sheets that Lenka Midnight had been forced to use. The first entry was dated 24th July 1919 and it appeared to be a disappointing day weather-wise.

Today the sky is grey and the sun is hiding and there's little prospect of change until the end of the week, but I don't care. The weather can do whatever it likes, it won't affect me. I have never felt so free. After breakfast I walked right around the gardens, intending to take stock in my head of the condition everything is in, but really all I was thinking was that this place is all mine. It belongs to me. There is nobody to organise my life for me, nobody to give me orders, nobody of whom I need ask permission. I am my own mistress.

And I will soon be a mistress to other people also. I must hire staff. I have decided I will have two indoors and two out – a housemaid, a cook, a gardener and another, a boy perhaps, who can be under-gardener and can also take over the outdoor jobs. This house ran with four servants before and I am sure it can run very well again. I do not want maids under my feet, scurrying all over the place. I shall tell them: Only open the rooms I need, and we'll leave the others closed up.

It is noon now and I will go to the village this afternoon. I have to some time. I have thought about this and decided to do it quickly, so that people can see me. I hope that will stop them speculating. Well, it won't, but perhaps it won't get out of hand. I have prepared a speech. I will say, "It is the Swiss way" or "In Switzerland, it is done like this". I think that ought to do the job. It doesn't matter a bit that they think I'm peculiar. I will wear a Cloak of Peculiarity. Better than being invisible, in my opinion. Certainly easier.

Maddy snorted. She was very opinionated when she was young, her grandmother. Very opinionated when she was old, too, it would seem. Fancy hiding your diaries with a neighbour because you didn't trust your son! The atmosphere in Unthank must have been a joy.

She had started reading at the first entry of the first volume but now flipped forward a few pages.

Effie has ruined the sheets and must wash them again. She tripped over with them in her arms and fell right down on top of the lot. It is only dirt, and it would all brush off once dry, but I am quite sure that is not the Swiss way so I told her to put them back in the copper. I'm finding this isn't always easy. However, I also told her that I would overlook imperfections this once. But Mrs McLeod is wonderful, a marvel. Her bread is much lighter than I have ever

Maddy didn't turn the page. Perhaps her grandmother's diaries weren't going to be riveting after all, not if they were all about the servants getting things wrong and getting things right. She flipped a few sections. It looked as if the author had abandoned the daily entry system pretty quick. Some days were empty and others ran over the whole week. Maddy picked out another volume and saw that despite being leather bound it did not have the dates printed but was a simple notebook into which her grandmother had written the dates when she had something to say: a journal rather than a diary.

She skimmed pages here and there. She seemed to have lived very quietly, with next to no socialising and hardly any trips away from Unthank. The Roaring Twenties didn't seem to have reached Kirkwitton. Maddy found herself wondering why her grandmother had come to England and taken up residence in this out-of-the-way corner where she knew no-one and did nothing. Why hadn't she sold Unthank and taken the money back to Switzerland? That would have been the obvious thing to do.

On the other hand, why hadn't she, Maddy, sold Unthank and taken the money back to London, also the obvious thing to do?

But I am making friends here, Maddy told herself. Marilena didn't seem to make friends with anyone. Well, Simpson, the gardener, perhaps – they seemed to be surprisingly relaxed with each other. *Forgot the time in the greenhouse this afternoon, taking cuttings with Simpson. He wants roses but I want more ground for root crops. I told him I am open to negotiation on many aspects but not on this. This won't be the end of it, I know. But he has very good hands, I have noticed.*

Very good hands, eh? Was 'taking cuttings' a euphemism? But probably not. Marilena's dairies gave a strong impression of having been written *by* her grand-mother *for* her grandmother and it seemed unlikely she would shrink from saying plainly what she was doing with the gardener. The tone wasn't passionate or coy either, but cool and matter-of-fact. Maddy was sure it was the gardening her grandmother had been passionate about, not the gardener.

Odd words jumped off the pages. Maddy's attention was caught when *whistling* appeared three times together.

The whistling still comes and goes. The strangest part is that it seems only I can hear it. Mrs McLeod and Effie say they have never heard anybody whistling in the house and Doctor Burden could not either when he came to change the dressing. I hear it most in the upper rooms and loudest in the attic, which is a nightmare for me in any case. I have continued to avoid it of course, but as always in winter it is worse, and knowing it is up there, behind that door, makes me uneasy. So I have had a lock put on the door, and I will leave the light on too.

That was creepy. So that was why the door to the attic had a lock. And the light, too. Maddy knew she would think about that, probably in the stilly watches of the long, dark night. Hmm. In the meantime, she turned back a few pages to find out what had happened to warrant the doctor, who was, of course, Edna's father.

If I could wind back time, now would be the day. I keep picturing myself not stumbling on the broken slab and staying upright instead of overbalancing and putting my hand through the glass of the cold frame. Because that is what I did. Blood all over the lettuces. Walter in a panic. Simpson very good, though, steady and calm. He sent Walter off at a run and was going to use his shirt but I told him to cut off some petticoat. I have more petticoats than he has shirts.

But Doctor Burden, here. I can't wear a veil indoors. What can I do?

Why did she want to wear a veil?

The next paragraph read:

So! No veil necessary and I can truly breathe now! An hour he was here, first cleaning and then stitching and finally binding. And I had no thought for my appearance once that needle started, that is for certain. But he thought nothing of me, of that I am perfectly sure, even though he looked full at me when he entered and again before he left. So whether or not my hand is throbbing – which it is – and I shall be restricted in what I do for weeks to come – which I will – I am light and carefree tonight. Doctor Burden in this very room and not two feet from me! It is a load off my shoulders. I begin to think I should have put my hand through some glass a year ago.

That was even weirder. Was she disfigured in some way? Maddy didn't think so, and her mother would have mentioned it, surely?

Further on there was reference to a bible and Maddy paused again to read.

I have been thinking about the bible because I need more money. There, it is said. I thought selling the paintings would bring enough for me to live on for years but I had not reckoned on the storm damage, or repairing the outside woodwork, or having the chimneys swept. There is always something needing money spent on it. Capital is not enough; I need an income.

Tell me about it, Maddy thought.

But I could not bear to sell the bible – the Unthank Bible, it is known as. Now I don't know why I should not. What is it to me, this old book about things I am not sure I believe in? If it is such a treasure, why should I not sell it to people who value it more? And yet when I consider doing such a thing I feel almost sick. It is as if there were a small creature curled asleep in my innards that wakes and protests. The Unthank Bible belongs here, it tells me. It has always been here and it must always remain here. And who am I, really, to tamper with that?

So her grandmother had a hamster in her stomach too! Maddy smiled. She was beginning to like her, or at least like the young version of her. But oh heavens yes, the need for an income…

Maddy set the diaries aside and went in search of her notebook. It was in the snug, and she cast a quick glance towards the bureau drawer where she had locked away the bible – the Unthank Bible. It was mystifying that it should have been considered so valuable sixty years ago and now not, and it seemed sensible to take care of it.

She curled herself up in the wing chair and turned to a fresh page. She had tried this before, many times: writing *Business Ideas* in capitals across the top and then scrawling down everything she could think of, however insane or impractical. So far it hadn't helped, but now something had changed.

There had been a couple of holiday-makers in the shop yesterday buying picnic stuff, their bicycles propped outside, and when she went in Joan had said, 'Here's the lady. Maddy, this gentleman wants to know where to go to get the best photographs of the Wall.'

Maddy had told him, having investigated Hadrian's Wall since her conversation with lovely Doug, and there had been several follow-on questions too that she was happy to help with. But after they had left and her purchases were being rung up, Joan said, 'There's lots of tourists come through here in the summer. You should run courses.'

Now Maddy wrote *Photographic Retreat*, underlined it, and began a list. As the list grew, images formed in her head.

TOPICS:

Get to Know Your Camera: Instamatics, SLRs

Basics:

Light, shade, shutter speed, focal length

Environmental Aspects:

Outdoors: Weather, time of day, sky

Indoors: Studio, lighting, backdrop

Subject:

Stationary, moving, landscape, animals, people

Processing for Beginners:

Film, chemistry, commercial developing, prints or slides

Darkroom Techniques:

Domestic darkroom, equipment, chemicals, papers

Printing:

Test strip, test print, dodge and burn, sepia, selenium

Presentation:

Mounting, framing, negative storage and cataloguing

FACILITIES AND EQUIPMENT NEEDED:

Convert other pantries to darkrooms

Second enlarger (third?)

Studio lights

Backdrops

Convert drawing room? Or second floor bedrooms?

*Lights expensive

Tart up courtyards (eventually gardens) for outside shoots

Typewriter

Photocopier for info sheets etc

DOMESTIC ARRANGEMENTS:

Bedrooms

Bathrooms and en-suites!!!

Dining room (breakfast)

Sitting room

*Combine these??

Boots and coats (bad weather)

Gatehouse for premium price??

Breakfast: Me!!

Lunch: Me? Anthea?

Dinner: Anthea? The Swaledale?

TO DO:

Research legal requirements B&B and full board

Kitchen?

Take cookery course (ugh)?

Insurance – equipment and public liability

Advertising

Local deals:

National Trust entry, private gardens, shops?

. . .

MADDY PAUSED and read it over. It was frightening, it would probably not work, and it would take a huge amount of effort – and money – to get off the ground. But for the first time since arriving at Unthank on that dark and stormy night she felt she could, maybe, perhaps, see a way through.

CHAPTER 26

So many days without writing! And now I have so much to set down! And in truth it is not what I wish to do, but I will regret it in future years if I do not.

Oh crumbs, Maddy thought, what are the parsnips up to now? She had reached 1921 and had read enough of her grandmother's diaries to recognise a garden story when it loomed. Triumph or disaster, matters of roots and shoots and fruits had occupied her grandmother to a degree Maddy found extraordinary. She had been no dabbler, and certainly not one to observe from her lofty patrician's pedestal, but had got down to work with soil under her fingernails and rain in her hair. Her knowledge seemed extensive. Maddy wondered whether Simpson had found her involvement in his domain a blessing or a curse.

There had been a hiatus in the dates of close to a week, and Maddy wondered what could have occurred in the garden in February that was so exciting it had drawn her wordaholic grandmother from her diary. Maddy had arrived in Northumberland in February and remembered well that the only thing out then had been snowdrops. Even Marilena couldn't be getting worked up over snowdrops.

She had been reading the diaries again, this time without so much hopping. It wasn't as though she didn't have time, and Liz had impressed upon her the significance of such an uninterrupted run of social commentary. Liz, Maddy knew, was itching to ask her to post the lot to her.

Maddy turned the page, expecting turnips and kale – soft fruit and flowers hadn't rung her grandmother's bells the way that root crops and greens had – and read on.

It happened – he happened – he arrived on Tuesday, just a Tuesday, not a special day, it could have been any day. A bright day at first, frost overnight, crisp and sparkling, perfect powder-blue sky, barely a breeze. Effie ironing, of course; Mrs McLeod making a pie; Simpson and Willy on maintenance; and me with no inkling at all, no suspicion, no premonition of what lay ahead. Just an ordinary day like any other, I thought. But how wrong was I!

(Not turnips then.)

I was on my way to the parlour when the doorbell rang and since I was passing, I answered. That is the one thing I have never been able to do – ignore a doorbell when I am closest. "Not the Swiss way", how many times have I used that excuse? But they are all used to me now. So I opened the door and he was there, and I did not recognise him at all. Not at all. He was just a man, a stranger, on the door step, bareheaded and smiling, and I believe, I really do, that he would have smiled and bowed like that had it been Effie who answered to him. In fact, I know it.

And he said, 'Good morning! I am sorry to trouble you. My name is Theo Lawrence and I am afraid I need your help.'

Theo Lawrence! My grandfather, Maddy thought. Well, well!

His motorcycle had broken down. It was outside the gates, he had pulled into the drive to get off the road. We walked down together, and I didn't send for Simpson first. Why not? Because an inkling had arrived after all? Oh, I don't know. How strange that already I have forgotten how this happened. Only days ago, yet all I know now is that when I stepped out of the porch he was just a passer-by with a problem, and by the time we reached the gates he was Theo, and I did not want him to go.

And he didn't. Not for four days.

How the trivial happenings of life hold sway over our destinies! Alf Armstrong travelled to Newcastle last week for the funeral of his grand-mother, who married again after her husband died to the undertaker that buried him. This is the truth! And then the undertaker retired to live with his cousin in the city and Alf's mother naturally went too. I wonder what that funeral was like and how much it cost; special rates, I hope.

So Alf had two days away, and in the meantime the blacksmith in Shilston has burned his arm (careless) and much of his work has come to Kirkwitton. And all of this means that Alf has more work than he can deal with right now and Theo's motorcycle part had to take its place in the queue.

So, he stayed.

We pushed the motorcycle through the gates and all the way along the drive, and it was so good to really work at something. To throw my weight into the job and use my strength. Theo hardly protested at all – a word of warning first, instinctive I think, but then he accepted my help with no awkwardness at all. For certain he is a rare man! I've seen enough of them to know that.

And in the afternoon, after we had walked to the forge and seen Alf, he — Theo — showed me his motorcycle and explained the parts. It is a Brough Superior SS80. It is a side-valve machine and has a three-speed four-stud gearbox, and Theo loves the low riding position. I have sat on it too, yesterday, with my skirt hitched up, and would you believe that a powerful desire to ride on it sprang up in me straight away? Well, it did. It must be wonderful.

Perhaps one day.

It has a name, like a horse: The Super. Theo says, "When The Super's ready". And I thought, when The Super's ready it will take him away from me. And it did.

But I think he will come back.

Well, he did, obviously. Maddy paused. The circumstances of the lovely guy with transport trouble were weirdly similar, except that Marilena had longer with hers. No breakdown service then, just the village blacksmith embracing a new, mechanised world.

Lucky Marilena.

Marilena was how she thought of the writer now, not *Grandmother*. The voice was too young, the time she was describing too distant. It was another world, another country as HE Bates put it; the diaries were like a story, not history, and it was a tussle to remember that these events happened here, in Unthank, where Maddy was now living. How odd that both Lenka Midnight and Marilena Bircher had felt driven to record their lives in words.

She returned to the page.

Theo Lawrence was absent for a month and then, late in August 1921, his motorcycle roared up the drive one happy Saturday evening and after dinner, no doubt hastily put together by a startled Mrs MacLeod, he proposed to Marilena and was accepted.

Five days' acquaintance and five weeks of consideration: what a plunge into the unknown! But as the weeks and months rolled on, it became clear that it had been the right decision. Marilena's voice quickly abandoned the excited, lovelorn tenor of that first Theo entry and reverted to the more acerbic narrator Maddy had come to know, but her passion for her new husband glowed. She never described him, as probably one wouldn't in a private journal, and Maddy found herself wondering what he had been like. Blond, apparently – Marilena talked about the sun on his hair – and tall because she mentioned looking up to him.

Tall and blond. Maddy thought of film actors with sparkling blue eyes and heaps of charm: Robert Redford and Anthony Andrews for a start. Then it occurred to her that Theo had probably passed on at least some aspects of his appearance to her own father, and perhaps to herself. She stood in front of the vast mirror in the bedroom she had been assuming was her grandmother's and took a critical look: longish nose, straight eyebrows she had to remember to lift for photographs, a chin kind people called 'strong'. She wasn't a beauty.

Of course, any of this could have been inherited from Marilena, not Theo. Maddy wished she had a photograph of her grandmother but so far none had shown up. It struck her as unusual for there to be no family photographs at all; cameras had become common items by the 1960s. Had Claude chucked everything out? Had Marilena destroyed them? And if so, why?

Theo had clearly been everything to Marilena; a whirl-wind romance it might have been but they built foundations swiftly. Theo had been in the Royal Flying Corps in the war, at first flying reconnaissance trips taking photographs on glass plates (interesting) and then in combat, finally flying a Sopwith Camel, like Biggles. After the Armistice he was desperate to continue flying but the odds were stacked against him, with thousands of pilots competing for only a handful of civil flying jobs. Nevertheless, he managed to keep his hand in, obtaining from somewhere a converted Vicker Vimy and odd-jobbing in the skies' transporting time-sensitive cargo like news reels, freshly killed grouse for Paris restaurants, and, occasionally, a wealthy passenger. Then in 1923, six months after they were married, he found a job delivering new private planes to the super-rich. It was inter-mittent work but reliable enough, and he appeared to be very willing to fill in with courier jobs on his motorcycle.

Not massively onerous work, Maddy thought. Theo clearly liked to have fun. He liked speed too, by the sound of things, and reading between the lines she suspected Marilena had put the brakes on his itch to race. Still, he fell in with her wishes and in due course became a lovely dad, enthusiastic about baby Claude when he arrived and far more hands-on than fathers in the nineteen-twenties were expected to be.

It wasn't all ribbons and champagne. Marilena's first pregnancy had resulted in a miscarriage mid-term, the still-born baby a girl. Theo's family were noticeably absent from the diaries too, never explained by Marilena. Then when Claude was born things perked up. There were picnics and day trips to the sea, and the little boy was introduced to sheep and traction engines at the agricultural shows, and sat in front of his father on The Super while they wobbled at walking speed around the courtyard. Marilena became pregnant for the third time, confiding in her diary that she hoped for a girl, and in the July of 1925 the small family spent a whole week in Eyemouth, travelling by rail and renting a cottage right on the harbour. They returned sun-tanned, relaxed and blissfully happy.

A fortnight and a day after their return to Unthank, a telegram arrived with a job for Theo. For the Lawrences, telegrams were not the dread harbinger of tragedy they had become for so many during the Great War, but they were not common either. The post service was swift and dependable then, and Maddy had gleaned from reading Marilena's journal that one could write a letter in full confidence that it would be delivered the following day. Most of Theo's assignments arrived by letter, but once in a while the firm wanted him at short notice and sent a telegram that would reach him within an hour.

Theo apparently was happy. *A de Havilland Moth,* Marilena had written, *new this year, he can't wait.* He had to set off immediately, and Marilena wrote that he had managed to leave his razor behind and would be stubbly when he returned the next evening *but I doubt the man buying the kite will notice, or care. Now I'm going to talk to Simpson about these apples.*

The rest of the page was left blank. Maddy turned over. The date at the top of the new page was 14th October. The style of writing had changed, the script more upright, less flowing. The words jolted her.

Theo is dead.

He was dead. Maddy had known it would happen soon but she had become lost in the journal and forgotten the dates.

Theo had delivered the plane as arranged to some viscount in the midlands, a very young man who had escaped the war. He planned to take the train home as usual, and the viscount offered to drive him to the station. Theo accepted. They crashed and both were killed.

Marilena set down those bald facts, her anger and grief knifing across the decades in that spiky, vertical script, and then abandoned the diary for months until at the end of February the following year there was something that had to be recorded.

Sunday, 22nd of February 1925. Ivan Joseph born.

Maddy's father.

CHAPTER 27

Summer had seemed to come late to Northumberland, but apparently so did autumn. At the end of September, the evenings were no longer the everlasting, drawn-out affairs of mid-summer, when daylight was still filtering through the curtains when Maddy went to bed at eleven and would wake her again at four. But they remained golden and mild, a gentle wrapping up of the day, and this was often the time that Maddy would walk round the gardens to see what progress had been made and to take stock.

The unofficial Unthank Gardening Club had worked wonders. The focus this first year had been to repair and prepare. Simply clearing away the rubbish had made a vast difference, spiritually as well as practically, although with the weeds and dead stuff gone the area seemed to Maddy even greater and more impossible to manage. However, she had stumped up for a couple of extra wheelbarrows – other tools were brought on site by the volunteers – and for replacement glass in the greenhouses, and someone's student son had given a week of his vacation to repair the roofing felt on the potting sheds and straighten up the raised beds.

The established plants like the fruit trees and gooseberry bushes had been pruned, and the rhubarb fed and mulched; the half-made compost had been turned and a new, fresh heap started; and the compost that had quietly been making itself for the past two or three years was spread around the cleared beds in one defined and manageable area that had been designated for immediate cultivation. Chris Beattie, Experienced Gardener, wanted vegetable growing to start as soon as possible because that would, he said, keep everyone's enthusiasm going, and Maddy felt sure he was right. There did seem something magical, even spooky, about tiny seedlings appearing where there had been bare earth and then swelling relentlessly into proper, sturdy little plants. To Maddy the soil with its lumps of matter and scattered stones looked dismally inhospitable, but not so to the lettuce and broad beans and chard, which spread their baby leaves to the sun and got on with the business of growing.

Three proper gardening clubs in neighbouring districts had requested visits, one of which arrived in a coach. Then Maddy had a letter from the headmistress of the Kirkwitton school asking if the children – all thirty-two of them – might be brought to see the project, and word clearly spread because before the end of the summer term two more village schools had come along. In early August Maddy spoke with someone from a special needs school and found herself talking to Chris and Evelyn about making paths wide enough not just for wheelbarrows but for wheelchairs too, and building some extra-high raised beds. It wasn't quite the authentic Edwardian restoration they had planned, but wider paths here and there were easy to manage and they agreed to make one of the walled gardens into a more contemporary, visitor-friendly version and put the new high-level beds there.

Then later in the month a stringer from the local newspaper turned up with a photographer to interview Maddy and Evelyn for a feature. His rejection of Maddy's bid to do the photography herself was galling, especially as the pictures published weren't up to much in her view, but she grudgingly supposed it was understandable; anyone might claim to be a competent photographer and he was hardly going to look through her portfolio first.

The feature came out the following week and Joan propped the page up on the counter. As a result, several new volunteers arrived including a retired history professor particularly interested in Victorian country house society, and an artist who wanted to capture the gardens in water-colours for greetings cards.

Restoring the Unthank kitchen gardens had developed a life of its own.

Also developing a life of its own was Maddy's idea of a photographic retreat.

Her original brainstorming had been followed by more considered plans. She had drawn up possible schedules for courses, a two-day weekend one and a five-day, taking care to cater for complete beginners ('This is called a shutter'), those with a little knowledge ('Now we'll use a light meter') and serious amateurs ('Who's heard of Ansel Adams' zone system?'). Darkroom techniques would feature heavily, and she was certain she would have to kit out at least two pantries, possibly three.

She could offer non-instructional camera holidays too, providing facilities like the dark rooms and studios but allowing guests to do their own photographic thing. She would loan out tripods, equip them with a printed guide to scenic hot spots and insider tips on the best places to set up, and provide an overnight contact print service so they knew what they'd got and whether they needed to retake, as well as being on hand to give advice and guidance on request.

Maddy had always enjoyed teaching photography; a venture like this could be perfect.

Not quite so perfect was what would have to accompany the tuition. She had shrunk from the notion of Unthank as a hotel and yet here she was, making plans to take residential guests. But it was different. A hotel is a hotel, open all the time, at the mercy of anyone's whim to come and stay. But by running courses and retreats, Maddy would be in control. She would have scheduled periods when she'd know guests would be here and other times when they definitely wouldn't.

The domestic side was daunting but she had an ace in her hand: Anthea.

In the months since she had known her, Maddy had come to realise Anthea was a lovely, reliable, ever-cheerful and loyal friend, but she was more even than that, because Anthea's best friend at school had had parents who ran a small guest house, and she was bubbling with hard, useful information. She was bubbling with enthusiasm too. And she was a cook.

'But I won't be able to do the breakfasts,' she said.

'I know,' Maddy said quickly. Anthea could hardly be expected to drive over at six o'clock every morning.

'But I'll teach you so that you can. And I'll do lunches, and packed lunches too. And afternoon tea.'

Tea and coffee with a kettle in their rooms and Anthea's homemade biscuits. Mid-morning cake. Constantly replenished fruit bowls. They'd hardly need dinner at all, and when they did, Maddy would send them to The Swaledale; Mike there was already getting excited.

There would, needless to say, be a frighteningly large price tag on getting the house ready to take guests. One cranky old bathroom was not going to do it. The good thing was that the bedrooms were huge and could easily give a few square metres to en-suite shower rooms. The bad thing was that installing en-suite shower rooms would be expensive, and the outlay wouldn't stop there. Maddy needed to buy new mattresses and bed linen, a fridge and freezer – giant ones – and more furniture of all kinds if Unthank was to be welcoming; rugs and cushions too, and some cosy, stylish accessories – vases and jugs and the like. People might think they were booking for the photography but she was sure Anthea was right when she said they'd only come back if they liked the setting too.

Anthea, wonderful Anthea, was going to invite her old school friend to stay and be interrogated in depth.

That was settled for next month. Today they were pushing furniture around in the bedrooms, experimenting with en-suite layouts. They told themselves it was necessary but they were playing really. In the room at the end, the one

Maddy had assumed had been her grandmother's because of the double bed and huge free-standing mirror, the main problem was that very mirror. It was easily six feet high, set into an oval frame of the heaviest wood going, and the castors had jammed solid. The floorboards were uneven underneath, and they were utterly unable to drag it.

Anthea said, 'Do you suppose these boards are uneven because there's a secret place underneath?'

She was intrigued by Claude's trail; Maddy was jaded.

'Who knows? Half the rooms in the house have wonky floors. I can't prise up all the boards.' Then she said, 'Look, if it won't come this way how about pushing it closer to the wall and then pulling it sideways?'

They did that, and with a groan the mirror shifted, the stuck castors screeching against the worn polish. Anthea let out her held breath with a pant. 'There!' she said with satisfaction, and then, 'Oh! Look!'

Maddy looked. On the wall behind the mirror, or rather on the wall behind where the mirror had recently been, the wallpaper was marked with a rectangular cut, about waist height, making a panel perhaps twelve inches tall and ten wide. The wall paper had curled away a little at the corners and the plaster was visible behind, a dirty pinkish brown.

Maddy stared. Why would you cut a rectangle in the wallpaper? *Just* the wallpaper?

She lifted a corner and pinched it back. There was an incision in the plaster too.

All right, why would you cut a rectangle in the plaster? Maddy thought she knew. She prised at the edge with her nails.

The plaster moved and became a door.

Anthea said, 'Oh,' a second time, and Maddy thought, *Here we go again.*

THE CUPBOARD in the wall was shallow and the small modern cashbox was upended to fit. Maddy shook the box and heard the key rattle. She sighed and noticed that Anthea was gazing at her with huge eyes and a face full of wonder.

I was like that once, Maddy thought.

'Come on then,' she said. 'The keys are downstairs.'

Key number seven fitted. Thank goodness for that. It had been bad enough at the start to be played along like this, but even worse since the boxes and keys got out of sync. Inside the cashbox was the new key, the eighth of the line, with the usual folded papers, and a small photograph of a woman with the soft, jaw-length haircut of the nineteen-twenties.

'Who is she?' Anthea breathed.

'No idea. Look at it later. First...'

Maddy crossed the snug to the corner under the window where she had set down the metal box from the priest hole. She hunkered down before it, tried the new key in the padlock and crowed with relief as it slipped in.

'Hallelujah!'

A new haul: the papers as expected, and a key of course, but a key with a difference. Maddy held it up in astonishment.

'Gosh,' Anthea said.

CHAPTER 28

I DO NOT LIKE THE NAME OF THIS HOUSE. SO UGLY. AND WHAT does it mean? It is not <u>grammatical</u>. English is not a pretty language.

'Hang on,' Maddy said. 'This isn't Lenka.'

They had put the key aside for the time being in order to read the latest instalment of the journal, Maddy cross-legged on the rug, Anthea looking over her shoulder. But it wasn't the latest instalment. The handwriting looked similar, but the language was quite different.

I would like to name it different. I would like to call it Bircher Hall from my family name but they would have to change the maps and the English authorities will not let me. In any case, people in the village do not use the name very much; they call it 'The German House', which shows how ignorant they are.

It's my grandmother! Just after she arrived here!'

'Shh, go on.'

'Hall' is what the English call a house when it is very large. This house is not very large, not as large as Alderhof. Not so many rooms, and all the rooms smaller. But it is certain the largest house at this village

and I expect my uncle's mother thought she was very special, very grand to be living here, even with only three servants. Three servants! To manage a house even this size! And one of them for the gardens only! It is truly not surprising that half the rooms were closed and the growing-houses so poor. I have had to order much glass to repair the broken ones.

I must find servants also. There were only two here at the end and both of them left when my grandmother died. I think they should have waited for me, but they did not and nobody in the village knows to where they went. Or nobody tells me; I think they know but do not want me to know. I think they do not like me.

But I am here now and I will stay. Why? If this house has a bad name and is not large as home and I must spend much money to make it good, why do I not sell it and go back to Switzerland?

Because it is mine, this house. I do not have to share with Jurgen and Katrin. I do not have to be quiet and nice and do whatever they want to do, just because Jurgen was born a boy and I was born a stupid girl. I do not have to go to parties and see Stefan with his stupid fiancée, looking and holding hands and sighing. And I do not have to embroider handkerchiefs and stick stupid scrapbooks because there is no proper work for me to do. Here there is many work, repairing the house and making the gardens good and learning English and learning about the English. That is why I have written all this in English, and it has hurt my brain. Enough! I will now finish for today.

Ich liebe nicht diese Füllfeder.

They looked at each other. Anthea said, 'She sounds angry.'

'Doesn't she just? I bet the village loved her. What's this at the end, that she doesn't like? Do you know any German? What's a Füllfeder?'

Anthea didn't, but Maddy said, 'Hang on, I've got a German dictionary.'

The battered book lay on the shelf, a primer rather than a dictionary, but it included a glossary at the back. Maddy flicked the pages. 'It's a pen. A fountain pen.'

'Not the butler then!'

'It doesn't sound like she's got a butler yet.'

Maddy picked up the second set of pages. Same hand-writing, same pen too going by the blots. Naughty Füllfeder!

Also, ich bin richt No! English!

So, I am right, they do not like me in the village. I asked at the grocer shop for help in obtaining servants, what is the way the English find servants, and I was told I must use an agency that is in Hexham and hire servants from a long way distance who will not run away home. Stupid! And then a girl came into the shop and she was the right age I think and I asked her if she had work, and she said no, and I said she could work for me and she said no again because her father is a doctor! She is too grand! But how could I know she was the daughter of a doctor?

So now I must go again to Hexham, many miles, and go to the agency. But today a woman from the village, Mrs Bell, will come here and make some meals for me, until I have a cook. She will be surprised I think to see the fire but it is the Swiss way to know how to make fire. All Swiss know how. I will tell her. It is good because it is cold today.

There is a horse here. It is in the field. It is the Swiss way to know how to put on harness. I will tell them.

Close to the bottom of the page there was a gap of an inch and a fresh feel to the handwriting as if written on a different day.

I have servants! Mrs McLeod is the cook. Effie Marley is the maid.

Simpson is the gardener. Walter Black is the outside boy. I have told them that I am Swiss and I do the Swiss way. Now all is better and I do not make fire or go in the kitchen. Tomorrow I will

And that was it. There was no second page and nothing on the back.

'Oh no!' Anthea protested. 'I want to know more!'

'Yes. Well. I've grown used to cliffhangers. Lenka Midnight was a master.'

Maddy tidied the sheets and lay them on the table. Later she would stick them in with her grandmother's diaries. In the meantime there was that mirror to move.

ANTHEA'S SCHOOL friend was called Sally. She was short, fierce, and worked in a laboratory somewhere looking at seeds through a microscope. She was *very* grown-up and Maddy found her slightly scary. She was glad Anthea was there to deflect.

'What a fabulous place!' Sally said first, which was grati-fying, but then she got down to business.

'I have to say this, so forgive me, but you do realise you'll absolutely have to buy carpets and curtains and furniture and so on? This is…quaint…but people won't want to come here if it's all metal bedsteads and threadbare brocade.'

They were sitting round the kitchen table, ready to be serious, a pot of coffee to hand. Maddy had her note pad out and pencil poised.

'I know,' Maddy said. She did. 'I've got the money from the sale of my flat. I've done the sums. It will – just about – cover replacing all that stuff as well as putting bathrooms in.'

It would, just about. But 'just about' would be good enough, provided an income started up quickly.

'Will you be offering meals?'

'Breakfast of course, and a packed lunch. For the evening meal I'll be sending them to the village. We've got a really nice pub that does lovely food.'

'Good. In that case you won't need a commercial kitchen. How many guests at a time?'

'I haven't decided yet,' Maddy said. 'It depends really on how many I can cater for with the dark rooms…'

'No, it doesn't. It depends on how many rooms you can get around in a morning. You are going to be teaching some of the day, yes? But you also have to hoover, make the beds and clean the bathrooms and loos. You'll have to hoover the public rooms too. And clear up after breakfast and make the lunches.'

'Lunches is me,' Anthea said. She added nobly, 'And I can hoover the dining room.'

'Okay, but still. Are you up for that?' Sally looked at Maddy. She had an unsettlingly clear gaze.

'Yes,' Maddy said, hearing the waver in her voice. 'Or I might get someone in for the rooms.'

'A chambermaid. Good. So you'll need to factor in her wages.'

Maddy made a note: *Pay for chambermaid.*

Sally went on. 'The regulations for bed-and-breakfast aren't anything like as strict as for a hotel, but there are some and you'll need to contact your local council to find out what's current. You probably won't need to apply for change of use, but you might. You'll need to check the fire regulations as well.'

Maddy wrote *Change of use. Fire regulations.*

'Now, bathrooms.'

And so it went on. Maddy listened, protested once in a while, in a half-hearted way, and took pages of notes. Much of what Sally had to tell her she already knew, but she had buried it, turned a blind eye, and it was depressing to be made to face facts. Unthank was easily large enough and had masses of potential but it was also shabby, ill-equipped and cold.

The problem was that she needed to get the place rewired by an electrician, but obviously that would be best scheduled for after the plumber had put in central heating, a proper boiler and some radiators. But the plumbing would have to include the new bathrooms (or possibly shower rooms, Maddy hadn't made her mind up yet), so first she needed a builder. And the builder would naturally need to work around the wiring, which dropped her back at the electrician again. She didn't know what order to do everything in, and in the meantime she was still camping, using two or three rooms and ignoring the rest, managing mostly by refusing to look at all the things that needed attention and getting by because it was summer and warm enough not to need heating. She was the grasshopper, singing away instead of working; suddenly she regretted not having been an ant.

It's a big job,' Sally said, no-nonsense. 'You need a project manager.'

'I think I ought to be the project manager,' Maddy said.

'I've got the time; it isn't like I'm doing anything else, and it would be much cheaper.'

'Have you got the knowledge though?'

Maddy said, 'No.'

Sally sort of shrugged with her eyebrows: *my point exactly*. 'You've got a lot going for you though,' she added, more cheerily. 'Lots of parking space!'

Maddy snorted.

Sally leaned back in her chair. 'I know. But seriously, if you get the basics covered, you could make yourself really special for guests so that they'll leave with a terrific impression and come back, and spread the word as well.'

'Like what?' *Aren't crenellations enough?* Maddy thought.

'Well, my parents took on an old coaching inn and they had to really squeeze en-suites in. The rooms were then too small to get the top star rating. Nothing they could do about that. But they put bathrobes as well as towels in all the rooms and had cut glass tumblers for tooth mugs, and proper fresh flowers all over the place.'

'I've got flowers!' Maddy said. 'Or will have by then. And I'll have home-grown salads!'

'There you go. Get proper art for the walls – local art clubs will usually clamour to have their members' watercolours and abstracts in a public place and they'll be way better than boring traditional prints. Books in the bedrooms – guests like second-hand books, they feel authentic, so buy them from the Oxfam shop, and get hardbacks, not paperbacks. Filter coffee. Starched napkins. Anthea will help you.'

Maddy might have been offended at that but she was too

sensible. Anthea would indeed be of enormous help. Thank goodness for Anthea!

It had been drizzling for much of the morning but now the sky had cleared and they went for a stroll around the grounds, Maddy pleased to be able to show off the size of her estate. Sally admired the gardens and asked a couple of rookie questions that even Maddy (these days) could answer, which also went some way to restoring Maddy's self-confidence. She had learned about gardening; she could learn about the bed-and-breakfast business too!

'There is one other thing,' Sally said as they headed for the door. 'You have had a survey done on this place?'

'No,' Maddy said. 'Not yet.' She remembered Mr Pattison's advice but had put it off along with all the other jobs.

'Mm. I'd get one if I were you. Old houses can look fine and still have nasty surprises in store.'

'Yes,' Maddy said firmly. 'Yes, it is on the list.'

Had been for months. She would shunt it up to the top.

CHAPTER 29

MADDY CONTINUED WORKING HER WAY THROUGH HER grandmother's diaries. It was remarkable how little of current affairs made its way into the entries. There was no mention of the General Strike, nor the Jarrow March ten years later; George V died, Edward VIII succeeded him, gave rise to a mighty scandal and abdicated, and George VI came to the throne, all without the smallest reference appearing in Marilena's diary. Instead, she recorded the departure of Walter, the Outside Boy, when he turned eighteen and went to work as a gardener on an estate near the coast, and talked at length about the training up of his replacement, called Percy. That was the same name as the one at Unthank when mad gipsy housekeeper Lenka Midnight arrived, Maddy thought, although apparently this one was kinder to animals.

Her grandmother did not talk much about her family either, although scraps of information dripped in and

Maddy realised all was not well. Claude began having health problems soon after his second birthday, when baby Ivan was in swaddling clothes and Marilena still grieving the loss of her beloved Theo. The toddler was slow to walk, slow to move generally, having never really cracked crawling with his bottom up, and in the spring of 1926 he began to suffer bouts when breathing became difficult. Doctor Burden toyed with croup and bronchitis but eventually plumped for asthma, which he pronounced to be psychosomatic and brought about by over-dependence on his mother. *He advised us all to be very firm with him,* Marilena wrote.

Poor little Claude – especially since even without Doctor Burden's advice, his mother seemed to have little patience for nursing him. There was something about that sentence, often repeated – *Claude is wheezy <u>again</u>* – that sounded exasperated rather than sympathetic. The woman Maddy remembered from childhood was gradually appearing in the lines of text, an impression slowly becoming solid. It was hard to pinpoint anything specific, yet Maddy sensed a discontented woman, and not just (just!) because she had been widowed so dreadfully young. The version of her grandmother that rose out of the diary entries seemed sometimes fearful, sometimes angry, even guilty at times, and there was a perpetual undercurrent of unease. Claude exasperated her; Ivan, Maddy's father, irritated her, often, as the years rolled on, deliberately. There were times when Maddy was sure he had gone out of his way to do the opposite of what his mother advised and wanted. In 1943, as soon as he was old enough, Ivan joined the RAF, hardly likely to appease his mother, and after the war his choice of career – importing sports cars and inevitably driving them too – also seemed designed to annoy her, although it seemed to Maddy that in this case Marilena's annoyance could be put down to fear. It must have been frightening to watch the son dabbling in what had caused his father's untimely death.

In the end, of course, it hadn't been fast cars that did for Ivan but undiagnosed meningitis. So sad.

Little mention was made in the diaries of the Second World War. Lots of bombs fell in the North of England but over the industrial areas and ports, not deep in the rural heartland. Similarly, the street parties that followed VE Day took place in the cities and suburbs but not so much in the villages, and if Kirkwitton celebrated it would have been without the stand-offish foreign woman in her castle.

Maddy wondered if there had been a repeat of the anti-German sentiment that had been aimed at Unthank during the first war. Her grandmother did not say so. Perhaps by the 1940s people were more sophisticated and understood that German-speaking Swiss were not actual Germans. Presumably by then Unthank had lost its local appellation of The German House. Certainly Marilena's written English had become fluent very quickly; how her accent had fared was another matter; Maddy had not noticed it as a child.

Claude never served in the war, excused on account of his asthma. By the time Ivan was released from the RAF in 1947, Claude had begun to tread his solitary path towards reclusion. Ivan never lived at Unthank again, abandoning his brother along with his mother. Maddy had no real memories of her father, but it struck her now that he had been not an entirely admirable person. If he had stayed in touch with his family, visited from time to time, would Claude have grown into the odd, secretive, desperately shy man he had been? Reading between the lines of the diaries, Maddy formed a strong impression that her grandmother and her uncle had lived quite separate lives under the same, admittedly large, roof, Claude with his codes and puzzles, Marilena with her gardening and her regrets.

In December 1952, instead of talking about Christmas preparations (had they even given one another presents?) her grandmother had written:

I am still working the magic. Not all that hocus-pocus about warts and harvests and lovemaking but <u>real</u> magic, serious magic, magic that actually works. Long-term magic that comes slowly. Because I never did for myself, I never thought to. I thought there would be time; I thought we could always try again.

Well. Wiser now. And it has been a year. I began as soon as they got married − I'd have started sooner if I'd known anything about the girl, but of course he told me nothing. Still, I've met her and my guess is she kept herself until after the wedding, so it's all to play for.

How mysterious...or was it? 'The girl', Maddy realised, must be her mother, Norma, and it seemed fairly obvious what 'kept herself until after the wedding' referred to. Marilena must have been thinking about Ivan's child.

Me.

Not mysterious then, but distinctly creepy. Not quite able to restrain herself, Maddy flipped forward to February. There was nothing relevant on the 15th, but on the 6th of March she found what she was looking for.

I have a girl! A little girl. Norma wrote − Ivan didn't. Healthy, seven and a half pounds. I've replied with a cheque. I told Norma I want her to be called Madeleine – first or second name, it doesn't matter – and that it would be better if Ivan doesn't know I've asked.

So, I can still do it!

Still do what? Work magic? Maddy shook her head in disbelief.

Mind you, she'd had her way, her grandmother, and Norma had given her baby the right name. Well, well.

THE SURVEYOR CAME ON FRIDAY.

Since Sally's visit Maddy had knuckled down and become an ant. There was a ton of work to be done before she could invite paying guests to Unthank and she had squandered the summer, drifting about luxuriating in proprietorship, basking in the extraordinary experience of having so much acreage, indoors and out, at her private command. But now the evenings were chilly and dusk came early; the clocks would go back soon and then the Northumbrian days would quickly grow short and the nights long, dark and cold.

She asked Joan in the shop if anyone local could recommend a builder, and got the number of a Bob Macdonald in Morpeth who had put an extension onto a house in the village and converted a stone barn into a pair of holiday cottages for a farmer down the road. He arrived promptly when arranged, which Maddy thought a good sign, and took his boots off at the door unasked. When he stepped over the threshold and stood at the same level as Maddy she realised he was barely taller than she was, but really broad. He was in his forties at a guess, with dense iron-grey hair cropped short, and the hand she shook was huge, the fingers blunt, the skin rough as if from handling bricks and stone. Whether he actually handled bricks and stone himself or shuffled paper and supervised other people handling bricks and stone Maddy did not know, but it was reassuring.

She gave him the tour, inside and out, explaining as they went what she had in mind, and in return learned to her chagrin that her Hamlet-like dithering over the past three months had been entirely unnecessary. He, Bob Macdonald, would put in all the wiring and sockets and radiators and pipes required for the bathrooms, or his electrician and plumber associates would, and if Maddy liked he would quote for bringing the rest of the house up to scratch too.

Maddy drew in a stiffening breath and said, 'About managing the project–'

'Oh, I do all that.'

She exhaled. 'Oh. Right. Good!'

'I'll get the estimates done next week and drop them round.' They reached his van. Bob Macdonald opened the door and then said almost conversationally, 'Have you had a survey done?'

'Not yet,' Maddy said, 'but I'm going to.'

The builder nodded. 'I would. Just one or two things, you know. Don't want any nasty surprises.'

Everyone talked about nasty surprises. And what one or two things? But he had slammed the door and started the engine.

Maddy watched the van disappear into the tunnel of cedars and then went to the snug and pulled out her shiny new Yellow Pages. It was barely a quarter of the thickness of the London version. She turned to Structural Surveyors, rang for a handful of quotes, and picked the one she liked the sound of best.

HIS NAME WAS Michael Smeaton and he looked like someone's geography teacher, with a tweed jacket and polished brogues. He was slightly built, had a receding hairline and his lower lip protruded ever so slightly, but his handshake was warm and dry and bony, and Maddy took to him. He had an air of quiet professionalism touched with academia, and somehow implied that they were equally well educated, which Maddy appreciated.

It was just as well she liked him because what he had to say was far from welcome.

After showing him round, just like Bob, indoors and out, Maddy left him to do what he had to do and tried to be busy. He took ages. Maddy made coffee and tracked him down in the servants' bedrooms, and he asked questions about the history of the house and its fabric to which she could only reply 'I don't know'. After a while she amended this to 'Sorry'. He seemed to get the picture.

Eventually he finished, packed his moisture meters and probes and notebook and rulers away and told her the report would be posted to her in due course. His voice was very even and he did not smile.

Unnerved, Maddy said brightly, 'It isn't going to fall round my ears tonight, then?'

'No, no. You're quite safe for now. The report will

explain what you need to know and if you have any questions then, just call me and I'll go through it with you.'

Once again Maddy watched a car swallowed up by her giant cedar trees with a sense of disquiet in her stomach.

She didn't at all like that *for now*.

CHAPTER 30

THE ENVELOPE WAS IN THE POST BOX AT THE GATE WHEN Maddy drove in. She had been in Durham all day with Anthea, a rare trip south to see an exhibition of art embroideries in the Cathedral. Anthea had heard about it and they had made it a mini-holiday, with a picnic on a rug and coffee and cake in a café. Baby Ben, a seasoned crawler by now, had been his usual smiley self, effortlessly charming passersby, and they had left the city early enough to avoid home-time traffic. A good day.

Now Maddy felt the weight of the manila envelope with misgiving, but told herself she was being needlessly pessimistic. The man had investigated everything thoroughly and had written it up, and with a property this size the result was bound to be a lot of words.

At the house Maddy made herself a mug of tea and sat at the kitchen table to open the envelope. The report was typed on thick paper and bound with a plastic spiral. Maddy read it from cover to cover while her abandoned tea stopped steaming and grew cold.

When she reached the end, after the conclusion summarising the issues and the photocopied pages with diagrams that Michael Smeaton had helpfully included, she got up and went out through the courtyard and walked to the field. She climbed the gate and sat on the top rail facing towards the grass, no longer the bright green it had been after the hay was cut but already tussocky again and fading in colour. The house was behind her; she didn't want accidentally to look at it.

It was October but could easily have been September still, the sunlight golden beyond the long shadows and the air warm. A bee was droning its way along the hedge and far away a crow was cawing, harsh across the fields.

She had been a fool. Obviously there had to be a catch. Had she really thought she could live in a castle for the rest of her life? Was she a character in some teenage novel, or a television drama? It had felt like Fairyland and it *was* Fairyland; now Michael Smeaton had burst the bubble and dropped her back to earth.

There was so much wrong with the house, her lovely house, that Maddy was surprised it was still standing. *You're quite safe for now*, he had said, but the report made it transparently clear that 'for now' didn't extend very far into the future, not very far at all.

Phrases so awful that they made her shiver now circled in her thoughts like a grim carousel...*external walls are built of a local stone that shows a tendency to porosity...it is self-evident that significant*

*areas – probably 80/90% - are in need of raking out and repointing...
rainwater goods are in iron and are in poor condition and need to be
replaced...gutters have been blocked by debris and have led to water penetra-
tion around window heads...no evidence of any remedial damp proofing
having been carried out...tests taken with a moisture meter went off the scale
in the majority of instances showing a water content in excess of 25%...roof
shows evidence of nail sickness and requires stripping and replacing...*

Unthank was a hulk of neglect. Why? Why had Uncle
Claude not tackled this years ago? Maddy understood that
he was a recluse, shy and reluctant to interact with people in
the outside world, but surely he would have realised that you
can't just stick your head in the sand and ignore everything
unpleasant?

Maddy could feel something trembling inside her midriff.
The hamster, shaking with anger?

What kind of person bequeaths a castle that is about to
fall down?

Michael Smeaton, helpful to the last, had included a line
about insurance. *Unfortunately most policies covering buildings carry
exclusions for damage from ageing, from general wear and tear, and from
willful neglect of the property, which I regret accounts for almost all of
the issues in this report.*

So it had to be cash. And she didn't have it, not enough
for this, nothing like.

Since February she had dreamed of keeping Unthank
and making it her home. Since that first snowfall had thawed
and yet she hadn't driven straight back to Twickenham, she
had been thinking and planning and hoping that she could
live in a castle, imagining solutions to the problem of
income, playing with ideas and schemes, and then finding a

way with the photographic retreats that looked possible, really did look possible. It would take work, she had known that, but it wouldn't be beyond her and in return, oh in return she would have her dream of Unthank come true.

But now the dream was over.

MADDY WASN'T a recluse but neither did she want to rush to share her pain. Tomorrow – tomorrow she would talk to someone, Anthea or Liz, or her mother. But she needed the initial shock to have eased, the dreadful rawness to have skinned over at least a little. At the moment she felt as if she were held in a kind of cold syrup that pressed upon her, weighting her limbs down and constricting her ribs. She moved slowly, walking or mounting steps or turning her head, as if taking immense care in everything she did would help matters.

Which was rubbish, of course. Nothing could help.

She read the report again, and then the tiny print of her buildings insurance policy, which confirmed Michael Smeaton's warning. She stood outside by the front porch and in the courtyard and on the terrace, staring at the stone with its sorry mortar, and indoors, in the front hall and the gallery and many of the rooms, she placed her palms against the panelling and plaster and knew, as she should have known months ago, that they were damp. She had no doubt that the condition of the roof was as the surveyor had said too, and the gutters and drainpipes, and the windows. The whole thing was a mess.

Still in shock, Maddy found she had returned to the

snug, growing dim now as the autumn twilight settled over the house. She didn't light the lamp. Instead, she stood by the little table, locked in inertia, her eyes slowly roaming over the objects that had accumulated there, the small accidents of daily life like pencils and a used mug and her current book, and the more permanent occupants that had taken up residence: the German dictionary, the box of keys and the bible.

The Unthank Bible.

Maddy pulled it towards her idly and opened the cover. There was the list of names, the ink permanent and final, still seeming to thoroughly modern Maddy a sacrilege. One simply did not write in books. It was a lesson drilled into her from childhood and one that caused her almost to wince every time she looked at this register of owners.

Owners and interlopers. *Lenka Midnight.* What a nerve. What had she been like, the mad housekeeper who kept the entire estate running single-handed, and then ran away with the gardener?

Except there hadn't been a gardener, had there? Not until Simpson was hired after Marilena arrived from Switzerland, and that was after Lenka Midnight had done a bunk. Pretty shameful really.

Maddy thought about the work being undertaken in the kitchen gardens by all the volunteers, and found herself mentally taking her hat off to the mysterious housekeeper nonetheless. Shameful or not, she must have been a prodigious worker. There had been the horse as well, and the cooking. Maddy knew she could never have kept so many plates spinning.

And presumably Marilena, Maddy's grandmother, had never known, or at least not until those journal pages were uncovered. Where were they hidden? And why did Lenka Midnight not take them with her, or burn them? On the other hand, she was long gone and, in any case, they were hardly incriminating – she hadn't done anything criminal, just been a bit woolly in the honesty department.

Marilena Johanna Bircher: 24th December 1897

She had been very pleased at owning Unthank, her grandmother. The disdain that was evident in that first note she had written, the one Uncle Claude had extracted and hidden in the cupboard behind the mirror, had quickly dissolved into appreciation in the proper diaries, and Maddy was in no doubt that her grandmother had begun to love Unthank almost immediately.

They all did, didn't they? First Lenka Midnight, then Grandmother Marilena, and now Maddy herself, who felt as if her heart would be wrenched from her body if she had to sell.

And she would have to, because the sum her flat had raised might just about cover the work to keep the house intact *or* pay for the improvements necessary to make it a viable business, but not both, never both. She couldn't live without an income, and the kind of job she was actually qualified to do – a shop assistant basically – would not bring in enough to maintain a castle.

Doom loomed before her.

Maddy dragged her thoughts away.

It was peculiar that her grandmother had not removed the housekeeper's name from the bible. Perhaps ink eradicator didn't exist then, but she could have crossed it out at least. It didn't sit with what Maddy knew of her character to let it stay there, interrupting the family succession.

Oh well. One never really knew what other people thought.

How peculiar that this bible was so famous, too. It was hard to see why it would be, but the pamphlet from the library had been effusive. *The Unthank Bible*, as if it were some historic treasure.

Maddy gazed at the title page.

The Holy Bible
Containing the Old and New Testaments
Translated Out of the Original Tongues:
And with the Former Translations
Diligently Compared and Revised
By His Majesty's Special Command
Published by The Society for Promoting Christian Knowledge

So far it sounded terribly Victorian and worthy. But there was that date: 1698. Sixteen ninety-eight! Just thirty years after the Plague and the Great Fire of London. Was Samuel Pepys still alive? Maddy's history was hazy. Did the end of the seventeenth century still count as The Restoration? And who was on the throne? James still, or William and Mary?

Without doubt the bible was an antique and was spookily ancient, but did that alone make it priceless? The antiquarian book dealer in Edinburgh had said not. There had been masses of these produced, and loads of them would have survived because people just do take care of bibles.

Perhaps there was a riddle hidden in there, buried in the dense text. It was possible. There were bibles with famous misprints, weren't there? One that left out the crucial 'not' from one of the Ten Commandments, and one that declaimed *Printers have persecuted me without a cause* when it should have been *Princes*. They must fetch high prices.

But Maddy was certain they were all much older than this one, and the dealer would have recognised it, surely. It was pointless looking for rescue there.

Oh, too many mysteries. That wretched key for one – the last one, the one in the box that she had found in the priest hole.

Maddy retrieved it from the box and turned it over in her hands. It was ridiculously large, probably six inches for the shaft alone and the shaft was thick too, the diameter of a pencil. The keyhole for this must let in one hell of a draught.

Well. There wasn't a keyhole for this at Unthank, Maddy was certain. It was far too big for any box or padlock and it simply wasn't possible that there was a door yet to be discovered. Whatever this key had been made to unlock was not here, and it was the end of the trail. Maddy had finished with games and riddles; frankly she had more pressing worries now.

CHAPTER 31

NINE MONTHS AGO, MADDY HAD IMAGINED THIS AND recoiled in horror. Now it was happening, and the horror was every bit as bad as she had feared.

She trailed around while the man measured the width and length of every room and wrote on the pad clipped to his folder. He was in his twenties, probably much the same age as Doug Ferguson had been but deeply unattractive, his suit too trendy, his lips too full, his after-shave too pungent. Deeply insensitive too, bubbly with enthusiasm, stock phrases flying forth: Beautiful house – wonderful windows – gorgeous grounds – highly desirable (*well, I know that*) – niche market (*No kidding*). Finally he told Maddy, 'Someone will see it and fall in love with it', and she thought, *I know, I already did.*

She went through the misery twice, feeling she must choose her agent carefully, but couldn't bear a third time and gave the job to the second lot, because the guy sent to take the details was less offensively ebullient and seemed at least faintly sensitive to Maddy's mood.

The next day a photographer came, and once again Maddy had to stand aside and watch someone else wield a camera when she knew she could have done a better job. She had all the photos she had taken for Brenda, the local history lady, for a start, but the agency said they liked to take their own. He was using a wide-angle lens and it was inevitable that the rooms would look stretched and lean ridiculously at the edges, but when she pointed this out he looked at her blankly and said there was no other way to give buyers a proper impression of the interiors. Maddy wanted to say *Define "proper"*, but she didn't.

A horrible calmness had settled on her. She thought the hamster had probably died.

ANTHEA CAME OVER. They sat in the huge drawing room so that there was a large tract of open floor for Baby Ben to crawl; the kitchen flagstones were freezing and in the snug they'd be perpetually retrieving him from under furniture.

Maddy knew her friend was handling her gently, like someone recently bereaved.

'Has there been any interest?' Anthea asked, using the customary euphemism.

Maddy sighed. 'Actually yes. A couple coming on Saturday. Mr and Mrs Gore.'

'Well, that's good.'

Was it? Maddy supposed so. It was just so hard to feel pleased.

The Gores were coming at the weekend because the husband worked in London and they had to travel up. If the appointment had been during the week Maddy would have asked – begged – Anthea to be there in support, to be the comfort blanket she so badly wanted, but it wasn't fair to ask her to give up family time.

Three weeks after it had hit the market, these were the first punters Unthank had pulled in. Maddy had instructed the agents to emphasise to enquirers that the property needed repair as well as refurbishment, because it would be pointless to plod down the path over and over again only to have buyers pull out when they had their own structural surveys done. Perhaps that accounted for the lack of response.

'I suppose everyone's put off by the condition,' she said. 'But it's still a castle. You'd think someone would want to live in a castle. I would. Wouldn't you?'

Anthea smiled sadly. 'I would.'

But she couldn't, of course. Matthew's salary from the National Park would never stretch to maintaining Unthank, let alone the repairs needed. Instead, they lived happily in a small stone cottage with idyllic views and a friendly village nearby.

Could Maddy do that? Even if she had to drop her price a lot, what she would get for selling Unthank would certainly buy her a stone cottage with a modest garden. Once upon a time Anthea's house would have looked like a dream, but that was in the past, that distant era to which one can never return, before she had been spoiled by riches.

Because that was what space, private space, amounted to, wasn't it? Forget the fact that the house was damp, draughty, and about to fall down, Unthank still offered masses and masses of beautiful, desirable, luxurious space indoors and out, and it was going to be desperately hard to turn her back on all that and hole herself up in a three-bedroom house you could walk right around in sixty seconds.

Could she settle for a cottage like Anthea's? She hadn't even started to plan her future, which was irresponsible, she knew, but seemed inevitable at present. Back to Twickenham and another flat? Or stay in wild, empty Northumberland and be a country bumpkin? Jobs would be more plentiful in London, although she hadn't managed to land one last February, but the North had its hold on her and she wasn't sure she could tear free.

Well. When Unthank sold there would be a few weeks' grace while the searches went through, and even after that she could rent somewhere while she wrestled with the big decisions.

Ben was trying to pull himself up by the curtains. Anthea retrieved him. 'We ought to be going.'

Maddy trailed her to the front door, where her lovely friend said, 'By the way, if you'd like some help when these people come, you will say, won't you? I can easily drive over.'

'Oh Anthea, really?' Maddy knew she sounded pathetic but didn't care. 'Won't you be busy?'

'No, of course not. Matthew can take Ben out. If you'd like me to come, that is.'

'Oh, I would, I would. Sorry. And thank you.'

So Anthea came, and her comfortable presence in the kitchen and occasionally drifting past as Maddy conducted the tour was as reassuring as Maddy had known it would be, especially as the Gores were horrible.

Well, perhaps not horrible, not truly, but Maddy did not find them in the remotest degree congenial. Mrs Gore – first names weren't on offer – was willowy and elegant with long, dark hair that was dead straight and very shiny. She wore a belted leather coat the colour of champagne and looked over Maddy's shoulder instead of meeting her eyes. Mr Gore was like the young estate agent, only older and with money. Some people really look like they never set foot outdoors, Maddy thought, and Mr Gore was one of them. What did they want with a castle in Northumberland?

A country address with show-off potential, it seemed, within commuting distance of Newcastle-upon-Tyne, where Mr Gore's office was relocating. Was Kirkwitton within commuting distance of Newcastle, Maddy wondered? Probably, if you drove a Mercedes like the gleaming monster parked in front of the porch.

'They did tell you that the house needs some structural work?' Maddy asked.

'Oh, we can get a little structural work done before we move in,' Mrs Gore said. She seemed to be leading the negotiations.

'Quite a lot,' Maddy said.

'No problem.'

The bargaining was the wrong way round, Maddy thought, with herself talking the house down and the buyer – potential buyer – dismissing the problems. But eventually the Gores drove away and two hours later Marlow and Black rang to say they had put in an offer only just below the asking price and recommended that Maddy accept it.

So she did.

And Unthank was sold.

CHAPTER 32

THE GARDENERS WERE APPALLED.

'Will they allow the restoration to continue?'

Maddy faced the delegation, petite Devyani wearing fuchsia pink, Evelyn looking stern in man's trousers and leather boots, Jed with his watery eyes. *Not in a million years*, is what she thought.

'I don't know,' she said. 'Maybe.' But she was honest enough not to smile.

Evelyn said, 'I'll put a report together. Explain what we're doing. How unusual this is, what a resource it is. Might help.'

'Yes, that's a good idea,' Maddy said, but it was a good idea mostly because then they would at least know they had done all they could. She thought cows would give birth to kittens before the Gores would allow outsiders into their domain.

The process trickled on. Buying property is never brisk. Maddy knew she would have to go through it all over again when she was ready to buy somewhere to live. She looked wretchedly in the windows of estate agents in Hexham – other estate agents, not Marlow and Black because she rather hated them now – and tried to get enthusiastic about narrow town houses and first-floor flats. She even made a couple of appointments to view.

The awful thing was that the houses were nice. Maddy had enough money to afford a reasonable rent and didn't have to pitch herself at the lowest end of the market. Hexham was way cheaper than Twickenham and she had a lot of money in the bank, just not enough to restore a crumbling castle.

But though the houses were well decorated, centrally heated, fully carpeted, they struck her as soulless and constricting. She would feel like a tiger in a cage. How could she go for a walk indoors? And outdoors was hardly better, the front doors barely two strides from the pavement, the back gardens thin strips between close-boarded fencing. It would be impossible to ramble, and Maddy realised that in the months she had lived at Unthank she had become a compulsive rambler.

She was going for a furnished let; it would be quicker to move into and much easier to leave later. She investigated the cost of storing furniture and found she could empty Unthank into a storage unit in Gateshead. That would have to do.

Then the Gores came again, this time talking casually about knocking through and tearing out and building on, about enlarging windows to let in more light and turning the stables into garages and building a tennis court and then a pool.

'A pond?' Maddy asked, trying to project polite interest.

'No, a *pool.*' Mrs Gore looked faintly annoyed at being interrupted. 'With a sauna,' she added, her attention back on her husband and away from Maddy again. 'Those old walled areas are perfect.'

So much for the restoration project. All that history, all that hard work, was going to be tarmacked and excavated and built over. Evelyn's report would fizzle into non-existence in nanoseconds, like a snowflake in a fire.

On leaving, as she opened the door of the Mercedes, Mrs Gore paused fractionally to toss a few words in Maddy's direction. 'Can you get on to your solicitor? He seems to be dragging his feet.'

'Of course,' Maddy said.

Cow, she thought. No way on earth would she try to hurry Mr Pattison.

An hour later Marlow and Black rang to tell her the Gores had dropped their offer. 'They say they have to consider the structural work the property needs,' the agent said.

Maddy gaped. 'But they knew about that. We told them about that at the start.'

The agent, to give him his due, sounded uncomfortable, but it was still just a job to him. 'They are the only prospective purchasers at present.'

'But…' Maddy felt as if weights were dragging her down. 'I can't believe…'

'Would you like me to accept the new offer?'

Maddy said, 'I'll ring you tomorrow.'

She put the phone down and stood in the snug expecting to have a cry, but tears wouldn't come. She felt hollow and hopeless. There were things she could have been doing but all of them required energy, and she had none, not even enough to walk to the kitchen and put the kettle on.

The light from the window was dim. It was probably past five but she couldn't be bothered to check her watch. She wasn't hungry, so supper needn't be considered yet; there was just the long, empty evening and then bed, with another day gone and the time she would leave Unthank forever one day closer.

Stay standing or sit down? It didn't really matter.

The box of keys was in its customary place on the card table. Maddy lifted the lid and stared at them, all the different sizes and ages and types, all the mysteries she had solved.

Except for one.

She took up the giant key, the ridiculous one, and turned it over in her hands, a small corner of her brain somehow able to haul itself away from her dismal future. She had been utterly unable to find any lock for this key. Something about it looked wrong, and not just its size. Maddy turned it over in her hand. The brass of the handle was dull while the shaft was polished and bright. Why would that be?

Maddy stroked the shaft. She wiggled it. Nothing was loose.

Anthea was very taken with secret compartments in furniture – tiny slots for bank notes and wills cleverly built into writing desks and armoires. Maddy had watched her go all over every piece of furniture in Unthank, probing and twisting and peering underneath. But this key was far too big for any secret compartment.

Too big for a secret compartment.

But not too big *to be* a secret compartment.

Maddy fingered the wards. Then she placed the handle on the card table and put the bible on top. Not enough, the key slipped. She fetched a handful of books from the shelves – hard backs, weighty ones – and stacked them on top of the bible. Then she gripped the wards and twisted them.

Nothing. The wards remained in the same horizontal plane.

Alright.

Maddy released the handle from under the books and flipped it, then leaning her elbow on the stack of books she tried again, pressing the wards to move out of their horizontal position and angle away.

And this time they did.

'Oh!'

Maddy almost jumped. The wards had turned and were now at thirty degrees or so, but the handle was still flat on the table.

She pushed again and the wards unscrewed. She pulled the key out from the books and carried on twisting, and the long, shiny shaft of the key drew away from the handle.

Maddy looked into a hollow tube. There was something inside.

∾

THE HAMSTER WAS awake and spinning; she told it (silently of course, she wasn't mad) to calm down and let her be, she needed all her attention to focus on breathing and making her legs work. The urge to hold her breath was almost overwhelming and she had to force her ribs to work, in and out, in and out.

Almost overwhelming, but not quite. Maddy breathed, held the rail in her free hand, and lifted her feet, one after another, to climb the stairs.

The hand that was not holding the rail gripped the torch. If there were to be another power cut she most definitely did not want to be left up there in the dark.

It was extraordinary, she now thought, that she could have been living serenely downstairs while all the time aware of this...oddity. Abnormality. The power of the human mind to turn away from that which is uncomfortable. Admirable? Or stupid? Either way she was having to face facts now, and it wasn't fun.

Breathe.

She reached the door at the top of the stair, unlocked it and pushed it open. The light from the naked bulb above her threw deep shadows behind the boxes and crates, the chairs and the rocking horse and the dressmaker's dummy, and they all seemed to be watching her.

Maddy forced herself forward.

SHE HAD the slip of paper in her back pocket but there were only seven words written on it and she had memorized those. The paper was thin, almost tissue, and had been rolled up to be inserted into the hollow shaft of the key. The words were aggravatingly cryptic. The last three were clear enough; it was the first four that left her feeling desperate.

Look for the lead in the attic.

Could Claude have possibly, in a decade of trying, been less helpful? *Look for the lead*, as if this were a murder mystery on television – detectives following leads to solve crimes by their intuition and hints dropped by indiscrete suspects. But what kind of lead was she looking for? A lead to what? Yet again Maddy found herself filled with a desire to shake her uncle by the throat.

What-was-he-thinking-of?

She should walk away, she really should, just chuck the keys away and write off the many, many hours of her life she had wasted on this ridiculous paper-chase.

Maddy switched on her torch and directed it into the depths, past the clutter, to where the rafters met the floorboards. But she had no idea what she was looking for.

AN HOUR later Maddy was finding it hard to breathe. The attic was bitter, but shivering was only part of the problem. The air seemed dense, like fog, pressing on her and dragging at her limbs. Her heart rate was too fast and her breaths too shallow, and she winced from the effort of blocking out fear.

But she was not miserable. She noticed that.

She was desperate to end the search, though.

After too long tiptoeing about and looking from a distance, she had decided that since she had no idea what form this lead would take she would have to examine absolutely everything, and would start with the biggest stuff. She had begun with a battered looking dressing table and investigated all of its little drawers, and then moved on to a chest and then a small, chunky cupboard like a bedside cabinet. This was facing into the eaves, so she tried to swivel it round the better to access it, and was surprised to find it was stuck.

She hunkered down and felt around the base for what was snagging it.

Nothing.

She had another go, wrapping her arms around it, and this time it shifted. It wasn't trapped at all, it was just heavy. Really heavy. Far too heavy for a simple wooden cabinet.

What was inside?

Maddy felt for the handle. It was a simple round one, like a flattened ball, but when she pulled the door remained closed.

A catch? She ran her fingers up and down the edge where the door met the panel but could feel nothing.

The torch. She leaned across the boards to grab the torch from where she had propped it against a suitcase and aimed the beam at the handle. Nope. No catch.

Maddy yanked again, thinking the mechanism must be stiff, and then tried turning the handle as if it were on a house door.

Bingo. A peculiar arrangement for such a small cupboard, though.

She opened the door of the cabinet and shone the torch inside. The compartment behind the door seemed smaller than one would have expected; the floor was raised several inches higher on the inside than outside.

Maddy rapped it. Not hollow. She stroked it. Not smooth either, but with raised metal triangles at the corners.

It wasn't the floor of the cupboard at all; it was a box almost the same dimensions as the floor. The gap between the edges of the box and the wall of the cabinet was barely quarter of an inch.

Maddy reached in, wormed her fingertips behind and took hold.

CHAPTER 33

MADDY'S FIRST EVER NIGHT AT UNTHANK HAD BEEN LONG and uncomfortable, rolled up in a sleeping bag on the hall floor, her mind buzzing with the strangeness of the present and the unguessableness of the future.

This night was worse.

Yes, she was in a bed and had a pillow instead of a bundled-up raincoat, but her mind was on overdrive, fizzing and popping as if on amphetamine, her thoughts tearing round and round the same track, unable to break free. Twice she gave up, switched on her bedside lamp, tried to read or took up her pad and pencil as if to begin a new list or spider chart, but she never managed to make a mark because the ideas hammering in her head were too frightening – or perhaps, just perhaps, too wonderful – to commit to paper. She couldn't let herself think about them, and they were all she could think about. She was stewing.

In the morning she felt awful. She had probably had barely two hours' actual sleep and yet was desperate to get going, but it only took forty minutes to drive there and park, and she ought to allow them at least five minutes to start the day before she burst in.

She didn't have an appointment. Surely he would squeeze her in somewhere though? She had better take a book for the wait…

The casket was impossible, far too heavy to carry them in, so Maddy used her overnight bag, a sturdy nylon hold-all with a zip, and then, on thinking about things, put the bag into a black plastic bin liner. She would now have to carry it bundled in her arms, but just suppose the heavens opened and there was a torrential downpour while she was in the open? The weather forecast was for a dry, sunny day but she couldn't take the risk of the nylon soaking through.

She set off at eight o'clock. It was too early but she would sit in the carpark.

THE RECEPTIONIST RECOGNISED HER.

'Oh, Miss Lawrence, I didn't know you had an appointment—'

'I don't,' Maddy said. 'But I'd really, really like one. Is there any chance I could just have five minutes sometime today?'

Her fingers were crossed under the bundle, where the receptionist couldn't see.

'Well…he has an appointment away from the office this morning, but I'm expecting him back for eleven o'clock. If he gets here earlier, he might be able to see you before eleven. Would that be any good? Otherwise there's a space on Wednesday…'

'This morning would be brilliant,' Maddy said firmly.

The waiting room was very small, with only two chairs and a tiny, low coffee table. She dropped into one of the chairs and hugged the bundle on her lap.

The receptionist looked surprised. 'Are you going to wait?'

'If that's all right.'

'Well, yes, of course.'

'Thanks.'

She had got here safely and had no intention of setting off again. The possibility of a car crash and being whipped off to hospital leaving the bundle behind had plagued her all the way down, and even in Hexham she had wondered about being mugged. Did Hexham harbour muggers? Probably not, but one never knew…

Anyway, she was here and staying. Surely, surely Mr Pattison wouldn't time his return too tight?

Was he truly in a meeting somewhere, Maddy wondered, or was that a euphemism for having a late start? How much business did solicitors conduct away from their offices? Of course, he had visited Unthank between Uncle Claude's departure and her arrival. Perhaps the same thing was happening now: an elderly resident dying, a house being made secure, a legatee informed; keys held, probate kicked off, the process unfolding all over again. It must be commonplace.

This isn't commonplace, though.

No, of that she was quite sure.

Maddy dragged the bin liner off the holdall, conscious of the noise she was making and how bizarre it must look, and bundled it up. She unzipped the bag, thrust the bin liner inside and took out her book.

She smiled at the receptionist.

But reading was hopeless. Maddy's eyes ran over the lines and reached the foot of the page without the least idea of what had been said. Pointless. But at least it looked like normal behaviour, so she stared at the print and turned pages from time to time, and tried hard not to keep checking the clock on the wall.

At twenty to eleven the door opened and Maddy glanced up in hope, but an elderly couple came in, shedding coats and scarves and talking in loud whispers. Maddy eaves-dropped fiercely. They were, of course, the eleven o'clock appointment.

The receptionist rose from her seat. 'I'll fetch another chair.'

Maddy jumped up. 'No, that's okay, I'll stand for a bit.'

'Are you sure?'

'Yes. Been sitting too long anyway.'

The couple sat down and Maddy, her bag in both hands, lurked in the opposite corner and felt desperate.

Please come, please, please.

And he came, with barely ten minutes to spare.

'Mr and Mrs Burroughs are here,' the receptionist said, 'and Miss Lawrence is hoping for a brief word.'

'Ah.'

'Five minutes,' Maddy said, her pleading face back on. It

wasn't intentional, it just seemed to happen. '*Really* quick. If you could.'

Mr Pattison, the loveliest solicitor in the world, made a kind of twisty nod with his head that managed to convey *All right* and *Come with me* and *I don't mind* all at once, and Maddy followed him into the office.

She shut the door behind her.

He took off his coat.

She unzipped the holdall.

He said, 'So, what's up?'

She put the bibles on the desk, side by side.

Mr Pattison said, 'What's this?'

He opened the front cover of the left hand one and turned a few pages. Then he closed it and sat down. For a moment longer he stared at the leather binding. Then he blinked, looked up at Maddy, and said nothing at all.

Maddy's hamster somersaulted. She thought, *He's speech-less. I'm not mad. This is real.*

She said, 'There's something called the Unthank Bible, and I think this is it.'

CHAPTER 34

THERE WAS A STEEP HILL DOWN FROM THE MARKET PLACE TO where Maddy had parked and she very nearly fell down it. Her legs had no strength – string, she thought, it was like walking with string for legs. She tried to organise them into supporting her but it wasn't easy.

Behind her, in the office, Mr Pattison was right now meeting with Mr and Mrs Burroughs and attending to their affairs. *Trying* to attend to their affairs. Maddy didn't know whether they were altering a will or selling their house or suing their window cleaner, but whatever it was couldn't possibly compete with her business. And they would never know – never know what the naughty girl without an appointment had said behind the closed door that made their solicitor three minutes late for their meeting.

A grin broke out and since there was nobody around Maddy indulged it. She felt breathless and giddy and very, very excited.

She didn't have to worry about muggings or car crashes

any more. 'Shall I keep this in our safe?' Mr Pattison had asked, and she had wanted to climb over the desk and hug him.

Then he had said, 'I should just say that we will have to bill you at some point for this. I have to count it as a new job. But,' he added, 'if this is what we think it is, you will be able to afford it.'

And they had smiled at each other, like collaborators, and then switched their expressions to neutral and Mr Pattison saw her politely out of the office.

He really was an extremely nice solicitor. She really was extremely lucky to have him. Good old Uncle Claude.

Good old Uncle Claude. How ironic. All these months, all this frustration, all the aggravation and irritation and at times *anger* she had felt about the wretched trail of hints and hiding places, and all the time he had been doing it to please her.

Alongside the two volumes in the lead-lined casket there had been a single sheet of paper.

Dear Madeleine,

You have now found the treasure!

You must be careful and treat it with care. The Unthank Bible has lived here for a great many years. Your grandmother would never sell it, although at times money has been tight, but I believe you should make up your own mind about that. It is part of your inheritance.

I hope you have enjoyed your treasure hunt as much as you did once before, and will forgive your old uncle, because he has his reasons. I love this house, you see, and I want you to love it too. Falling in love takes time, and I had to find a way to make you stay a little while.

Have you solved the riddle yet?

Your uncle,

Claude Lawrence

It had taken three read-throughs, sitting on the attic floor, before she had been able to get to grips with it. *I hope you enjoyed your treasure hunt…Falling in love takes time.* The cunning old wretch.

The casket had been far too heavy to waltz about with, being lined top, bottom and sides with lead, so Maddy had lifted the first item out and turned it over in her lap, under the yellow tungsten light. It was large, heavy, smelled not musty exactly but old, and was covered in tooled leather.

It was a book.

She had opened the cover and found four blank pages the colour of weak tea, and then a page printed with two columns of the most dense black text she had ever seen, edged with a delicate, swirling pattern in muted colours.

That was when the hamster jumped.

Maddy had closed the book.

She took out the second volume, which looked exactly like the first, and shone the torch into the empty casket and back into the cabinet too, making sure nothing had been missed. Then, tucking Claude's letter inside one of the volumes, she made her way back to the stairs.

IN THE KITCHEN, Maddy had spread on the table two tea towels, clean and fresh from the drawer, and positioned the two books carefully on top. Then she made herself some coffee and first set the mug on the dresser behind her but then changed her mind and put it on the draining board six feet away.

She was taking no chances.

She opened the first volume again and began turning pages.

They were bibles. On the leather covers were stamped the words **BIBLIA SACRA LATINA**, and even her mostly-forgotten O-level Latin could handle that.

They weren't in English, so not the King James version, and the type-face, font, whatever one called it in centuries past, was of the sort called 'black letter', although Maddy didn't know whether there were different variations of that. Probably there were. It was familiar to her, of course, from embossed, shiny gold lettering on Christmas cards: *Christus est natus*, *Season's Greetings*. Looking at it now, it occurred to her that if someone had set out to design lettering as difficult to read as possible, they couldn't have done a better job. That anyone had ever read this fluently seemed miraculous.

She turned the pages.

The text was set out in two columns with wide margins all around. Occasionally capital letters at the start of paragraphs were in red ink, but apart from that first page, there was no other ornament. Unable to decipher the writing, to Maddy every page looked much the same.

She closed the book.

Her mug was still waiting. The coffee was cold but she drank it anyway, standing at the sink and staring across the kitchen to the books on the table.

The Unthank Bible.

This was what the Warwickshire Traveller had raved

about. This was what her grandmother had not wanted to separate from the house. It was never the commonplace family bible at all.

It seemed laughable now. The pages of that bible were thin, weak, poor things, the print small and crowded with little space and no...importance. The pages of the Unthank Bible had importance in truck-loads.

How old was it? The paper looked pretty old to Maddy, but the binding was whole and smelled of decent leather, not whatever centuries-old leather must surely smell like. It didn't smell of tombs.

Still...those pages, that text, the decoration on the front page, and that lead-lined casket...Someone had believed these volumes to be precious.

So she had taken them to the person nearest to her that she had come to trust as knowledgeable and dependable. And Mr Pattison believed them to be precious too.

Maddy stocked up in the supermarket on the things Joan's village shop didn't sell – bitter chocolate, smoked salmon and a bottle of Sauvignon blanc.

She felt a celebration was in order.

MR PATTISON TELEPHONED the next day. Maddy was still having breakfast. After that first sleepless night, yesterday evening she had gone off the moment she lay down and had slept like a baby until late. She glanced at the clock on the wall as she picked up the phone. Nine forty. Oh dear.

'I've got some news,' Mr Pattison said. 'Will you be free on Friday morning?'

Will she be free? Bless him!

'Yes,' she said.

'Then perhaps you'd like to come in. I've arranged for someone to examine the books – a specialist who will tell us exactly what they are.'

'Great,' Maddy said, thinking about the dealer in Edinburgh and his corduroy jacket. 'It isn't a Mr Murray, is it?'

Mr Pattison sounded nonplussed. 'No, a Doctor Garland. Lead Curator of Incunabula and Early Printed Books at the British Museum. I think she'll know what's what.'

Dr Garland did.

She hadn't jumped on a train at once. First, she had asked Mr Pattison to do a few checks. Apparently he had had to count the number of lines in each column (forty-two), measure precisely the height and width of each column, and also measure the distance between the two columns. He had offered to measure the outside margins, but had been told no, the pages might have been trimmed.

He had described the books in detail and explained how Maddy had found them. And then Dr Garland said she would come.

Maddy was to meet her at the station and walk her to the office. One does not expect a Lead Curator of Incunabula and Early Printed Books to find her own way in a strange town.

'What are incunabula anyway?' Maddy had asked on the phone.

'Incunabula, plural of incunabulum, meaning swaddling clothes and also the early stages of development of a thing – that's the general meaning – and specifically a book printed before 1501.'

'Wow,' Maddy said.

'Shorter Oxford English Dictionary,' Mr Pattison said.

'*Shorter?*'

'Still two hefty volumes of very small print.'

Maddy thought. She said, 'But this Dr Garland's title is curator of incunabula *and* early printed books. That's tautological.'

'Um…I see what you mean…but books printed after 1501 are still going to be considered "early". Movable type didn't arrive until about then, did it? And it must have been decades, centuries even, before everyone was doing it.'

A time before printed books.

'What a thought,' Maddy said.

'Indeed.'

Now she waited, dazzlingly early, outside the station for someone who looked like an expert in early printed material. It was drizzly and she had two umbrellas, the one over her head and a spare. She hoped the rain would not put Dr Garland in a bad mood. How old was she? What would she look like? Maddy was conscious of trying not to fall into the trap of picturing her as elderly, bespectacled, tweedy, severe.

A train pulled in and the first passengers emerged from the station. Maddy felt a fool holding her notepad in front of her chest: *Pattison*, like at an airport, but how else could poor Dr Garland find her?

People passed her paying no attention. Then a woman

appeared from the doorway, glanced Maddy's way and set a course directly for her. She began to smile. Maddy began to smile too.

'Doctor Garland?'

'Miss Lawrence!'

Maddy fumbled the notepad and freed up her hand to shake. 'Maddy. Thank you so much for coming.'

'Thank *you* so much for getting in touch. I'm looking forward to seeing your bible.'

Not tweedy and severe at all, just ordinary, Maddy thought: forty-ish, minimal make up, wearing black trousers and a quilted waterproof coat. No glasses. And her manner was comfortable yet breezy.

Maddy attempted some small talk. 'Did you have a good trip?'

'Yes, thank you. I come up to Edinburgh quite often.'

'Oh, right. Well. The office isn't far. There is a bit of a hill though.'

'So Mr Pattison warned me.'

But Dr Garland didn't slow down noticeably and had enough puff at the top to say, 'How lovely!' as she arrived in the market place and saw the Abbey.

Maddy guided her to the side road. 'Do you think,' she asked, unable to help herself, 'that you will be able to identify it today?'

'Authenticate your bible? Not conclusively. But I'll be able to tell you whether it's worth taking further. Then it's your choice.'

'My choice?'

'What to do next.'

'Oh. Right.'

What I want to do next, Maddy thought, is turn it into money. But she felt that was not quite the thing to say.

They arrived at the office and Maddy followed her captured academic inside to where her tame solicitor was waiting, talking to his receptionist. He came forward to shake hands.

'Doctor Garland, Robert Pattison, pleased to meet you. This way.'

And they were off.

CHAPTER 35

THIS TIME MADDY HAD TO TELL SOMEONE. NOT ANYONE specific; she just needed to say it out loud to somebody who didn't yet know.

Her mother. But it would be awfully early in New York and in any case, her mother didn't have the back story. 'There was a crisis, it's now resolved' wouldn't elicit the required degree of wonder and jubilation.

The gardeners: Evelyn and Devyani. But until it was absolutely definite − until Maddy knew for sure, and how much − it would be better not to raise hopes that might even now be dashed.

Oh please, I hope not!

No, this nugget, this gem-stone of news needed to be kept confidential until…well, until the money arrived, basically.

Anthea.

Maddy noticed her hand was trembling as she dialled.

Breathe.

'Hello?'

'Anthea,' Maddy said, 'can you spare five minutes? I've got some news.'

DR GARLAND HAD TAKEN the bible, both volumes of it, away for analysis in her lab or whatever it was called, but she had told them she was pretty certain what it was: a Gutenberg bible.

Maddy had opened her mouth before she had time to consider how dim her question would make her sound.

'What *is* a Gutenberg bible?'

She had heard of it, of course, and knew it was ancient and rare and valuable, but if pushed to provide a definition she knew she was wanting.

Dr Garland, lovely woman, did not gasp with horror nor chortle at such ignorance. She simply said, in a matter-of-fact tone that Maddy blessed her for, 'Johann Gutenberg invented movable type. Before that, printed books could only be produced from large print blocks of a complete page. The blocks could be printed from many times but only for that one purpose. Movable type means individual letters and symbols that can be rearranged into whatever text you like.'

'Printing as we know it,' Mr Pattison put in.

'Exactly. And the first text Gutenberg printed was the bible, to be bound in two volumes. I believe yours is one of those.'

Maddy's mouth was dry. 'So how old are they? What date are we talking about?'

'Mid-fifteenth century. The first were in the 1450s.'

Five hundred years old.

Maddy looked down at the two volumes lying on the desk. Mr Pattison had spread a white cloth for them to lie on; it looked like a folded tablecloth – he must have brought it from home.

Dr Garland went on. 'Don't worry about the binding. Leather deteriorates much faster than paper. The text blocks of almost all these early bibles have been rebound, usually more than once. Your binding looks early 19th century – at a guess I'd say between 1810 and 1840.' She clasped her hands together and rested them on the edge of the desk. 'They have been reasonably well stored. They are in reasonably good condition.'

'How should they be looked after now?' Mr Pattison asked.

'Ah. Well. Rare book depositories nowadays can control temperature and humidity to provide the optimum conditions for preservation.'

Five hundred years old.

Maddy said, 'So no-one gets to see them anymore?'

'Not necessarily. You can make a display case with the right conditions and the volume can be exhibited open at a page. One changes the page frequently, of course, to protect the spine.'

Maddy dragged her gaze away from the books and discovered Mr Pattison was looking at her. He cocked an eyebrow.

Oh yes.

She said, 'So…how would I go about selling them? And how much do you think…'

'It will fetch?' Dr Garland took her hands back into her lap. 'You will understand that at present I have not definitely authenticated this bible, although I would be very surprised if it is not a Gutenberg. You will also understand that items of this rarity are immensely difficult to value. It is truly unique, because the condition of each one still in existence will be particular. I believe no *sections* are missing from this one, but I have yet to verify that no individual *pages* have been lost. However.' She was weighing her words, Maddy thought. 'On the assumption this bible is complete – no sections or pages missing – and is a genuine Gutenberg, then we have a fair idea of what it would fetch because a similar two-volume complete bible was sold at Christie's in 1978.'

She paused…for thought or for dramatic effect?

'Yes?' Maddy prompted.

Nice Dr Garland smiled.

'AND?' Anthea said. 'Go on, tell me, what did she say?'

'She doesn't know for sure. She said she still has to run through some more things with the pages first.'

'I know that. You said that. But?'

'Anthea, you mustn't tell anyone, I don't want rumours to get out before I know for sure.'

'Absolutely. Cross my heart and hope to die. But?'

All alone in the kitchen, Maddy grinned stupidly. She saw again Dr Garland, ordinary and friendly, as she smiled across Mr Pattison's desk at her, and told her what the 1978 sale had made.

Now she repeated the same words to Anthea. 'A similar

one sold in 1978 went for two point two million dollars. At the time, roughly one and a half million pounds.'

There was silence at the other end of the phone line. Then Anthea said, 'Oh Maddy.' Then she said, 'But what about the–'

'They're not having it,' Maddy said. 'I've already done that. The deal's off.'

She had walked with Dr Garland back to the railway station, which Dr Garland had said was entirely unnecessary but which Maddy felt was the courteous – and slavishly grateful – thing to do, and then climbed back up the hill and made straight for Marlow and Black's office, where she thrust open the door knowing exactly what she was going to say but not at all how she was going to say it. Ordinarily she liked to prepare for business discussions so that she came across as efficient and intelligent; this time she honestly didn't care.

The bloke at the desk nearest the door greeted her with a bright, commercial smile and said, 'Good morning! Can I help you?'

But across the floor the one she knew, Steve, the one who had measured up and arranged the viewings with the dreaded Gores, had recognised her and was already walking towards her, wearing the same smile, though tempered by her prevarication over accepting the Gores' new, lower offer.

How mean of them, how dishonourable, to agree a figure and then seek to reduce it. They had tried to turn the screw on Maddy, and had it not been for the extraordinary events of the last three days they would have succeeded. In a week or so she would have been signing contracts.

Not now.

Steve had extended his hand and Maddy had shaken it. It was, after all, goodbye.

'They weren't happy,' she told Anthea now.

'I should think not!'

'But there are plenty of other estate agents, should I ever need one.'

'Of course. But you won't need one now, will you?'

The Unthank Bible had yet to be proven to be a Gutenberg, but Dr Garland had been explicit: even if not one of those amazing first-ever products of a movable-type printing press, it was still very early, very rare, and very, very valuable.

Maddy said, 'No. Absolutely not.'

She smiled.

Unthank was hers again, and this time she was keeping it.

CHAPTER 36

Maddy had been right: if you never knew there was a problem, news of the solution is no news at all.

The gardeners, or at any rate the committee who had known Unthank was to be sold, were relieved and jubilant, but they had not known the Gores' plans for the walled gardens. Maddy had never quite got around to telling Joan in the shop that she was selling at all, nor her mother, who was interested but only mildly so.

'Goodness! Funny old Claude!'

Maddy hadn't confided in Liz either, and felt guilty about that. She called her one evening and brought her up to date with events. Liz, she was sure, would be interested in the bible and she was right.

'A Gutenberg! You are kidding! I can't believe it! And you never showed it to me!'

'I didn't know about it when you were here. Actually, I only held it a handful of times myself.'

That was true. In retrospect it was odd and faintly

annoying that the Unthank Bible had been whisked away only hours after she discovered it, first by Mr Pattison (lovely Mr Pattison) and then by Dr Garland (nice Dr Garland). She would, all being well, fingers crossed and all that, never hold it again, never even see it again in the flesh.

In the paper.

But of course that was what had to happen. You can't keep your cake – or five-hundred-year-old Gutenberg bible – and eat it too, and Maddy had no doubts at all about choosing to eat.

The British Museum had decided it was the real thing. Then Christie's had taken it, and now they were letting the world know that it existed and would be put up for auction in due course. One did not simply add something like this to next month's sale catalogue; one had to allow time for knowledge of its existence to percolate to those bodies that might be in the market for such a thing. An institute of learning would get it in the end, for sure, and that was A Good Thing, Maddy knew.

So she was in limbo. She did not want to set the wheels of structural repair in motion just in case. It was unlikely that anything would go wrong at this point, but Maddy was financially cautious and could put up with condensation on the windows and freezing cold rooms for another few months.

In the meantime there was little she could do. She had returned to planning her photography retreats, and also had in mind a running project to document the renovations that lay ahead, taking photographs of the under-layers of the structure as they were revealed – the internal walls, beneath the floorboards, the ceilings – and approach the Sunday supplements, or even perhaps make a book. If she put her mind to it and asked enough questions while the work was happening, she could definitely put together a good talk on the subject and see if there were any takers – Women's Institutes, local history societies and so on. If nothing else it would be a lovely record for herself in years to come.

Her children, too?

Hm. Well.

In any case she had become much more interested in history – social history, domestic – than ever before, and had decided to read her grandmother's diaries again, paying more attention this time. She would begin at the beginning and not skip, and would make notes of anything important.

She set to on a grey Wednesday afternoon in mid-December. She was feeling scrubbed and rosy because after a morning in the darkroom she had stretched her legs walking to the gatehouse and got caught in a downpour, and had been so wet the only way she could get dry was by having a bath.

In comfy clothes, she settled down in the snug, tucked her legs underneath her in the big wing chair, and took onto her lap the first of Marilena's diaries.

Maddy tried to imagine how her grandmother must have felt, so newly arrived in England, knowing she was an outsider, so young still and yet having inherited this great pile of stone.

Just like Maddy herself in some ways.

She opened the cover and loose sheets of paper slid onto her stomach. Oh yes – the detached pages, the ones Uncle

Claude had left her in the wall hidden by the mighty Victorian mirror and in the priest hole. Her grandmother's very first reactions to Unthank.

Better be thorough. Later she would stick them into this first bound diary.

She began at the top.

I do not like the name of this house. So ugly. And what does it mean? It is not grammatical. English is not a pretty language.

I would like to name it different. I would like to call it Bircher Hall from my family name but they would have to change the maps and the English authorities will not let me. In any case, people in the village do not use the name very much; they call it 'The German House', which shows how ignorant they are.

Poor old Marilena! She really hadn't been happy. Maddy found herself smiling at the indignation expressed in every sentence. It was impossible not to hear the German accent as she read.

'Hall' is what the English call a house when it is very large. This house is not very large, not as large as Alderhof. Not so many rooms, and all the rooms smaller. But it is certain the largest house at this village and I expect my uncle's mother thought she was very special, very grand to be living here, even with only three servants. Three servants! To manage a house even this size! And one of them for the gardens only! It is truly not surprising that half the rooms were closed and the growing-houses so poor. I have had to order much glass to repair the broken ones.

I must find servants also. There were only two here at the end and both of them left when my grandmother died. I think they should have waited for me, but they did not and nobody in the village knows to where they went. Or nobody tells me; I think they know but do not want me to know. I think they do not like me.

Ah yes, the mystery of the Disappearing Housekeeper. But only the housekeeper, because mad Lenka Midnight's last instalment had made it clear she was both the house-keeper and the enigmatic gardener both.

What a woman! You had to admire her.

Maddy finished the loose pages and began on the diary.

It's done, finished, in the past. I've been here two weeks now and can put it all behind me.

Today the sky is grey and the sun is hiding and there's little prospect of change until the end of the week, but I don't care. The weather can do whatever it likes, it won't affect me. I have never felt so free. After breakfast I walked right around the gardens, intending to take stock in my head of the condition everything is in, but really all I was thinking was that this place is now mine. It belongs to me. There is nobody to organise my life for me, nobody to give me orders, nobody of whom I need ask permission. I am my own mistress.

And I will soon be a mistress to other people also. I must hire staff. I have decided I will have two indoors and two out – a housemaid, a cook, a gardener and another, a boy perhaps, who can be under-gardener and can also take over the outdoor jobs. This house ran with four servants before and I'm sure they'll cope perfectly well. I do not want maids under my feet, scurrying all over the place. I shall tell them: Only open the rooms I need, and we'll leave the others closed up.

Maddy frowned. She picked up the last loose sheet again and reread the final paragraph.

I have servants! Mrs McLeod is the cook. Effie Marley is the maid. Simpson is the gardener. Walter Black is the outside boy. I have told them that I am Swiss and I do the Swiss way. Now all is better and I do not make fire or go in the kitchen. Tomorrow I will

She already had the servants. What was all this about

deciding who to employ? Unless the loose sheet had been written after the diary entry, but why would you do that?

The diary was dated 24th July 1919. There was no date on the loose page, but it must have been much earlier; the language was quite different, not to mention the tone.

Yes, very different.

Maddy looked from one to the other. The handwriting was very similar, but one old-fashioned, forward-slanting cursive is much like another, isn't it? The sheet was full of grammatical misuse - *I would like to name it different; nobody in the village knows to where they went* – and even when correct, the sentences seemed un-English, stilted and alien. But the first diary entry flowed. It was full of contractions for a start – *It's done; I don't care; it won't affect me* – and the vocabulary was wider and incorporated expressions like *they'll cope very well* and *scurrying all over the place.* It was text written by a native speaker, or at least someone very fluent in English; it had not been written by someone who had learned the language in the classroom or from books.

Nobody could go from one to the other in the space of a couple of weeks, let alone days. What was going on?

It's done, finished, in the past. I've been here two weeks now and can put it all behind me.

Two weeks? And can put all what behind me? What was done, finished and in the past?

Something stirred at the back of Maddy's mind, almost like an idea waking up, turning over and scratching. She felt uneasy without knowing why.

She returned to the diary and read on, not skipping any pages this time. The language continued to be fluent and colloquial, allowing for a degree of formality that could be put down to the six decades that separated 1984 from 1920. The feeling of unease remained. It was so odd that Marilena had been writing about finding and interviewing and selecting and hiring her servants when she had apparently already done this while still writing in schoolgirl English. Had she got someone else to write in the diary for her? Interpret her meaning and translate it?

No, that was absurd.

She reached the first week of August and recognised a paragraph she had read before.

Effie has ruined the sheets and must wash them again. She tripped over with them in her arms and fell right down on top of the lot. It is only dirt, and it would all brush off once dry, but I am quite sure that is not the Swiss way so I told her to put them back in the copper. I'm finding this isn't always easy. However, I also told her that I would overlook imperfections this once. But Mrs McLeod is wonderful, a marvel. Her bread is much lighter than I have ever

This time Maddy turned the page.

managed to bake myself, despite using the same horrible range in the same horrible kitchen.

EVERYTHING SHE HAD FOUND during the course of following Uncle Claude's treasure hunt was in the snug: the keys, the papers, the photographs and the book. Maddy spread them out on the card table.

The book was the German primer. Maddy checked it again. Yes, definitely written to help English people learn

German, not the other way about. That had made no sense at all at the time; now perhaps it did.

The first loose document had been the builder's invoice. Reading it again now, Maddy realised it referred to building cupboards into the walls of the chimney and the bedroom, the first being the one discovered by the chimney sweep, the second the one concealed by the huge mirror. She could see no other relevance. Probably Uncle Claude had intended it to help her find those two caches, and probably it would have if only she had spent longer trying to understand the faded typing.

After that had come the photocopies of notes about Marilena's family, her parents and siblings. The information did not seem controversial, but the existence of the information in this form? Evidence that someone had been investigating…what, exactly? And all the stuff about travellers, which should have no connection and yet Claude must have thought relevant.

On top of that was the letter about the other Marilena's death – still a puzzle.

She left the two photographs until last, setting them side by side and moving the standard lamp so that its light fell on them. On the left, Lenka the mad housekeeper with Lily and Sam Biddle; on the right, Marilena Lawrence, née Bircher. Lenka would have been in her very early twenties; Marilena in her thirties.

Maddy stared. After a few moments she rose and fetched her loupe from the darkroom. Placing it over each picture in turn, she examined the magnified features.

Both women faced the camera. Neither woman smiled.

Both women had long faces with straight noses and straight eyebrows, and both had straight, wide shoulders. But if you really looked, Lenka Midnight's jaw was a little asymmetrical, one side – her left side – more prominent than the other. "Jutted" was too strong a word, but that was what it did – the corner of the bone below the ear jutted out a tiny bit more on that side.

And when she turned her attention back to the other photograph, Marilena's jaw did that too.

CHAPTER 37

Nobody knew. Really, who knew? Nobody. Just Maddy. Claude, obviously, and he was dead. Her father must have known – she presumed – although perhaps not, because he had cut himself off from his family at a very young age. If he had known, though, had he told Norma when he married her? Maddy didn't think so. Her mother had never sounded as if she knew. If she had, then she must have forgotten or surely she would have mentioned it over this past eleven months? And how could you forget a thing like that?

Did anyone in the village know? Had anyone known, or guessed, at the time? The doctor, for instance?

Maddy flipped through the pages; she had read something about him…There: summer 1920, when her grandmother had put her hand through the glass.

So! No veil necessary and I can truly breathe now! An hour he was here, first cleaning and then stitching and finally binding. And I had no thought for my appearance once that needle started, that is for certain. But he thought nothing of me, of that I am perfectly sure, even though he looked full at me when he entered and again before he left. So whether or not my hand is throbbing – which it is – and I shall be restricted in what I do for weeks to come – which I will – I am light and carefree tonight. Doctor Burden in this very room and not two feet from me! It is a load off my shoulders. I begin to think I should have put my hand through some glass a year ago.

So Dr Burden had not recognised Marilena Bircher as the dishevelled housemaid who had opened the door to him two years earlier, and whom he had suspected of taking a tumble in the hot beds with the gardener.

Maddy could empathise with Marilena's relief. She must have been living in constant fear of discovery.

It seemed highly likely that nobody in England suspected her of being anyone other than Fräulein Marilena Bircher from Switzerland who had inherited Unthank legitimately, not half-gipsy Lenka Midnight who had stolen it.

What about the real owners? Had anyone in Switzerland wondered what had happened to (Maddy checked the names in the front of the family bible) Anders Wilhelm Bircher's English estate? Had someone been sitting at home in the Alps wondering why they had been passed over? Would that person not have made enquiries? Come to England to investigate? Challenge what had happened?

How had Lenka done it? She was a servant, had been a field-labourer and before that a traveller's child in a caravan with a wastrel for a father. How could she have passed herself off as a Swiss heiress and waltzed away with a castle? It was insane.

Or maybe it was Maddy who was insane, and all this was some wild and ridiculous mistake. That's what anyone would say – anyone normal, well-adjusted and sensible. She was imagining things; she had to be.

Except…

She used the loupe again, crossing from one face to the other.

It was the same woman.

Maddy abandoned the photographs abruptly and reached for the box file she had been given by Brenda MacWhatsit, the aged local historian she had visited in Gosforth. There had been more photographs in there.

She tipped them onto the table in a slithering heap. One by one she examined the faces of all the people, long dead, using the loupe and looking carefully.

She found Marilena in one, looking away this time but still, Maddy felt sure, her grandmother aged thirty-ish. The young man on the motorcycle, the Lawrence of Arabia bloke, turned up again too, and it seemed obvious now that he was her grandfather, Theo.

But mostly she looked at the unknown, unguessed faces, comparing them, paying close attention, until she was quite certain. People are *not* all alike. Even in old, faded, blurry photographs, faces don't merge into one another. That Lenka Midnight and Marilena Bircher shared the same features, the same asymmetry, was not her imagination. It was because they were the same person.

Maddy was the great-granddaughter of Jeremiah Midnight.

And that meant Unthank wasn't hers at all.

IT WAS WORSE THIS TIME, so much worse. Unthank was not hers, so if she sold it the money raised would also not be hers.

The Unthank Bible wasn't hers either, so the million or two that was worth also wouldn't be hers.

She owned nothing but the money from selling her flat, and when eventually she used that to buy whatever she was going to live in, in wherever she was going to live, she would be right back where she had been a year ago, with no job, no qualifications, and no prospects.

She was being pathetic and she knew it but couldn't stop.

You will own a house, she told herself desperately, *and how many people your age own their home outright? Get a job in a supermarket, find out if a bank will train you, ask what it takes to be a postman. Buck up!*

But she couldn't buck up; she was in mourning.

The simple truth was that she had been living for almost a whole year in a fairy tale, albeit one with flaws. She had believed Unthank to be hers, *her* castle. But it wasn't and never had been.

Don't tell them, her inner voice nagged. *Don't tell anyone. Who's to know?*

Nobody knew. She could live, as she now realised her grandmother had lived, anxious and uncertain in the grip of a guilty secret, ever fearful of discovery, constantly expecting to be found out and evicted from her home with nothing, nothing at all.

It was no way to exist. Maddy began to understand why her grandmother had been bitter and difficult. She had lost her lovely Theo, all but lost her elder son, and had lived in a state of trepidation that she might lose her beloved home. Maddy's grandmother had built her life on shifting sands and had known it.

'I don't want to be like her,' Maddy said aloud, over and over, and the voice in her head responded.

So, what are you going to do, Maddy? What?

CHAPTER 38

ANTHEA INVITED HER TO SPEND CHRISTMAS DAY WITH THEM. It was very kind of her.

Maddy declined. She said she was going to be super-indulgent and have long hot baths with a book, roaring open fires, the biggest Christmas tree in the world, sloppy clothes, and wine, Stilton and bitter chocolate.

She wasn't sure Anthea believed her, but she accepted it. 'If you change your mind, just come anyway.'

Liz invited her down south. That was also very kind.

Maddy declined again.

'It is an awful long way and the weather might be rotten.' She added, 'And I've been invited to my friend Anthea's for Christmas Day.'

Not strictly a lie, but said in a lying kind of way that made her feel ashamed.

If you can't be happy with even a little lie, how are you going to cope with a massive one?

In the village shop, Joan said cheerily, 'Going home for

Christmas, Maddy?' She hadn't ever really understood that 'home' for Maddy was now Unthank.

'I've been invited to a friend's,' Maddy said again, taking the coward's course, and plodded home with her shopping.

CHRISTMAS WAS HORRIBLE, as bad as she had expected and then more. She did buy a Christmas tree but it was only a small one because there was only her to carry it in and make it stand up. She dug out the box of decorations that had moved with her from Twickenham, but the snug was too cramped to accommodate even this small tree and in the cavern of the drawing room the tree was dwarfed. It looked ridiculous. And anyway, the drawing room was cold.

She lived off ready-meals and easy things like eggs and cheese on toast, and yes, she splurged on creamy Stilton in a ceramic pot and designer chocolates, and it was all quite useless. Slopping about the cold house in legwarmers and baggy jumpers didn't make her feel cosy and relaxed but weak and vulnerable, and a hot bath is less entrancing when it's taken in a bitterly cold bathroom.

And all the time, oh, all the time it was there: the fear, the grief, the nasty nagging knowledge that she was in receipt of stolen goods and had no right to be there at all.

Christmas sort of extends until New Year's Day. Many people, probably including solicitors, don't work on the days between Boxing Day and the New Year. Maddy existed for one more week, and then on the second of January she drove to Hexham and presented herself in the office to ask, again, to talk to Mr Pattison even though she had no appointment.

VERY FEW PEOPLE want a meeting with their solicitor on the second of January. Mr Pattison saw her straight away.

'Happy New Year,' he said, waving her to sit down. 'I hope you had a good Christmas.'

Maddy dropped into the chair. He was smiling and looked as nice as he always did.

He had no idea at all.

In this moment, she thought, this moment right now, I'm not committed. I haven't told him yet and I don't have to. I could say I've come to ask if he's heard from Dr Garland, that I was in Hexham anyway and thought I'd drop in. Nobody knows. Really, who knows? Nobody.

I know.

Maddy said, 'I had a terrible Christmas and I think I'm going to cry.'

She did. She could feel it in her throat and behind her eyes.

Say it now, quickly, now.

She said, 'Unthank doesn't belong to me. My grandmother stole it.'

Done. Committed. The tears spilled over.

Mr Pattison switched out of his easy, friendly mood to one of minor alarm. He pushed a box of tissues towards her. 'Goodness! I think you're mistaken.'

Maddy shook her head miserably. 'I'm not, I'm not. It's in her diaries, and there are photographs. My grandmother was the housekeeper, the one that ran away. Lenka Midnight.'

'Lenka Midnight!'

Maddy had forgotten Mr Pattison had never heard the name. She remembered her own astonishment on hearing it for the first time.

'Yes. She was sort of half-gipsy, I think. She was a bondager on a farm, and then she came to Unthank and worked in the gardens, and then the housekeeper, the proper one, and the gardener went to York for the day and disappeared and never came back and Lenka Midnight took over and ran the whole place on her own.'

'Good heavens.'

'And I don't know how but when the old woman died – the owner, the Swiss woman – she, Lenka, must have passed herself off as Marilena Bircher and inherited it. Everything. I can't think how she got away with it. But she did, and now I know and I can't live like her, knowing it doesn't belong to me and expecting to be found out.' Maddy blew her nose. 'Unthank isn't mine. It belongs to some Swiss person.' She swallowed. 'So the Bible isn't mine either.'

Mr Pattison was looking at her. His eyebrows were raised a little, as if registering his surprise at her story, but he didn't look stricken. Why would he? The castle and the fortune had never been his. Still, when he did at last speak Maddy felt he might have sounded more troubled.

'Just a minute.'

He left the office.

Maddy took another tissue. Talking was what kicked off

the tears; once she stopped doing that she could stop crying too, although her eyes were a bit leaky.

Mr Pattison was absent for nearly five minutes. Then he returned carrying a pink card folder.

He took his seat and placed the folder on the desk. Dismally, Maddy watched him open it and pull out a manila envelope, and from that he drew forth papers.

'Here we are.' He turned the papers to face her. 'The deeds. Take a look.'

The deeds.

Maddy read. Then she looked up.

'I…but this…I don't understand.'

'I don't think there's anything to understand, is there? Those are the deeds to Unthank Hall. Your uncle asked us to keep them when he inherited. That's quite normal, by the way – we have a fireproof safe, lots of people ask solicitors to keep the originals of documents. I should have asked you, but I rather assumed you'd want us to carry on.'

Maddy was finding breathing a trial. She felt tight and air hungry.

Deeds. She thought Mr Pattison was being kind here because she had vague recollections of his asking her months ago if she wanted him to hold on to the deeds for her, and she had said yes. Of course she had. He might even have shown them to her, but it had seemed a small thing at the time and she had paid scant attention.

Now she said, 'But it still doesn't mean she had any right to it, does it? If she stole it, took possession fraudulently, then when she died and Uncle Claude inherited, it wouldn't be his either.'

Mr Pattison had returned his attention to the folder. 'Here we are.'

Maddy took another piece of paper from him. It was a letter – no, a receipt written in the form of a letter. There was a company name across the top, with an address in Bonn, and it was dated 14th January 1924.

Dear Mr Lawrence,

I am pleased to write on behalf of my client Herr Paul Bircher confirming your purchase outright of the property known as Unthank House, Kirkwitton, Northumberland, England.

Yours faithfully,

M Rengel

Maddy raised her eyes.

'There you go,' Mr Pattison said. 'All better.'

...

BOOK THREE

CHAPTER 39

Maddy opened the book and turned the first page. She smoothed it back and readied her pen. She had decided it was too scary to jump straight in but would have a title page – the dates, for a start, and probably her name and address – and she would think how to lay that out attractively later.

How to begin?

My name is Lenka Midnight and this is my story.

Maddy shrugged and wrote: *My name is Madeleine Lawrence and this is my story.* It was mad, but then the whole thing was mad.

She wrote.

My name is Madeleine Lawrence and this is my story.

I'm going to have a go at keeping a diary, or rather a journal, because I strongly doubt I'll manage to write in it every day. But Lenka/Marilena did it, and I'm game for a try.

Yesterday was my birthday. I'm now thirty. And I'm not dead yet. They didn't manage it after all, not the chimney – which I will explain in a moment – nor the train door, not even that sports car on the hill outside Bath. I've beaten the record, beaten Fate, and beaten Dad and Theo. I made it.

I'm writing a journal partly because now I've achieved thirty I don't see why I can't make ninety, or a hundred even. Got to give it a go. And partly because the last twelve months have been astonishing, the stuff of novels, and I am already wishing I'd kept a record of them as lived. Well, I didn't, and tackling the job retrospectively is a terrible idea, but the next twelve months are going to be pretty packed too, and I don't want to be regretting even more this time next year. However, I will start this journal as if it were the beginning of the year. It's tidier that way. So…

1985: New Year's Day

Awful, ghastly day full of misery and despair.

2ND JANUARY

The day Mr Pattison set me straight. Unthank deeds in order, clear documentary evidence that Theo Lawrence purchased the estate from the poor Swiss man who should have inherited it in the first place but knew nothing about it. Actually, not that poor because the money Theo paid him would have come out of the blue and it's unlikely he had any ambitions to live in England anyway.

· · ·

3ʳᴰ January

The First Day of the Rest of my Life: freedom from care and luxuriating in it.

4ᵀᴴ January

Back to work planning the future.

THAT'S ENOUGH OF THAT. I'll recap the rest.

The Unthank Bible will be auctioned by Christie's at the end of April. They have already had interest from universities in Belgium and Tokyo and from a mysterious private collector in the USA. There has been inflation since 1978 when the last copy was sold, and Dr Garland says the prices of books this rare tend to go up anyway because everyone knows that with each discovery, the chances of yet another being discovered are even more vanishingly rare.

Christies are predicting it will go for over three million. That's pounds, not dollars. *Three million.* So I will be able to afford those new boots.

February was nasty because of my birthday. If anything was going to kill me off, it was running out of time. I thought of hiding at home, but on the twentieth I went in to Hexham with Anthea and we were walking past some scaffolding outside the bank, in single file because the pavement is narrow there, when someone shouted and there was the most enormous crash followed by billowing dust, because a great chunk of the chimney had fallen off the roof right in front of us. And the thing is, if we hadn't stopped to wipe Ben's nose I'd have been under it.

But I wasn't.

What else?

We're waiting for the weather to improve before the workmen start but I've got Bob Macdonald, the builder, lined up. And the extraordinary thing is that I won't have to explain to him about the attic light, because it goes off now.

By which I mean that it goes off and stays off. Even after I've gone.

This is the truth. Also the truth, although a bit more subjective, is that the air up there is fresher, and although it is cold, it's no colder nowadays than the air on the stairs. The shadows are less scary too, although I admit that could just be me.

Anyway, nothing to explain to a sceptical builder.

And I'm having cookery lessons from Anthea. We've started with breakfast but I suspect we'll branch out in due course and I have high hopes of becoming adept at boeuf-en-daube and tarte au citron too. Mum and Bill are coming over at Easter and it will be good to be able to impress them with my burgeoning domestic skills.

I think we'll go to The Swaledale too, though.

The thing is, the realisation has finally sunk in that I am the granddaughter of an amazing woman. Lenka/Marilena was a powerhouse. Not only had she the physical strength and energy to operate this huge place single-handed at a time when all your vegetables came from seeds you had sown and keeping the kitchen running was a full-time job in itself, but she had the wits and imagination to pull off a spectacular fraud. Okay, so the fraud itself is not admirable, but having the ability to perform it is pretty appealing.

I've been rereading the diaries, and with hindsight there is a lot revealed between the lines. She did feel guilty, I'm sure of that. If only Theo had told her what he had done. Why didn't he? I'll never know, but at a guess I would say it was because Marilena didn't know that he had uncovered her secret, and he didn't want her to know that he knew. The purchase was definitely made in his name alone – not so uncommon then, no doubt, but given my grandmother's independent nature it does raise the question of whether she was party to it.

Perhaps she wasn't aware he had the funds to do it. Perhaps he had an inheritance that made it possible without her knowing. Sudden, undreamt-of inheritances can arrive in one's lap, I have heard.

I asked the reference librarian to look up 'Lenka Midnight'. After he stopped saying 'Lenka Midnight, wow!' he searched but couldn't find any trace of her, nor of Jeremiah Midnight, which was hardly surprising. I also asked where the name Lenka originates, and together we learned that it is, I quote, 'a common Slavic diminutive of Lena, from Magdalena', which appears as a Christian name in many countries from Scandinavia to Spain.

Magdalena is, of course, a form of Madeleine, the name my grandmother urged on my parents. It isn't a million miles away from Marilena, either.

While there I looked up the origin of the name Unthank too. It has Anglo-Saxon roots and means 'land held without consent', or in plain terms, a squat, so Doug was right. No further comment required, I think.

I've kept the other lovely news to last...almost last.

A week ago, I had a letter from the USA but in a strange hand, not Mum's and not Bill's either. When I opened it, it was from someone informing me that his sabbatical at MIT was coming to a close in April and that he would be returning to Durham then and hoped he might come up to Kirkwitton.

Doug. He said he'd love to see Unthank by daylight. And he said he'd love to see me too.

But that isn't the absolutely final bit of news to bring this journal up to date, because last Tuesday I went to see Mr Pattison at his behest for a change.

When I took my place across the desk – it feels quite homely to me now – we exchanged the usual pleasantries and then he slid an envelope towards me.

'I am now performing my final action on behalf of Claude Lawrence,' he said, pompously I thought. 'With this action, the contract between R J Pattison and Company and Claude Lawrence is fulfilled and terminated. There you go.'

The envelope was not sealed and I opened it. Inside was another envelope and this one was sealed but had written on it:

To be given in person to Madeleine Lawrence on the first anniversary of my death.

'That's today,' Mr Pattison said.

I tore open the flap. There was a single sheet of paper inside, handwritten.

Dear Madeleine,

This letter is no more than a safety net. I am sure you will have solved the riddle and followed the trail to the treasure by now, but just in case, I have left instructions that you be given this letter one year on.

The Unthank Bible is in a lead-lined box in a small cabinet in the attic. It is very rare and very valuable. My mother never felt she could separate it from the house, but you might think differently.

In case you have not solved the riddle, you will find the document that explains all in the gatehouse. It is under the hearthrug in the parlour.

Enjoy your inheritance. Unthank is a special place.

Your uncle, Claude Lawrence

I had to ask. 'This really is the final end? Finally?'

'This really is the final end.'

'Well thank heavens for that!'

I went home, unlocked the gatehouse, lifted the rug and found the plastic folder. I drove back up to the house, made coffee and began to read.

CHAPTER 40

And so we come to that first question. Why did I not leave of my own accord and return to life on the land? The answer: because I had fallen in love.

You will be wondering if you have missed something now. Who was there at Kirkwitton for poor Lenka Midnight to have fallen in love with? The neighbouring farmer's son? The knife grinder? Did the doctor who called on Madam as she grew older and more frail have a handsome young locum to assist him in his practice?

No. It was not that kind of love that afflicted me. It was the house I had fallen in love with. Unthank itself.

By then it was more than the practicality of being able to shelter from the wild weather without being afraid the sky would fall on me. I had almost forgotten those days now, so accustomed was I to walking tall and fearless indoors, although I knew the terror would return were I to venture under low ceilings again. The very house had found its way into my heart, and now, with Lily and Sam gone and only Madam shuffling between her three rooms, it felt, yes, I admit it felt like mine.

But Madam was not immortal. One day, perhaps next year, or five years hence, or perhaps next week, she would die. The Birchers would return from Switzerland to take up residence here or to sell the estate to new owners, and I would be out. It was a prospect I could not bear to think on.

And then came the letter. It was a shock for Madam, that was plain, and it was momentous for other reasons too. But first I must explain about that winter.

I had been in charge of Unthank for over a year by then and running the place, being my own master, making decisions and managing had all become normal; it was simply what I did. Unthank was its own world and it had become my world.

But for a world it was terribly underpopulated. I have always liked my own company, but after two years even I craved a friend. I could not look beyond the walls, I thought, for fear that I would be discovered, so I kept my contact with the people of Kirkwitton to a minimum. I dealt with delivery boys swiftly and brusquely, greeted Dr Burden when he called with downcast eyes and mumbled speech – I'm sure he thought me an idiot – and returned the shopkeepers' pleasantries with short answers and no smiles.

So there we were, two solitary women rattling about in an empty house, and what did we do? Inevitably I now think, we began to talk. It started so gradually I could not point to the day I first ventured to say something other than 'Your breakfast, Madam,' or 'Your dinner, Madam,' or even 'Good morning, Madam'. There was certainly a time when she caught cold (how and where from, goodness knows) and for some days I had to spend time helping her along. I wouldn't call it nursing, but I took her hot drinks and tried to be solicitous to a point – not easy to fit into my daily schedule. She was uncharacteristically meek and somehow we never quite returned to our old way of being.

I began to ask her how she was each morning, and one day, to my

362

amazement, she enquired as to the apple crop. It was the first indication she had ever shown that she understood where her food came from. I said I would ask the gardener.

By then it was winter, the quietest time in the garden, and although my days were still filled with labour, I was able to squeeze in twenty minutes or so of conversation with Madam most evenings. I can't say it was the high point of my day, and I daresay it was not hers either, but we did it, so it must have suited us to some degree. And although I hid from her the fact that her household was reduced to the two of us alone, we got to know each other a tiny bit.

At first it was finding out how much of the world she did not like: hot summers; cold winters; wet springs; windy autumns; meat with fat on it, fish that was over-salted, bread too dense (these were directed at me, no doubt). She found fault with the vicar for coming too often and with the doctor for not coming often enough.

She had little good to say about her family either. Anders, her son, had married a woman she had no time for at all, and she had, she told me, been relieved when they left her in peace and returned to Switzerland. Her grandsons too, feckless and idiotic she said they were, and noisy to boot.

But her granddaughter, Marilena, the little bird as they all called her, she was the one, the sole person that Madam liked, and even loved, it seemed to me. Marilena - little Marilena, pretty Marilena, funny Marilena - was everything to her poor lonely grandmother, stuck through her own obstinate nature in a foreign land, and whether Madam remembered her truly or was indulging in a dream of an ideal child who had never existed, it was Marilena of whom she talked.

And it was Marilena to whom she had bequeathed her estate. 'Gertrud will have none of it,' she told me often enough. 'I have left it all to Marilena.'

As that winter wore on Madam would tell me some evenings to bring out 'the Family Box', and would show me the three photographs of Marilena that fed her memories. The first was a stiff portrait of the family, baby Marilena, fat and frilled, sitting on her mother's lap, her father standing behind and her brothers flanking her. The second was Marilena as a toddler, staring wide-eyed at the camera, stoutly standing on wide, sturdy legs below her lacy gown. And the third showed Marilena just before she departed Unthank in 1914, a slim young woman with a clear gaze, posed in front of the porch.

There were papers in the box too and I asked once what they were, innocently I assure you. 'Certificates,' Madam answered dismissively. 'Just certificates. They left them behind. Too much haste.'

And then in February came the letter. I delivered it to the parlour as I did all letters, and left Madam alone with it. I had bread to bake that day and took what work I could to the kitchen to deal with while the dough was proving; I was cleaning silverware, I recall. At midday I abandoned the forks and spoons to make Madam's cold tray and took it to the parlour to find the old woman staring across the room in a way that made my innards jump. I cannot say exactly what alerted me, but there was something about that distant gaze that made the hairs on my arms stand up.

She looked around when I spoke, but slowly, as if from a great distance.

The letter, lying open, was on her lap and I moved it so that I could set the tray before her.

Madam swivelled her eyes to me.

'The little bird is dead,' she said.

I didn't at once understand. 'Which little bird is this?' I asked, crisply, thinking she was rambling and I could buck her up. I unfolded her napkin and spread it on her lap. I wanted to be quick because my own meal was waiting.

'My little bird. Little Marilena. She is dead and only now they have told me.'

So you see, she did understand. This is important. She really did understand that day when she first read the letter. But by the time a week had gone by, it was as though the letter had never come. Madam spoke of Marilena-this and Marilena-that just as she always had, and when I – gently, I hope – reminded her that her granddaughter was no more, she argued with me. What did I know? and What a stupid girl I was! She pulled out the Family Box and thrust her will at me: 'Marilena will inherit all that I have. Of course she is not dead!' And so I left it alone. Arguing was pointless, and anyway, why not let the old woman find comfort in denial?

February passed, and March, and looking back it seems obvious to me that the letter changed things. Madam's fragile health took a downwards turn and my working day expanded to include washing her and helping her to dress. It was not work that suited me, and I was impatient, and we bickered more like colleagues than mistress and servant. At times I despaired of life ever improving, and both longed for Madam to make up her mind and die, and also dreaded that day when I would have to relinquish my beloved Unthank forever.

And in the last week of April, I thought that day had come.

MARILENA BIRCHER MIGHT HAVE BEEN CALLED the Little Bird, but her grandmother really resembled one, still and white in her bed. She could have weighed hardly more than a child, and her neck was scrawny, her face wizened, her wispy hair fine as down. I was standing above her, staring at her little clutching fingers, trying to come to terms with my *fate, when I realised she was not dead after all but was still breathing. But little breaths, shallow breaths, breaths that did not convey confidence in continuing life.*

Dr Burden when he examined her gave me to understand that death was near – 'Perhaps tomorrow, perhaps a week hence.' He showed me how to wet her mouth, but said he believed she would not eat or drink again. 'Send for me when the end comes,' he instructed, and left.

It seemed everything now could go hang but for feeding the hens and Tom the cob, keeping the range alight, the monster, and waiting for an old lady to finish her life. So I cleared away the paraphernalia of needlework and medicines and afternoon tea, and put the letter that had been the start of the end into the Family Box with the photographs and the certificates Madam had dismissed, and found myself looking at the Will.

Everything to Marilena, and Marilena dead.

I looked at the letter. It was signed by Anders, Madam's son, who had married the dreadful Gertrud that Madam did not want to have her money.

I looked at the Will again.

What were the certificates?

I pushed the photographs aside and drew out the faded, folded papers beneath. Even in German it was plain to see what they were: Madam's marriage certificate to Herr Stefan Bircher; Stefan Bircher's death certificate seven years later; and the last one, a certificate of birth this time, to a girl child named Marilena.

I looked again at the old woman in the bed, her eyes closed, her mouth open, labouring towards her last breath which soon would come.

In my possession I had her Last Will and Testament and the birth certificate of her sole beneficiary.

And nobody knew.

AT FIRST IT WAS A GAME, I think. I played with what would have to be done as if it were an exercise, a test. The letter must be destroyed, obviously, and I must go through Madam's papers and destroy any that could direct people to Anders' address. I had no idea what kind of person would assume responsibility for tracing her descendants but felt certain Dr Burden would know, and it would be he that would set the ball rolling.

My only chance was to arrive before the hunt had begun, brandishing the Will and proof of my identity. And I must be convincing as a Swiss heiress.

Me – Lenka Midnight, the bondager and outside boy! You can see why it felt like a game.

There was money in the house. Madam kept a strong box and I knew where the key lived. That meant I had funds to use without interfering with the household accounts.

There were clothes too. I went hunting and found several outfits in one of the bedroom wardrobes. They were old-fashioned, but fitted me well enough. I could say that Swiss fashion was a little behind English fashion. Who in Kirkwitton would contradict me?

And thus I hit upon my stalwart ally: the unknowable oddness of The Swiss. A young woman of twenty-three travelling to a strange country to claim her inheritance all alone? It is the Swiss way. Such a journey with just one portmanteau? It is the Swiss way. A wealthy woman paying her accounts with cash? But of course, because it is the Swiss way.

I purchased a German-English grammar and taught myself some basic German, how they put their sentences together, how they pronounce things and some vocabulary. I practised my accent, a mixture of Madam's own guttural English with Lily's embellishments, and played with switching the order of sentences around and using words that were a little wrong. Marilena Bircher had to be able to get by in English, but if she found it awkward it would serve to discourage conversation.

And I wrote a page or two of Marilena's first thoughts on arriving at Unthank, full of disdain and bad temper, and tossed in the hint of a failed romance and discontentment at home to lend weight to her decision to keep rather than sell her inheritance. It seemed thin to me, but who really would care? I folded the pages and secured them in my luggage.

Madam died in the second week of June and I was ready.

FIRST, I released the hens and turned Tom out in the pasture. The hens would have to run their luck with the fox and Tom would cope until someone – I was sure Dr Burden would organise this – came to care for him. I let the range die. I closed the portmanteau and lugged it to the gatehouse where I hid it in the larder, and then I walked to the village and knocked on Dr Burden's door.

Then I twisted my ankle.

Not truly, of course. But I stumbled sideways and shouted out, and the good doctor tutted and told me to follow on behind, then set off briskly along the lane.

A lady, you see, always takes precedence over a servant, even when the lady is dead and the servant is in pain.

When he was out of sight I slipped into the gatehouse and waited. He must have looked for me at length in the house for it was almost an hour before I heard his footsteps outside. I closed myself into the bedroom wardrobe and held my breath. This was my turning point, the moment when all was at stake – if discovered, I would be hard put to convince the doctor I had a legitimate reason for loitering in the gatehouse with a suitcase stuffed with stolen clothes.

But already he had stopped expecting to find me. He merely opened the door and shouted 'Is anyone here?', paused for a moment, and then shut the door and was gone.

I stayed in the gatehouse all afternoon, and then, when darkness fell, I began the long walk to the railway station.

The rest went as planned, beautifully so, such that I might have believed it was all meant to happen. I stayed in Newcastle, in a boarding house, for seven days, keeping to my room and having food sent up, and on the eighth day I returned to Hexham speaking accented English and holding my head high.

'It is the Swiss way.'

I said it every time with a sniff to imply that the Swiss way was far superior to poor English customs.

I made enquiries and was directed to the legal man in Shilton, who was confused and impressed by my appearance and manner, and who read the Will, looked at my birth certificate, and handed over the keys.

And that is how I became mistress of Unthank.

So now I know.

It is extraordinary. How ironic that they were so alike, old Frau Bircher and the woman who was born Lenka Midnight and turned herself into Marilena Bircher, my grandmother. Both were widowed early. Both had mighty bust-ups with their sons and to all intents and purposes lost them. Both independent, both prickly. And yet they were not related at all.

I find myself wondering about inherited traits. Have I

anything in common with my grandmother? I don't think I'm prickly, but I wouldn't mind her strength of mind, energy and sheer bloody determination to succeed. If, when she was Lenka, she could do all that, then surely I can learn to cook and make beds?

There are still questions, of course. Why did she have secret hiding places built into the chimney and the wall? Why did she give her diaries to Colin Chapman to guard? And why did she feel so strongly that the Unthank Bible should not be sold?

Answers might come in her diaries, now that I'm reading them properly, but I think the knowledge that she had cheated made her feel vulnerable, and secrecy helped. I think she was superstitious too, and heaven knows that attic light and The Whistler haunt us both.

But we agree, both of us, that Unthank is worth a little haunting.

AUTHOR'S NOTE

I hope you liked this book. If you did, please leave a review online, as this will help other readers find it – just a few words will be a huge help to me and very much appreciated!

A free book is available exclusively to members of my Reader's Group, who have signed up to my monthly newsletter. To receive your free copy of Emily's Story, read about the inspiration and personal stories behind my books, and hear advance notification of new releases, sign up to my newsletter at www.joanna-oneill.com. You can unsubscribe at any time.

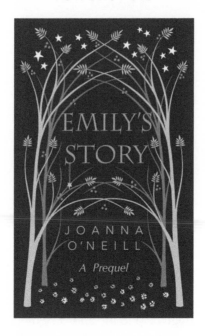

"I went through the woods that day…"

In 1839, thirteen-year-old Emily sets out to visit her grandmother and meets a dark and intriguing stranger in the woods.

Twelve years later and a hundred miles away, she meets him again, and this time he will take her on a magical journey that will alter the course of her life and the lives of generations to come.

Visit here to get started: joanna-oneill.com

Emily's Story stands alone but is connected to my World trilogy: A World Invisible, A World Denied and A World Possessed.

A World Invisible was my first published book, but of course it was not the first book I ever wrote, and there is a very old typescript of a rather poor story buried in a drawer somewhere here!

Having been intensely secret about everything else I had written over the years, sending A World Invisible out into the world was one of the bravest things I have ever done. There is nowhere for an author to hide, and it matters so much that people like it, or at least don't think it's ridiculous. Positive feedback is tremendously morale-boosting, but more than that, it enables other people to discover the book.

With millions of titles now available, it is only reviews that can lift a book to where it can be seen on Amazon and other on-line stores. Reviews from readers are not the same as reviews in newspapers and magazines; no analysis or summary is needed, just a line or two about whether you l liked it. I do hope you will leave a review.

Thanks!

Joanna

THE STRANGER BOOKSHOP

In a remote Northumbrian village, struggling to run a bookshop
that was once the home of cult author Edith Waterfield, Bryony is
short, opinionated, death to software and desperate for help.
Passing through and with time on her hands, Rosalind is hesitant,
competent with computers and unable to say 'No'.

This might work.

While in 1921 young Edith falls hopelessly in love with the hero
she has created in her own novel, in the present day Bryony and
Rosalind are just as distracted by the mysteries that beset them:
Why did Edith stop writing in her fifties? Why are her
photographs so blurry? Where did all her cats go when she died?
And above all, what was in the chapter torn out of the sole
surviving first edition of the novel that launched her?

This is a story about the magic of imagination. It is also about
books, cats, wood-engraving and bad photography. But most of all
it is about a secret.

As Bryony and Rosalind delve into the past, the truth that begins
to emerge is stranger than dreams, for it isn't only the living who
leave ghosts.

Paperback: ISBN 978-1-9163476-7-0

ebook: ISBN 978-1-9163476-9-4

ALSO BY JOANNA O'NEILL

A WORLD INVISIBLE

(Book 1 of The World trilogy)

You're telling me the Victoria and Albert Museum only exists because seven Victorians needed to hide a handful of objects for a hundred years?

Finding she can draw nothing but vines, Rebecca reluctantly puts her ambitions as an illustrator on hold when she is drawn into the machinations of a Victorian secret society founded to make safe an interface between parallel worlds.

But first she has to grow up.

Dragged into helping a cause in which she barely believes, Rebecca finds herself playing Hunt-the-Thimble amongst England's oldest institutions. Over one summer she will break a code, discover her astonishing ancestry, and half fall in love – twice.

But what begins as a game will shake her to the core.

Hardback: ISBN 978-1-9163476-4-9

Paperback: ISBN 978-0-9564432-8-1

ebook: ISBN 978-1-9163476-1-8

ALSO BY JOANNA O'NEILL

A WORLD DENIED

(Book 2 of The World trilogy)

'Stand on the island of glass and look toward the great circle.'

Three years ago Rebecca was drawn into hunting for a doorway to another world, and cannot forget the terrible consequences of finding it. And it seems she is still involved.

When the heating in her flat breaks down, Rebecca pays a visit to her friend in Oxford – good company, a change of scene, and warmth; what could be better? But by Sunday the university boathouse has burned down, there are reports of a strange animal loose on the streets, and three old Oxford professors are showing far too much interest in her.

What is being built amid the ashes on the riverbank? Who is the mysterious tramp in outlandish clothes? And what is the significance of the Queen of Clubs?

Soon Rebecca has embarked on a quest for another rift between the worlds, and this time she fears she is alone. But the World Invisible stretches wide, and there is a stranger in Vermont who is trying to reach England…

Hardback: ISBN 978-1-9163476-5-6

Paperback: ISBN 978-0-9564432-9-8

ebook: ISBN 978-1-9163476-2-5

ALSO BY JOANNA O'NEILL

A WORLD POSSESSED

(Book 3 of The World trilogy)

I always said I'd never do this. Why am I doing this?

On New Year's Day, outside the Royal Festival Hall where she is enjoying an innocent holiday among the buskers and street performers, Rebecca receives the first message, slipped into her pocket by sleight of hand while she is unaware.

And so the riddle begins. From London's South Bank to the Colleges of Oxford, from a hotel in the Peak District to her beautiful home on the Isle of Skye, Rebecca cannot evade the questions that hurtle at her thick and fast.

How many ways can you use a knife? Where did Shakespeare meet his Dark Lady? What is the point of a telescope with polarised lenses? Are foxes heroes or villains? And above all who, or what, is the Jack of Hearts?

As the significance of the messages emerges, Rebecca comes to realise that her path was laid long ago and the time is coming when she must tread it.

Hardback: ISBN 978-1-9163476-6-3

Paperback: ISBN 978-1-9163476-0-1

ebook: ISBN 978-1-9163476-3-2

Lightning Source UK Ltd.
Milton Keynes UK
UKHW011851230421
382518UK00002B/108

9 781838 438708